Book Four of The Malloreon

SORCERESS OF DARSHIVA

By David Eddings
Published by Ballantine Books

THE BELGARIAD

THE MALLOREON

THE ELENIUM

HIGH HUNT

* *Forthcoming*

Book Four of The Malloreon

SORCERESS OF DARSHIVA

DAVID EDDINGS

A Del Rey Book

Ballantine Books • New York

A Del Rey Book
Published by Ballantine Books

Copyright © 1989 by David Eddings
Maps by Shelly Shapiro

Library of Congress Cataloging-in-Publication Data
Eddings, David.
    The sorceress of Darshiva / David Eddings.—1st ed.
        p.   cm.—(The Malloreon ; bk. 4)
    "A Del Rey book."
    ISBN 0-345-33005-6
    I. Title. II. Series: Eddings, David.   Malloreon ; bk. 4
PS3555.D38S6   1989
813'.54—dc20   89-6705
                                                           CIP

Design by Holly Johnson

Manufactured in the United States of America

First Edition: December 1989
10 9 8 7 6 5 4 3 2 1

For Oscar William Patrick Janson-Smith:
Welcome to our world!
Much love,
Dave and Leigh

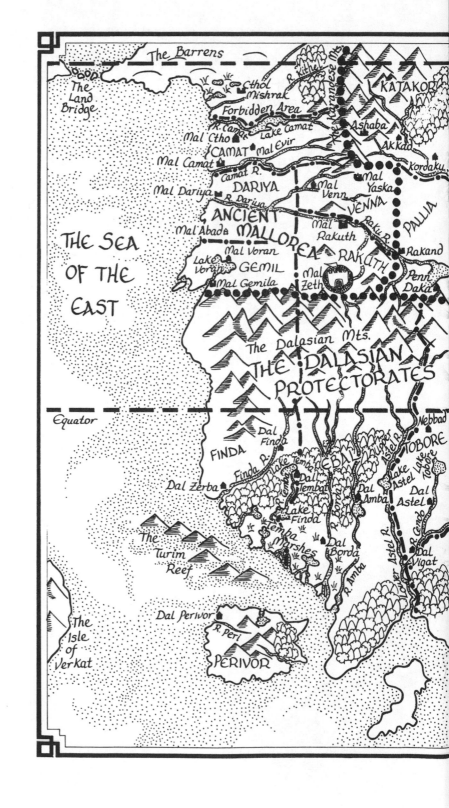

PROLOGUE

Being a Brief History of the Eastern Empire.
—from Emperors of Melcena and Mallorea
University of Melcene Press

The origins of the Melcene Empire are forever lost to us. Some legends maintain that the precursors of the Melcenes came in rude canoes out of the vast sea lying east of the Melcene Islands; others contend that the ancestral Melcene was an offshoot of that curious culture existing in Dalasia. Whatever the source, however, Melcena stands as the oldest civilization on the earth.

Melcena has always been closely allied with the sea, and her original home lay in the islands off the east coast of the Mallorean continent. The capital at Melcena was a city of light and culture when Tol Honeth was a rude village and Mal Zeth was only a shabby cluster of tents. Only Kell stood in contemplation of the heavens to rival the ancestral home of the Melcenes.

It was the advent of a catastrophe which caused Melcena to abandon its splendid isolation. At a time estimated to be five thousand years ago, a disaster occurred far to the west. The Angaraks and Alorns blame this on a theological dispute between the Gods. Such explanation is not to be taken seriously, but it does give some insight into the gropings of primitive minds to explain the forces of nature.

Whatever the source, the cataclysm involved a great split in the protocontinent and engendered colossal tidal waves. The seas first fell, then rose, and ultimately came to rest at more or less the present shoreline. For Melcena, this was disastrous. Fully half the land area of ancient Melcena was lost to the sea. Although the loss of property was enormous, the bulk of the people were saved. This left a pitifully overcrowded population clinging to the remnants of their former islands. The capital at Melcena had been a fair city in the mountains, where affairs could be managed without the debilitating effects of the climate in the tropical lowlands. Following the catastrophe, Melcena was a shattered city, destroyed by earthquake and flood, lying no more than a league from the new coast.

After a period of rebuilding, it became clear that the shrunken homeland could no longer support the population. Thus the Melcenes turned to the mainland. Southeastern Mallorea lay closest, a region populated by peoples of their own racial stock with a compatible, though corrupted, language; to that region the Melcenes turned their attention. There were five primitive kingdoms in the area—Gandahar, Darshiva, Celanta, Peldane, and Rengel. These were quickly overrun by the technologically superior Melcenes and were absorbed into their growing empire.

The dominating force in the Melcene Empire was the bureaucracy. While there were drawbacks to a bureaucratic form of government, it provided the advantages of continuity and a clear-eyed pragmatism more concerned with finding the most practical way to get the job done than with whim, prejudice, and egocentricity, which so frequently move other forms of government. Melcene bureaucracy was practical almost to a fault. The concept of "an aristocracy of talent" dominated Melcene thinking. If one bureau ignored a talented individual, another was almost certain to snap him up.

The various departments of the Melcene government rushed into the newly conquered mainland provinces to winnow through the population in search of genius. The conquered peoples were thus absorbed directly into the mainstream of the life of the empire. Always pragmatic, the Melcenes left the royal houses of the five mainland provinces in place, preferring to operate through established lines of authority rather than set up new ones.

For the next fourteen hundred years, the Melcene Empire prospered, far removed from the theological and political squabbles of the western continent. Melcene culture was secular, civilized, and highly educated. Slavery was unknown, and trade with the Angaraks and their subject peoples in Karanda and Dalasia was extremely profitable. The old capital at Melcena became a major center of learning. Unfortunately, some Melcene scholars turned toward the arcane. Their summoning of evil spirits went far beyond the mumbo-jumbo of the Morindim or the Karandese and began to delve into darker and more serious areas. They made progress in witchcraft and necromancy. But the major interest lay in the field of alchemy.

The first encounter with the Angaraks took place during this period. Although victorious in that first meeting, the Melcenes realized that eventually the Angaraks would overwhelm them by sheer weight of numbers.

While the Angaraks bent most of their efforts to the establishment of the Dalasian Protectorates, there was a wary, tentative peace. The trade contacts between the two nations yielded a somewhat better understanding of each other, though the Melcenes were amused by the preoccupation with religion of even the most worldly Angarak. Over the next eighteen hundred years relations between the two nations deteriorated into little wars, seldom lasting more than a year or two. Both sides scrupulously avoided committing their full forces, obviously not wishing all-out confrontation.

To gain more information about each other, the two nations developed a tradition of exchanging the children of various leaders for certain periods of time. The sons of high-ranking Melcene bureaucrats were sent to Mal Zeth to live with the families of Angarak generals, and the generals' sons were sent to the imperial capital to be raised. The result was a group of young men with cosmopolitanism which later became the norm for the ruling class of the Mallorean Empire.

One such exchange toward the end of the fourth millennium ultimately resulted in the unification of the two peoples. At about the age of twelve, a youth named Kallath, son of a high-ranking Angarak general, was sent to Melcena to spend his formative years in the household of the Imperial Minister of Foreign Affairs. The minister had frequent official and social contacts with the imperial family, and Kallath soon became a welcome guest at the imperial palace. Emperor Molvan was an elderly man with but one surviving child, a daughter named Danera, perhaps a year younger than Kallath. Matters between the two youngsters progressed in a not uncommon fashion until Kallath was recalled at eighteen to Mal Zeth to begin his military career. Kallath rose meteorically through the ranks to the position of Governor-General of the District of Rakuth by the time he was twenty-eight, thereby becoming the youngest man ever elevated to the General Staff. A year later he journeyed to Melcene, where he and Princess Danera were married.

In the years that followed, Kallath divided his time between Melcena and Mal Zeth, building a power base in each, and when Emperor Molvan died in 3829, he was ready. There had been others in line for the throne, but most of these had died—frequently under mysterious circumstances. It was, nonetheless, over the violent objections of many noble families of Melcena that Kallath was declared Emperor of Melcena in 3830; these objections were quieted with brutal efficiency by Kallath's cohorts. Danera had produced seven healthy children to insure that Kallath's line would continue.

Journeying to Mal Zeth the following year, Kallath brought the Melcene army to the border of Delchin, where it stood poised. At Mal Zeth, Kallath delivered an ultimatum to the General Staff. His forces comprised the army of his own district of Rakuth and of the eastern principalities in Karand, where the Angarak military governors had sworn allegiance to him. Together with the army on the Delchin border, these gave him absolute military supremacy. His demand was to be appointed OverGeneral of the armies of Angarak. There were precedents. In the past, an occasional general had been granted that office, though it was far more common for the General Staff to rule jointly. But Kallath's demand brought something new into the picture. His position as emperor was hereditary, and he insisted that the OverGeneralship of Angarak also be passed to his heirs. Helplessly, the generals acceded to his demands. Kallath stood supreme on the continent as Emperor of Melcene and Commander in Chief of Angarak.

The integration of Melcene and Angarak was turbulent, but in the end, Melcene patience won out over Angarak brutality, as it became evident over the years that the Melcene bureaucracy was infinitely more efficient than Angarak military administration. The bureaucracy first moved on such mundane matters as standards and currency. From there it was but a short step to establishing a continental Bureau of Roads. Within a few hundred years, the bureaucracy ran virtually every aspect of life on the continent. As always, it gathered up talented men and women from every corner of Mallorea, regardless of race; soon administrative units comprised of Melcenes, Karands, Dalasians, and Angaraks were not at all uncommon. By 4400, the bureaucratic ascendancy was complete. In the interim, the title of OverGeneral had begun to fall into disuse, perhaps because the bureaucracy customarily addressed all communications to "the Emperor." There appears to have been no specific date when the Emperor of Melcena became the Emperor of Mallorea, and such usage was never formally approved until after the disastrous adventure in the West which ended in the Battle of Vo Mimbre.

The conversion of Melcenes to the worship of Torak was at best superficial. They pragmatically accepted the *forms* of Angarak worship out of political expediency, but the Grolims were unable to command the abject submission to the Dragon God which had always characterized the Angaraks.

In 4850, Torak himself suddenly emerged from his eons of seclusion at Ashaba. A vast shock ran through Mallorea as the living God, his maimed face concealed behind a polished steel mask, appeared at the gates of Mal Zeth. The Emperor was disdainfully set aside, and Torak assumed full authority as "Kal"—King and God. Messengers were dispatched to Cthol Murgos, Mishrak ac Thull, and Gar og Nadrak, and a council of war was held at Mal Zeth in 4852. The Dalasians, Karands, and Melcenes were stunned by the appearance of a figure they had always thought purely mythical, and their shock was compounded by the presence of Torak's disciples.

Torak was a God and did not speak, except to issue commands. But the Disciples, Ctuchik, Zedar, and Urvon, were men and they probed and examined everything with a kind of cold disdain. They saw at once that Mallorean society had become almost totally secular—and took steps to rectify the situation. A reign of terror descended upon Mallorea. Grolims were everywhere, and secularism was a form of heresy to them. The sacrifices, long virtually unknown, were renewed with fanatic enthusiasm; soon not a village in all Mallorea did not have its altar and reeking bonfire. In one stroke, Torak's disciples overturned millennia of military and bureaucratic rule and returned absolute dominion to the Grolims. Soon there was not one facet of Mallorean life that did not bow abjectly to the will of Torak.

The mobilization of Mallorea in preparation for the war with the West virtually depopulated the continent, and the disaster at Vo Mimbre wiped out an entire generation. The catastrophic campaign, coupled with the apparent death of Torak at the hands of the Rivan Warder, utterly demoralized Mallorea. The doddering old emperor emerged from retirement to try to rebuild the shattered bureaucracy. Grolim efforts to maintain control were met with universal hatred. Without Torak, they had no real power. Most of the emperor's sons had perished at Vo Mimbre, but one gifted child remained, a boy of seven, the son of his old age. The emperor spent his few remaining years instructing and preparing his son for the task of ruling. When age finally rendered the emperor incompetent, Korzeth, then about fourteen, callously deposed his father and ascended the imperial throne.

After the war, Mallorean society had fractured back to its original components of Melcena, Karanda, Dalasia, and Mallorea Antiqua. There was even a movement to disintegrate further into the prehistoric kingdoms which had existed before the coming of the Angaraks. This movement was particularly strong in the principality of Gandahar in southern Melcena, in Zamad and Voresebo in Karanda, and in Perivor in the Dalasian Protectorates. Deceived by Korzeth's youth, these regions rashly declared independence from the imperial throne at Mal Zeth, and other principalities gave indications that they would soon follow suit. Korzeth moved immediately to stem the tide of revolution. The boy emperor spent the rest of his life on horseback in perhaps the greatest bloodbath in history; but when he was done, he delivered a reunified Mallorea to his successor to the throne.

The descendants of Korzeth brought a different kind of rule to the continent. Before the disastrous war, the Emperor of Mallorea had often been little more than a figurehead, and power had largely rested with the bureaucracy. But now the imperial throne was absolute. The center of power shifted from Melcena to Mal Zeth in keeping with the military orientation of Korzeth and his descendants. As is usual when power rests in the hands of one supreme ruler, intrigue became commonplace. Plots and conspiracies abounded as various functionaries schemed to discredit rivals and gain imperial favor. Rather than trying to stop these palace intrigues, Korzeth's descendants encouraged them, perceiving that men divided by mutual distrust could never unite to challenge the power of the throne.

The present emperor, Zakath, assumed the throne during his eighteenth year. Intelligent, sensitive, and capable, he gave early promise of enlightened rule. A personal tragedy, however, turned him from that course and made him a man feared by half the world. Now he is obsessed with the concept of power; the idea of becoming Overking of all the Angaraks has dominated his thoughts for the past two decades. Only time will determine if Zakath will succeed in asserting dominance over the Western Angarak Kingdoms, but if he succeeds, the history of the entire world may be profoundly altered.

Part One

MELCENA

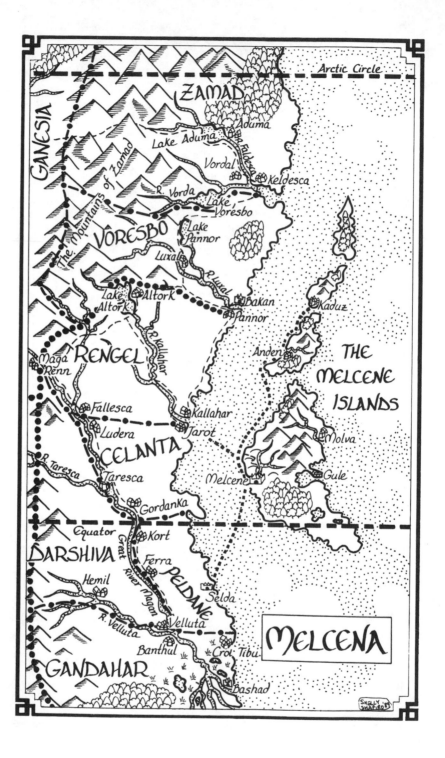

CHAPTER ONE

Her Majesty, Queen Porenn of Drasnia, was in a pensive mood. She stood at the window of her pink-frilled sitting room in the palace at Boktor watching her son Kheva and Unrak, the son of Barak of Trellheim, at play in a garden drenched with morning sunlight. The boys had reached that age where sometimes it seemed almost possible to see them growing, and their voices wavered uncertainly between boyish soprano and manly baritone. Porenn sighed, smoothing the front of her black gown. The Queen of Drasnia had worn black since the death of her husband. "You would be proud of him, my dear Rhodar," she whispered sadly.

There was a light knock at her door.

"Yes?" she replied, not turning.

"There's a Nadrak here to see you, your Majesty," the aged butler at the door reported. "He says you know him."

"Oh?"

"He says his name is Yarblek."

"Oh, yes. Prince Kheldar's associate. Show him in, please."

"There's a woman with him, your Majesty," the butler said with a disapproving expression. "She uses language your Majesty might prefer not to hear."

Porenn smiled warmly. "That must be Vella," she said. "I've heard her swear before. I don't know that she's really all that serious about it. Show them both in, if you would, please."

"At once, your Majesty."

Yarblek was as shabby as ever. At some point, the shoulder seam of his long black overcoat had given way and had been rudimentarily repaired with a piece of rawhide thong. His beard was coarse and black and scraggly, his hair was unkempt, and he looked as if he didn't smell very good. "Your Majesty," he said grandly, attempting a bow which was marred a bit by an unsteady lurch.

"Drunk already, Master Yarblek?" Porenn asked him archly.

"No, not really, Porenn," he replied, unabashed. "It's just a little carry-over from last night."

The queen was not offended by the Nadrak's use of her first name. Yarblek's grip on formality had never been very firm.

The woman who had entered with him was a stunningly beautiful Nadrak with blue-black hair and smoldering eyes. She was dressed in tight-fitting leather trousers and a black leather vest. A silver-hilted dagger protruded from each of her boot tops, and two more were tucked under the wide leather belt about her waist. She bowed with infinite grace. "You're looking tired, Porenn," she observed. "I think you need more sleep."

Porenn laughed. "Tell that to the people who bring me stacks of parchment every hour or so."

"I made myself a rule years ago," Yarblek said, sprawling uninvited in a chair. "Never put anything down in writing. It saves time as well as keeping me out of trouble."

"It seems to me that I've heard Kheldar say the same thing."

Yarblek shrugged. "Silk's got a good grip on reality."

"I haven't seen you two for quite some time," Porenn noted, also sitting.

"We've been in Mallorea," Vella told her, wandering around the room and looking appraisingly at the furnishings.

"Isn't that dangerous? I've heard that there's plague there."

"It's pretty much confined to Mal Zeth," Yarblek replied. "Polgara persuaded the Emperor to seal up the city."

"Polgara?" Porenn exclaimed, coming to her feet. "What's she doing in Mallorea?"

"She was going in the general direction of a place called Ashaba the last time I saw her. She had Belgarath and the others with her."

"How did they get to Mallorea?"

"By boat, I'd imagine. It's a long swim."

"Yarblek, am I going to have to drag every single scrap of information out of you?" Porenn demanded in exasperation.

"I'm getting to it, Porenn," he said, sounding a little injured. "Do you want the story first or the messages? I've got lots of messages for you, and Vella's got a couple more that she won't even talk about—at least not to me."

"Just start at the beginning, Yarblek."

"Any way you want it." He scratched at his beard. "The way I got the story is that Silk and Belgarath and the others were in Cthol Murgos. They got captured by the Malloreans, and Zakath took them all to Mal Zeth. The young fellow with the big sword—Belgarion, isn't it? Anyway, he and Zakath got to be friends—"

"Garion and Zakath?" Porenn asked incredulously. "How?"

"I wouldn't know. I wasn't there when it happened. To make it short, they were friends, but then the plague broke out in Mal Zeth. I managed to sneak Silk and the others out of the city, and we went north. We separated before we got to Venna. They wanted to go to this Ashaba place, and I had a caravan load of goods I wanted to get to Yar Marak. Made a fairly good profit, actually."

"Why were they going to Ashaba?"

"They were after some woman named Zandramas—the one who abducted Belgarion's son."

"A *woman?* Zandramas is a woman?"

"So they told me. Belgarath gave me a letter for you. It's all in there. I told him that he shouldn't write it down, but he wouldn't listen to me." Yarblek unwound himself from his chair, fished around inside his overcoat, and handed a rumpled and none-too-clean piece of parchment to the queen. Then he strolled to the window and looked out. "Isn't that Trellheim's boy down there?" he asked. "The husky one with the red hair?"

Porenn was reading the parchment. "Yes," she said absently, trying to concentrate on the message.

"Is he here? Trellheim, I mean?"

"Yes. I don't know if he's awake yet, though. He stayed up rather late last night and he was a little tipsy when he went to bed."

Yarblek laughed. "That's Barak, all right. Has he got his wife and daughters with him, too?"

"No," Porenn said. "They stayed in Val Alorn, making the preparations for his oldest daughter's wedding."

"Is she that old already?"

"Chereks marry young. They seem to think it's the best

way to keep a girl out of trouble. Barak and his son came here to get away from all the fuss."

Yarblek laughed again. "I think I'll go wake him up and see if he's got anything to drink." He touched his forefinger to the spot between his eyes with a pained look. "I'm feeling a little delicate this morning, and Barak's a good man to get well with. I'll stop back when I'm feeling better. Besides, you've got your mail to read. Oh," he said, "I almost forgot. Here are some others." He started rummaging around inside his shabby coat. "One from Polgara." He tossed it negligently on the table. "One from Belgarion. One from Silk, and one from the blond girl with the dimples—the one they call Velvet. The snake didn't send anything—you know how snakes are. Now, if you'll excuse me, I'm *really* not feeling too good." He lurched to the door and went out.

"That is the most exasperating man in the world," Porenn declared.

"He does it on purpose." Vella shrugged. "He thinks it's funny."

"Yarblek said that you have some messages for me, too," the queen said. "I suppose I should read them all at once— get all the shocks over with at one time."

"I've only got one, Porenn," Vella replied, "and it isn't in writing. Liselle—the one they call Velvet—asked me to tell you something when we were alone."

"All right," Porenn said, putting down Belgarath's letter.

"I'm not sure how they found out about this," Vella said, "but it seems that the King of Cthol Murgos is *not* the son of Taur Urgas."

"What are you saying, Vella?"

"Urgit isn't even related to that frothing lunatic. It seems that a number of years ago, a certain Drasnian businessman paid a visit to the palace in Rak Goska. He and Taur Urgas' second wife became friendly." She smiled with one eyebrow slightly raised. "Very friendly. I've always had that suspicion

15

about Murgo women. Anyway, Urgit was the result of that friendship."

A terrible suspicion began to dawn on Queen Porenn.

Vella grinned impishly at her. "We all knew that Silk had royal connections," she said. "We just didn't know how many royal families he was connected to."

"No!" Porenn gasped.

Vella laughed. "Oh, yes. Liselle confronted Urgit's mother with it, and the lady confessed." The Nadrak girl's face grew serious. "The whole point of Liselle's message is that Silk doesn't want that bony fellow, Javelin, to find out about it. Liselle felt that she had to report it to somebody. That's why she told me to pass it on to you. I guess *you're* supposed to decide whether to tell Javelin or not."

"How very kind of her," Porenn said drily. "Now they want me to keep secrets from the chief of my own intelligence service."

Vella's eyes twinkled. "Liselle's in a kind of difficult situation, Porenn," she said. "I know that I drink too much and I swear a lot. That makes people think that I'm stupid, but I'm not. Nadrak women know the world, and I have very good eyes. I didn't actually catch them at it, but I'd be willing to wager half the money I'll get when Yarblek sells me that Silk and Liselle are keeping company."

"*Vella!*"

"I couldn't prove it, Porenn, but I know what I saw." The Nadrak girl sniffed at her leather vest and made a sour face. "If it's not too much trouble, I would really like to take a bath. I've been in the saddle for weeks. Horses are nice enough animals, I suppose, but I really don't want to smell like one."

Porenn's mind was working very fast now; to give herself time to think, she rose and approached the wild Nadrak girl. "Have you ever worn satin, Vella?" she asked. "A gown, perhaps?"

16

"Satin? Me?" Vella laughed coarsely. "Nadraks never wear satin."

"Then you might be the very first." Queen Porenn reached out her small white hands and lifted Vella's wealth of blue-black hair into a tumbled mass atop her head. "I'd give my soul for hair like that," she murmured.

"I'll trade you," Vella offered. "Do you know what price I could bring if I were blond?"

"Hush, Vella," Porenn said absently. "I'm trying to think." She twined the girl's hair loosely about her hands, startled at how alive it felt. Then she reached out, lifted Vella's chin, and looked into her huge eyes. Something seemed to reach out and touch the Queen of Drasnia, and she suddenly knew the destiny of this half-wild child before her. "Oh, my dear," she almost laughed, "what an amazing future you have in store for you. You'll touch the sky, Vella, the very sky."

"I really don't know what you're talking about, Porenn."

"You will." Porenn looked at the perfect face before her. "Yes," she said, "satin, I think. Lavender would be nice."

"I prefer red."

"No, dear," Porenn told her. "Red just wouldn't do. It definitely has to be lavender." She reached out and touched the girl's ears. "And I think amethyst here and here."

"What are you up to?"

"It's a game, child. Drasnians are very good at games. And when I'm done, I'll double your price." Porenn was just a bit smug about it. "Bathe first, then let's see what we can do with you."

Vella shrugged. "As long as I can keep my daggers."

"We'll work that out."

"Can you really do something with a lump like me?" Vella asked, almost plaintively.

"Trust me," Porenn said, smiling. "Now go bathe, child. I have letters to read and decisions to make."

After the Queen of Drasnia had read the letters, she sum-

17

moned her butler and issued a couple of orders. "I want to speak with the Earl of Trellheim," she said, "before he gets any drunker. I also need to talk with Javelin just as soon as he can get to the palace."

It was perhaps ten minutes later when Barak appeared in her doorway. He was a bit bleary-eyed, and his vast red beard stuck out in all directions. Yarblek came with him.

"Put away your tankards, gentlemen," Porenn said crisply. "There's work to be done. Barak, is the *Seabird* ready to sail?"

"She's always ready," he said in an injured tone.

"Good. Then round up your sailors. You have a number of places to go. I'm calling a meeting of the Alorn Council. Get word to Anheg, Fulrach, and Brand's son Kail at Riva. Stop off in Arendia and pick up Mandorallen and Lelldorin." She pursed her lips. "Korodullin's not well enough to travel, so bypass Vo Mimbre. He'd get out of his deathbed to attend if he knew what was going on. Go to Tol Honeth instead and get Varana. I'll send word to Cho-Hag and Hettar myself. Yarblek, you go to Yar Nadrak and get Drosta. Leave Vella here with me."

"But—"

"No buts, Yarblek. Do exactly as I say."

"I thought you said this was a meeting of the Alorn Council, Porenn," Barak objected. "Why are we inviting the Arends and the Tolnedrans—and the Nadraks?"

"We've got an emergency on our hands, Barak, and it concerns everybody."

They stood staring stupidly at her.

She clapped her hands together sharply. "Quickly, gentlemen, quickly. We don't have any time to waste."

Urgit, High King of Cthol Murgos, sat on his garish throne in the Drojim Palace in Rak Urga. He was dressed in his favorite purple doublet and hose, he had one leg negligently cocked over the arm of the throne, and he was absently tossing his crown back and forth between his hands as he listened to the droning voice of Agachak, the cadaverous-looking Hierarch of Rak Urga. "It's going to have to wait, Agachak," he said finally. "I'm getting married next month."

"This is a command of the Church, Urgit."

"Wonderful. Give the Church my regards."

Agachak looked taken a bit aback. "You don't believe in anything now, do you, my King?"

"Not very much, no. Is this sick world we live in ready for atheism yet?"

For the first time in his life, Urgit saw doubt on the face of the Hierarch. "Atheism's a clean place, Agachak," he said, "a flat, gray, empty place where man makes his own destiny, and let the Gods go hang. I didn't make them; they didn't make me; and we're quits on all of that. I wish them well, though."

"This is unlike you, Urgit," Agachak said.

"No, not really. I'm just tired of playing the clown." He stretched out his leg and tossed his crown at his foot like a hoop. He caught it and kicked it back again. "You don't really understand, do you, Agachak?" he said as he caught the crown out of midair.

The Hierarch of Rak Urga drew himself up. "This is not a request, Urgit. I'm not *asking* you."

"Good. Because I'm not going."

"I *command* you to go."

"I don't think so."

"Do you realize to whom you're talking?"

"Perfectly, old boy. You're the same tiresome old Grolim who's been boring me to tears ever since I inherited the throne from that fellow who used to chew on the carpets back in Rak Goska. Listen carefully, Agachak. I'll use short words and simple sentences so that I don't confuse you. I am *not* going to Mallorea. I've never had any intention of going to Mallorea. There's nothing I want to see in Mallorea. There's nothing I

19

want to do there. I most definitely do not intend to put myself anywhere near Kal Zakath, and he's gone back to Mal Zeth. Not only that, they have demons in Mallorea. Have you ever seen a demon, Agachak?"

"Once or twice," the Hierarch replied sullenly.

"And you're *still* going to Mallorea? Agachak, you're as crazy as Taur Urgas was."

"I can make you king of all of Angarak."

"I don't *want* to be king of all of Angarak. I don't even want to be King of Cthol Murgos. All I want is to be left alone to contemplate the horror that's about to descend on me."

"Your marriage, you mean?" Agachak's face grew sly. "You could evade that by coming to Mallorea with me."

"Have I been going too fast for you, Agachak? A wife is bad enough. Demons are much worse. Did anybody ever tell you what that thing did to Chabat?" Urgit shuddered.

"I can protect you."

Urgit laughed scornfully. "You, Agachak? You couldn't even protect yourself. Even Polgara had to have help from a God to deal with that monster. Do you plan to resurrect Torak to give you a hand? Or maybe you could appeal to Aldur. He's the one who helped Polgara. I don't really think He'd like you, though. *I* don't even like you, and I've known you all my life."

"You go too far, Urgit."

"No. Not far enough, Agachak. For centuries—eons, probably—you Grolims have held the upper hand in Cthol Murgos, but that was when Ctuchik was still alive, and Ctuchik is dead now. You did know about that, didn't you, old boy? He tried his hand against Belgarath, and Belgarath disassembled him right down to the floor. I may be the only Murgo alive who's ever met Belgarath and lived to talk about it. We're actually on fairly good terms. Would you like to meet him? I could probably arrange an introduction, if you'd like."

Agachak visibly shrank back.

"Much better, Agachak," Urgit said smoothly. "I'm delighted at your grasp of the realities of the situation. Now, I'm certain that you can raise your hand and wiggle your fingers at me, but now I know how to recognize that sort of thing. I watched Belgarion rather closely while we were trotting across Cthaka last winter. If your hand moves even a fraction of an inch, you're going to get about a bushel basket full of arrows right in the middle of the back. The archers are already in place, and their bows are already drawn. Give it some thought, Agachak—while you're leaving."

"This is not like you, Urgit," Agachak said, his nostrils white with fury.

"I know. Delightful, isn't it? You may go now, Agachak."

The Hierarch spun on his heel and started toward the door.

"Oh, by the way, old boy," Urgit added. "I've had news that our dear brother Gethel of Thulldom recently died— probably something he ate. Thulls eat almost anything that swims, flies, crawls, or spawns on rotten meat. It's a pity, actually. Gethel was one of the few people in the world I could bully. Anyway, he's been succeeded on the throne by his half-wit son, Nathel. I've met Nathel. He has the mentality of an earthworm, but he's a true Angarak king. Why don't you see if *he* wants to go to Mallorea with you? It might take you a while to explain to him where Mallorea is, since I think he believes that the world is flat, but I have every confidence in you, Agachak." Urgit flipped his hand at the fuming Hierarch. "Run along now," he said. "Go back to your temple and gut a few more Grolims. Maybe you can even get the fires started in your sanctum again. If nothing else, I'm sure it will calm your nerves."

Agachak stormed out, slamming the door behind him.

Urgit doubled over, pounding on the arm of his throne and howling in glee.

"Don't you think you might have gone just a bit too far,

my son?'' Lady Tamazin asked from the shadowy alcove where she had been listening.

"Perhaps so, mother," he agreed, still laughing, "but wasn't it fun?"

She limped into the light and smiled fondly at him. "Yes, Urgit," she agreed, "it was, but don't push Agachak too far. He can be a dangerous enemy."

"I've got lots of enemies, mother," Urgit said, tuggling unconsciously at his long, pointed nose. "Most of the people in the world hate me, but I've learned to live with that. It's not as if I had to run for reelection, you know."

The bleak-faced seneschal, Oskatat, also came out of the shadowed alcove. "What are we going to do with you, Urgit?" he said wryly. "What did Belgarion teach you, anyway?"

"He taught me how to be a king, Oskatat. I may not last very long, but by the Gods, as long as I'm here, I'm going to *be* a king. They're going to kill me anyway, so I might as well enjoy myself while I can."

His mother sighed, then raised her hands helplessly. "There's no reasoning with him, Oskatat," she said.

"I suppose not, my Lady Tamazin," the gray-haired man agreed.

"Princess Prala wants to speak with you," Tamazin said to her son.

"I am at her immediate disposal," Urgit said. "Not only immediate, but perpetual, if I understand the terms of the marriage contract."

"Be nice," Tamazin chided.

"Yes, mother."

The Princess Prala of the house of Cthan swept in through a side door. She wore a riding habit consisting of a calf-length black skirt, a white satin blouse and polished boots. Her heels hit the marble floor like little hammers. Her long black hair swayed at her back, and her eyes were dangerous. She held a parchment scroll in her hands.

"Will you assist me, my Lord Oskatat?" Lady Tamazin asked, holding one hand out to the seneschal.

"Of course, my Lady," he replied, offering his arm to Urgit's mother with tender solicitude. The two of them withdrew.

"Now what?" Urgit warily asked his bride-to-be.

"Am I disturbing your Majesty?" Prala asked. She did not bother to curtsy. The princess had changed. She was no longer a properly submissive Murgo lady. The time she had spent with Queen Ce'Nedra and the Margravine Liselle had definitely corrupted her, Urgit felt, and the unwholesome influence of Polgara the sorceress showed in her every move and gesture. She was, however, Urgit concluded, absolutely adorable now. Her black eyes flashed, her delicate white skin seemed to reflect her mood, and her wealth of black hair seemed almost alive as it flowed down her back. Rather surprisingly, Urgit found that he was very fond of her.

"You always disturb me, my beloved," he answered her question, spreading his arms extravagantly.

"Stop that," she snapped. "You sound like your brother."

"It runs in the family."

"Did you put this in here?" she demanded, waving the scroll at him like a club.

"Did I put what in where?"

"This." She unrolled the scroll. "'It is agreed that Princess Prala of the House of Cthan shall be his majesty's most favored wife,'" she read. "Most favored wife" came out from between clenched teeth.

"What's wrong with that?" he asked, a little surprised at the girl's vehemence.

"The implication is that there will be others."

"It's the custom, Prala. I didn't make the rules."

"You're the king. Make different rules."

"Me?" He swallowed hard.

"There will *be* no other wives, Urgit—or royal concubines."

Her usually gentle voice seemed to crackle. "You are *mine*, and I'm not going to share you with anybody."

"Do you really feel that way?" he asked, a bit amazed.

"Yes, I do." She lifted her chin.

"Nobody's ever felt that way about me before."

"Get used to it." Her voice was flat and had the overtone of daggers in it.

"We'll amend the passage," he agreed quickly. "I don't need more than one wife anyway."

"Definitely not, my Lord. A very wise decision."

"Naturally. All royal decisions are wise. It says so in the history books."

She tried very hard not to smile, but finally gave up, laughed, and hurled herself into his arms. "Oh, Urgit," she said burrowing her face into his neck, "I do love you."

"You do? What an amazing thing." Suddenly an idea came to him, and its sheer purity almost blinded him. "What's your feeling about a double wedding, love?" he asked her.

She pulled her face back from where she had been grazing on his neck. "I don't quite follow you," she admitted.

"I'm the king, right?"

"A little more than you were before you met Belgarion," she admitted.

He let that pass. "I've got this female relative," he said. "I'm going to be busy being married."

"*Very* busy, my love," she agreed.

He coughed nervously. "Anyway," he rushed on. "I'm not really going to have all that much time to look after this certain female relative, am I? Wouldn't it be better if I married her off to some deserving fellow who's always held her in the highest regard?"

"I don't quite follow you, Urgit. I didn't think you had any female relatives."

"Only one, my princess," he grinned. "Only one."

She stared at him. "Urgit!" she gasped.

24

He gave her a rat-faced little grin. "I'm the king," he said grandly. "I can do anything I want to do, and my mother's been alone for far too long, wouldn't you say? Oskatat's loved her since she was a girl, and she's at least fond of him—although I think it might go a little farther than that. If I order them to get married, they'd have to do it, wouldn't they?"

"That's absolutely brilliant, Urgit," she marveled.

"It comes from my Drasnian heritage," he admitted modestly. "Kheldar himself couldn't have come up with a neater scheme."

"It's perfect," she almost squealed. "This way I won't have a mother-in-law interfering when I start changing you."

"Changing?"

"Just a few little things, love," she said sweetly. "You have a few bad habits, and your taste in clothing is terrible. Whatever possessed you to start wearing purple?"

"Anything else?"

"I'll bring the list with me next time I visit."

Urgit began to have second thoughts at that point.

His Imperial Majesty, Kal Zakath of Mallorea, had a busy morning that day. Most of the time, he was closeted with Brador, Chief of the Bureau of Internal Affairs, in a small, blue-draped office on the second floor of the palace.

"It's definitely subsiding, your Majesty," Brador reported when the subject of the plague came up. "There hasn't been a new case in the past week, and a surprising number of people are actually recovering. The plan of walling off each separate district of the city seems to have worked."

"Good," Zakath said. He turned to another matter. "Is there any further word out of Karanda?"

Brador shuffled through the papers he was holding. "Mengha hasn't been seen for several weeks now, your Majesty." The Chief of the Bureau of Internal Affairs smiled briefly. "That particular plague also seems to be subsiding.

The demons appear to have left, and the fanatics are losing heart." He tapped one of the papers against his pursed lips. "This is only an educated guess, your Majesty, since I can't get any agents into the region, but the turmoil appears to have shifted to the east coast. Shortly after Mengha disappeared, large bodies of Karandese irregular troops, along with Urvon's Temple Guardsmen and his Chandim, crossed the Mountains of Zamad, and all communications out of Voresebo and Rengel have broken down."

"Urvon?" Zakath asked.

"It appears so, your Majesty. I'd say that the Disciple is moving into position for a final confrontation with Zandramas. One is tempted to suggest that we just let them fight it out. I don't think that the world would miss either of them very much."

A faint, icy smile touched Zakath's lips. "You're right, Brador," he said. "It *is* tempting, but I don't think we should encourage that sort of thing—just as a matter of policy. Those principalities are a part of the empire and they're entitled to imperial protection. It might start some ugly rumors if we were to just stand idly by and let Urvon and Zandramas rip up the countryside. If anybody brings military force to bear in Mallorea, it's going to be me." He leafed through the papers on the table in front of him, picked one up, and frowned at it. "I suppose we'd better deal with this," he said. "Where have you got Baron Vasca?"

"He's in a cell with a splendid view," Brador replied. "He can look out at the executioner's block. I'm sure it's been most educational."

Zakath remembered something then. "Demote him," he said.

"That's a novel word for the procedure," Brador murmured.

"That's not exactly what I meant," Zakath said with another chill smile. "Persuade him to tell us where he hid all the money he extorted from the people he dealt with. We'll transfer the funds to the imperial treasury." He turned to look at the large map on the wall of his study. "Southern Ebal, I think."

"Your Majesty?" Brador looked puzzled.

"Assign him to the post of Minister of Trade in southern Ebal."

"There isn't any trade in southern Ebal, your Majesty. There aren't any seaports, and the only thing they raise in the Temba marshes is mosquitoes."

"Vasca's inventive. I'm sure he'll come up with something."

"Then you don't want him—" Brador made a suggestive gesture across his throat with one hand.

"No," Zakath said. "I'm going to try something Belgarion suggested. I may need Vasca again someday and I don't want to have to dig him up in pieces." A faintly pained look crossed the Emperor's face. "Has there been any word about him?" he asked.

"Vasca? I just—"

"No. Belgarion."

"They were seen shortly after they left Mal Zeth, your Majesty. They were traveling with Prince Kheldar's Nadrak partner, Yarblek. Not long after that, Yarblek sailed for Gar og Nadrak."

"It was all a ruse, then," Zakath sighed. "All Belgarion really wanted was to get back to his own country. That wild story of theirs was made up out of whole cloth." Zakath passed a weary hand before his eyes. "I really liked that young man, Brador," he said sadly. "I should have known better."

"Belgarion didn't go back to the West, your Majesty," Brador informed him, "at least not with Yarblek. We always check that fellow's ships rather closely. So far as we're able to determine, Belgarion has not left Mallorea."

Zakath leaned back with a genuine smile on his face. "I'm

not sure why, but that makes me feel better. The thought that he'd betrayed me was quite painful for some reason. Any idea about where he's gone?"

"There was some turmoil in Katakor, your Majesty—up around Ashaba. It was the sort of thing one might associate with Belgarion—strange lights in the sky, explosions, that sort of thing."

Zakath laughed out loud, a delighted kind of laugh. "He *can* be a little ostentatious when he's irritated, can't he? He blew the whole wall out of my bedchamber in Rak Hagga one time."

"Oh?"

"He was trying to make a point."

There was a respectful rap on the door.

"Come," Zakath replied shortly.

"General Atesca has arrived, your Majesty," one of the red-garbed guards at the door reported.

"Good. Send him in."

The broken-nosed general entered and saluted smartly. "Your Majesty," he said. His red uniform was travel-stained.

"You made good time, Atesca," Zakath said. "It's good to see you again."

"Thank you, your Majesty. We had a good following wind, and the sea was calm."

"How many men did you bring with you?"

"About fifty thousand."

"How many men do we have now?" Zakath asked Brador.

"Something in excess of a million, your Majesty."

"That's a solid number. Let's stage up the troops and get ready to move." He rose and went to the window. The leaves had begun to turn, filling the garden below with bright reds and yellows. "I want to quiet things down on the east coast," he said, "and it's turning into autumn now, so I think we want to move the troops before the weather starts to deteriorate. We'll go on down to Maga Renn and send out scouting parties from there. If the circumstances are right, we'll march. If not, we can wait at Maga Renn for more troops to come back from Cthol Murgos."

"I'll get started on that immediately, your Majesty." Brador bowed and quietly left the room.

"Sit down, Atesca," the Emperor said. "What's happening in Cthol Murgos?"

"We're going to try to hold the cities we've already taken, your Majesty," Atesca reported, drawing up a chair. "We've gathered the bulk of our forces near Rak Cthan. They're waiting there for transport to bring them back to Mallorea."

"Any chance that Urgit might try a counterattack?"

"I wouldn't think so, your Majesty. I don't believe he'll gamble his army in open country. Of course, you never know what a Murgo might do."

"That's true," Zakath agreed. He kept his knowledge that Urgit was not actually a Murgo to himself. He leaned back. "You captured Belgarion for me once, Atesca," he said.

"Yes, your Majesty."

"I'm afraid you're going to have to do it again. He managed to get away. Careless of me, I suppose, but I had a lot on my mind at the time."

"We'll just have to pick him up again then, won't we, your Majesty?"

The Alorn Council met at Boktor that year. Somewhat uncharacteristically, Queen Porenn took charge. The tiny blond queen of Drasnia, dressed in her usual black, walked quietly to the head of the table in the red-draped council chamber in the palace and took the chair normally reserved for the Rivan King. The others stared at her in astonishment.

"Gentlemen," she began crisply, "I recognize the fact that this flies in the face of tradition, but our time is limited. Certain information has come to me that I think you should be

29

made aware of. We have decisions to make and very little time in which to make them."

Emperor Varana leaned back in his chair with an amused twinkle in his eyes. "We will now pause while the Alorn kings go into collective apoplexy," he said.

King Anheg scowled at the curly-haired emperor for a moment, then laughed. "No, Varana," he said wryly. "We all got that out of our systems when Rhodar persuaded us to follow Ce'Nedra into Mishrak ac Thull. It's Porenn's house; let her run things."

"Why, thank you, Anheg." The Queen of Drasnia actually sounded a little surprised. She paused, gathering her thoughts. "As I'm sure you've noticed, our gathering this year includes kings who would not normally attend. The matter before us, however, concerns us all. I've recently received communications from Belgarath, Belgarion, and the others."

There was an excited stir in the room. Porenn held up one hand. "They're in Mallorea, close on the trail of the abductor of Belgarion's son."

"That young man can move faster than the wind sometimes," King Fulrach of Sendaria observed. The years had given Fulrach a tendency toward portliness, and his brown beard was now streaked with silver.

"How did they get to Mallorea?" King Cho-Hag asked in his quiet voice.

"It seems that they were captured by Kal Zakath," Porenn replied. "Garion and Zakath became friends, and Zakath took them with him when he returned to Mal Zeth."

"Zakath actually became *friends* with somebody?" King Drosta of Gar og Nadrak demanded incredulously in his shrill voice. "Impossible!"

"Garion has a way about him, sometimes," Hettar murmured.

"The friendship, however, may have run its course," Porenn continued. "Late one night, Garion and his friends slipped out of Mal Zeth without saying good-bye to the Emperor."

"With the whole imperial army on their trail, I'd imagine," Varana added.

"No," Porenn disagreed. "Zakath can't leave Mal Zeth just now. Tell them, Yarblek."

Silk's rangy partner rose to his feet. "They've got plague in Mal Zeth," he said. "Zakath has sealed up the city. No one can go in or out."

"Prithee," Mandorallen asked, "how then was it possible for our friends to make good their escape?"

"I'd picked up an itinerant comedian," Yarblek said sourly. "I didn't think much of him, but he amused Vella. She's fond of bawdy stories."

"Be careful, Yarblek," the Nadrak dancer warned. "You still have your health, but I can fix that for you." She put one hand suggestively on a dagger hilt. Vella wore a stunning lavender gown. There were a few concessions to Nadrak customs in her dress, however. She still wore polished leather boots—with daggers in their tops—and the customary wide leather belt about her waist was still adorned with similar knives. The men in the room, however, had all been surreptitiously eyeing her since she had entered. No matter how she was dressed, Vella still had the power to attract every eye.

"Anyway," Yarblek hurried on, "the fellow knew of a tunnel that runs from the palace to an abandoned quarry outside the city. It got us all out of Mal Zeth with no one the wiser."

"Zakath won't like that," Drosta said. "He hates to let people go once he's caught them."

"There's been an uprising of some sort in the Seven Kingdoms of Karanda in northern Mallorea," Porenn went on. "I understand that there are demons involved."

"Demons?" Varana said skeptically. "Oh, come now, Porenn."

"That's what Belgarath reports."

"Belgarath has a warped sense of humor, sometimes," Varana scoffed. "He was probably just joking. There's no such thing as a demon."

"You're wrong, Varana," King Drosta said with uncharacteristic soberness. "I saw one once—up in Morindland when I was a boy."

"What did it look like?" Varana did not sound convinced.

Drosta shuddered. "You really don't want to know."

"At any rate," Porenn said, "Zakath has ordered the bulk of his army back from Cthol Murgos to put down this uprising. It won't be very long until he floods the entirety of Karanda with troops, and that's the area where our friends are. That's why I've called this meeting. What are we going to do about it?"

Lelldorin of Wildantor came to his feet. "We'll need fast horses," he said to Hettar.

"Why?" Hettar asked.

"To get to their aid, of course." The young Asturian's eyes were flashing with excitement.

"Uh—Lelldorin," Barak said gently, "the Sea of the East is between here and Mallorea."

"Oh," Lelldorin said, looking slightly abashed. "I didn't know that. We'll need a boat, too, won't we?"

Barak and Hettar exchanged a long look. "Ship," Barak corrected absently.

"What?"

"Never mind, Lelldorin," Barak sighed.

"We can't," King Anheg said flatly. "Even if we could get through, we'd destroy Garion's chances of winning in the fight with the Child of Dark. That's what the Seeress told us at Rheon, remember?"

"But this is different," Lelldorin protested, tears standing in his eyes.

"No," Anheg said. "It's not. This is exactly what we were warned against. We can't go near them until this is over."

"But—"

"Lelldorin," Anheg said. "I want to go as much as you do, but we can't. Would Garion thank us if we were responsible for the loss of his son?"

Mandorallen rose to his feet and began to pace up and down, his armor clinking. "Methinks thy reasoning is aright, your Majesty," he said to Anheg. "We may not join with our friends, lest our presence imperil their quest, and we would all give up our lives to prevent that. We *may*, however, journey straightaway to Mallorea and, without going near them, place ourselves between them and the hordes of Kal Zakath. We can thereby bring the unfriendly advance of the Malloreans to a precipitous halt and thus allow Garion to escape."

Barak stared at the great knight, whose face shone with unthinking zeal. Then he groaned and buried his face in his hands.

"There, there," Hettar murmured, patting the big man sympathetically on the shoulder.

King Fulrach rubbed at his beard. "Why does it seem that we've done this before?" he asked. "It's the same as last time. We have to create a diversion to help our friends get through. Any ideas?"

"Invade Mallorea," Drosta said eagerly.

"Sack Zakath's coastline," Anheg said just as eagerly.

Porenn sighed.

"We could invade Cthol Murgos," Cho-Hag suggested thoughtfully.

"Yes!" Hettar agreed fiercely.

Cho-Hag held up his hand. "Only as a ruse, my son," he said. "Zakath has committed forces to the conquest of Cthol Murgos. If the armies of the West moved into that region, he'd almost be obliged to try to counter us, wouldn't he?"

Varana slid lower in his chair. "It's got possibilities," he admitted, "but it's already autumn, and the mountains of Cthol Murgos are brutal in the winter. It's a bad time to move troops around down there. An army can't move very fast on frozen feet. I think we might be able to accomplish the same thing by diplomacy—without risking a single toe."

"Trust a Tolnedran to be devious," Anheg growled.

"Do you *like* freezing, Anheg?" Varana asked.

Anheg shrugged. "It's something to do in the wintertime," he said.

Varana rolled his eyes ceilingward. "Alorns," he said.

"All right," Anheg said by way of apology. "I was only joking. What's this brilliantly devious plan of yours?"

Varana looked across the room at Javelin. "How good is the Mallorean intelligence service, Margrave Khendon?" he asked bluntly.

Javelin rose to his feet, straightening his pearl-gray doublet. "By himself, Brador is very good, your Imperial Majesty," he replied. "His people are sometimes awkward and obvious, but he has a lot of them. He has unlimited money to work with." He cast a slightly reproachful glance at Queen Porenn.

"Be nice, Khendon," she murmured. "I'm on a tight budget."

"Yes, ma'am." He bowed with a faint smile, then straightened and spoke in a crisp, businesslike manner. "Mallorean intelligence is crude by our standards, but Brador has the resources to put as many agents in the field as he needs. Neither Drasnian nor Tolnedran intelligence has that luxury. Brador sometimes loses a hundred people in the process, but he can usually get the information." He sniffed disdainfully. "I prefer a neater type of operation, personally."

"Then this Brador has operatives in Rak Urga?" Varana pressed.

"Almost certainly," Javelin replied. "I have four in the Drojim Palace at this time myself—and your Majesty's service has two that I know of."

"I didn't know that," Varana said with an innocent look. "Really?"

Varana laughed. "All right," he went on, "what would Zakath do if word reached Mal Zeth that the Kingdoms of the West were about to conclude a military alliance with the King of Murgodom?"

Javelin began to pace up and down. "It's very hard to know exactly what Zakath will do in any given situation," he mused. "A lot depends on just how serious his domestic problems are, but an alliance between the Murgos and the West would pose a major threat to Mallorea. He'd almost have to come back immediately and make an all-out effort to crush the Murgos before our troops could reinforce them."

"Ally ourselves with the Murgos?" Hettar exclaimed. "Never!"

"Nobody's suggesting a real alliance, my Lord Hettar," Kail, the son of the Rivan Warder, told him. "All we want to do is distract Zakath for long enough to give Belgarion the time to slip past him. The negotiations can drag on and then fall apart later on."

"Oh," Hettar said, looking a bit abashed, "that's different, then—I suppose."

"All right," Varana went on crisply. "Perhaps we can persuade Zakath that we're about to conclude an alliance with Urgit—if we do it right. Javelin, have your people kill a few Mallorean agents in the Drojim palace—not all of them, mind you—just enough to convince Mal Zeth that this is a serious diplomatic effort."

"I understand perfectly, your Majesty." Javelin smiled. "I have just the man—a recently recruited Nyissan assassin named Issus."

"Good. A possible alliance will serve the same purpose as a real one. We can distract Zakath without the loss of a single man—unless we count this Issus fellow."

"Don't worry about Issus, your Majesty," Javelin assured him. "He's a survivor."

"I think we're missing something," Anheg growled. "I wish Rhodar were here."

"Yes," Porenn agreed in a voice near to tears.

"Sorry, Porenn," Anheg said, engulfing her tiny hand in his huge one, "but you know what I mean."

"I have a diplomat in Rak Urga," Varana continued. "He can make the overtures to King Urgit. Do we know anything useful about the King of the Murgos?"

"Yes," Porenn said firmly. "He'll be amenable to the suggestion."

"How do you know, your Majesty?"

Porenn hesitated. "I'd rather not say," she said with a quick glance at Javelin. "Just take my word for it."

"Of course," Varana agreed.

Vella rose and walked to the window, her satin gown filling the room with its music. "You people of the West always want to complicate things," she said critically. "Zakath's your problem. Send somebody to Mal Zeth with a sharp knife."

"You should have been a man, Vella." Anheg laughed.

She turned and looked at him with smoldering eyes. "Do you really think so?" she asked.

"Well," he hesitated, "maybe not."

She leaned disconsolately against the window casing. "I wish I had my juggler here to entertain me," she said. "Politics always give me a headache." She sighed. "I wonder whatever happened to him."

Porenn smiled, watching the girl intently and remembering the sudden insight she had when the Nadrak girl first arrived in Boktor. "Would you be terribly disappointed to find out that your juggler was not who he seemed to be?" she asked. "Belgarath mentioned him in his letter."

Vella looked at her sharply.

"Belgarath would have known him, of course," Porenn went on. "It was Beldin."

Vella's eyes went wide. "The hunchbacked sorcerer?" she exclaimed. "The one who can fly?"

Porenn nodded.

Vella said a number of things that no genteel lady would have said. Even King Anheg turned slightly pale at her choice of language. Then she drew a dagger and advanced on Yarblek, her breath hissing between her teeth. Mandorallen, clad all in steel, stepped in front of her, and Hettar and Barak seized her from behind and wrested the knife from her grasp.

"You idiot!" she shrieked at the cringing Yarblek. "You absolute idiot! You could have sold me to him!" Then she collapsed weeping against Barak's fur-clad chest, even as Hettar prudently relieved her of her other three daggers.

Zandramas, the Child of Dark, stood gazing across a desolate valley where shattered villages smoked and smoldered under a lead-gray sky. The eyes of the Child of Dark were hooded, and she looked unseeing at the devastation spread before her. A lusty wail came from behind her, and she set her teeth together. "Feed him," she said shortly.

"As you command, mistress," the man with white eyes said quickly in a mollifying tone.

"Don't patronize me, Naradas," she snapped. "Just shut the brat up. I'm trying to think."

It had been a long time. Zandramas had worked everything out so very carefully. Now she had come half around the world, and, despite her best efforts, the Godslayer with his dreadful sword was but a few days behind her.

The sword. The flaming sword. It filled her sleep with nightmares—and the burning face of the Child of Light terrified her even more. "How *does* he stay so close behind?" she exploded. "Will nothing slow him?"

She thrust her hands out in front of her and turned them palms-up. A myriad of tiny points of light seemed to swirl beneath the skin of her hands—swirling, glittering like a constellation of minuscule stars spinning in her very flesh. How long would it be until those constellations invaded her entire body and she ceased even to be human? How long until the dreadful spirit of the Child of Dark possessed her utterly? The child wailed again.

"I told you to shut him up!" she half shouted.

"At once, mistress," Naradas said.

The Child of Dark went back to the contemplation of the starry universe enclosed in her flesh.

Eriond and Horse rode out at the first light before the others had awakened, cantering across a mountain meadow in the silvery dawn-light. It was good to ride alone, to feel the surge and flow of Horse's muscles under him and the wind against his face without the distraction of talk.

He reined in atop a knoll to watch the sun rise, and that was good, too. He looked out over the sun-touched mountains of Zamad, drinking in the beauty and solitude, then gazed at the fair sight of the bright green fields and forests. Life was good here. The world was filled with loveliness and with people he loved.

How could Aldur have forced Himself to leave all this? Aldur had been the God who must have loved this world above all things, since He had refused to take a people to worship Him, but had chosen to spend His time alone to study this fair world. And now He could only visit occasionally in spiritual form.

But Aldur had accepted the sacrifice. Eriond sighed, feeling that perhaps no sacrifice could be truly unbearable if it were made out of love. Eriond took comfort in that belief.

Then he sighed again and slowly rode back toward the little lake and the cluster of tents where the others slept.

CHAPTER TWO

They rose late that morning. The turmoil of the past several weeks seemed finally to have caught up with Garion, and, even though he could tell by the light streaming in through the front of the tent that the sun was already high, he was reluctant to move. He could hear the clinking of Polgara's cooking utensils and the murmur of voices. He knew that he was going to have to get up soon anyway. He considered trying to doze off to catch a last few moments of sleep, but he decided against it. He moved carefully to avoid waking Ce'Nedra as he slid out from under their blankets. He leaned over and gently kissed her hair, then he pulled on his rust-colored tunic, picked up his boots and sword, and ducked out of the tent.

Polgara, in her gray traveling dress, was by her cook-fire. As usual, she hummed softly as she worked. Silk and Belgarath were talking quietly nearby. Silk had, for some reason, changed clothes and he now wore the soft, pearl-gray doublet which marked him as a prosperous businessman. Belgarath, of course, still wore his rust-colored tunic, patched hose, and mismatched boots. Durnik and Toth were fishing, lacing the blue surface of the little mountain lake with their lines, and Eriond was brushing the gleaming chestnut coat of his stallion. The rest of their friends had apparently not arisen yet.

"We thought you were going to sleep all day," Belgarath said as Garion sat on a log to pull on his boots.

"I gave it some thought," Garion admitted. He stood up and looked across the sparkling lake. There was a grove of aspens on the far side, their trunks the color of new snow. The leaves had begun to turn and they shimmered in the morning sun like beaten gold. The air was cool and slightly damp. Suddenly he wished that they could stay here for a few days. He sighed and walked over to join his grandfather and Silk near the fire. "Why the fancy clothes?" he asked the rat-faced little Drasnian.

Silk shrugged. "We're moving into an area where I'm fairly well known," he replied. "We might be able to take advantage of that—as long as people recognize me. Are you absolutely sure the trail goes toward the southeast?"

Garion nodded. "There was a little confusion right at first, but I got it sorted out."

"Confusion?" Belgarath asked.

"The Sardion was here, too—a long time ago. For a few moments, the Orb seemed to want to follow both trails at the same time. I had to speak with it rather firmly about that." Garion draped the sword belt over his shoulder and buckled it. Then he shifted the scabbard slightly until it was more comfortable. The Orb on the pommel of the sword was glowing a sullen red color.

"Why's it doing that?" Silk asked curiously.

"Because of the Sardion," Garion told him. He looked over his shoulder at the glowing stone. "Stop that," he said.

"Don't hurt its feelings," Silk warned. "We could be in a great deal of trouble if it decides to start sulking."

"What lies off to the southeast?" Belgarath asked the little man.

"Voresebo," Silk replied. "There isn't much there except some caravan tracks and a few mines up in the mountains. There's a seaport at Pannor. I land there sometimes on my way back from Melcena."

"Are the people there Karands?"

Silk nodded. "But they're even cruder than the ones back in the central kingdoms—if that's possible."

The blue-banded hawk came spiraling out of a bright morning sky, flared, and shimmered into the form of Beldin as soon as the talons touched the ground. The hunchbacked little sorcerer was dressed in his usual rags tied on with bits of thong, and twigs and straw clung to his hair and beard. He shivered. "I *hate* to fly when it's cold," he grumbled. "It makes my wings ache."

"It's not really that cold," Silk said.

"Try it a couple thousand feet up." Beldin pointed toward the sky, then turned, and spat out a couple of soggy gray feathers.

"Grazing again, uncle?" Polgara asked from her cook-fire.

"Just a bite of breakfast, Pol," he replied. "There was a pigeon that got up too early this morning."

"You didn't have to do that, you know." She tapped meaningfully on the side of her bubbling pot with a long-handled wooden spoon.

Beldin shrugged. "The world isn't going to miss one pigeon."

Garion shuddered. "How can you stand to eat them raw like that?"

"You get used to it. I've never had much luck trying to build a cook-fire with my talons." He looked at Belgarath. "There's some trouble up ahead," he said, "a lot of smoke and groups of armed men wandering around."

"Could you see who they were?"

"I didn't get that close. There's usually a bored archer or two in any crowd like that, and I'd prefer not to have my tail feathers parted with an arrow just because some idiot wants to show off his skill."

"Has that ever happened?" Silk asked curiously.

"Once—a long time ago. My hip still aches in cold weather."

"Did you do something about it?"

"I had a chat with the archer. I asked him not to do it any more. He was breaking his bow across his knee when I left." He turned back to Belgarath. "Are we sure the trail goes on down to that plain?"

"The Orb is."

"Then we'll have to chance it." The little man looked around. "I thought you'd have struck the tents by now."

"I decided it might not hurt to let everybody get some sleep. We've been traveling hard and we're going to have to do it some more, I think."

"You always want to pick these idyllic spots for your rest stops, Belgarath," Beldin observed. "I think you're secretly a romantic."

Belgarath shrugged. "Nobody's perfect."

"Garion," Polgara called.

"Yes, Aunt Pol?"

"Why don't you wake the others? Breakfast's almost ready."

"Right away, Aunt Pol."

After breakfast, they broke camp and started out about midmorning with Beldin flying on ahead to scout out possible trouble. It was pleasantly warm now, and there was the pungent smell of evergreens in the air. Ce'Nedra was strangely quiet as she rode along beside Garion with her dark gray cloak pulled tightly around her.

"What's the matter, dear?" he asked her.

"She didn't have Geran with her," the little queen murmured sadly.

"Zandramas, you mean? No, she didn't, did she?"

"Was she really there, Garion?"

"In a way, but in a way she wasn't. It was sort of the way Cyradis was here and not here at the same time."

"I don't understand."

"It was more than a projection, but less than actually being there. We talked it over last night, and Beldin explained it. I didn't understand very much of what he said. Beldin's explanations get a little obscure sometimes."

"He's very wise, isn't he?"

Garion nodded. "But he's not a very good teacher. He gets impatient with people who can't keep up with him. Anyway, this business of being somewhere between a projection and the real thing makes Zandramas very dangerous. We can't hurt her, but she can hurt us. She came very close to killing you yesterday, you know—until Poledra stopped her. She's very much afraid of Poledra."

"That's the first time I've ever seen your grandmother."

"No, actually it's not. She was there at Aunt Pol's wedding, remember? And she helped us in Ulgoland when we had to fight the Eldrak."

"But one time she was an owl, and the other time she was a wolf."

"In Poledra's case, I don't think that really matters."

Ce'Nedra suddenly laughed.

"What's so funny?"

"When this is all over and we're back home with our baby, why don't you change into a wolf for a while?" she suggested.

"Why?"

"It might be nice having a big gray wolf lying before the fire. And then on cold nights, I could burrow my feet into your fur to keep them warm."

He gave her a long steady look.

"I'd scratch your ears for you, Garion," she offered by way of inducement, "and get you nice bones from the kitchen to chew on."

"Never mind," he said flatly.

"But my feet get cold."

"I've noticed."

Just ahead of them as they rode up through a shady mountain pass, Silk and Sadi were engaged in a heated discussion. "Absolutely not," Silk said vehemently.

"I really think you're being unreasonable about this, Kheldar," Sadi protested. The eunuch had discarded his iridescent silk robe and now wore western-style tunic and hose and stout boots. "You have the distribution system already in place, and I have access to unlimited supplies. We could make millions."

"Forget it, Sadi. I won't deal in drugs."

"You deal in everything else, Kheldar. There's a market out there just waiting to be tapped. Why let scruples stand in the way of business?"

"You're Nyissan, Sadi. Drugs are a part of your culture, so you wouldn't understand."

"Lady Polgara uses drugs when she treats the sick," Sadi pointed out defensively.

"That's different."

"I don't see how."

"I could never explain it to you."

Sadi sighed. "I'm very disappointed in you, Kheldar. You're a spy, an assassin, and a thief. You cheat at dice, you counterfeit money, and you're unscrupulous with married women. You swindle your customers outrageously and you soak up ale like a sponge. You're the most corrupt man I've ever known, but you refuse to transport a few harmless little compounds that would make your customers very happy."

"A man has to draw the line somewhere," Silk replied loftily.

Velvet shifted in her saddle to look back at them. "That was one of the more fascinating conversations I've ever heard, gentlemen," she complimented them. "The implications in the field of comparative morality are absolutely staggering." She gave them a sunny smile with her dimples flashing into view.

"Uh—Margravine Liselle," Sadi said. "Do you happen to have Zith again?"

"Why, yes, Sadi, as a matter of fact, I do." The honey-blond girl held up one hand to head off his objections. "*But* I didn't steal her this time. She crawled into my tent in the middle of the night and crept into her favorite hiding place all on her own. The poor dear was actually shivering."

Silk turned slightly pale.

"Would you like to have her back?" Velvet asked the shaved-headed eunuch.

"No," Sadi sighed, rubbing his hand over his scalp, "I suppose not. As long as she's happy where she is, we might as well leave her there."

"She's very happy. In fact, she's purring." Velvet frowned slightly. "I think you should watch her diet just a bit, Sadi," she said critically. "Her little tummy seems to be getting bigger." She smiled again. "We wouldn't want a fat snake on our hands, would we?"

"Well, excuse me!" Sadi said, sounding very offended.

There was a large snag at the top of the pass, and the blue-banded hawk perched on a dead limb, busily preening his feathers with his hooked beak. As they approached, he swooped down, and Beldin stood in the trail in front of them, muttering curses.

"Something wrong, uncle?" Polgara asked him.

"I got caught in a crosswind," he growled. "It scrambled my feathers a bit. You know how that goes."

"Oh, goodness yes. It happens to me all the time. Night breezes are so unpredictable."

"Your feathers are too soft."

"I didn't design the owl, uncle, so don't blame me about the feathers."

"There's a crossroads tavern just up ahead," Beldin said to Belgarath. "Did you want to stop and see if we can find out what's going on down there on the plain?"

"That might not be a bad idea," Belgarath agreed. "Let's not ride into trouble if we don't have to."

"I'll wait for you inside then," Beldin said and soared away again.

Polgara sighed. "Why must it *always* be a tavern?" she complained.

"Because people who've been drinking like to talk, Pol," Belgarath explained in a reasonable tone. "You can gather more information in five minutes in a tavern than you can in an hour in a tearoom."

"I knew you'd be able to find a reason for it."

"Naturally."

They crossed over the top of the wooded pass and on down the shade-splotched trail to the tavern. It was a low building made of logs crudely chinked with mud. The roof was low, and its shingles had curled with the weather and the passage of years. Buff-colored chickens scratched at the dirt in the dooryard, and a large speckled sow lay in a mud puddle, nursing a litter of happily grunting piglets. There were a few spavined nags tied to a hitch rail in front of the tavern, and a Karand dressed in moth-eaten furs snored on the front stoop.

Polgara reined in her horse as they approached the tavern

and the first whiff of its reeking interior reached her nostrils. "I think, ladies, that we might prefer to wait over there in the shade."

"There *is* a certain fragrance coming out that door, isn't there?" Velvet agreed.

"You, too, Eriond," Polgara said firmly. "There's no need for you to start picking up bad habits this early in life." She rode over toward a grove of tall fir trees some distance away from the tavern and dismounted in the shade. Durnik and Toth exchanged a quick glance, then joined her there with Velvet, Ce'Nedra, and Eriond.

Sadi started to dismount in front of the tavern. Then he sniffed once and gagged slightly. "This is not my sort of place, gentlemen," he said. "I think I'll wait outside as well. Besides, it's Zith's feeding time."

"Suit yourself," Belgarath shrugged, dismounting and leading the way toward the building. They stepped over the snoring Karand on the stoop and went on inside. "Split up and spread out," the old man muttered. "Circulate and talk to as many as you can." He looked at Silk. "We're not here to make a career out of this," he cautioned.

"Trust me," Silk said, moving away.

Garion stood just inside the door, blinking to let his eyes adjust to the dimness. The tavern showed no signs of ever having been cleaned. The floor was covered with moldy straw that reeked of spilled beer, and scraps of rotting food lay in heaps in the corners. A crudely built fireplace smoked at the far end, adding its fumes to the generally unpleasant odor of the place. The tables consisted of rough-hewn planks laid on trellises, and the benches were half logs with sticks drilled into their undersides for legs. Garion saw Beldin talking with several Karands over in one corner and he started over to join him.

As he passed one of the tables, his foot came down on

something soft. There was a protesting squeal and a sudden scramble of hoofed feet.

"Don't step on my pig," the bleary-eyed old Karand sitting at the table said belligerently. "I don't step on your pig, do I?" He pronounced it "peg," and Garion had a little trouble sorting out his dialect.

"Watch yer fate," the Karand said ominously.

"Fate?" Garion shrank back from that word just a bit.

"Fate. Them thangs you got on the end of yer laigs."

"Oh. Feet."

"That's what I just said—fate."

"Sorry," Garion apologized. "I didn't quite understand."

"That's the trouble with you outlanders. You can't even understand the language when she's spoke to you plain as day."

"Why don't we have a tankard of ale?" Garion suggested. "I'll apologize to your pig just as soon as he comes back."

The Karand squinted at him suspiciously. The old man was bearded and he wore clothing made of poorly tanned furs. He wore a hat made from the whole skin of a badger—with the legs and tail still attached. He was very dirty, and Garion could clearly see the fleas peeking out of his beard.

"I'm buying," Garion offered, sitting down across the table from the pig's owner.

The old Karand's face brightened noticeably.

They had a couple of tankards of ale together. Garion noticed that the stuff had a raw, green flavor to it, as if it had been dipped from the vat a week or so too soon. His host, however, smacked his lips and rolled his eyes as if this were the finest brew in the world. Something cold and wet touched Garion's hand, and he jerked it away. He looked down into a pair of earnest blue eyes fenced in by bristly white eyelashes. The pig had recently been to the wallow and he carried a powerful odor with him.

The old Karand chortled. "That's just my peg," he said.

"He's a good-natured young peg, and he don't hold no grudges." The fur-clad fellow blinked owlishly. "He's a orphan, y'know."

"Oh?"

"His ma made real good bacon, though." The old man snuffled and wiped his nose on the back of his hand. "Sometimes I miss her real bad," he admitted. He squinted at Garion. "Say, that's a mighty big knife you got there."

"Yes," Garion agreed. He absently scratched the half-grown pig's ears, and the animal closed his eyes in bliss, laid his head in Garion's lap, and grunted contentedly.

"We were coming down the trail out of the mountains," Garion said, "and we saw a lot of smoke out on the plain. Is there some kind of trouble out there?"

"The worst kinda trouble there is, friend," the old man said seriously. He squinted at Garion again. "You're not one of them Mal-or-eens, are you?"

"No," Garion assured him, "not Mallorean. I come from farther west."

"I didn't know there *was* anythin' to the west of the Mal-or-eens. Anyhow, there's whole bunches of people down there on the plains havin' some kind of a argument about religion."

"Religion?"

"I don't hold much with it myself," the Karand admitted. "There's them as do and them as don't, and I'm one of them as don't. Let the Gods take care of theirselves, I say. I'll take care of me and mine, and we're quits on the whole business."

"Seems like a good way," Garion said carefully.

"Glad you see it like that. Anyhow, there's this Grolim named Zandramas down in Dar-sheeva. This Zandramas, she come up into Voresebo and started talkin' about this here new God of Angarak—Torak bein' dead an' all, y'know. Now, I'm just about as interested in all that as my peg is. He's a smart peg and he knows when people is talkin' nonsense."

Garion patted the pig's muddy flank, and the plump little

animal made an ecstatic sound. "Good pig," Garion agreed. "Peg, that is."

"I'm fond of him. He's warm and good to snuggle up against on a cold night—and he don't hardly snore none at all. Well, sir, this Zandramas, she come up here and started preachin' and yellin' and I don't know what all. The Grolims all gives out a moan and falls down on their faces. Then, a while back, a whole new bunch of Grolims comes over the mountains, and they says that this Zandramas is dead wrong. They says that there's gonna be a new God over Angarak, right enough, but that this Zandramas don't have the straight of it. That's what all the smoke down there on the plains is about. Both sides is a-burnin' and a-killin' and a-preachin' about *their* idea of who the new God's gonna be. I'm not gonna have anythin' to do with either side. Me and my peg are gonna go back up in the mountains and let them folks kill each other. When they get it all sorted out, we'll come back and nod at whichever altar comes out on top as we go by."

"You keep calling this Zandramas 'she,'" Garion noted.

"Would you believe it's a *woman*?" the Karand snorted. "That's the foolishest thing I ever heard tell of. Women got no business mixin' up in men's affairs."

"Have you ever seen her?"

"Like I say, I don't mess around in religious stuff. Me and my peg, we just kinda keep to ourselves when it comes to that."

"Good way to get along," Garion said to him. "My friends and I have to go through that plain down there, though. Are Grolims all we need to worry about?"

"I can see you're a stranger," the Karand said, suggestively looking down into his empty tankard.

"Here," Garion said, "let's get another one." He fished another coin out of the pouch at his waist and signaled the servingman.

"The whole thang, friend," the garrulous owner of the pig

went on, "is that in this part of the country, them Grolims always has troops with 'em. The ones as follows Zandramas, they got the army of the king of Voresebo with 'em. The old king, he didn't hold with none of this religious stuff, but he got hisself de-posed. His son decided the old man was gettin' too silly to run the country, so he set his pa aside and took the throne for hisself. The son's a squinty-eyed sort and he's lookin' to put hisself on the side most likely to win. He's throwed in with Zandramas, but then this Urvon fella, he comes along, and he's got this whole army out of Jenno and Ganesia and folks in armor and some real ugly big black dogs with him—not to mention all the Grolims. It's mean down there on the plains, friend. They're killin' and burnin' and sacrificin' prisoners on this altar or that. If it was me, I'd go a long way around all that foolishness."

"I wish I could, friend," Garion told him sincerely. "We heard that there were demons up in Jenno—off toward Callida. Have any of them shown up around here?"

"Demons?" The Karand shuddered, making the sign against evil. "None that I ever heard tell of. If I had, me and my peg would already be so far back in the mountains that they'd have to ship daylight in to us by pack train."

Despite himself, Garion found that he liked this gabbly old fellow. There was an almost musical flow to his illiterate speech, a kind of warm inclusiveness that paid no attention to any kind of social distinctions, and a shrewd, even penetrating, assessment of the chaos around him. It was almost with regret that Garion briefly acknowledged Silk's jerk of the head in the direction of the door. Gently, he removed the pig's head from his lap. The animal made a small, discontented sound. "I'm afraid I'm going to have to go now," he told the Karand as he rose to his feet. "I thank you for your company—and the loan of your pig."

"Peg," the Karand corrected.

"Peg," Garion agreed. He stopped the servingman who was

51

going by and handed him a coin. "Give my friend and his peg whatever they'd like," he said.

"Why, thank you, my young friend." The old Karand grinned expansively.

"My pleasure," Garion said. He looked down. "Have a nice day, pig," he added.

The pig grunted rather distantly and clattered around the table to his master.

Ce'Nedra wrinkled her nose as he approached the shady spot where the ladies had been waiting. "What on earth have you been doing, Garion?" she asked. "You smell awful."

"I was getting acquainted with a pig."

"A pig?" she exclaimed. "Whatever for?"

"You almost had to have been there."

As they rode along exchanging the information they had gleaned, it became evident that the owner of the pig had offered a surprisingly complete and succinct perception of the situation in Voresebo. Garion repeated the conversation, complete with dialect.

"He didn't *really* talk that way, did he?" Velvet giggled incredulously.

"Why, no'm," Garion said, exaggerating just a bit, "when you get right down to the core of it, he didn't. There was 'theses' and 'thoses' and 'themses' that I can't quite get the hang of. Me and the pig got along good, though."

"Garion," Polgara said a bit distantly, "do you suppose you could ride back there a ways?" She gestured toward the rear of the column. "Several hundred yards or so, I'd say."

"Yes, ma'am," he said. He reined Chretienne in. The big gray horse, he noted, also seemed a bit offended by something in the air.

By general request, Garion bathed that night in a shockingly cold mountain stream. When he returned, shivering, to the fire, Belgarath looked at him and said, "I think you'd better put your armor back on. If half of what your friend with the pig said is true, you might need it."

"Peg," Garion corrected.

"What?"

"Never mind."

The next morning dawned clear and definitely chilly. The mail coat felt clammy even through the padded tunic Garion always wore under it, and it was heavy and uncomfortable. Durnik cut him a lance from a nearby thicket and leaned it against a tree near where the horses were picketed.

Belgarath came back from a small hilltop where he had been surveying the plains below. "From what I can see, the turmoil is fairly general down there, so there isn't much point in trying to avoid people. The quicker we get past Voresebo, the better, so we might as well ride straight on through. We'll try to talk our way out of any difficulties first; and, if that doesn't work, we'll do it the other way."

"I suppose I'd better go find another club." Sadi sighed.

They rode out with Garion jingling along in the lead. His helmet was in place, and his shield was strapped to his left arm. The butt of his lance rested beside his foot in his stirrup, and he affected a menacing scowl. The sword strapped across his back pulled steadily at him, indicating that they were still on the trail of Zandramas. When they reached the edge of the foothills, the winding mountain track became a narrow, rutted road stretching off toward the southeast. They picked up their pace and moved along the road at a brisk trot.

A few miles out onto the plain, they passed a burning village set back about a half mile from the road. They did not stop to investigate.

About noon, they encountered a party of armed men on foot. There were about fifteen of them, and they wore clothing which vaguely resembled uniforms.

"Well?" Garion said back over his shoulder, tightening his grip on his lance.

53

"Let me talk to them first," Silk said, moving his horse forward. "Try to look dangerous." The little man walked his horse towards the strangers. "You're blocking the road," he told them in a flat, unfriendly tone.

"We have orders to check everyone who passes," one of them said, looking at Garion a little nervously.

"All right, you've checked us. Now stand aside."

"Which side are you on?"

"Now, that's a stupid question, man," Silk replied. "Which side are *you* on?"

"I don't have to answer that."

"Then neither do I. Use your eyes, man. Do I look like a Karand—or a Temple Guardsman—or a Grolim?"

"Do you follow Urvon or Zandramas?"

"Neither one. I follow money, and you don't make money by getting mixed up in religion."

The roughly dressed soldier looked even more uncertain. "I have to report which side you're on to my captain."

"That's assuming that you've seen me," Silk told him, bouncing a purse suggestively on the palm of his hand. "I'm in a hurry, friend. I have no interest in your religion. Please do me the same courtesy."

The soldier was looking at the purse in Silk's hand with undisguised greed.

"It would be worth quite a bit to me not to be delayed," Silk suggested slyly. He theatrically wiped his brow. "It's getting hot out here," he said. "Why don't you and your men go find some shade to rest in? I'll 'accidentally' drop this purse here, and you can 'find' it later. That way, you make a nice profit, and I get to move along without interference and without having someone in authority find out that I've passed."

"It *is* getting warm out here," the soldier agreed.

"I thought you might have noticed that."

The other soldiers were grinning openly.

"You won't forget to drop the purse?"

stop to think. He discarded his lance, drew Iron-grip's sword, cautioned the Orb to avoid display, and then charged.

The Grolim was apparently so caught up in his religious frenzy that he neither heard nor saw Garion bearing down on him. He screamed once as Chretienne thundered over the top of him. The soldiers took one startled look at Garion, threw away their weapons, and fled. That did not seem to satisfy his anger, however. Implacably, he pursued them. His anger was not so great, though, as to goad him into killing unarmed men. Instead, he simply rode them down one by one. When the last had tumbled beneath the big gray's hooves, Garion wheeled, freed the prisoners, and cantered back to the road.

"Don't you think that was a little excessive?" Belgarath demanded angrily.

"Not under the circumstances, no," Garion snapped back. "At least I'm fairly sure that *one* group of soldiers in this stinking country won't be dragging civilians to the altar—at least not until all the broken bones mend."

Belgarath snorted in disgust and turned away.

Still enraged, Garion glared belligerently at Polgara. "Well?" he demanded.

"I didn't say anything, dear," she said mildly. "Next time, though, don't you think you should let your grandfather know what you're planning? These little surprises set his teeth on edge sometimes."

Beldin came flaring in. "What happened out there?" he asked curiously when he had resumed his own form. He pointed at the groaning soldiers dotting the nearby field.

"My horse needed some exercise," Garion said flatly. "Those soldiers got in his way."

"What's got you so foul-tempered this morning?"

"This is all so stupid."

"Of course it is, but get ready for some more of it. The border of Rengel is just ahead, and things are just as bad down there as they are here."

CHAPTER THREE

They paused at the border to consider their alternatives. The guardpost at the boundary was deserted, but black columns of smoke rose from burning villages, and they could clearly see large groups of men moving across the landscape, looking tiny in the distance.

"Things are a little more organized down here," Beldin reported. "About all we saw in Voresebo were fairly small bands, and they were more interested in loot than fighting. The groups are bigger on up ahead, and there's a certain semblance of discipline. I don't think we'll be able to bluff our way through Rengel the way we did Voresebo."

Toth made a series of obscure gestures.

"What did he say?" Belgarath asked Durnik.

"He suggests that we travel at night," Durnik replied.

"That's an absurd notion, Toth," Sadi protested. "If things are dangerous in the daytime, they'll be ten times more dangerous at night."

Toth's hands began to move again. For some reason, Garion found that he could almost understand what the huge mute was trying to say.

"He says that you looked at the idea too fast, Sadi," Durnik translated. "We've got certain advantages." The smith frowned slightly, and he looked back at his friend. "How did you find out about that?" he asked.

Toth gestured again.

"Oh," Durnik nodded. "I guess she *would* know, wouldn't she?" He turned to the others. "He says that Belgarath, Pol, and Garion can lead the way in their other forms. The darkness wouldn't be that big a problem for a pair of wolves and an owl."

Belgarath tugged thoughtfully at one earlobe. "It's got possibilities," he said to Beldin. "We could avoid just about anybody out there that way. Soldiers don't move around in the dark very much."

"They post sentries, though," the hunchback pointed out.

"Garion, Pol, and I wouldn't have much trouble locating them and leading the rest of you around them."

"It's going to be slow going," Velvet said. "We won't be able to travel at a gallop, and we'll have to detour around every sentry we come across."

"You know," Silk said, "now that I think about it, it's not such a bad idea. I sort of like it."

"You always enjoy sneaking around in the dark, Kheldar," Velvet said to him.

"Don't you?"

"Well—" Then she smiled at him. "I suppose I do, yes—but then, I'm a Drasnian, too."

"It would take too long," Ce'Nedra protested. "We're only a little way behind Zandramas. If we try to sneak, she'll get ahead again."

"I don't see that we've got much choice, Ce'Nedra," Garion told her gently. "If we just try to plow our way across Rengel, sooner or later we're going to run into more soldiers than we can handle."

"You're a sorcerer," she said accusingly. "You could wave your hand and just knock them out of our way."

"There are limits to that, Ce'Nedra," Polgara said. "Both Zandramas and Urvon have Grolims in the region. If we tried to do it that way, everybody in Rengel would know exactly where we were."

Ce'Nedra's eyes filled with tears, and her lower lip began to tremble. She turned and ran blindly away from the road, sobbing.

"Go after her, Garion," Polgara said. "See if you can get her calmed down."

They took shelter for the rest of the day in a grove of beech trees about a mile from the road. Garion tried to sleep, knowing that the night ahead of them would be very long; but after about an hour, he gave up and wandered restlessly about the camp. He shared Ce'Nedra's impatience. They were so close to Zandramas now, and moving at night would slow their pace to a crawl. Try though he might, however, he could think of no alternative.

As the sun was going down, they struck camp and waited at the edge of the beech grove for it to get dark.

"I think I've just hit a flaw in the plan," Silk said.

"Oh?" Belgarath asked.

"We need the Orb to be able to follow Zandramas. If Garion turns into a wolf, the Orb won't be able to tell him which way to go—or will it?"

Belgarath and Beldin exchanged a long look. "I don't know," Belgarath admitted. "Do you?"

"I haven't got the slightest idea," Beldin said.

"Well, there's only one way to find out," Garion said. He handed Chretienne's reins to Durnik and went some distance away from the horses. Carefully, he created the image of the wolf in his mind, then he began to focus his will upon the image. He seemed, as always, to go through a peculiar sensation of melting, and then it was done. He sat on his haunches for a moment, checking himself over to make sure everything was there.

His nose suddenly caught a familiar fragrance. He turned his head and looked back over his shoulder. Ce'Nedra stood there, her eyes very wide and the fingertips of one hand to her lips. "I-is that still really you, Garion?" she stammered.

He rose to his feet and shook himself. There was no way he could answer her. Human words would not fit in the mouth of a wolf. Instead, he padded over to her and licked her hand. She sank to her knees, wrapped her arms about his head, and laid her cheek against his muzzle. "Oh, Garion," she said in a tone of wonder.

On an impulse born out of sheer mischief, he deliberately licked her face from chin to hairline. His tongue was quite long—and quite wet.

"Stop that," she said, giggling in spite of herself and trying to wipe her face. He momentarily touched his cold nose to the side of her neck. She flinched away. Then he turned and loped off toward the road where the trail was. He paused in the bushes beside the road and carefully peered out, his ears alert and his nose searching for the scent of anyone in the vicinity. Then, satisfied, he slipped out of the bushes with his belly low to the ground to stand in the middle of the road.

It was not the same, of course. There was a subtle difference to the pulling sensation, but it was still there. He felt a peculiar satisfaction and had to restrain an urge to lift his muzzle in a howl of triumph. He turned then and loped back toward where the others were hidden. His toenails dug into the turf, and he exulted in a wild sense of freedom. It was almost with regret that he changed back into his own shape.

"Well?" Belgarath asked as he walked toward them in the gathering dusk.

"No problem," Garion replied, trying to sound casual about it. He suppressed the urge to grin, knowing that his offhand manner would irritate his grandfather enormously.

"Are you really sure we need him along on this trip?" Belgarath asked his daughter.

"Ah—yes, father," she said. "He is sort of necessary."

"I was afraid you might feel that way about it." He looked at the others. "All right," he said. "This is the way it works. Pol and Durnik can keep in touch with each other over quite some distance, so he'll be able to warn you if we run across any soldiers—or if the trail moves off the road. Move at a walk to keep down the noise, and be ready to take cover on short notice. Garion, keep your mind in contact with Pol's and don't forget that you've got a nose and ears as well as eyes. Swing back to the road from time to time to make sure we're still on the trail. Does anybody have any questions?"

They all shook their heads.

"All right then, let's go."

"Do you want me to go along?" Beldin offered.

"Thanks all the same, uncle," Polgara declined, "but hawks don't really see all that well in the dark. You wouldn't be much help after you'd flown head-on into a few trees."

It was surprisingly easy. The first impulse of any group of soldiers when setting up for the night is to build fires, and the second is to keep them going until the sun comes up. Guided by these cheery beacons, Garion and Belgarath were able to locate the night encampments of all the bands of troops in the area and to sniff out the sentries. As luck had it, in most cases the troops had set up some distance from the road, and the party was able to ride through undetected.

It was well into the night. Garion had crept to the top of a hill to survey the next valley. There were a fair number of campfires out there, winking at him in the darkness.

"Garion?" Ce'Nedra's voice seemed right on top of him. With a startled yelp, he jumped high in the air.

It took him a moment to regain his composure. "Ce'Nedra," he whined plaintively, "*please* don't do that. You almost scared me out of my fur."

"I just wanted to be sure you were all right," she said defensively. "If I have to wear this amulet, I may as well get some use out of it."

"I'm fine, Ce'Nedra," he said in a patient tone. "Just don't startle me like that. Wolves are edgy animals."

"Children," Polgara's voice cut in firmly. "You can play some other time. I'm trying to hear Durnik, and you're drowning him out with all this chatter."

"Yes, Aunt Pol," Garion replied automatically.

"I love you, Garion," Ce'Nedra whispered by way of farewell.

They traveled by night and sought cover as dawn began to stain the eastern sky for the next several days. It all became so easy that finally Garion grew careless. He was padding through a thicket on the fourth night and accidentally stepped on a dry twig.

"Who's there?" The voice was downwind of him, and the soldier's scent had not reached his nostrils. The fellow came pushing into the thicket, making a great deal of noise. He was warily holding a spear out in front of him. Angry more at himself than at the clumsy sentry, Garion shouldered the spear aside, raised up on his hind legs, and put his forepaws on the terrified man's shoulders. Then he swore at some length, his oaths coming out as a horrid growling and snarling.

The soldier's eyes bulged as Garion's awful fangs snapped

within inches of his face. Then he screamed and fled. Garion slunk guiltily out of the thicket and loped away.

Polgara's voice came to him. "What was that?"

"Nothing important," he replied, more than a little ashamed of himself. "Tell Durnik and the others to swing out to the west for a while. This group of soldiers is camped fairly close to the road."

It was nearly dawn on the following night when the night breeze brought the smell of frying bacon to Garion's nostrils. He crept forward through the tall grass, but before he could get near enough to see who was cooking, he encountered his grandfather.

"Who is it?" he asked in the manner of wolves.

"A couple hundred soldiers," Belgarath replied, "and a whole herd of pack mules."

"They're right on the road, aren't they?"

"I don't think that's going to be a problem. I heard a couple of them talking. It seems that they work for Silk."

"Silk's got his own army?" Garion asked incredulously.

"So it would seem. I wish that little thief wouldn't keep secrets from me." Garion felt the old man's thought reaching out. "Pol, tell Durnik to send Silk up here." Then he looked at Garion. "Let's go back to the road. I want to have a little talk with the pride of Drasnia."

They loped back to the road, resumed their own shapes, and intercepted Silk. Belgarath, Garion thought, showed enormous restraint. "There's a large group of soldiers wearing blue tunics just up ahead," he said in a level tone. "Would you by any chance know who they are?"

"What are they doing here?" Silk asked with a puzzled frown. "They've been told to avoid any area where there's trouble."

"Maybe they didn't hear you." Belgarath's tone was sarcastic.

"It's a standing order. I'm definitely going to talk with the captain about this."

"You've got a private army?" Garion asked the little man.

"I don't know that I'd call it an army, exactly. Yarblek and I hired some mercenaries to guard our caravans, is all."

"Isn't that terribly expensive?"

"Not nearly as expensive as losing those caravans would be. Highway robbery is a cottage industry in Karanda. Let's go talk with them."

"Why don't we?" Belgarath's tone was flat—even unfriendly.

"You're not taking this very well, old friend."

"Don't crowd it, Silk. I've been slinking through wet grass for five nights running. I've got burrs in my coat and a snarl in my tail that's going to take me a week to chew out, and all this time you've had an armed escort within shouting distance."

"I didn't know they were here, Belgarath," Silk protested. "They're not supposed to be here."

Belgarath stalked away muttering curses under his breath.

The muleteers in the camp had begun to load their animals when Silk, with Garion walking on one side of him and Belgarath on the other, rode in. A hard-bitten looking man with a pockmarked face and thick wrists approached them and saluted. "Your Highness," he said to Silk, "we didn't know that you were in this part of Mallorea."

"I move around a lot," Silk said. "Is it all right if we join you, Captain Rakos?"

"Of course, your Highness."

"The rest of our party will be along shortly," Silk told him. "What are we having for breakfast this morning?"

"Bacon, fried eggs, chops, hot bread, jam—the usual, your Highness."

"No gruel?"

"I can have the cook mix some up for you, if you'd like, your Highness," Rakos replied.

"No, thanks, Captain," Silk said. "I think I can live without gruel, for today anyway."

"Would your Highness care to inspect the troops?"

Silk made a face, then sighed. "They sort of expect it, don't they?"

"It's good for morale, your Highness," Rakos assured him. "An uninspected trooper begins to feel unappreciated."

"Right you are, Captain," Silk said, dismounting. "Fall them in if you would please, and I'll boost their morale."

The captain turned and bellowed an order.

"Excuse me," Silk said to Belgarath and Garion. "Certain formalities are the price of command." He smoothed down his hair with the palm of his hand and carefully adjusted his clothing. Then he followed Captain Rakos toward the ranks of soldiers standing at attention beside the road. His manner was grand as he inspected his troops, and he rather meticulously pointed out missing buttons, unshaved faces, and boots not polished to perfection. Durnik, Polgara, and the others arrived while he was progressing down the last rank. Belgarath quickly explained the situation to them.

When Silk returned, he had a certain self-satisfied look on his face.

"Was all that really necessary?" Velvet asked him.

"It's expected." He shrugged. He looked rather proudly at his men. "They look good, don't they? I may not have the biggest army in Mallorea, but I've got the sharpest. Why don't we go have some breakfast?"

"I've eaten soldiers' rations before," Beldin told him. "I think I'll go look for another pigeon."

"You're jumping to conclusions, Beldin," the little man assured him. "Bad food is the greatest cause of dissatisfaction in the ranks in any army. Yarblek and I are very careful to hire only the best cooks and to provide them with the finest food available. Dry rations might be good enough for Kal Zakath's army, but not for mine."

Captain Rakos joined them for breakfast. Rakos was obviously a field soldier and he had certain difficulties with his utensils.

"Where's the caravan bound?" Silk asked him.

"Jarot, your Highness."

"What are we carrying?"

"Beans."

"Beans?" Silk sounded a little startled.

"It was your order, your Highness," Rakos said. "Word came from your factor in Mal Zeth before the plague broke out that you wanted to corner the market in beans. Your warehouses in Maga Renn are overflowing with them, so lately we've been transferring them to Jarot."

"Why would I do that?" Silk said, scratching his head in bafflement.

"Zakath was bringing his army back from Cthol Murgos," Garion reminded him. "He was going to mount a campaign in Karanda. You wanted to buy up all the beans in Mallorea so that you could gouge the Bureau of Military Procurement."

"Gouge is such an ugly word, Garion," Silk protested with a pained look. He frowned. "I thought I'd rescinded that order."

"Not that I've heard, your Highness," Rakos said. "You've got tons of beans pouring into Maga Renn from all over Delchin and southern Ganesia."

Silk groaned. "How much longer is it going to take us to reach Jarot?" he asked. "I've got to put a stop to this."

"Several days, your Highness," Rakos replied.

"And the beans will just keep piling up the whole time."

"Probably, your Highness."

Silk groaned again.

They rode on down through the remainder of Rengel with no further incidents. Silk's professional soldiers apparently had a wide reputation in the region, and the poorly trained troops of the varying factions there gave them a wide berth. Silk rode at the head of the column like a field marshal, looking about with a lordly manner.

"Are you going to let him get away with that?" Ce'Nedra asked Velvet after a day or so.

"Of course not," Velvet replied, "but let him enjoy it for now. Time enough to teach him the realities of the situation later on."

"You're terrible," Ce'Nedra giggled.

"Naturally. But didn't you do the same thing to our hero here?" Velvet looked pointedly at Garion.

"Liselle," Polgara said firmly, "you're giving away secrets again."

"Sorry, Lady Polgara," Velvet replied contritely.

The trail of Zandramas was soon joined by the sullen scarlet trail of the Sardion, and both proceeded down across Rengel to the River Kallahar and the border of Celanta. The trails also seemed to be going toward Jarot.

"Why is she going toward the sea?" Garion worriedly asked Belgarath.

"Who knows?" the old man replied shortly. "She's read the Ashabine Oracles, and I haven't. It could be that she knows where she's going, and I'm just floundering along in the rear."

"But what if—"

"Please don't 'what if' me, Garion," Belgarath said. "I've got enough problems already."

They crossed the River Kallahar aboard a cluster of ferries that seemed to belong to Silk and arrived in the port city of Jarot on the Celanta side. As they rode through the cobbled streets, crowds came out to cheer. Silk rode at the head of the column graciously waving his acknowledgment of the cheers.

"Have I missed something?" Durnik asked.

"His people love him very much," Eriond explained.

"*His* people?"

"Who owns a man, Durnik?" the blond young man asked sadly. "The one who rules him, or the one who pays him?"

Silk's offices in Jarot were opulent—even ostentatious. Mallorean carpets lay thick upon the floors, the walls were paneled in rare, polished woods, and officials in costly livery were everywhere.

"One sort of has to keep up appearances," the little man explained apologetically as they entered. "The natives are so impressed by show."

"Of course," Belgarath said drily.

"Surely you don't think—"

"Just let it pass, Silk."

"But it's all so much fun, Belgarath." Silk grinned.

Belgarath then did something Garion had never thought he would see him do. He raised his hands imploringly, assumed a tragic expression, and said, "Why me?"

Beldin chortled.

"Well?" Belgarath said crossly to him.

"Nothing," Beldin replied.

Silk's factor in Jarot was a baggy-eyed Melcene named Kasvor. Kasvor walked as if he had the weight of the world on his shoulders and he sighed often. He came wearily into the office where Silk sat as if enthroned behind a very large writing desk and the rest of them lounged in comfortable chairs along the walls. "Prince Kheldar," Kasvor said, bowing.

"Ah, Kasvor," Silk said.

"I've seen to the rooms your Highness wanted." Kasvor sighed. "The inn is called the Lion. It's two streets over. I've taken the entire top floor for you."

Durnik leaned over and whispered to Garion. "Wasn't that inn we stayed at in Camaar also called the Lion?" he asked. "The place where Brendig arrested us that time?"

"I'd imagine that you could find a Lion Inn in just about every city in the world," Garion replied.

69

"Capital, Kasvor. Capital," Silk was saying.

Kasvor smiled faintly.

"How's business?" Silk asked.

"We're showing a fair profit, your Highness."

"How fair?"

"About forty-five percent."

"Not bad. I need to talk to you about something else, though. Let's stop buying beans."

"I'm afraid it's a little late for that, your Highness. We own just about every bean in Mallorea already."

Silk groaned and buried his face in his hands.

"The market's up ten points, though, your Highness."

"It is?" Silk sounded startled, and his eyes brightened. "How did that happen?"

"There have been all manner of rumors going about and some tentative inquiries from the Bureau of Military Procurement. Everyone's been scrambling around trying to buy up beans, but we've got them all."

"Ten points, you say?"

"Yes, your Highness."

"Sell," Silk said.

Kasvor looked startled.

"We bought up the bean crop in the expectation of an imperial military campaign in Karanda. There won't be one now."

"Can your Highness be sure?"

"I have access to certain sources of information. When the word gets out, the market in beans is going to sink like a rock, and we don't really want several million tons of beans on our hands, do we? Have there been any offers?"

"The Melcene consortium has expressed some interest, your Highness. They're willing to go two points above the market."

"Negotiate with them, Kasvor. When they get to three

points above the market price, sell. I don't want to have to eat all those beans myself."

"Yes, your Highness."

Belgarath cleared his throat meaningfully.

Silk glanced at the old man and nodded. "We just came down through Voresebo and Rengel," he said. "Things are a bit chaotic up there."

"So I've heard, your Highness," Kasvor replied.

"Is there unrest anywhere else in the region? We have some things to do in this part of the world and we don't want to have to do them in a war zone if we don't have to."

Kasvor shrugged. "Darshiva's in an uproar, but there's nothing new about that. Darshiva's been in an uproar for the past dozen years. I took the liberty of pulling all our people out of that principality. There's nothing left there that's worth our while." He looked toward the ceiling in mock piety. "May Zandramas grow a boil on her nose," he prayed.

"Amen," Silk agreed fervently. "Is there any place else we ought to avoid?"

"I've heard that northern Gandahar is a bit nervous," Kasvor answered, "but that doesn't affect us, since we don't deal in elephants."

"Smartest decision we ever made," Silk said to Belgarath. "Do you have any idea how much an elephant can eat?"

"Peldane is also reported to be in turmoil just now, your Highness," Kasvor reported. "Zandramas is spreading her infection in all directions."

"Have you ever seen her?" Silk asked him.

Kasvor shook his head. "She hasn't come this far east yet. I think she's trying to consolidate her position before she comes this way. The Emperor won't mourn the loss of Darshiva, Rengel, and Voresebo very much, and Peldane and Gandahar are more trouble than they're worth. Celanta—and certainly Melcena—are altogether different matters, though."

"Truly," Silk agreed.

71

Kasvor frowned. "I did hear something, though, your Highness," he said. "There's a rumor going around the waterfront that Zandramas' cohort, Naradas, hired a ship for Melcena a few days ago."

"Naradas?"

"Your Highness may never have seen him, but he's fairly easy to pick out of a crowd. He has absolutely white eyes." Kasvor shuddered. "Gruesome-looking fellow. Anyway, he's reputed to have been with Zandramas since the beginning and, as I understand it, he's her right arm. There are some other rumors as well, but I don't think I should repeat them in the presence of the ladies." He looked apologetically at Polgara, Ce'Nedra, and Velvet.

Silk tapped his forefinger thoughtfully on his chin. "So Naradas went to Melcena," he said. "I think I'd like to get a few more details about that."

"I'll circulate some people around the waterfront, your Highness," Kasvor said. "I'm sure we'll be able to find someone who can give us more information."

"Good," Silk said, rising to his feet. "If you find someone, send him to me at the Lion Inn. Tell him that I'll be very generous."

"Of course, your Highness."

Silk hefted the leather pouch at his belt. "I'll need some money," he noted.

"I'll see to it at once, Prince Kheldar."

As they left the building and walked down the polished stone steps toward their horses, Beldin made a disgusted sound. "It's unwholesome," he muttered.

"What is?" Belgarath asked him.

"How lucky you are."

"I don't quite follow you."

"Isn't it remarkable that Kasvor just *happened* to remember the one thing you really had to know? He threw it out almost as an afterthought."

"The Gods have always been fond of me," Belgarath re-plied complacently.

"You think of luck as a God? Our Master would put you on bread and water for several centuries if he heard you talking like that."

"It may not have been entirely luck," Durnik said thought-fully. "This prophecy of ours has nudged people a bit now and then. I remember one time in Arendia when Ce'Nedra was supposed to give a speech. She was so terrified she was almost sick until a drunken young nobleman insulted her. Then she got angry, and her speech set fire to the whole crowd. Pol said that maybe the prophecy had made him get drunk so that he'd insult Ce'Nedra in order to make her angry enough to give the speech. Couldn't this have been sort of like that? Fate instead of luck?"

Beldin looked at the smith, his eyes suddenly alight. "This man is a jewel, Belgarath," he said. "I've been looking for someone to talk philosophy with for centuries now, and here he is, right under my nose." He put his large, gnarled hand on Durnik's shoulder. "When we get to that inn, my friend," he said, "you and I are going to begin a very long conversation. It might just go on for several centuries."

Polgara sighed.

The Lion Inn was a large building with walls of yellow brick and a red tile roof. A broad stairway led up to an imposing main door attended by a liveried footman.

"Where are the stables?" Durnik asked, looking about.

"Probably around back," Silk replied. "Melcene architec-ture is a bit different from the style in the West."

As they dismounted, two grooms came trotting around the building to take their horses. Silk mounted the stairs, and the footman at the door bowed deeply to him. "This house is honored by your presence, Prince Kheldar," he said. "My master's waiting inside to greet you."

"Why, thank you, my good man," Silk replied, giving him

a coin. "There may be someone along later to see me. It's possible that he'll be a sailor or a longshoreman. When he arrives, would you be so good as to send him to me immediately?"

"Of course, your Highness."

The top floor of the inn was palatial. The rooms were large and deeply carpeted. The walls were covered with white mortar, and the windows were draped with blue velvet. The furnishings were massive and comfortable-looking. The doorways were arched.

Durnik wiped his feet carefully before entering. He looked around.

"They seem to be awfully fond of arches," he noted. "I've always preferred post-and-lintel construction myself. For some reason, I just don't quite trust an arch."

"It's perfectly sound, Durnik," Silk assured him.

"I know the theory," Durnik said. "The trouble is that I don't know the man who built the arch, so I don't know if he can be trusted."

"Do you still want to talk philosophy with him?" Belgarath said to Beldin.

"Why not? Solid practicality has a place in the world, too, and sometimes my speculations get a little airy."

"I think the word is windy, Beldin. Windy."

"You didn't really have to say that, did you?"

Belgarath looked at him critically. "Yes," he replied. "I think I did."

Polgara, Ce'Nedra, and Velvet retired to an elaborate bath that was even larger than those in their quarters in the imperial palace at Mal Zeth.

While the ladies were bathing, Silk excused himself. "There are a few other things I need to attend to," he explained. "I won't be very long."

It was after bath time, but before suppertime, when a wiry little fellow in a tar-smeared canvas smock was escorted into the main sitting room. "I was told that there was a Prince Kheldar as was wantin' words with me," he said, looking around. He spoke in a brogue almost identical to Feldegast's.

"Ah—" Garion floundered, "the prince has stepped out for a moment."

"I surely don't have all day to sit around coolin' me heels, me boy," the little fellow objected. "I've things to do an' people to see, don't y' know."

"I'll handle this, Garion," Durnik said mildly.

"But—"

"It's no problem at all," Durnik said just a bit more firmly. He turned to the little dockhand. "The prince just had a few questions, is all," he said in an almost lazy tone. "It's nothing that you and I can't take care of without bothering his Highness." He laughed. "You know how these highborn people are—excitable."

"Now that's the truth, surely. There's nothin' like a title t' iob a man of his good sense."

Durnik spread his hands. "What can I say?" he said. "Why don't we sit down and talk a bit? Would you take a spot of ale?"

"I've been known t' take a sup from time t' time." The little fellow grinned. "Yer a man after me own heart, me friend. What trade is it ye follow?"

Durnik held out his callused and burn-scarred hands. "I'm a blacksmith," he admitted.

"Whoosh!" the dockhand exclaimed. "'Tis a hot an' heavy line o' work ye've chose fer yerself. I labor on the docks, meself. 'Tis heavy enough, but at least it's out in the open air."

"It is indeed," Durnik agreed in that same easygoing fashion. Then he turned and snapped his fingers at Belgarath. "Why don't you see if you can find some ale for my friend and me?" he suggested. "Get some for yourself, too—if you're of a mind."

Belgarath made a number of strangling noises and went to the door to talk to the servant waiting outside.

"A relative of my wife's," Durnik confided to the tar-smeared man. "He's not quite bright, but she insists that I keep him on. You know how that goes."

"Oh, by the Gods, yes. Me own dear wife's got cousins by the score who can't tell one end of a shovel from another. They kin surely find the ale barrel an' supper table, though."

Durnik laughed. "How's the work?" he asked. "On the docks, I mean?"

"'Tis cruel hard. The masters keep all the gold fer their-selves, and we git the brass."

Durnik laughed ironically. "Isn't that always the way of it?"

"It is indeed, me friend. It is indeed."

"There's no justice in the world," Durnik sighed, "and a man can only bow to the ill winds of fortune."

"How truly ye speak. I see that ye've suffered under un-kind masters yerself."

"A time or two," Durnik admitted. He sighed. "Well," he said, "on to the business at hand, then. The prince has got a certain interest in a fellow with white eyes. Have you ever seen him?"

"Ah," the dockhand said, "*that* one. May he sink in a cess-pool up to the eyebrows."

"You've met him, I take it."

"An' the meetin' gave me no pleasure, I kin tell ye."

"Well, then," Durnik said smoothly, "I can see that we're of the same opinion about this fellow."

"If it's in yer mind t' kill him, I'll lend ye me cargo hook."

"It's a thought." Durnik laughed.

Garion stared in amazement at his honest old friend. This was a side of Durnik he had never seen before. He glanced quickly to one side and saw Polgara's eyes wide with astonishment.

At that moment, Silk came in, but stopped as Velvet motioned him to silence.

"However," Durnik went on slyly, "what better way to upset somebody that we both dislike than to overturn a scheme he's been hatching for a year or more?"

The dockhand's lips peeled back from his teeth in a feral grin. "I'm listenin', me friend," he said fervently. "Tell me how to spoke the white-eyed man's wheel, an' I'm with ye to the end." He spat in his hand and held it out.

Durnik also spat on his palm, and the two of them smacked their hands together in a gesture as old as time. Then the smith lowered his voice confidentially. "Now," he said, "we've heard that this white-eyed one—may all of his teeth fall out—hired a ship for Melcena. What we need to know is when he left, on what ship, who went with him, and where he was to land."

"Simplicity in itself," the dockhand said expansively, leaning back in his chair.

"You, there," Durnik said to Belgarath, "is that ale on the way?"

Belgarath made a few more strangling noises.

"It's so hard to get good help these days." Durnik sighed.

Polgara tried very hard to stifle a laugh.

"Well, now," the dockhand said, leaning forward in that same confidential manner, "this is what I seen with me own two eyes, so I'm not handin' along secondhand information. I seen this white-eyed one come to the docks on a mornin' about five days ago. 'Twas about daybreak, it was, an' one of them cloudy mornin's when ye can't tell the difference between fog an' smoke, an' ye don't want to breathe too deep of either. Anyway, the white-eyed one, he had a woman with him in a black satin robe with a hood coverin' her head, an' she had a little boy with her."

"How do you know it was a woman?" Durnik interrupted.

"Have ye no eyes, man?" the dockhand laughed. "They

don't walk the same as we do. There's a certain swayin' of the hips that no man alive could imitate. 'Twas a woman, right enough, an' ye have me word on that. An' the little boy was as fair as a mornin' sunrise, but he seemed a little sad. Sturdy little lad he was, an' looked fer all the world as if he wished he could put his hands on a sword to rid hisself of them as he didn't like too much. Anyway, they went aboard ship, an' the ship, she slipped her hawsers an' rowed off into the fog. Word was that they was bound fer the city of Melcena—or some well-hid cove nearby, smugglin' not bein' unknown in these parts, don't y' know."

"And this was five days ago?" Durnik asked.

"Five or four. Sometimes I lose track of the days."

Durnik seized the man's tar-smeared hand warmly. "My friend," he said, "between us, we'll kick all the spokes out of the white-eyed man's wheel yet."

"I'd surely like to help with the kickin'," the dockhand said a bit wistfully.

"You have, friend," Durnik said. "You definitely have. I'll kick a time or two for you myself. Silk," the smith said very seriously, "I think our friend here should have something to pay him for his trouble."

Silk, looking a bit awed, shook a few coins out of his purse.

"Is that the best you can do?" Durnik asked critically.

Silk doubled the amount. Then, after a glance at Durnik's disapproving expression, doubled that in gold.

The dockhand left, his fist clutched protectively around his coins.

Velvet rose wordlessly to her feet and curtsied to Durnik with profound respect.

"Where did you learn how to do that?" Silk demanded.

Durnik looked at him with some surprise. "Haven't you ever traded horses at a country fair before, Silk?" he asked.

"As I told ye, me old friend," Beldin said gaily, "the old

speech has not died out yet altogether, an' 'tis music to me
ears t' hear it again."

"Must you?" Belgarath said in a highly offended tone. He
turned to Durnik. "What was all that folksy business?"

Durnik shrugged. "I've met that sort of man many times,"
he explained. "They can be very helpful, if you give them a
reason to be—but they're very touchy, so you have to approach them just right." He smiled. "Given a little time, I
could have sold that fellow a three-legged horse—and convinced him that he'd got the best of the bargain."

"Oh, my Durnik," Polgara said, throwing her arms about
the smith's neck. "What would we ever do without you?"

"I hope we never have to find out," he said.

"All right," Belgarath said, "now we know that Zandramas
went to Melcena. The question is why."

"To get away from us?" Silk suggested.

"I don't think so, Kheldar," Sadi disagreed. "Her center
of power is in Darshiva. Why should she run off in the other
direction?"

"I'll work on that."

"What's in Melcena?" Velvet asked.

"Not too much," Silk replied, "unless you count all the
money in Melcena itself—most of the world's supply, last
time I heard."

"Would Zandramas be interested in money?" the blond girl
asked.

"No," Polgara said very firmly. "Money would have no
meaning to her—not at this point. It's something else."

"The only thing that means anything to Zandramas right
now is the Sardion, isn't it?" Garion said. "Could the Sardion
be out there in the islands someplace?"

Beldin and Belgarath exchanged a look. "What *does* that
phrase mean?" Beldin demanded in exasperation. "Think,
Belgarath. What does it mean when they say the 'Place Which
Is No More'?"

"You're smarter than I am," Belgarath retorted. "You answer the riddle."

"I hate riddles!"

"I think about all we can do at this point is trail along behind and find out," Silk said. "Zandramas seems to know where she's going, and we don't. That doesn't leave us much choice, does it?"

"The Sardion came to Jarot as well," Garion mused. "It was a long time ago, but the Orb picked up its trail just outside of town. I'll go down to the docks and see if both trails are still running together. It's possible that Zandramas has some way of following the Sardion, the same as we do. She might not really know where it's going. Maybe she's just following it."

"He's got a point there," Beldin said.

"If the Sardion is hidden somewhere out there in Melcena, this could all end before the week is out," Garion added.

"It's too early," Polgara said flatly.

"Too early?" Ce'Nedra exclaimed. "Lady Polgara, my baby's been gone for over a year now. How can you say it's too early?"

"It has nothing to do with that, Ce'Nedra," the sorceress replied. "You've waited a year for the return of your baby. I waited a thousand years and more for Garion. Fate and time and the Gods pay no attention to our years, but Cyradis said at Ashaba that we still had nine months until the final meeting, and it hasn't been that long yet."

"She might have been wrong," Ce'Nedra objected.

"Perhaps—but only by a second or so either way."

CHAPTER FOUR

It was foggy in the harbor the next morning, one of those thick early autumn fogs that always hovers on the verge of rain. As they were loading the horses, Garion glanced up and found that he could see no more than a few feet up the masts of the ship they were boarding. Silk stood on the aft deck talking with the ship's captain.

"It should clear off when we get a few leagues out to sea, your Highness," the captain was saying as Garion approached. "There's a fairly steady wind that always blows down the passage between the coast and Melcena."

"Good," Silk said. "I wouldn't want to run into anything. How long is it likely to take us to get to Melcena?"

"Most of the day, your Highness," the captain replied. "It's a fair distance, but the prevailing wind works to our advantage. The return voyage takes several days, though."

"We'll be all loaded shortly," Silk told him.

"We can leave any time you're ready, your Highness."

Silk nodded and joined Garion at the rail. "Are you feeling any better?" he asked.

"I don't quite follow you."

"You were just a bit grumpy when you got up this morning."

"Sorry. I've got a lot on my mind."

"Spread it around," Silk suggested. "Worries get lighter when you've got people to share them with you."

"We're getting closer," Garion said. "Even if this meeting doesn't happen out here in the islands, it's still only a matter of a few more months."

"Good. I'm getting a little tired of living out of a saddlebag."

"But we don't know what's going to happen yet."

"Of course we do. You're going to meet Zandramas, divide her down the middle with that big knife of yours, and take your wife and son back to Riva where they belong."

"But we don't *know* that, Silk."

"We didn't know you were going to win the duel with Torak either, but you did. Anyone who goes around picking fights with Gods has very little to fear from a second-rate sorceress."

"How do we know she's second-rate?"

"She's not a disciple, is she? Or would the word be disciple-ess?"

"How would I know?" Garion smiled faintly, then grew serious again. "I think Zandramas has stepped over disciple-ship. She's the Child of Dark, and that makes her a bit more serious than an ordinary disciple." He banged his fist down on the rail. "I *wish* I knew what I'm supposed to do. When I went after Torak, I knew. This time I'm not sure."

"You'll get instructions when the time comes, I'm sure."

"But if I knew, I could sort of get ready."

"I get the feeling that this is not the sort of thing you can get ready for, Garion." The little man glanced over the rail at the garbage bobbing in the water beside the ship. "Did you follow the trail all the way to the harbor last night?" he asked.

Garion nodded. "Yes—both of them. Both Zandramas and the Sardion left from here. We're fairly sure that Zandramas is going to Melcena. Only the Gods know where the Sardion went."

"And probably not even they."

A large drop of water fell from the rigging lost in the fog overhead and landed with a splat on Silk's shoulder.

"Why is it always me?" the little man complained.

"What?"

"Anytime something wet falls out of the sky, it lands on me."

"Maybe somebody's trying to tell you something," Garion grinned.

Toth and Durnik led the last of the horses up the gangway and on down into the hold.

"That's the lot, Captain," Silk called. "We can leave any time now."

"Yes, your Highness," the captain agreed. He raised his voice and started shouting orders.

"I've been meaning to ask you about something," Garion said to Silk. "Always before, you acted almost as if you were ashamed of your title. Here in Mallorea, though, you seem to want to wallow in it."

"What a fascinating choice of words."

"You know what I mean."

Silk tugged at one earlobe. "In the West, my title's an

inconvenience. It attracts too much attention, and it gets in my way. Things are different here in Mallorea. Here, nobody takes you seriously unless you've got a title. I've got one, so I use it. It opens certain doors for me and permits me to have dealings with people who wouldn't have time for Ambar of Kotu or Radek of Boktor. Nothing's really changed, though.''

"Then all of that posturing and pomposity—pardon the terms—are just for show?"

"Of course they are, Garion. You don't think I've turned into a complete ass, do you?"

A strange thought came to Garion. "Then Prince Kheldar is as much a fiction as Ambar and Radek, isn't he?"

"Of course he is."

"But where's the real Silk?"

"It's very hard to say, Garion." Silk sighed. "Sometimes I think I lost him years ago." He looked around at the fog. "Let's go below," he said. "Murky mornings always seem to start off these gloomy conversations."

A league or so beyond the breakwater, the sky turned a rusty color, and the fog began to thin. The sea lying to the east of the coast of Mallorea rolled in long, sullen swells that spoke of vast stretches of uninterrupted water. The ship ran before the prevailing wind, her prow knifing through the swells, and by late afternoon the coast of the largest of the Melcene Islands was clearly visible on the horizon.

The harbor of the city of Melcena was crowded with shipping from all over Mallorea. Small and large, the vessels jostled against each other in the choppy water as Silk's captain carefully threaded his way toward the stone quays thrusting out from the shore. It was dusk by the time they had unloaded, and Silk led them through the broad streets toward the house he maintained there. Melcena appeared to be a sedate, even stuffy city. The streets were wide and scrupulously clean. The houses were imposing, and the inhabitants all wore robes in sober hues. There was none of the bustle here that was evident in other cities. The citizens of Melcena moved through the streets with decorum, and the street hawkers did not bawl their wares in those strident voices that helped so much to raise that continual shouted babble that filled the streets of less reserved cities. Although Melcena lay in tropic latitudes, the prevailing breeze coming in off the ocean moderated the temperature enough to make the climate pleasant.

Silk's house here was what might more properly be called a palace. It was constructed of marble and was several stories high. It was fronted by a large formal garden and flanked by stately trees. A paved drive curved up through the garden to a porch lined with columns, and liveried servants stood attentively at the entryway.

"Opulent," Sadi noted as they dismounted.

"It's a nice little place," Silk admitted in an offhand way. Then he laughed. "Actually, Sadi, it's mostly for show. Personally, I prefer shabby little offices in back streets, but Melcena takes itself very seriously, and one has to try to fit in, if one plans to do business here. Let's go inside."

They went up the broad steps and through an imposing door. The foyer inside the door was very large, and the walls were clad with marble. Silk led them on through the foyer and up a grand staircase. "The rooms on the ground floor are given over to offices," he explained. "The living quarters are up here."

"What sort of business do you do here?" Durnik asked. "I didn't see anything that looked like a warehouse."

"There aren't many warehouses in Melcena," Silk said as he opened a door and led them into a very large, blue-carpeted sitting room. "The decisions are made here, of course, but the goods are normally stored on the mainland. There's not much point in shipping things here and then turning around and shipping them back again."

"That makes sense," Durnik approved.

The furnishings of the room they had entered were ornate.

Divans and comfortable chairs were clustered in little group-
ings here and there, and wax candles burned in sconces along
the wood-paneled walls.

"It's a little late to be wandering around the streets looking
for Zandramas," Silk observed. "I thought we might have
something to eat, get a good night's sleep, and then Garion
and I can start out early in the morning."

"That's probably the best way to go at it," Belgarath
agreed, sinking down onto a well-upholstered divan.

"Could I offer you all something to drink while we're waiting for dinner?" Silk asked.

"I thought you'd never ask," Beldin growled, sprawling in
a chair and scratching his beard.

Silk tugged at a bellpull, and a servant entered immediately. "I think we'll have some wine," Silk told him.

"Yes, your Highness."

"Bring several varieties."

"Have you got any ale?" Beldin asked. "Wine sours my
stomach."

"Bring ale for my messy friend as well," Silk ordered, "and
tell the kitchen that there'll be eleven of us for dinner."

"At once, your Highness." The servant bowed and quietly
left the room.

"You have bathing facilities, I assume?" Polgara asked, removing the light cloak she had worn on the voyage.

"You bathed just last night in Jarot, Pol," Belgarath pointed
out.

"Yes, father," she said dreamily. "I know."

"Each suite has its own bath," Silk told her. "They're not
quite as large as the ones in Zakath's palace, but they'll get
you wet."

She smiled and sat on one of the divans.

"Please, everybody, sit down," Silk said to the rest of them.

"Do you think any of your people here might know what's
going on in the world?" Belgarath asked the little man.

"Naturally."

"Why naturally?"

"My boyhood occupation was spying, Belgarath, and old habits die hard. All of my people are instructed to gather information."

"What do you do with it?" Velvet asked him.

He shrugged. "I sort through it. I get almost as much pleasure from handling information as I do from handling money."

"Do you forward any of this information to Javelin in Boktor?"

"I send him a few crumbs now and then—just to remind him that I'm still alive."

"I'm sure he knows that, Silk."

"Why don't you send for someone who can bring us up to date?" Belgarath suggested. "We've been out of touch for quite a while, and I'd sort of like to know what certain people are up to."

"Right," Silk agreed. He tugged the bellpull again, and another liveried servant responded. "Would you ask Vetter to step in here for a moment?" Silk asked.

The servant bowed and left.

"My factor here," Silk said, taking a seat. "We lured him away from Brador's secret police. He's got a good head for business and he's had all that training in the intelligence service."

Vetter proved to be a narrow-faced man with a nervous tic in his left eyelid. "Your Highness wanted to see me?" he asked respectfully as he entered the room.

"Ah, there you are, Vetter," Silk said. "I've been back in the hinterlands and I was wondering if you could fill me in on what's been happening lately."

"Here in Melcena, your Highness?"

"Perhaps a bit more general than that."

"All right." Vetter paused, gathering his thoughts. "There was a plague in Mal Zeth," he began. "The Emperor sealed the city to prevent the spread of the disease, so, for a time, we couldn't get any information out of the capital. The plague has subsided, however, so the gates have been opened again. The Emperor's agents are moving freely around Mallorea now.

"There was an upheaval in central Karanda. It appeared to have been fomented by a former Grolim named Mengha. The Karands all believed that there were demons involved, but Karands think that there's a demon behind any unusual occurrence. It does appear, though, that there were at least a few supernatural events in the region. Mengha hasn't been seen for quite some time, and order is being gradually restored. The Emperor took the business seriously enough to summon the army back from Cthol Murgos to put down the uprising."

"Has he rescinded that order yet?" Silk asked. "If things are quieting down in Karanda, he's not going to need all those troops, is he?"

Vetter shook his head in disagreement. "The troops are still landing at Mal Gemila," he reported. "The word we've been getting out of Mal Zeth is that the Emperor has lost his enthusiasm for the conquest of Cthol Murgos. He had personal reasons for the campaign in the first place, and those reasons don't seem to be as pressing anymore. His major concern at the moment seems to be the impending confrontation between the Disciple Urvon and Zandramas the Sorceress. That situation is about to come to a head. Urvon seems to be suffering from some form of mental instability, but his subordinates are moving large numbers of people into the region in preparation for something fairly major. Zandramas is also marshaling her forces. Our best assessment of the situation is that it's only going to be a matter of time before the Emperor moves his forces out of Mal Zeth to restore order. There have been reports of supplies being stockpiled at Maga

Renn. It's apparent that Kal Zakath intends to use it as a staging area."

"Were we able to capitalize on that in any way?" Silk asked intently.

"To some degree, your Highness. We sold a part of our bean holdings to the Bureau of Military Procurement just today."

"What was the price?"

"About fifteen points above what we paid."

"You'd better get word to Kasvor in Jarot," Silk said with a sour expression. "I told him to sell at thirteen. The Melcene consortium has been making offers. Is the price likely to go higher?"

Vetter spread one hand and rocked it back and forth uncertainly.

"Let the word get out that we sold at fifteen and tell Kasvor to hold out for that figure. Even if the price goes to sixteen, we'll have still taken most of the profit out of the transaction."

"I'll see to it, your Highness." Vetter frowned a bit. "There's something going on in Dalasia," he continued his report. "We haven't been able to get the straight of it yet, but the Dalasians all seem to be very exited about it. Kell has been sealed off, so we can't get anybody there to investigate, and Kell is the source of just about everything that goes on in Dalasia."

"Any news from the West?" Garion asked.

"Things are still stalemated in Cthol Murgos," Vetter replied. "Kal Zakath is reducing his forces there and he's called all his generals home. He's still holding the cities in eastern Cthol Murgos, but the countryside is reverting. It's not certain whether King Urgit is going to take advantage of the situation. He has other things on his mind."

"Oh?" Silk asked curiously.

"He's getting married. A princess from the House of Cthan, as I understand it."

Silk sighed.

"King Gethel of Mishrak ac Thull died," Vetter went on, "and he was succeeded by his son, Nathel. Nathel's a hopeless incompetent, so we can't be sure how long he'll last." Vetter paused, scratching at his chin. "We've had reports that there was a meeting of the Alorn Council at Boktor. The Alorns get together once a year, but it's usually at Riva. About the only other thing unusual about it was the fact that a fair number of non-Alorn monarchs attended."

"Oh?" Belgarath said. "Who?"

"The king of the Sendars, the Emperor of Tolnedra, and King Drosta of Gar og Nadrak. The king of Arendia was ill, but he sent representatives."

"*Now* what are they up to?" Belgarath muttered.

"We weren't able to get our hands on the agenda," Vetter told him, "but not long afterward, a delegation of diplomats from their kingdoms went to Rak Urga. There are rumors that some fairly serious negotiations are going on."

"What are they *doing*?" Belgarath demanded in an exasperated voice.

"I've told you over and over not to go off and leave the Alorns untended," Beldin said. "If there's any way at all for them to do something wrong, they'll do it."

"The price of gold is up," Vetter continued, "and the price of Mallorean crowns is down. Melcene imperials are holding steady, but the diamond market is fluctuating so wildly that we've withdrawn our investments in that commodity. That's more or less what's current, your Highness. I'll have a more detailed report on your desk first thing in the morning."

"Thank you, Vetter," Silk replied. "That's all for right now."

Vetter bowed and quietly left.

Belgarath began to pace up and down, swearing to himself.

"There's nothing you can do about it, father," Polgara told him, "so why upset yourself?"

"Perhaps they have some reason for what they're doing," Silk suggested.

"What possible reason could they have to be negotiating with the Murgos?"

"I don't know." Silk spread his hands. "I wasn't there when they made the decision. Maybe Urgit offered them something they wanted."

Belgarath continued to swear.

About a half-hour later, they adjourned to the dining room and took seats near one end of a table that could easily have accommodated a half a hundred. The linen was snowy white, the knives and forks were solid silver, and the porcelain plates were edged in gold. The service was exquisite, and the meal was of banquet proportions.

"I must talk with your cook," Polgara said as they lingered over dessert. "He appears to be a man of talent."

"I should hope so," Silk replied. "He's costing me enough."

"I'd say you can afford it," Durnik noted, looking around at the luxurious furnishings.

Silk leaned back in his chair, toying with the stem of a silver goblet. "It doesn't really make much sense to maintain a place like this when I only come here about twice a year," he admitted, "but it's expected, I guess."

"Doesn't Yarblek use it, too?" Garion asked him.

Silk shook his head. "No. Yarblek and I have an agreement. I give him free rein in the rest of the world as long as he stays out of Melcena. He doesn't really fit in here, and he insists on taking Vella with him everyplace he goes. Vella really shocks the Melcenes."

"She's a good wench, though," Beldin said, grinning. "When this is all over, I might just buy her."

"That's disgusting!" Ce'Nedra flared.

"What did I say?" Beldin looked confused.

"She's not a cow, you know."

"No. If I wanted a cow, I'd buy a cow."

"You can't just buy people."

"Of course you can," he said. "She's a Nadrak woman. She'd be insulted if I didn't try to buy her."

"Just be careful of her knives, uncle," Polgara cautioned. "She's very quick with them."

He shrugged. "Everybody has a few bad habits."

Garion did not sleep well that night, although the bed he shared with Ce'Nedra was deep and soft. At first he thought that might be part of the problem. He had been sleeping on the ground for weeks now, and it seemed reasonable that he was just not used to a soft bed. About midnight, however, he realized that the bed had nothing to do with his sleeplessness. Time was moving on inexorably, and his meeting with Zandramas marched toward him with a measured, unstoppable pace. He still knew little more than he had at the beginning. He was, to be sure, closer to her than he had been at the start—no more than a week at most behind, if the reports were correct—but he was still trailing after her and he still did not know where she was leading him. Darkly, he muttered a few choice oaths at the madman who had written the Mrin Codex. Why did it all have to be so cryptic? Why couldn't it have been written in plain language?

"Because if it had been, half the world would be waiting for you when you got to the place of the meeting," the dry voice in his mind told him. *"You're not the only one who wants to find the Sardion, you know."*

"I thought you'd left for good."

"Oh, no, I'm still around."

"How far behind Zandramas are we?"

"About three days."

Garion felt a wild surge of hope.

"Don't get too excited," the voice said, *"and don't just dash off as soon as you find the trail again. There's something else that has to be done here."*

"*What?*"

"*You know better than to ask that, Garion. I can't tell you, so quit trying to trick me into answering.*"

"*Why can't you just tell me?*"

"*Because if I tell you certain things, the other spirit will be free to tell other things to Zandramas—like the location of the Place Which Is No More, for instance.*"

"*You mean she doesn't know?*" Garion asked incredulously.

"*Of course she doesn't know. If she knew, she'd be there by now.*"

"*Then the location isn't written down in the Ashabine Oracles?*"

"*Obviously. Pay attention tomorrow. Somebody's going to say something in passing that's very important. Don't miss it.*"

"*Who's going to say it?*"

But the voice was gone.

It was breezy the following morning when Silk and Garion set out, wearing long robes of a sober blue color. At Silk's suggestion, Garion had detached the Orb from the hilt of his sword and carried it concealed beneath his robe. "Melcenes rarely wear arms inside the city," the little man had explained, "and your sword is very conspicuous." They did not take their horses, but rather walked out into the street to mingle with the citizens of Melcena.

"We might as well start along the waterfront," Silk suggested. "Each wharf is owned by a different group of businessmen, and if we can find out which wharf Zandramas landed on, we'll know whom to question for more information."

"Sounds reasonable," Garion said shortly, striding off toward the harbor.

"Don't run," Silk told him.

"I'm not."

"You're moving too fast," the little man said. "People in Melcena go at a more stately pace."

"You know, Silk, I really don't care what the people here think of me. I'm not here to waste time."

Silk took hold of his friend's arm with a firm grip. "Garion," he said seriously, "we know that Zandramas and her underling have come here. She knows that we're after her, and there are people in Melcena who can be hired for various kinds of mischief. Let's not make it easy for them by standing out in the crowd."

Garion looked at him. "All right," he said. "We'll do it your way."

They walked at an infuriatingly slow pace down a broad avenue. At one point, Silk stopped with a muttered oath.

"What's wrong?" Garion asked him.

"That fellow just ahead—the one with the big nose—he's a member of Brador's secret police."

"Are you sure?"

Silk nodded. "I've known him for quite some time." The little man squared his shoulders. "Well, there's no help for it, I guess. He's already seen us. Let's move along."

But the man with the large, bulbous nose moved forward to stand in their path. "Good morning, Prince Kheldar," he said, bowing slightly.

"Rolla," Silk replied distantly.

"And your Majesty," Rolla added, bowing more deeply to Garion. "We weren't expecting you to appear here in Melcena. Brador will be very surprised."

"Surprises are good for him." Silk shrugged. "An unsurprised man gets complacent."

"The Emperor was most put out with you, your Majesty," Rolla said reproachfully to Garion.

"I'm sure he'll survive it."

"In Mallorea, your Majesty, it's the ones who offend Kal Zakath who need to be concerned about survival."

"Don't make threats, Rolla," Silk warned. "If his Majesty here decides that your report to the Chief of the Bureau of

94

Internal Affairs would be embarrassing, he might decide to take steps to keep you from ever writing it. His Majesty is an Alorn, after all, and you know how short-tempered they can be."

Rolla stepped back apprehensively.

"Always nice talking with you, Rolla," Silk said in a tone of dismissal. Then he and Garion walked on. Garion noticed that the big-nosed man had a slightly worried look on his face as they passed him.

"I love to do that to people," Silk smirked.

"You're easily amused," Garion said. "You do know that when his report gets to Mal Zeth, Zakath's going to flood this whole region with people trying to find us."

"Do you want me to go back and kill him for you?" Silk offered.

"Of course not!"

"I didn't think so. If you can't do something about a situation, there's no point in worrying about it."

When they reached the harbor, Garion tightened his grip on the Orb. The pulling of Iron-grip's sword had sometimes been quite strong, and Garion had no desire to have the stone jump out of his hand. They walked northward along the wharves with the salt tang of the sea in their nostrils. The harbor of Melcena, unlike that of most of the port cities in the world, was surprisingly clear of floating garbage. "How do they keep it so clean?" Garion asked curiously. "The water, I mean?"

"There's a heavy fine for throwing things in the harbor," Silk replied. "Melcenes are compulsively tidy. They also have workmen with nets in small boats patrolling the waterfront to scoop up any floating debris. It helps to maintain full employment." He grinned. "It's a nasty job and it's always assigned to people who aren't interested in finding regular work. A few days in a small boat full of garbage and dead fish increases their ambition enormously."

"You know," Garion said, "that's really a very good idea. I wonder if—" The Orb suddenly grew very warm in his hand. He pulled his robe open slightly and looked at it. It was glowing a sullen red.

"Zandramas?" Silk asked.

Garion shook his head. "The Sardion," he replied.

Silk nervously tugged at his nose. "That's a sort of dilemma, isn't it? Do we follow the Sardion or Zandramas?"

"Zandramas," Garion said. "She's the one who's got my son."

"It's up to you." Silk shrugged. "That's the last wharf just up ahead. If we don't pick up the trail there, we'll go on and check the north gate."

They passed the last wharf. The Orb gave no indication of interest.

"Could they have landed on one of the other islands?" Garion asked with a worried frown.

"Not unless they changed course once they were at sea," Silk replied. "There are plenty of other places to land a ship along this coast. Let's go have a look at the north gate."

Once again they moved through the streets at that frustratingly leisurely pace. After they had crossed several streets, Silk stopped. "Oh, no," he groaned.

"What is it?"

"That fat man coming this way is Viscount Esca. He's one of the senior members of the Melcene Consortium. He's bound to want to talk business."

"Tell him we have an appointment."

"It wouldn't do any good. Time doesn't mean that much to Melcenes."

"Why, there you are, Prince Kheldar," the fat man in a gray robe said, waddling up to them. "I've been looking all over the city for you."

"Viscount Esca," Silk said, bowing.

"My colleagues and I have stood in awe of your recent venture into the commodities market," Esca said admiringly.

Silk's eyes grew sly, and his long nose twitched. Then he assumed a pained expression. "A blunder, actually, my dear Viscount," he said mournfully. "There's little profit to be made in something as bulky as farm produce."

"Have you been keeping abreast of the market?" Esca asked, his face taking on a transparent cast of neutrality, but his eyes filled with undisguised greed.

"No," Silk lied, "not really. I've been upcountry, and I haven't had the chance to talk with my factor as yet. I left instructions for him to take the first offer that comes along, though—even if we have to take a loss. I need my warehouses, and they're all filled to the rafters with beans."

"Well, now," Esca said, rubbing his hands together, "I'll speak with my colleagues. Perhaps we can make you a modest offer." He had begun to sweat.

"I couldn't let you do that, Esca. My holdings are virtually worthless. Why don't we let some stranger take the loss? I couldn't really do that to a friend."

"But, my dear Prince Kheldar," Esca protested in a tone verging on anguish, "we wouldn't really expect to make a *vast* profit. Our purchase would be more in the nature of long-term speculation."

"Well," Silk said dubiously, "as long as you're fully aware of the risks involved—"

"Oh, we are, we are," Esca said eagerly.

Silk sighed. "All right, then," he said. "Why don't you make your offer to Vetter? I'll trust you not to take advantage of my situation."

"Oh, of course, Kheldar, of course." Esca bowed hastily. "I really must be off now. Pressing business, you understand."

"Oh," Silk said, "quite."

Esca waddled off at an unseemly rate of speed.

"Hooked him!" Silk chortled. "Now I'll let Vetter land him."

"Don't you ever think about anything else?" Garion asked.

"Of course I do, but we're busy right now and we didn't have all morning to listen to him babble. Let's move along, shall we?"

A thought occurred to Garion. "What if Zandramas avoided the city?" he asked.

"Then we'll get our horses and check the coastline. She had to have landed somewhere."

As they approached the north gate of Melcena, the press in the street grew noticeably heavier. Carriages and people on horseback began to become more frequent, and the normally sedate citizens began to move more rapidly. Garion and Silk found it necessary to push their way through the throng.

"Anything?" Silk asked.

"Not yet," Garion replied, taking a firmer grip on the Orb. Then, as they passed a side street, he felt the now-familiar pulling. "She's been here," he reported. "She came out of that street—or went into it. I can't quite tell which yet." He went a few steps up the side street. The Orb tried to push him back. He turned around and rejoined his rat-faced friend. The steady pull of the Orb drew him toward the gate. "She went out this way," he reported as they reached the arched opening.

"Good," Silk said. "Let's go back and get the others. And then maybe we can find out why Zandramas came to Melcena."

CHAPTER FIVE

It seemed somehow that Garion's impatience had communicated itself to Chretienne. The big gray stallion was restive as they left Silk's house and rode into the street and he flicked his ears in irritation as Garion tried to curb him with the reins. Even the sound of his steel-shod hooves on the cobblestones came as a kind of restless staccato. As Garion leaned forward to lay a calming hand on the arched gray neck, he could feel the nervous quivering of his horse's muscles under the sleek skin. "I know," he said. "I feel the same way, but we have to wait until we're outside the city before we can run."

Chretienne snorted and then made a plaintive whinnying sound.

"It won't take that long," Garion assured him.

They rode in single file through the busy streets with Silk in the lead. The breeze swirling through the streets carried with it the dusty smell of autumn.

"What are all those buildings over there?" Eriond called ahead to Silk. The blond young man pointed toward a large complex of structures that seemed to be set in the center of a lush green park.

"The University of Melcena," Silk replied. "It's the largest institution of higher learning in the world."

"Even bigger than the one in Tol Honeth?" Garion asked.

"Yes, much. The Melcenes study everything. There are branches of learning at that university that the Tolnedrans won't even admit exist."

"Oh? Such as what?"

"Applied alchemy, astrology, necromancy, fundamentals of witchcraft, that sort of thing. They've even got an entire college devoted to the reading of tea leaves."

"You're not serious."

"I'm not, but they are."

Garion laughed and rode on.

The streets of Melcena grew even busier, but there was a decorum to the bustle. No matter how urgent his affairs might be, a Melcene businessman was never so preoccupied that he didn't have time for a friendly chat with one of his competitors. The snatches of conversation Garion heard as they rode along the boulevards ranged in subject from the weather to politics to flower arrangement. The major concentration that morning, however, seemed to be centered on the price of beans.

When they reached the north gate, the great sword strapped across Garion's back began to pull at him. Despite Silk's critical look, Garion had decided that he was not going out into the countryside without the sword. Zandramas had a way of

leaving traps behind her, and Garion definitely did not want
to walk into one of them unprepared. As they passed through
the gate, he nudged Chretienne forward to ride beside Silk.
"The trail seems to be following this road," he said, pointing
up a broad highway stretching off to the north.

"At least it doesn't go across open country," Silk said. "The
ground gets a little marshy in spots up here, and I hate to ride
through mud."

Belgarath had said nothing since they had left Silk's house,
but had ridden along with an irritated expression on his face.
Now he came forward to join Silk and Garion. He looked
around to make sure that none of the local citizens were close
enough to overhear what they were saying and then spoke to
Garion. "Let's go over it again—step by step this time. Exactly what did your friend say?"

"Well," Garion replied, "he started out by saying that all
the prophecies are cryptic in order to keep the information
out of the wrong hands."

"That makes a certain amount of sense, Belgarath," Beldin
said from just behind them.

"It might make sense," Belgarath said, "but it doesn't
make things any easier."

"Nobody promised you easy."

"I know. I just wish they'd stop going out of their way to
make it difficult. Go ahead, Garion."

"Then he said that we're only three days behind Zandramas," Garion told him.

"That means that she's left the island," Silk noted.

"How did you arrive at that conclusion?" Belgarath asked.

"Melcena's a big island, but not that big. You can ride from
one end of it to the other in two days. She might have gone
on to one of the northern islands, but if we're three days
behind her, she isn't on this one any more."

Belgarath grunted. "What else did he say?" he asked
Garion.

"He said that there's something else we have to do here—besides finding the trail, I mean."

"I gather he wasn't very specific."

"No. He explained why not, though. He said if he told me what it was, the other prophecy could tell Zandramas certain things she didn't know yet. That's when he told me that she doesn't know where the Place Which Is No More is, and that the location's not in the Ashabine Oracles."

"Did he give you any clues at all about this task of ours?"

"Only that somebody's going to say something to us today that's very important."

"Who?"

"He wouldn't tell me. All he said was that somebody was going to say something in passing that we shouldn't miss. He said that we should be alert for that kind of thing."

"Anything else?"

"No. That's when he left."

The old man started to swear.

"I felt pretty much the same way myself," Garion agreed.

"He's done as much as he can, Belgarath," Beldin said. "The rest is up to us."

Belgarath made a wry face. "I suppose you're right."

"Of course I'm right. I'm always right."

"I wouldn't go that far. Well, first things first, I guess. Let's find out where Zandramas went. Then we can start analyzing every casual remark we hear." He turned in his saddle. "Keep your ears open today, all of you." Then he nudged his mount into a trot.

A rider in sober blue galloped past, going toward the city with uncharacteristic haste. Silk began to laugh after the man had passed them.

"Who was that?" Durnik asked.

"A member of the Consortium," Silk replied gaily. "It appears that Viscount Esca's called an emergency session."

"Is this something I ought to know about?" Belgarath asked.

"Not unless you're interested in the market price of beans."

"*Will* you keep your mind on what we're here for and stop playing?"

"It was sort of necessary, Grandfather," Garion came to his friend's defense. "The Viscount stopped us in the street while we were looking for the trail. He'd have talked all day if Silk hadn't sent him off on a fool's errand."

"Did he say anything at all that might be what we're looking for?"

"No. He just talked about beans."

"Did you meet anybody else today? Share these little encounters with us, Garion."

"We ran into one of Brador's secret policemen. I'd imagine that his messenger is already on the way to Mal Zeth."

"Did *he* say anything?"

"He made a few veiled threats, is all. I guess Emperor Zakath's a little unhappy with us. The policeman recognized me, but I suppose that's only natural. Silk was going to kill him, but I said no."

"Why?" Beldin asked bluntly.

"We were in the middle of a busy street for one thing. Killing somebody's the sort of thing you ought to do in private, wouldn't you say?"

"You were a much nicer boy before you developed this clever mouth," Beldin snapped.

Garion shrugged. "Nothing ever stays the same, uncle."

"Be polite, Garion," Polgara called from behind.

"Yes, ma'am."

A black carriage rattled by. The team of white horses drawing it was moving at a dead run and they were flecked with foam.

"Another bean buyer?" Belgarath asked.

Silk smirked and nodded.

Durnik had been looking around. "I don't see any signs that this land is being farmed," he said.

Silk laughed. "Land in Melcena's too valuable to be wasted on farming, Durnik. The people here import all their food from the mainland. About all we'll find out here are the estates of the very wealthy—retired businessmen, nobles, that sort of thing. The whole countryside's one huge park. Even the mountains have been landscaped."

"That doesn't seem very practical," Durnik said disapprovingly.

"The people who live on the estates spent a great deal of money for them, so I guess they can do what they like with the land."

"It still seems wasteful."

"Of course it is. That's what rich people do best—waste things."

The green hills to the north of the city were gently rolling and were dotted with artistically placed groves of trees. Many of the trees had been carefully pruned to accentuate their pleasing shapes. Garion found this tampering with nature somehow offensive. It appeared that he was not alone in this feeling. Ce'Nedra rode with a stiff look of disapproval on her face and frequently made little sounds of disgust, usually at the sight of a well-trimmed oak tree.

They moved into a canter, following the trail north along a road surfaced with gleaming white gravel. The road curved gently from hillside to hillside and in level spots it frequently made wide bends, evidently for no other purpose than to relieve the monotony of long straight stretches. The houses set far back from the road were universally constructed of marble and were usually surrounded by parks and gardens. It was a sunny autumn day, and the prevailing breeze carried with it the smell of the sea, a smell Garion found very familiar. He suddenly felt a sharp pang of homesickness for Riva.

As they cantered past one estate, a large number of gaily

dressed people crossed the road ahead of them at a gallop, chasing after a pack of barking dogs. The people jumped fences and ditches with what appeared to be reckless abandon.

"What are they doing?" Eriond called to Silk.

"Fox hunting."

"That doesn't really make any sense, Silk," Durnik objected. "If they don't farm, they don't raise chickens. Why are they worried about foxes?"

"It makes even less sense in view of the fact that the fox isn't native to these islands. They have to be imported."

"That's ridiculous!"

"Of course it is. Rich people are always ridiculous, and their sports are usually exotic—and often cruel."

Beldin gave an ugly little chuckle. "I wonder how sporting they'd find chasing a pack of Algroths—or maybe an Eldrak or two."

"Never mind," Belgarath told him.

"It wouldn't really take much effort to raise a few, Belgarath." The hunchback grinned. "Or maybe some Trolls," he mused. "Trolls are great fun, and I'd love to see the look on the face of one of those overdressed butterflies when he jumped a fence and came face to face with a full-grown Troll."

"Never mind," Belgarath repeated.

The road forked at one point, and the Orb pulled toward the left. "She's headed toward the ocean again," Silk noted. "I wonder what it is that makes her so fond of water. She's been hopping from island to island ever since we started out after her."

"Maybe she knows that the Orb can't follow her over water," Garion said.

"I don't think that would be her major concern at this point," Polgara disagreed. "Time's running out—for her as well as us. She doesn't have the leisure for side trips."

The road they were following led down toward the cliffs, and finally the Orb pulled Garion onto a long, paved drive that curved down toward an imposing house set at the very edge of a precipitous drop and overlooking the ocean far below. As they rode toward the house, Garion loosened his sword in its scabbard.

"Expecting trouble?" Silk asked.

"I just like to be ready," Garion replied. "That's a big house up ahead, and a lot of people could be hiding inside."

The men who came out of the cliff-top villa, however, were not armed and they were all garbed in purple livery. "May I ask your business?" one of them asked. He was tall and thin and had an imposing mane of snowy white hair. He carried himself with an air of self-importance, that kind of air usually assumed by senior servants accustomed to ordering grooms and maids about.

Silk pushed forward. "My friends and I have been out for a morning ride," he said, "and we were struck by the beauty of this house and its location. Is the owner about perhaps?"

"His Lordship, the Archduke is away at present," the tall man replied.

"What a shame," Silk said. He looked around. "I'm really taken with this place," he said. Then he laughed. "Maybe it's as well that he's not at home. If he were, I might be tempted to make him an offer for his house."

"I don't know that his Grace would be very interested," the servant said.

"I don't believe I know his Grace," Silk said artfully. "Do you suppose you could tell me his name?"

"He's the Archduke Otrath, sir," the servant answered, puffing himself up slightly. "He's a member of the imperial family."

"Oh?"

"He's the third cousin—twice removed—of his Imperial Majesty, Kal Zakath."

"Really? What an amazing thing. I'm so sorry to have

106

missed him. I'll tell his Majesty that I stopped by the next time I see him, though."

"You know his Majesty?"

"Oh, yes. We're old friends."

"Might I ask your name, honored sir?"

"Oh, sorry. How very stupid of me. I'm Prince Kheldar of Drasnia."

"*The* Prince Kheldar?"

"I certainly hope there aren't any others." Silk laughed. "I can get into enough trouble all by myself."

"His Grace will be very sorry to have missed you, your Highness."

"I'll be in Melcena for several weeks," Silk said. "Perhaps I can call again. When do you expect his Grace to return?"

"That's very hard to say, your Highness. He left not three days ago with some people from the mainland." The white-haired servant paused thoughtfully. "If you and your friends wouldn't mind waiting for a few moments, Prince Kheldar, I'll go advise her Grace, the Archduke's wife, that you're here. Her Grace has so few visitors out here, and she loves company. Won't you please come inside? I'll go to her at once and tell her that you're here."

They dismounted and followed him into a broad entryway. He bowed rather stiffly and went off down a corridor lined with tapestries.

"Very smooth, Kheldar," Velvet murmured admiringly.

"They don't call me Silk for nothing," he said, polishing his ring on the front of his pearl-gray doublet.

When the tall servant returned, he had a slightly pained look on his face. "Her Grace is a bit indisposed at the moment, your Highness," he apologized to Silk.

"I'm sorry to hear that," Silk replied with genuine regret. "Perhaps another time, then."

"Oh, no, your Highness. Her Grace insists on seeing you, but please forgive her if she seems a bit—ah—disoriented."

One of Silk's eyebrows shot up.

"It's the isolation, your Highness," the servant confided, looking embarrassed. "Her Grace is not happy in this somewhat bucolic locale, and she's resorted to a certain amount of reinforcement in her exile."

"Reinforcement?"

"I trust I can count on your Highness' discretion?"

"Of course."

"Her Grace takes some wine from time to time, your Highness, and this appears to be one of those times. I'm afraid she's had a bit more than is really good for her."

"This early in the morning?"

"Her Grace does not keep what one might call regular hours. If you'll come with me, please."

As they followed the servant down a long corridor, Silk murmured back over his shoulder to the rest of them. "Follow my lead on this," he said. "Just smile and try not to look too startled at what I say."

"Don't you just love it when he gets devious?" Velvet said admiringly to Ce'Nedra.

The archduchess was a lady in her mid-thirties. She had luxurious dark hair and very large eyes. She had a pouting lower lip and an ever-so-slightly overgenerous figure which filled her burgundy gown to the point of overflowing. She was also as drunk as a lord. She had discarded her goblet and now drank directly from a decanter. "Prince Kheldar," she hiccuped, trying to curtsy. Sadi moved sinuously to catch her arm to prevent a disaster.

"'Scuse me," she slurred to him. "So nice of you."

"My pleasure, your Grace," the eunuch said politely.

She blinked at him several times. "Are you really bald— or is that an affectation?"

"It's a cultural thing, your Grace," he explained, bowing.

"How disappointing," she sighed, rubbing her hand over

108

his head and taking another drink from the decanter. "Could I offer you all something to drink?" she asked brightly.

Most of them declined with faint headshakes. Beldin, however, stumped forward with his hand extended. "Why not?" the grotesque little man said. "Let's try a rip of that, me girl." For some reason he had lapsed into Feldegast's brogue.

Belgarath rolled his eyes ceilingward.

The archduchess laughed uproariously and passed over the decanter.

Beldin drained it without stopping for breath. "Very tasty," he belched, tossing the decanter negligently into a corner, "but ale's me preference, y'r ladyship. Wine's hard on the stomach so early of a morning."

"Ale it shall be, then," she crowed happily. "We'll all sit around and swill ourselves into insensibility." She fell back on a couch, exposing a great deal of herself in the process. "Bring ale," she commanded the embarrassed servant, "lots and lots of ale."

"As your Grace commands," the tall man replied stiffly, withdrawing.

"Nice enough fellow," the archduchess slurred, "but he's so terribly stuffy sometimes. He absolutely refuses to take a drink with me." Her eyes suddenly filled with tears. "Nobody wants to drink with me," she complained. She held out her arms imploringly to Beldin, and he enfolded her in an embrace. "*You* understand, don't you, my friend?" she sobbed, burying her face in his shoulder.

"Of course I do," he said, patting her shoulder. "There, there, me little darlin'," he said, "'twill all be right again soon."

The noblewoman regained her composure, sniffed loudly, and fished for a handkerchief. "It's not that I *want* to be like this, your Highness," she apologized, trying to focus her eyes on Silk. "It's just that I'm so absolutely *bored* out here. Otrath has all the social grace of an oyster, so he's imprisoned me out here in the hinterlands with nothing but the booming of the surf and the screeching of gulls for company. I so miss the balls and the dinner parties and the conversation in Melcena. What am I to do with myself out here?"

"'Tis cruel hard, me darlin'," Beldin agreed. He took the small cask of ale the servant cringingly brought, placed it between his knees, and bashed in the top with his gnarled fist. "Would ye care fer a sup, sweeting?" he asked the duchess politely, holding out the cask.

"I'd drown if I tried to drink out of that," she protested with a silly little laugh.

"Right y' are," he agreed. "You there," he said to Belgarath. "Get the poor girl a cup or somethin'."

Belgarath scowled at his gnarled brother, then wordlessly fetched a silver tankard from a sideboard.

Beldin dipped deeply into the cask with the tankard, wiped off the bottom with his sleeve, and offered it to their hostess. "To yer good health, me darlin'," he said, drinking from the cask.

"You're *so* kind," she hiccuped. Then she drained off about half the tankard with foamy ale spilling out of the corners of her mouth and down the front of her gown.

"We were very sorry to have missed his Grace," Silk said, obviously a little nonplussed by Beldin's rough-and-ready approach to a highborn, though tipsy, lady.

"You didn't miss a thing, your Highness," she burped, politely covering her mouth. "My husband's a fat green toad with all the charm of a dead rat. He spends his time trying to decipher his proximity to the imperial throne. Kal Zakath has no heir, so all the imperial cousins sit around waiting for one another to die and trying to cement alliances. Have you ever been in Mal Zeth, your Highness? It's an absolutely ghastly place. Frankly, imperial crown or no, I'd sooner live in Hell." She drained her tankard and handed it wordlessly back to Beldin. Then she looked around brightly, her eyes slightly unfocused. "But my dear Prince Kheldar," she said, "you haven't introduced me to your friends as yet."

"How terribly forgetful of me, your Grace," he exclaimed, slapping his hand to his forehead. He rose formally to his feet. "Your Grace, I have the honor to present her Grace, the Duchess of Erat." He held his hand out grandly to Polgara, who rose and curtsied.

"Your Grace," she murmured.

"Your Grace," the archduchess replied, trying to rise, but not quite succeeding.

"There, there, me darlin'," Beldin said, pressing down on her shoulder to keep her more or less in place. "'Tis early, an' we're all friends. There's no need at all fer us t' be goin' through all these tiresome formalities."

"I *like* him," the noblewoman said, pointing at Beldin with one hand and dipping out more ale with the other. "Can I keep him?"

"Sorry, your Grace," Belgarath said. "We might need him later on."

"So grim a face," she observed, looking at the ancient sorcerer. She grinned roguishly. "I'll wager I could make you smile."

Silk rushed on. "Her Highness, Princess Ce'Nedra of the House of Borune," he said, "and the Margravine Liselle of Drasnia. The young man with the sword is known as the Lord of the Western Sea—an obscure title, I'll grant you, but his people are an obscure sort of folk."

Garion bowed deeply to the tipsy archduchess.

"So great a sword you have, my Lord," she said.

"It's a family heirloom, your Grace," he replied. "I'm more or less obliged to carry it."

"The others have no titles they care to acknowledge," Silk said. "They're business associates, and we don't worry about titles where money is concerned."

"Do *you* have a title?" the lady asked Beldin.

"Several, me little darlin'," he replied in an offhand way, "but none from any land ye'd be recognizin' the name of—most of 'em havin' disappeared long ago." He raised the cask again and drank noisily.

"What a dear little man you are," she said in a smoldering sort of voice.

"'Tis me charm, darlin'," he replied with a resigned sort of sigh. "'Tis always been me bane, this charmin' quality about me. Sometimes I must actually hide myself t' keep off the maids overpowered with unreasonin' passion." He sighed again, then belched.

"We might want to talk about that one of these days," she suggested.

Silk was obviously out of his depth here. "Ah—" he said lamely, "—as I was saying, we're sorry to have missed the archduke."

"I can't for the life of me think why, your Highness," the lady said bluntly. "My husband's an unmitigated ass, and he doesn't bathe regularly. He has wild aspirations about the imperial throne and very little in the way of prospects in that direction." She held out her tankard to Beldin. "Would you, dear?"

He squinted down into the cask. "It could just be that we'll need another, me darlin'," he suggested.

"I've got a cellar full," she sighed happily. "We can go on like this for days, if you'd like."

Belgarath and Beldin exchanged a long look. "Never mind," Belgarath said.

"But—"

"Never mind."

"You were saying that your husband has imperial ambitions, your Grace," Silk floundered on.

"Can you imagine that idiot as emperor of Mallorea?" She sneered. "Half the time he can't even get his shoes on the right feet. Fortunately, he's a long way down the line of succession."

Garion suddenly remembered something. "Has anyone ever suggested anything to him that might have encouraged these ambitions?" he asked.

"*I* certainly didn't," she declared. She frowned blearily at the far wall. "Now that you mention it, though, there *was* a fellow who came through here a few years ago—a fellow with white eyes. Have you ever seen anybody with eyes like that? It makes your blood run cold. Anyway, he and the archduke went off to my husband's study to talk." She snorted derisively. "Study! I don't think my idiot husband can even read. He can barely talk to me, but he calls the room his study. Isn't that absurd? Well, at any rate, that happened at a time when I was still curious about the oaf's affairs. I'd had one of the footmen drill a hole through the wall so I could watch— and hear—what the fool was up to." Her lower lip began to tremble. "Not long after that, I saw him in there with the upstairs maid." She threw her arms out tragically, sloshing ale on Beldin. "Betrayed!" she cried. "In my own house!"

"What were they talking about?" Garion asked her gently. "Your husband and the white-eyed man, I mean?"

"White-eyes told my husband that somebody named Zandramas could guarantee him succession to the throne in Mal Zeth. That name sounds familiar for some reason. Has anybody ever heard it before?" She looked around, trying to focus her eyes.

"Not that I recall," Silk lied blandly. "Have you ever seen this white-eyed man again?"

The archduchess was busily trying to dip the last bit of ale out of the cask. "What?" she asked.

"The white-eyed man," Belgarath said impatiently. "Did he ever come back?"

"Of course." The lady leaned back and lustily drained her tankard. "He was here just a few days ago. He came here with some woman in a black satin robe and a little boy." She belched modestly. "Could you give that bellpull over there a bit of a jerk, my twisted little friend?" she asked Beldin. "I think we've used up all of this cask, and I'm still sort of thirsty."

"I'll see to it at once, me darlin'!" The hunchback stumped to the bellpull.

"It's so very nice to have friends about," the archduchess said dreamily. Then her head drooped to one side and she began to snore.

"Wake her up, Pol," Belgarath said.

"Yes, father."

It was a very light surge, but the tipsy noblewoman's eyes popped open immediately. "Where was I?" she asked.

"Ah—you were telling us about the visit of the white-eyed man a few days back, your Grace," Silk supplied.

"Oh, yes. He came in about dusk—him and that hag in black satin."

"Hag?" Silk asked.

"She must have been a hag. She went to a lot of trouble to keep her face covered. The little boy was adorable, though—reddish-blond curls and the bluest eyes you ever saw. I got some milk for him, because he was hungry. Anyway, White-eyes and the hag went off along with my husband, and then they all took horses and rode off. The toad, my husband, told me that he was going to be gone for a while and that I should send for my dressmaker—something about a gown suitable for an imperial coronation. I forget exactly."

"What happened to the little boy?" Ce'Nedra asked in a very tense voice.

The archduchess shrugged. "Who knows? As far as I know, they did take him with them." She sighed. "I'm suddenly so sleepy," she murmured.

"Did your husband give you any hint about where they were going?" Silk asked her.

She waved her hands helplessly. "I stopped listening to him years ago," she said. "We have a small yacht in a cove about a mile from here. It's gone, so I think they took that. My husband was saying something about those commercial wharves south of the city." She looked around. "Has that other cask of ale got here yet?" she asked drowsily.

"'Twill only be a moment or two, me darlin'," Beldin assured her in a gentle voice.

"Oh, good."

"You need anything more?" Silk quietly asked Belgarath.

"I don't think so." The old man turned to his daughter. "Put her to sleep again, Pol," he said.

"There's no need, father," she replied. She looked rather sadly at the lush-bodied noblewoman, who had once again wrapped her arms about Beldin's neck, burrowed her face into his shoulder, and was lightly snoring. Gently, the dwarfed hunchback disengaged her arms and laid her softly on the couch. He straightened her gown, then crossed the room, picked up a comforter from a divan, returned, and covered her with it. "Sleep well, my Lady," he murmured, touching her face with one sad hand. Then he turned and glared pugnaciously at Belgarath. "Well?" he demanded in the tone of a man ready to fight.

"I didn't say anything," Belgarath said to him.

Wordlessly, Ce'Nedra rose, went to the hideous little man, embraced him, and kissed him on the cheek.

"What was that all about?" he asked suspiciously.

"I didn't say anything either," she replied, absently picking a few pieces of straw out of his beard and handing them to him.

115

CHAPTER SIX

As they emerged from the house, Garion went immediately to Chretienne and swung up into his saddle.

"What have you got in mind?" Silk asked him.

"I'm going to stay on the trail," Garion replied.

"Why? All it's going to do is run down to that cove the lady
mentioned and then go out to sea again."

Garion looked at him helplessly.

"I'd say that the best thing for us to do right now is get
back to Melcena as quickly as possible. I have a lot of people
working for me there. I'll saturate those commercial wharves
with men—the same way we did in Jarot. Naradas won't be
hard to follow."

"Why don't I just take the Orb and go down to the wharves myself?" Garion protested.

"Because all you'll find out that way is which wharf she sailed from. We need more than that." Silk looked sympathetically at his friend. "I know you're impatient, Garion— we all are—but my way's going to be faster, actually. My people can find out when Zandramas sailed and where she was going. That's the thing we really have to know."

"All right, then," Belgarath said, "let's ride."

They mounted quickly and rode at a canter back up the drive to the road. Then they went south toward Melcena at a gallop.

It was about noon when they reached the north gate and not long after that when they dismounted in front of Silk's house. They went inside and on up the stairs to the sitting room. "Would you ask Vetter to come up?" the little man asked a passing servant as they entered the room.

"At once, your Highness."

"I'd say we'd better pack again," Silk suggested, removing his businessman's robe. "As soon as we find out where Zandramas is going, I think we'll be leaving again."

Sadi smiled faintly. "Poor Zith," he murmured. "She's getting very tired of traveling."

"She's not the only one," Velvet said a bit ruefully. "When this is all over, I don't think I'll ever want even to *look* at another horse."

There was a polite knock at the door, and Vetter opened it. "You wanted to see me, your Highness?" he asked.

"Yes, Vetter. Come in, please." Silk was pacing up and down, his eyes deep in thought. "We've been looking for some people," he said.

"I surmised as much, your Highness."

"Good. We know that these people came to Melcena not too long back. Then they left again about three days ago. We need to know where they went."

117

"Very well, your Highness. Can you give me a description?"

"I was just getting to that. There were two men, a woman, and a small boy. One of the men was the Archduke Otrath. Do you know him?"

Vetter nodded. "I can give our people an accurate description of him, yes."

"Very good, Vetter. The other man is named Naradas."

"I've heard the name, your Highness, but I don't think I've ever seen him."

"You wouldn't have forgotten him. His eyes are totally white."

"He's a blind man?"

"No, but his eyes have no color to them."

"That should make things simpler."

"I thought it might. The woman's been going to some trouble to keep her face covered, but she'll be with the archduke and Naradas. We've picked up the information that they may have sailed from one of the commercial wharves to the south of the city. Start out by concentrating the search there. Send every man you can put your hands on down there. Have them talk with everybody on those wharves. We need information and we need it fast. Spread money around if you have to. I want to know when they left, on which ship, and where they were going. If the ship happens to be back in port, bring me one of the sailors—or even better yet, the captain. Speed is essential, Vetter."

"I'll see to it at once, your Highness. I'll have several hundred men on those wharves within the hour and I'll keep you posted about the progress of the search. Will there be anything else?"

Silk frowned. "Yes," he decided. "We came to Melcena aboard one of our own ships. It should still be down in the harbor. Send someone to the captain and tell him to make

118

ready to sail again. We'll be leaving as soon as we get the information."

"I'll attend to it." Vetter bowed and quietly left the room.

"He seems like a good man," Beldin noted.

"One of the best," Silk agreed. "He gets things done and he never gets excited." The little man smiled. "I've heard that Brador's been trying to lure him back, but I've got more money than Brador has."

Beldin grunted and looked at Belgarath. "We've got some things to sort out," he said. "Why is Zandramas saddling herself with this archduke? This whole side trip of hers didn't make any sense at all."

"Of course it did."

"I'm sure you'll explain that to me—sometime in the next week or so."

Belgarath fished around inside his tunic and pulled out a tattered scrap of paper. He looked at it. "This is it," he grunted. He held the paper out in front of him. "'Behold:'" he read. "'In the days which shall follow the ascension of the Dark God into the heavens shall the King of the East and the King of the South do war upon each other, and this shall be a sign unto ye that the day of the meeting is at hand. Hasten therefore unto the Place Which Is No More when battles do rage upon the plains of the South. Take with thee the chosen sacrifice and a King of Angarak to bear witness to what shall come to pass. For lo, whichever of ye cometh into the presence of Cthrag Sardius with the sacrifice and an Angarak king shall be exalted above all the rest and shall have dominion over them. And know further that in the moment of sacrifice shall the Dark God be reborn, and he shall triumph over the Child of Light in the instant of his rebirth.'"

"What a fascinating piece of gibberish," Beldin said. "Where did you come by it?"

"We picked it up in Cthol Murgos." Belgarath shrugged.

"It's a part of the Grolim Prophecies of Rak Cthol. I told you about it before."

"No," Beldin disagreed, "as a matter of fact, you didn't."

"I must have."

"I'm sorry, Belgarath," the grubby little man said from between clenched teeth, "you didn't."

"What an amazing thing." Belgarath frowned. "It must have completely slipped my mind."

"We knew it was going to happen eventually, Pol," Beldin said. "The old boy's finally slipped over the line into senility."

"Be nice, uncle," she murmured.

"Are you *positive* I didn't tell you about this?" Belgarath said a little plaintively.

"There's no such thing as positive," Beldin replied, automatically, it seemed.

"I'm awfully glad you said that," Belgarath said just a bit smugly.

"Stop that."

"Stop what?"

"Don't try to use my own prejudices against me. Where does this Grolim insanity put us?"

"Grolims obey orders beyond the point of reason."

"So do we, when you get down to it."

"Perhaps, but at least we question the orders now and then. Grolims don't. They follow instructions blindly. When we were in Rak Urga, we saw the Hierarch Agachak bullying King Urgit about this. Agachak knows that he has to have an Angarak king in tow if he's going to have any chance at all when he gets to this place of the final meeting. He's going to take Urgit, even if he has to drag him by the hair. Up until now, Zandramas hasn't bothered herself about the requirement."

"She must be planning to kill Zakath, then," Durnik said, "and then put this archduke on the throne in his place."

"She won't even have to do that, Durnik. All you need to be called a king in Angarak society is a hint of royal blood, a

coronation ceremony, and recognition by a major Grolim priest. Back in the old days, every clan-chief was a king. It didn't really matter that much, because all the power was in the hands of Torak anyway. They all had crowns and thrones, though. Anyway, Zandramas is a recognized Grolim priest— or priestess, in this case. Otrath is of royal blood. A coronation, spurious or not, would qualify him as a King of Angarak, and that would satisfy the prophecy."

"It still seems a little questionable to me," Durnik said.

"This comes from a man whose people elected a rutabaga farmer as their first king," Beldin said.

"Actually, Fundor the Magnificent wasn't a bad king," Belgarath said. "At least, once he got the hang of it all. Farmers always make good kings. They know what's important. At any rate, Otrath will be king enough to fulfill the prophecy, and that means that Zandramas has everything she needs now. She has Geran and an Angarak king."

"Do we need one, too?" Durnik asked. "An Angarak king, I mean?"

"No. We'd need an Alorn King. I think Garion qualifies."

"It wasn't this complicated last time, was it?"

"Actually it was. Garion was already the Rivan King as well as the Child of Light. Torak was both king and God, *and* he was the Child of Dark."

"Who was the sacrifice, then?"

Belgarath smiled affectionately at the good man. "You were, Durnik," he said gently. "Remember?"

"Oh," Durnik said, looking a bit embarrassed. "I forget about that sometimes."

"I wouldn't be at all surprised," Beldin growled. "Getting killed is the sort of thing that might tend to make one's memory wander just a bit."

"That's enough of that, uncle," Polgara said dangerously, putting a protective arm about Durnik's shoulders.

Garion suddenly realized that not one of them had ever

spoken with Durnik about that terrible time between the moment Zedar had killed him and the moment when the Orb and the Gods had returned him to life. He had the very strong feeling that Polgara fully intended to keep it that way.

"She's completed all her tasks then, hasn't she?" Ce'Nedra asked sadly. "Zandramas, I mean. She has my son and an Angarak king. I do so wish I could see him one more time before I die."

"Die?" Garion asked incredulously. "What do you mean, die?"

"One of us is going to," she said simply. "I'm sure it's going to be me. There's no other reason for me being along, is there? We all have tasks to perform. Mine is to die, I think."

"Nonsense!"

"Really?" She sighed.

"Actually, Zandramas still has several more tasks," Belgarath told her. "She has to deal with Urvon at the very least."

"And Agachak, I think," Sadi added. "He wants to play, too, as I recall."

"Agachak's in Cthol Murgos," Silk objected.

"So were we—until some months back," the eunuch pointed out. "All it takes to get to Mallorea from Cthol Murgos is a boat and a little luck with the weather."

"Zandramas has one other thing she has to do as well," Velvet said, moving over until she was beside Ce'Nedra and wrapping her arms about the sad little queen.

"Oh?" Ce'Nedra said without much interest. "What's that?"

"The prophecy told Garion that she still doesn't know where the Place Which Is No More is. She can't go there until she finds out, can she?"

Ce'Nedra's face brightened just a bit. "That's true, isn't it?" she conceded. "I suppose it's something," she said, laying her head against Velvet's shoulder.

"Zandramas isn't the only one with things left to do," Bel-

garath said. "I still have to find an unmutilated copy of the Ashabine Oracles." He looked at Silk. "How long do you think it's going to take your men to find out what we need to know?"

Silk spread his hands. "It's a little hard to say," he admitted. "A lot could depend on luck. A day at the most, I'd imagine."

"How fast is that ship of yours?" Garion asked him. "I mean, can it go any faster than it did when we were coming here?"

"Not by very much," Silk replied. "Melcenes are better shipbuilders than Angaraks, but that ship was built to carry cargo, not to win races. If the wind gets too strong, the captain's going to have to shorten his sails."

"I'd give a lot to have a Cherek warship right now," Garion said. "A fast boat could make up for a lot of lost time." He gazed thoughtfully at the floor. "It wouldn't really be too hard, would it?" he suggested. He looked at Belgarath. "Maybe you and I could put our heads together, and—" He made a kind of vague gesture with his hand.

"Uh—Garion," Durnik interrupted him, "even if you did have a Cherek boat, who would you find to sail her? I don't think the sailors here would understand what's involved."

"Oh," Garion said glumly. "I hadn't thought about that, I guess."

There was a light rap at the door, and Vetter entered carrying a sheaf of parchments. "The men have been dispatched to the south wharves, your Highness," he reported. "You suggested that the matter was of some urgency, so I took the liberty of posting couriers on fast horses to central locations near the waterfront. As soon as anyone gets news of any kind, the word should reach us here within five minutes." He glanced at Ce'Nedra. "I hope that will relieve some of her Majesty's anxiety," he added.

"Her—" Silk burst out, then controlled himself. He stared

at his factor for a moment, then burst out laughing. "How did you find out, Vetter?" he asked. "I didn't introduce anybody."

"Please, your Highness," Vetter replied with a pained look. "You didn't engage me in this position to be stupid, did you? I've maintained certain contacts with my former associates in Mal Zeth, so I more or less know who your guests are and what your mission is. You chose not to mention the matter, so I didn't make an issue of it, but you aren't paying me to keep my eyes and ears closed, are you?"

"Don't you just love Melcenes?" Velvet said to Sadi.

Sadi, however, was already looking at Vetter with a certain interest. "It may just happen that in time I'll be able to resolve the slight misunderstanding I presently have with my queen," he said delicately to Silk's factor. "Should that happen, I might want to make you aware of certain employment opportunities in Sthiss Tor."

"Sadi!" Silk gasped.

"Business is business, Prince Kheldar," Sadi said blandly.

Vetter smiled. "There are these few documents, your Highness," he said to Silk, handing over the parchments he carried. "As long as you're waiting, I thought you might want to glance at them. A few require your signature."

Silk sighed. "I suppose I might as well," he agreed.

"It does save time, your Highness. Sometimes it takes quite a while for things to catch up with you."

Silk riffled through the stack. "This all seems fairly routine. Is there anything else of note going on?"

"The house is being watched, your Highness," Vetter reported. "A couple of Rolla's secret policemen. I imagine they'll try to follow you when you leave."

Silk frowned. "I'd forgotten about him. Is there some way to get them off our trail?"

"I think I can manage that for your Highness."

"Nothing fatal, though," Silk cautioned. "The Rivan King here disapproves of random fatalities." He grinned at Garion.

"I think we'll be able to deal with the situation without bloodshed, your Highness."

"Anything else I should know about?"

"The Consortium will make an offer on our bean holdings tomorrow morning," Vetter replied. "They'll start at three points below market and go as high as five above it."

"How did you find that out?" Silk looked amazed.

"I've bribed one of the members." Vetter shrugged. "I promised to give him a quarter point commission on everything over ten—a bit generous, perhaps, but we may need him again sometime, and now I'll have a hold on him."

"That's worth a quarter of a point right there."

"I thought so myself, your Highness." Vetter laughed suddenly. "Oh, one other thing, Prince Kheldar. We have this investment opportunity."

"Oh?"

"Actually, it's more in the nature of a charitable contribution."

"I gave at the office," Silk said with an absolutely straight face. Then his nose twitched slightly. "It wouldn't hurt to hear about it, though, I guess."

"There's a very grubby little alchemist at the university," Vetter explained. "He absolutely swears that he can turn brass into gold."

"Well, now." Silk's eyes brightened.

Vetter held up a cautioning hand. "The cost, however, is prohibitive at this time. It doesn't make much sense to spend two pieces of gold to get back one."

"No, I wouldn't say so."

"The little clubfoot maintains that he can reduce the cost, though. He's been approaching every businessman in Melcena about the project. He needs a rich patron to underwrite the cost of his experiments."

125

"Did you look into the matter at all?"

"Of course. Unless he's a very skilled trickster, it appears that he actually *can* turn brass into gold. He has a rather peculiar reputation. They say that he's been around for centuries. He's got a bad temper and he smells awful—the chemicals he uses, I understand."

Belgarath's eyes suddenly went very wide. "What did you call him?" he demanded.

"I don't believe I mentioned his name, Ancient One," Vetter replied. "He's called Senji."

"I don't mean his name. Describe him."

"He's short and mostly bald. He wears a beard—though most of his whiskers have been singed off. Sometimes his experiments go awry, and there have been explosions. Oh, and he has a clubfoot—the left one, I believe."

"That's it!" Belgarath exclaimed, snapping his fingers.

"Don't be cryptic, father," Polgara said primly.

"The prophecy told Garion that somebody was going to say something to us in passing today that was very important. This is it."

"I don't quite—"

"At Ashaba, Cyradis told us to seek out the clubfooted one because he'd help us in our search."

"There are many men with clubfeet in the world, father."

"I know, but the prophecy went out of its way to introduce this one."

"Introduce?"

"Maybe that's the wrong word, but you know what I mean."

"It does sort of fit, Pol," Beldin said. "As I remember, we were talking about the Ashabine Oracles when Cyradis told us about this clubfoot. She said that Zandramas has one uncut copy, Nahaz has another, and that this clubfoot has the third—or knows where it is."

"It's pretty thin, Belgarath," Durnik said dubiously.

"We've got time enough to chase it down," the old man replied. "We can't go anywhere until we find out where Zandramas is going anyway." He looked at Vetter. "Where do we find this Senji?"

"He's on the faculty of the College of Applied Alchemy at the university, Ancient One."

"All right, I'll take Garion and we'll go there. The rest of you might as well get ready to leave."

"Grandfather," Garion protested, "I have to stay here. I want to hear the word about Zandramas with my own ears."

"Pol can listen for you. I might need you along to help persuade the alchemist to talk to me. Bring the Orb, but leave the sword behind."

"Why the Orb?"

"Let's just call it a hunch."

"I'll come with you," Beldin said, rising to his feet.

"There's no need of that."

"Oh, yes there is. Your memory seems to be failing a bit, Belgarath. You forget to tell me things. If I'm there when you locate the Oracles, I'll be able to save you all the time and trouble of trying to remember."

CHAPTER SEVEN

The University of Melcena was a sprawling complex of buildings situated in a vast park. The buildings were old and stately, and the trees dotting the close-clipped lawns were gnarled with age. There was a kind of secure serenity about the place that bespoke a dedication to the life of the mind. A calm came over Garion as he walked with the two old sorcerers across the green lawn, but there was a kind of melancholy as well. He sighed.

"What's the problem?" Belgarath asked him.

"Oh, I don't know, Grandfather. Sometimes I wish I might have had the chance to come to a place like this. It might be kind of nice to study something for no reason except that you want to know about it. Most of my studying has been pretty urgent—you know, find the answer, or the world will come to an end."

"Universities are overrated places," Beldin said. "Too many young men attend simply because their fathers insist, and they spend more time carousing than they do studying. The noise is distracting to the serious student. Stick to studying alone. You get more done." He looked at Belgarath. "Have you got even the remotest idea where we're going to find this Senji?"

"Vetter said that he's a member of the faculty of the College of Applied Alchemy. I'd imagine that's the place to start."

"Logic, Belgarath? You? The next question that pops to mind is where we're going to find the College of Applied Alchemy."

Belgarath stopped a robed scholar who was walking across the lawn with an open book in his hand. "Excuse me, learned sir," he said politely, "but could you direct me to the College of Applied Alchemy?"

"Umm?" the scholar said, looking up from his book.

"The College of Applied Alchemy. Could you tell me where I could find it?"

"The sciences are all down that way," the scholar said, "near the theology department." He waved rather vaguely toward the south end of the campus.

"Thank you," Belgarath said. "You're too kind."

"It's a scholar's duty to provide instruction and direction," the fellow replied pompously.

"Ah, yes," Belgarath murmured. "Sometimes I lose sight of that."

They walked on in the direction the scholar had indicated.

"If he doesn't give his students any more specific directions than that, they probably come out of this place with a rather vague idea of the world," Beldin observed.

The directions they received from others gradually grew more precise, and they finally reached a blocky-looking building constructed of thick gray rock and solidly buttressed along its walls. They went up the steps in front and entered a hallway that was also shored up with stout buttresses.

"I don't quite follow the reason for all the interior reinforcement," Garion confessed.

As if in answer to his question, there came a thunderous detonation from behind a door partway up the hall. The door blew outward violently, and clouds of reeking smoke came pouring out.

"Oh," Garion said. "Now I understand."

A fellow with a dazed look on his face and with his clothes hanging from his body in smoking tatters came staggering out through the smoke. "Too much sulfur," he was muttering over and over again. "Too much sulfur."

"Excuse me," Belgarath said, "do you by any chance know where we might find the alchemist Senji?"

"Too much sulfur," the experimenter said, looking blankly at Belgarath.

"Senji," the old man repeated. "Could you tell us where to find him?"

The tattered fellow frowned. "What?" he said blankly.

"Let me," Beldin said. "Can you tell us where to find Senji?" he bellowed at the top of his lungs. "He's got a clubfoot."

"Oh," the man replied, shaking his head to clear his befuddlement. "His laboratory's on the top floor—down toward the other end."

"Thank you," Beldin shouted at him.

"Too much sulfur. That's the problem, all right. I put in too much sulfur."

"Why were you shouting at him?" Belgarath asked curiously as the three of them went on down the hall.

"I've been in the middle of a few explosions myself." The

hunchback shrugged. "I was always deaf as a post for a week or two afterward."

"Oh."

They went up two flights of stairs to the top floor. They passed another door that had only recently been exploded out of its casement. Belgarath poked his head through the opening. "Where can we find Senji?" he shouted into the room.

There was a mumbled reply.

"Last door on the left," the old man grunted, leading the way.

"Alchemy seems to be a fairly dangerous occupation," Garion noted.

"Also fairly stupid," Beldin growled. "If they want gold so badly, why don't they just go dig it up?"

"I don't think that's occurred to very many of them," Belgarath said. He stopped before the last door on the left, a door showing signs of recent repair. He knocked.

"Go away," a rusty-sounding voice replied.

"We need to talk with you, Senji," Belgarath called mildly.

The rusty voice told him at some length what he could do with his need to talk. Most of the words were very colorful.

Belgarath's face grew set. He gathered himself up and spoke a single word. The door disappeared with a shocking sound.

"Now that's something you don't see around here very much," the grubby little man sitting in the midst of the splintered remains of his door said in a conversational tone. "I can't remember the last time I saw a door blow *in*." He started picking splinters out of his beard.

"Are you all right?" Garion asked him.

"Of course, just a little surprised is all. When you've been blown up as many times as I have, you sort of get used to the idea. Does one of you want to pull this door off me?"

Beldin stumped forward and lifted the remains of the door.

"You're an ugly one, aren't you?" the man on the floor said.

131

"You're no beauty yourself."

"I can live with it."

"So can I."

"Good. Are you the one who blew my door in?"

"He did." Beldin pointed at Belgarath and then helped the fellow to his feet.

"How did you manage that?" the grubby little man asked Belgarath curiously. "I don't smell any chemicals at all."

"It's a gift," Belgarath replied. "You're Senji, I take it?"

"I am. Senji the clubfoot, senior member of the faculty of the College of Applied Alchemy." He thumped on the side of his head with the heel of his hand. "Explosions always make my ears ring," he noted. "You—my ugly friend," he said to Beldin. "There's a barrel of beer over there in the corner. Why don't you bring me some? Get some for yourself and your friends as well."

"We're going to get along fairly well," Beldin said.

Senji limped toward a stone table in the center of the room. His left leg was several inches shorter than his right, and his left foot was grotesquely deformed. He leafed through several sheets of parchment. "Good," he said to Belgarath. "At least your explosion didn't scatter my calculations all over the room." He looked at them. "As long as you're here, you might as well find something to sit down on."

Beldin brought him a cup of beer, then went back to the corner where the barrel was and filled three more cups.

"That is *really* an ugly fellow," Senji noted, hauling himself up and sitting on top of the table. "I sort of like him, though. I haven't met anybody quite like that for almost a thousand years."

Belgarath and Garion exchanged a quick look. "That's quite a long time," Belgarath said cautiously.

"Yes," Senji agreed, taking a drink from his cup. He made a face. "It's gone flat again," he said. "You there," he called to Beldin. "There's an earthenware jar on the shelf just above the barrel. Be a good fellow and dump a couple handfuls of that powder into the beer. It wakes it up again.'' He looked back at Belgarath. "What was it you wanted to talk about?" he asked. "What's so important that you have to go around blowing doors apart?"

"In a minute," Belgarath said. He crossed to where the little clubfoot sat. "Do you mind?" he asked. He reached out and lightly touched his fingertips to the smelly man's bald head.

"Well?" Beldin asked.

Belgarath nodded. "He doesn't use it very often, but it's there. Garion, fix the door. I think we'll want to talk in private."

Garion looked helplessly at the shattered remains of the door. "It's not in very good shape, Grandfather," he said dubiously.

"Make a new one then."

"Oh. I guess I forgot about that."

"You need some practice anyway. Just make sure that you can get it open later. I don't want to have to blow it down again when the time comes to leave."

Garion gathered in his will, concentrated a moment, pointed at the empty opening, and said, "Door." The opening was immediately filled again.

"Door?" Beldin said incredulously.

"He does that sometimes," Belgarath said. "I've been trying to break him of the habit, but he backslides from time to time."

Senji's eyes were narrow as he looked at them. "Well, now," he said. "I seem to have some talented guests. I haven't met a real sorcerer in a long, long time."

"How long?" Belgarath asked bluntly.

"Oh, a dozen centuries or so, I guess. A Grolim was here giving lectures in the College of Comparative Theology. Stuffy sort of fellow, as I recall, but then, most Grolims are."

133

"All right, Senji," Belgarath said, "just how old *are* you?"

"I think I was born during the fifteenth century," Senji replied. "What year is it now?"

"Fifty-three seventy-nine," Garion told him.

"Already?" Senji said mildly. "Where does the time go?" He counted it up on his fingers. "I guess that would make me about thirty-nine hundred or so."

"When did you find out about the Will and the Word?" Belgarath pressed.

"The what?"

"Sorcery."

"Is that what you call it?" Senji pondered a bit. "I suppose the term is sort of accurate, at that," he mused. "I like that. The Will and the Word. Has a nice ring to it, doesn't it?"

"When did you make the discovery?" Belgarath repeated.

"During the fifteenth century, obviously. Otherwise I'd have died in the normal course of time, like everybody else."

"You didn't have any instruction?"

"Who was around in the fifteenth century to instruct me? I just stumbled over it."

Belgarath and Beldin looked at each other. Then Belgarath sighed and covered his eyes with one hand.

"It happens once in a while," Beldin said. "Some people just fall into it."

"I know, but it's so discouraging. Look at all the centuries our Master took instructing us, and this fellow just picks it up on his own." He looked back at Senji. "Why don't you tell us about it?" he suggested. "Try not to leave too much out."

"Do we really have time, Grandfather?" Garion asked.

"We have to *make* time," Beldin told him. "It was one of our Master's final commandments. Any time we come across somebody who's picked up the secret spontaneously, we're supposed to investigate. Not even the Gods know how it happens."

Senji slid down from the table and limped over to an overflowing bookcase. He rummaged around for a moment and
finally selected a book that looked much the worse for wear.
"Sorry about the shape it's in," he apologized. "It's been
blown up a few times." He limped back to the table and
opened the book. "I wrote this during the twenty-third century," he said. "I noticed that I was starting to get a little
absentminded, so I wanted to get it all down while it was still
fresh in my memory."

"Makes sense," Beldin said. "My grim-faced friend over
there has been suffering from some shocking lapses of memory
lately—of course, that's to be expected from somebody who's
nineteen thousand years old."

"Do you mind?" Belgarath said acidly.

"You mean it's been longer?"

"Shut up, Beldin."

"Here we are," Senji said. Then he began to read aloud.
"'For the next fourteen hundred years the Melcene Empire
prospered, far removed from the theological and political
squabbles of the western part of the continent. Melcene culture was secular, civilized, and highly educated. Slavery was
unknown, and trade with the Angaraks and their subject peoples in Karanda and Dalasia was extremely profitable. The
old imperial capital at Melcena became a major center of learning.'"

"Excuse me," Belgarath said, "but isn't that taken directly
from *Emperors of Melcena and Mallorea*?"

"Naturally," Senji replied without any embarrassment.
"Plagiarism is the first rule of scholarship. Please don't
interrupt."

"Sorry," Belgarath said.

"'Unfortunately,'" Senji read on, "'some of the thrust of
Melcene scholarship turned toward the arcane. Their major
field of concentration lay in the field of alchemy.'" He looked
at Belgarath. "This is where it gets original," he said. He

135

cleared his throat. "'It was a Melcene alchemist, Senji the clubfooted, who inadvertently utilized sorcery during the course of one of his experiments.'"

"You speak of yourself in the third person?" Beldin asked.

"It was a twenty-third-century affectation," Senji replied. "Autobiography was considered to be in terribly bad taste—immodest, don't you know. It was a very boring century. I yawned all the way through it." He went back to reading. "'Senji, a fifteenth-century practitioner of alchemy at the university in the imperial city, was notorious for his ineptitude.'" He paused. "I might want to edit that part just a bit," he noted critically. He glanced at the next line. "And this just won't do at all," he added. "'To be quite frank about it,'" he read with distaste, "'Senji's experiments more often turned gold into lead than the reverse. In a fit of colossal frustration at the failure of his most recent experiment, Senji accidentally converted a half ton of brass plumbing into solid gold. An immediate debate arose, involving the Bureau of Currency, the Bureau of Mines, the Department of Sanitation, the faculty of the College of Applied Alchemy and the faculty of the College of Comparative Theology about which organization should have control of Senji's discovery. After about three hundred years of argumentation, it suddenly occurred to the disputants that Senji was not merely talented, but also appeared to be immortal. In the name of scientific experimentation, the varying bureaus, departments, and faculties agreed that an effort should be made to have him assassinated to verify that fact.'"

"They didn't!" Beldin said.

"Oh, yes," Senji replied with a grim smugness. "Melcenes are inquisitive to the point of idiocy. They'll go to any lengths to prove a theory."

"What did you do?"

Senji smirked so hard that his long nose and pointed chin almost touched. "'A well-known defenestrator was retained

136

to throw the irascible old alchemist from a high window in one of the towers of the university administration building,'" he read. "'The experiment had a threefold purpose. What the curious bureaus wished to find out was: (A) if Senji *was* in fact unkillable, (B) what means he would take to save his life while plummeting toward the paved courtyard, and (C) if it might be possible to discover the secret of flight by giving him no other alternative.'" The clubfooted alchemist tapped the back of his hand against the text. "I've always been a little proud of that sentence," he said. "It's so beautifully balanced."

"It's a masterpiece," Beldin approved, slapping the little man on the shoulder so hard that it nearly knocked him off the table. "Here," he said, taking Senji's cup, "let me refill that for you." His brow creased, there was a surge, and the cup was full again. Senji took a sip and fell to gasping.

"It's a drink that a Nadrak woman of my acquaintance brews," Beldin told him. "Robust, isn't it?"

"Very," Senji agreed in a hoarse voice.

"Go on with your story, my friend."

Senji cleared his throat—several times—and went on. "'What the officials and learned men actually found out as a result of their experiment was that it is extremely dangerous to threaten the life of a sorcerer—even one as inept as Senji. The defenestrator found himself suddenly translocated to a position some fifteen hundred meters above the harbor, five miles distant. At one instant he had been wrestling Senji toward the window; at the next, he found himself standing on insubstantial air high above a fishing fleet. His demise occasioned no particular sorrow—except among the fishermen, whose nets were badly damaged by his rapid descent.'"

"That was a masterful passage," Beldin chortled, "but where did you discover the meaning of the word 'translocation'?"

"I was reading an old text on the exploits of Belgarath the

137

Sorcerer, and I—" Senji stopped, going very pale, turned, and gaped at Garion's grandfather.

"It's a terrible letdown, isn't it?" Beldin said. "We always told him he ought to try to look more impressive."

"You're in no position to talk," the old man said.

"You're the one with the earthshaking reputation." Beldin shrugged. "I'm just a flunky. I'm along for comic relief."

"You're really enjoying this, aren't you, Beldin?"

"I haven't had so much fun in years. Wait until I tell Pol."

"You keep your mouth shut, you hear me?"

"Yes, O mighty Belgarath," Beldin said mockingly.

Belgarath turned to Garion. "Now you understand why Silk irritates me so much," he said.

"Yes, Grandfather, I think I do."

Senji was still a little wild-eyed.

"Take another drink, Senji," Beldin advised. "It's not nearly so hard to accept when your wits are half-fuddled."

Senji began to tremble. Then he drained his cup in one gulp without so much as a cough.

"Now there's a brave lad," Beldin congratulated him. "Please read on. Your story is fascinating."

Falteringly, the little alchemist continued. "'In an outburst of righteous indignation, Senji then proceeded to chastise the department heads who had consorted to do violence to his person. It was finally only a personal appeal from the emperor himself that persuaded the old man to desist from some fairly exotic punishments. After that, the department heads were more than happy to allow Senji to go his own way unmolested.

"'On his own, Senji established a private academy and advertised for students. While his pupils never became sorcerers of the magnitude of Belgarath, Polgara, Ctuchik, or Zedar, some of them were, nonetheless, able to perform some rudimentary applications of the principle their master had inadvertently discovered. This immediately elevated them far above the magicians and witches practicing *their* art forms within the confines of the university.'" Senji looked up. "There's more," he said, "but most of it deals with my experiments in the field of alchemy."

"I think that's the crucial part," Belgarath said. "Let's go back a bit. What were you feeling at the exact moment that you changed all that brass into gold?"

"Irritation," Senji shrugged, closing his book. "Or maybe more than that. I'd worked out my calculations so very carefully, but the bar of lead I was working on just lay there not doing anything. I was infuriated. Then I just sort of pulled everything around me inside, and I could feel an enormous power building up. I shouted 'Change!'—mostly at the lead bar, but there were some pipes running through the room as well, and my concentration was a little diffused."

"You're lucky you didn't change the walls, too," Beldin told him. "Were you ever able to do it again?"

Senji shook his head. "I tried, but I never seemed to be able to put together that kind of anger again."

"Are you always angry when you do this sort of thing?" the hunchback asked.

"Almost always," Senji admitted. "If I'm not angry, I can't be certain of the results. Sometimes it works and sometimes it doesn't."

"That seems to be the key to it, Belgarath," Beldin said. "Rage is the common element in every case we've come across."

"As I remember, *I* was irritated the first time I did it as well," Belgarath conceded.

"So was I," Beldin said. "With you, I think."

"Why did you take it out on that tree, then?"

"At the last second I remembered that our Master was fond of you, and I didn't want to hurt his feelings by obliterating you."

"That probably saved your life. If you'd said 'be not,' you wouldn't be here now."

Beldin scratched at his stomach. "That might explain why we find so few cases of spontaneous sorcery," he mused. "When somebody's enraged at something, his first impulse is usually to destroy it. This might have happened many, many times, but the spontaneous sorcerers probably annihilated themselves in the moment of discovery."

"I wouldn't be at all surprised that you've hit it," Belgarath agreed.

Senji had gone pale again. "I think there's something I need to know here," he said.

"It's the first rule," Garion told him. "The universe won't let us unmake things. If we try, all the force turns inward, and *we're* the ones who vanish." With a shudder he remembered the obliteration of Ctuchik. He looked at Beldin. "Did I get that right?" he asked.

"Fairly close. The explanation is a little more complex, but you described the process pretty accurately."

"Did that by any chance happen to any of your students?" Belgarath asked Senji.

The alchemist frowned. "It *might* have," he admitted. "Quite a few of them disappeared. I thought they'd just gone off someplace, but maybe not."

"Are you taking any more students these days?"

Senji shook his head. "I don't have the patience for it any more. Only about one in ten could even grasp the concept, and the rest stood around whining and sniveling and blaming me for not explaining it any better. I went back to alchemy. I almost never use sorcery any more."

"We were told that you can actually do it," Garion said. "Turn brass or lead into gold, I mean."

"Oh, yes," Senji replied in an offhand way. "It's really fairly easy, but the process is more expensive than the gold is worth. That's what I'm trying to do now—simplify the process and substitute less expensive chemicals. I can't get any-one to fund my experiments, though."

Garion felt a sudden throbbing against his hip. Puzzled, he looked down at the pouch in which he was carrying the Orb. There was a sound in his ears, an angry sort of buzz that was unlike the shimmering sound the Orb usually made.

"What's that peculiar sound?" Senji asked.

Garion untied the pouch from his belt and opened it. The Orb was glowing an angry red.

"Zandramas?" Belgarath asked intently.

Garion shook his head. "No, Grandfather. I don't think so."

"Does it want to take you someplace?"

"It's pulling."

"Let's see where it wants to go."

Garion held the Orb out in his right hand and it drew him steadily toward the door. They went out into the corridor with Senji limping along behind them, his face afire with curiosity. The Orb led them down the stairs and out the front door of the building.

"It seems to want to go toward that building over there," Garion said, pointing toward a soaring tower of pure white marble.

"The College of Comparative Theology," Senji sniffed. "They're a sorry group of scholars with an inflated notion of their contribution to the sum of human knowledge."

"Follow it, Garion," Belgarath instructed.

They crossed the lawn. Startled scholars scattered before them like frightened birds after one look at Belgarath's face.

They entered the ground floor of the tower. A thin man in ecclesiastical robes sat at a high desk just inside the door. "You're not members of this college," he said in an outraged voice. "You can't come in here."

Without even slowing his pace, Belgarath translocated the

officious doorman some distance out onto the lawn, desk and all.

"It does have its uses, doesn't it?" Senji conceded. "Maybe I should give it a little more study. Alchemy's beginning to bore me."

"What's behind this door?" Garion asked, pointing.

"That's their museum." Senji shrugged. "It's a hodge-podge of old idols, religious artifacts, and that sort of thing."

Garion tried the handle. "It's locked."

Beldin leaned back and kicked the door open, splintering the wood around the lock.

"Why did you do that?" Belgarath asked him.

"Why not?" Beldin shrugged. "I'm not going to waste the effort of pulling in my will for an ordinary door."

"You're getting lazy."

"I'll put it back together, and you can open it."

"Never mind."

They went into the dusty, cluttered room. There were rows of glass display cases in the center, and the walls were lined with grotesque statues. Cobwebs hung from the ceiling and dust lay everywhere.

"They don't come in here very often," Senji noted. "They'd rather cook up addlepated theories than look at the real effects of human religious impulses."

"This way," Garion said as the Orb continued to pull steadily at his hand. He noticed that the stone was glowing redder and redder, and it was getting uncomfortably warm.

Then it stopped before a glass case where a rotting cushion lay behind the dusty panes. Aside from the cushion, the case was empty. The Orb was actually hot now, and its ruddy glow filled the entire room.

"What was in this case?" Belgarath demanded.

Senji leaned forward to read the inscription on the corroded brass plate attached to the case. "Oh," he said, "now I re-

142

member. This is the case where they used to keep Cthrag Sardius—before it was stolen."

Suddenly, without any warning, the Orb seemed to jump in Garion's hand, and the glass case standing empty before them exploded into a thousand fragments.

CHAPTER EIGHT

"How long was it here?" Belgarath asked the shaken Senji, who was gaping in awe first at the still sullenly glowing Orb in Garion's hand, then at the shattered remains of the case.

"Senji," Belgarath said sharply, "pay attention."

"Is that what I think it is?" the alchemist asked, pointing at the Orb with a trembling hand.

"Cthrag Yaska," Beldin told him. "If you're going to play this game, you may as well learn what's involved. Now answer my brother's question."

Senji floundered. "I'm not—" he began. "I've always been just an alchemist. I'm not interested in—"

"It doesn't work that way," Belgarath cut him off. "Like it or not, you're a member of a very select group. Stop thinking about gold and other nonsense, and start paying attention to what's important."

Senji swallowed hard. "It was always just a kind of game," he quavered. "Nobody ever took me seriously."

"We do," Garion told him, holding out the Orb to the now-cringing little man. "Do you have any idea of the kind of power you've stumbled over?" He was suddenly enormously angry. "Would you like to have me blow down this tower— or sink the Melcene Islands back into the sea—just to show you how serious we are?"

"You're Belgarion, aren't you?"

"Yes."

"The Godslayer?"

"Some people call me that."

"Oh, my God," Senji whimpered.

"We're wasting time," Belgarath said flatly. "Start talking. I want to know just where Cthrag Sardius came from, how long it was here, and where it went from here."

"It's a long story," Senji said.

"Abbreviate it," Beldin told him, kicking aside the glass shards on the floor. "We're a little pressed for time right now."

"How long was the Sardion here?" Belgarath asked.

"Eons," Senji replied.

"Where did it come from?"

"Zamad," the alchemist responded. "The people up there are Karands, but they're a little timid about demons. I think a few of their magicians were eaten alive. Anyway—or so the legends say—at about the time of the cracking of the world some five thousand years or so ago . . ." he faltered again, staring at the two dreadful old men facing him.

"It was noisy," Beldin supplied distastefully. "A lot of steam and earthquakes. Torak was always ostentatious—some kind of character defect, I think."

"Oh, my God," Senji said again.

145

"Don't keep saying that," Belgarath told him in a disgusted tone. "You don't even know who your God is."

"But you will, Senji," Garion said in a voice that was not his own, "and once you have met Him, you will follow Him all the days of your life."

Belgarath looked at Garion with one raised eyebrow.

Garion spread his hands helplessly. "Get on with this, Belgarath," the voice said through Garion's lips. "Time isn't waiting for you, you know."

Belgarath turned back to Senji. "All right," he said. "The Sardion came to Zamad. How?"

"It's said to have fallen out of the sky."

"They always do," Beldin said. "Someday I'd like to see something rise up out of the earth—just for the sake of variety."

"You get bored too easily, my brother," Belgarath told him.

"I didn't see you sitting over Burnt-face's tomb for five hundred years, my brother," Beldin retorted.

"I don't think I can stand this," Senji said, burying his face in his trembling hands.

"It gets easier as you go along," Garion said in a comforting tone. "We're not really here to make your life unpleasant. All we need is a little information and then we'll go away. If you think about it in the right way, you might even be able to make yourself believe that this is all a dream."

"I'm in the presence of three demigods, and you want me to pass it off as a dream?"

"That's a nice term," Beldin said. "Demigod. I like the sound of it."

"You're easily impressed by words," Belgarath told him.

"Words are the core of thought. Without words there *is* no thought."

Senji's eyes brightened. "Now, we might want to talk about that a little bit," he suggested.

146

"Later," Belgarath said. "Get back to Zamad—and the Sardion."

"All right," the clubfooted little alchemist said. "Cthrag Sardius—or the Sardion, whatever you want to call it—came out of the sky into Zamad. The barbarians up there thought that it was holy and built a shrine to it and fell down on their faces and worshiped it. The shrine was in a valley up in the mountains, and there was a grotto and an altar and that sort of thing."

"We've been there," Belgarath said shortly. "It's at the bottom of a lake now. How did it get to Melcena?"

"That came years later," Senji replied. "The Karands have always been a troublesome people, and their social organization is fairly rudimentary. About three thousand years ago—or maybe a little longer—a King of Zamad began to feel ambitious, so he assimilated Voresebo and started looking hungrily south. There were a series of raids in force across the border into Rengel. Of course, Rengel was a part of the Melcene Empire, and the emperor decided that it was time to teach the Karands a lesson. He mounted a punitive expedition and marched into Voresebo and then Zamad at the head of a column of elephant cavalry. The Karands had never seen an elephant before and they fled in panic. The emperor systematically destroyed all the towns and villages up there. He heard about the holy object and its shrine and he went there and took Cthrag Sardius—more I think to punish the Karands than out of any desire to possess the stone for himself. It's not really very attractive, you know."

"What does it look like?" Garion asked him.

"It's fairly large," Senji said. "It's sort of oval-shaped and about so big." He indicated an object about two feet in diameter with his hands. "It's a strange reddish sort of color, and kind of milky-looking—like certain kinds of flint. Anyway, as I said, the emperor didn't really want the thing, so when he got back to Melcena, he donated it to the university.

It was passed around from department to department, and it finally ended up here in this museum. It lay in that case for thousands of years, collecting dust, and nobody really paid any attention to it."

"How did it leave here?" Belgarath asked.

"I was just getting to that. About five hundred years ago there was a scholar in the College of Arcane Learning. He was a strange sort who heard voices. At any rate, he became absolutely obsessed with Cthrag Sardius. He used to sneak in here at night and sit for hours staring at it. I think he believed that it was talking to him."

"It's possible," Beldin said. "It could probably do that."

"This scholar grew more and more irrational and he finally came in here one night and stole Cthrag Sardius. I don't think anyone would have noticed that it was missing, but the scholar fled the island as if all the legions of Melcena were on his heels. He took ship and sailed south. His ship was last seen near the southern tip of Gandahar, and it seemed to be bound in the direction of the Dalasian Protectorates. The ship never came back, so it was generally assumed that she went down in a storm somewhere in those waters. That's all I really know about it."

Beldin scratched reflectively at his stomach. "It sort of fits together, Belgarath. The Sardion has the same kind of power that the Orb has. I'd say that it's been taking conscious steps to move itself from place to place—probably in response to certain events. It's my guess that if we pinned it down, we'd find that this Melcene emperor took it out of Zamad at just about the time that you and Bear-shoulders went to Cthol Mishrak to steal back the Orb. Then that scholar Senji mentioned stole it from here at just about the time of the Battle of Vo Mimbre."

"You speak as if it were alive," Senji objected.

"It is," Beldin told him, "and it can control the thoughts

148

of people around it. Obviously it can't get up and walk by itself, so it has men do the picking and carrying."

"It's pretty speculative, Beldin," Belgarath said.

"That's what I do best. Shall we move along? We've got a boat to catch, you know. We can sort all this out later."

Belgarath nodded and looked at Senji. "We've been advised that you might be able to help us," he said.

"I can try."

"Good. Someone told us that you might be able to put your hands on an uncut copy of the Ashabine Oracles."

"Who said so?" Senji asked warily.

"A Dalasian seeress named Cyradis."

"Nobody believes anything the seers say," Senji scoffed.

"I do. In seven thousand years, I've never known a seer to be wrong—cryptic, sometimes, but never wrong."

Senji backed away from him.

"Don't be coy, Senji," Beldin told him. "Do you know where we can find a copy of the Oracles?"

"There used to be one in the library of this college," the alchemist replied evasively.

"Used to be?"

Senji looked around nervously. Then he lowered his voice to a whisper. "I stole it," he confessed.

"Does it have any passages cut out of it?" Belgarath asked intently.

"Not that I could see, no."

Belgarath let his breath out explosively. "Well, finally," he said. "I think we just beat Zandramas at her own game."

"You're going up against Zandramas?" Senji asked incredulously.

"Just as soon as we can catch up with her," Beldin told him.

"She's terribly dangerous, you know."

"So are we," Belgarath said. "Where's this book you stole?"

"It's hidden in my laboratory. The university officials are

149

very narrow about people from one department pilfering from other people's libraries.''

"Officials are always narrow." Beldin shrugged. "It's one of the qualifications for the job. Let's go back to your laboratory. My ancient friend here has to read that book.''

Senji limped toward the door and back out into the hallway again.

The thin man in ecclesiastical robes had somehow managed to get his desk back where it belonged and he sat at it again. Garion noticed that his eyes were a little wild.

"We'll be leaving now," Belgarath told him. "Any objections?''

The thin man shrank back.

"Wise decision," Beldin said.

It was late afternoon by now, and the autumn sun streamed down on the well-maintained lawn.

"I wonder if the others have traced down Naradas yet," Garion said as they walked back toward the College of Applied Alchemy.

"More than likely," Belgarath replied. "Silk's people are very efficient.''

They entered the reinforced building again to find the halls full of smoke and several more splintered doors lying in the corridor.

Senji sniffed at the smoke. "They're putting in too much sulfur," he noted professionally.

"A fellow we ran into was saying exactly the same thing," Garion told him. "It was right after he blew himself up, I think.''

"I've told them over and over again," Senji said. "A little sulfur is necessary, but put in too much and—poof!''

"It looks as if there's been a fair amount of poofing going on in here," Beldin said, fanning at the smokey air in front of his face with one hand.

"That happens frequently when you're an alchemist,''

150

Senji replied. "You get used to it." He laughed. "And you never know what's going to happen. One idiot actually turned glass into steel."

Belgarath stopped. "He did what?"

"He turned glass into steel—or something very much like it. It was still transparent, but it wouldn't bend, break, or splinter. It was the hardest stuff I've ever seen."

Belgarath smacked his palm against his forehead.

"Steady," Beldin told him. Then he turned to Senji. "Does this fellow happen to remember the process?"

"I doubt it. He burned all his notes and then went into a monastery."

Belgarath was making strangling noises.

"Do you have any idea what a process like that would be worth?" Beldin asked Senji. "Glass is just about the cheapest stuff in the world—it's only melted sand, after all—and you can mold it into any shape you want. That particular process might just have been worth more than all the gold in the world."

Senji blinked.

"Never mind," Beldin said to him. "You're a pure scholar, remember? You're not interested in money, are you?"

Senji's hands began to shake.

They climbed the stairs and reentered Senji's cluttered laboratory. The alchemist closed and locked the door, then limped to a large cabinet near the window. Grunting, he moved it out from the wall a few inches, knelt, and reached behind it.

The book was not thick and it was bound in black leather. Belgarath's hands were shaking as he carried it to a table, sat, and opened it.

"I couldn't really make very much out of it," Senji confessed to Beldin. "I think whoever wrote it might have been insane."

"He was," the hunchback replied.

"You know who he was?"

Beldin nodded. "Torak," he said shortly.

"Torak's just a myth—something the Angaraks dreamed up."

"Tell that to him," Beldin said, pointing at Garion.

Senji swallowed hard, staring at Garion. "Did you really— I mean—?"

"Yes," Garion answered sadly. Oddly enough, he found that he still regretted what had happened at Cthol Mishrak over a dozen years ago.

"It's uncut!" Belgarath exclaimed triumphantly. "Somebody copied from the original before Torak had time to mutilate it. The missing passages are all here. Listen to this: 'And it shall come to pass that the Child of Light and the Child of Dark shall meet in the City of Endless Night. But that is not the place of the final meeting, for the choice will not be made there, and the Spirit of Dark shall flee. Know, moreover, that a new Child of Dark shall arise in the east.'"

"Why would Torak cut that passage?" Garion asked, puzzled.

"The implications of it aren't good—at least not for him," Belgarath replied. "The fact that there was going to be a new Child of Dark hints rather strongly that he wouldn't survive the meeting at Cthol Mishrak."

"Not only that," Beldin added, "even if he did survive, he was going to be demoted. That might have been just a little hard for him to swallow."

Belgarath quickly leafed through several pages.

"Are you sure you're not missing things?" Beldin asked him.

"I know what that copy at Ashaba said, Beldin. I have a very good memory."

"Really?" Beldin's tone was sardonic.

"Just let it lie." Belgarath read another passage rapidly. "I can see why he cut this one," he said. "'Behold, the stone which holds the power of the Dark Spirit will not reveal itself to that Child of Dark who shall come to the City of Endless Night, but will yield instead only to Him who is yet to come.'" He scratched at his beard. "If I'm reading this right, the Sardion concealed itself from Torak because he wasn't intended to be the ultimate instrument of the Dark Prophecy."

"I imagine that hurt his ego just a little." Beldin laughed.

But Belgarath had already moved on. His eyes suddenly widened, and his face paled slightly. "'For lo,'" he read, "'only one who hath put his hand to Cthrag Yaska shall be permitted to touch Cthrag Sardius. And in the moment of that touch, all that he is or might have become shall be sacrificed, and he shall become the Vessel of the Spirit of Dark. Seek ye, therefore, the son of the Child of Light, for he shall be our champion in the Place Which Is No More. And should he be chosen, he shall rise above all others and shall bestride the world with Cthrag Yaska in one hand and Cthrag Sardius in the other, and thus shall all that was divided be made one again, and he will have lordship and dominion over all things until the end of days.'"

Garion was thunderstruck. "So *that's* what they mean by the word 'sacrifice'!" he exclaimed. "Zandramas *isn't* going to kill Geran."

"No," Belgarath said darkly. "She's going to do something worse. She's going to turn him into another Torak."

"It goes a little further than that, Belgarath," Beldin growled. "The Orb rejected Torak—and burned off half his face in the process. The Sardion didn't even let Torak know that it was around. But the Orb *will* accept Geran, and so will the Sardion. If he gets his hands on both those stones, he'll have absolute power. Torak was a baby compared to what he'll be." He looked somberly at Garion. "That's why Cyradis told you at Rheon that you might have to kill your son."

"That's unthinkable!" Garion retorted hotly.

153

"Maybe you'd better start thinking about it. Geran won't be your son any more. Once he touches the Sardion, he'll be something totally evil—and he'll be a God."

Bleakly, Belgarath read on. "Here's something," he said. "'And the Child of Dark who shall bear the champion to the place of choosing shall be possessed utterly by the Dark Spirit, and her flesh shall be but a husk, and all the starry universe shall be contained therein.'"

"What does that mean?" Garion asked.

"I'm not sure," Belgarath admitted. He leafed through a couple more pages. He frowned. "'And it shall come to pass that she who gave birth unto the champion shall reveal unto ye the place of the final meeting, but ye must beguile her 'ere she will speak.'"

"Ce'Nedra?" Garion asked incredulously.

"Zandramas has tampered with Ce'Nedra before," Belgarath reminded him. "We'll have Pol keep an eye on her." He frowned again. "Why would Torak cut out that passage?" he asked with a baffled look.

"Torak wasn't the only one with a sharp knife, Belgarath," Beldin said. "That's a fairly crucial bit of information. I don't think Zandramas would have wanted to leave it behind, do you?"

"That confuses the issue, doesn't it," Belgarath said sourly. "I read a book at Ashaba that had two editors. I'm surprised there was anything left of it at all."

"Read on, old man," Beldin said, glancing at the window. "The sun's going down."

"Well, finally," Belgarath said after reading for a moment more. "Here it is. 'Behold, the place of the final meeting shall be revealed at Kell, for it lies hidden within the pages of the accursed book of the seers.'" He thought about it. "Nonsense!" he burst out. "I've read parts of the Mallorean Gospels myself, and there are dozens of copies scattered all over the world. If this is right, *anybody* could have picked up the location."

"They're not all the same," Senji murmured.

"*What?*" Belgarath exploded.

"The copies of the Mallorean Gospels aren't all the same," the alchemist repeated. "I used to look through all these holy books. Sometimes the ancients ran across things that could prove helpful in my experiments. I've gathered up a fair library of that sort of thing. That's why I stole the book you've got in your hands."

"I suppose you've even got a copy of the Mrin Codex," Beldin said.

"Two, actually, and they're identical. That's the peculiar thing about the Mallorean Gospels. I've got three sets, and no two copies are the same."

"Oh, fine," Belgarath said. "I knew there was a reason not to trust the seers."

"I think they do it on purpose." Senji shrugged. "After I started running across discrepancies, I went to Kell, and the seers there told me that there are secrets in the Gospels that are too dangerous to have out there for just anyone to read. That's why every copy is different. They've all been modified to hide those secrets—except for the original, of course. That's always been kept at Kell."

Beldin and Belgarath exchanged a long look. "All right," Beldin said flatly, "we go to Kell."

"But we're right behind Zandramas," Garion objected.

"And that's where we'll stay if we don't go to Kell," Beldin told him. "*Behind* her. Going to Kell is the only way we can get ahead of her."

Belgarath had turned to the last page of the Oracles. "I think this is a personal message, Garion," he said in an awed sort of voice, holding out the book.

"What?"

"Torak wants to talk to you."

155

"He can talk all he wants. I'm not going to listen to him. I almost made that mistake once—when he tried to tell me he was my father, remember?"

"This is a little different. He's not lying this time."

Garion took hold of the book, and a deathly chill seemed to run up through his hands and into his arms.

"Read it," Belgarath said implacably.

Compelled—driven, even—Garion lowered his eyes to the spidery script on the page before him. "'Hail, Belgarion,'" he read aloud in a faltering voice. "'If it should ever come to pass that thine eyes fall upon this, then it means that I have fallen beneath thy hand. I mourn that not. I will have cast myself into the crucible of destiny, and, if I have failed, so be it. Know that I hate thee, Belgarion. For hate's sake I will throw myself into the darkness. For hate's sake will I spit out my last breath at thee, my damnéd brother.'" Garion's voice failed him. He could actually feel the maimed God's towering hatred reaching down to him through the eons. He now understood the full import of what had happened in the terrible City of Endless Night.

"Keep reading," Belgarath told him. "There's more."

"Grandfather, this is more than I can bear."

"Read!" Belgarath's voice was like the crack of a whip.

Helplessly, Garion again lifted the book. "'Know that we *are* brothers, Belgarion, though our hate for each other may one day sunder the heavens. We are brothers in that we share a dreadful task. That thou art reading my words means that thou hast been my destroyer. Thus must I charge *thee* with the task. What is foretold in these pages is an abomination. Do not let it come to pass. Destroy the world. Destroy the universe if need be, but do not permit this to come to pass. In thy hand is now the fate of all that was; all that is; and all that is yet to be. Hail, my hated brother, and farewell. We will meet—or have met—in the City of Endless Night, and there will our dispute be concluded. The task, however, still lies before us in the Place Which Is No More. One of us must go there to face the ultimate horror. Should it be thou, fail us not. Failing all else, thou must reave the life from thine only son, even as thou hath reft mine from me.'"

The book fell from Garion's hands as his knees failed and he sank to the floor, weeping uncontrollably. He howled a wolflike howl of absolute despair and hammered at the floor with both his fists and with tears streaming openly down his face.

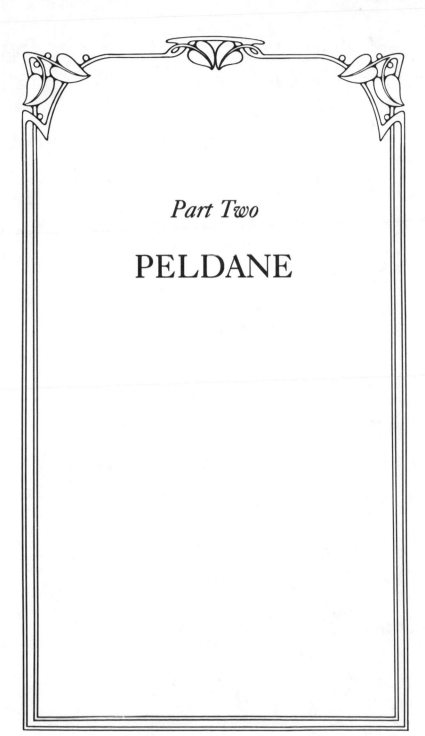

Part Two

PELDANE

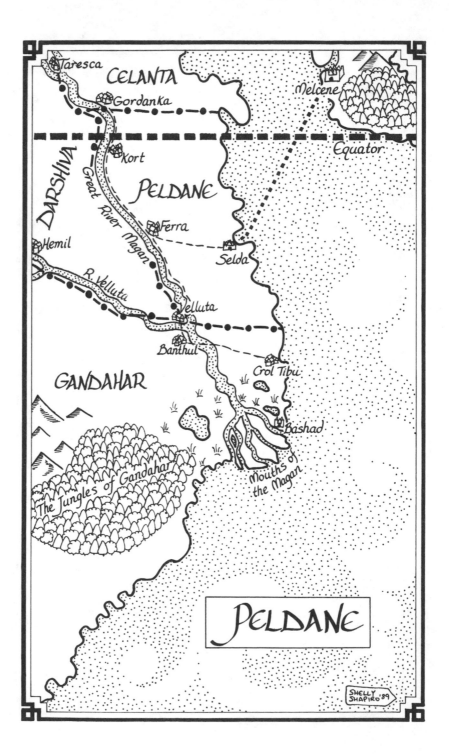

Taresca
CELANTA
Gordanka
Melcene
Equator
DARSHIVA
Kort
PELDANE
Great River Magan
Ferra
Hemil
Selda
R. Velluta
Velluta
Banthul
GANDAHAR
Crol Tibu
Bashad
The Jungles of Gandahar
Mouths of
the Magan

PELDANE

SHELLY
SHAPIRO '89

CHAPTER NINE

There was a man in a sea coat talking alone with Silk in the second floor sitting room when Garion, Belgarath, and Beldin returned. The man was stocky. He had silver-shot hair and beard and he wore a large gold earring in his left ear.

"Ah, there you are," Silk said, looking up as the three of them entered. The rat-faced little man had changed clothes and now wore plain doublet and hose of a nondescript brown. "This is Captain Kadian. He's the one who took our friends to the mainland." He looked back at the seaman. "Why don't you tell them what you just told me, Captain?" he suggested.

"If you want me to, your Highness," Kadian agreed. He

161

had that rusty sort of voice seafaring men often have—the result of bad weather and strong drink, Garion surmised. He took a swallow from the silver tankard he was holding. "Well, sir," he began, "it was three days ago when it happened. I'd just come up from Bashad in Gandahar. It's down by the mouth of the Magan." He made a face. "It's an unhealthy sort of a place—all swamps and jungles. Anyhow, I'd carried a cargo of ivory up here for the Consortium, and we'd just off-loaded, so I was sort of looking around for a cargo. A ship doesn't make any money for her owner when she's tied up to a wharf, y'know. I went to a certain tavern I know of. The tavern keeper's an old friend of mine—we was shipmates when we was younger—and he sort of keeps his ear to the ground for me. Well sir, I no sooner got there and set myself down, when my friend, he comes over to me and he asks me if I'd be interested in a short, easy voyage at a good price. I says to him that I'm always interested in that kind of prop- osition, but that I'd want to know what kind of cargo was involved before I made up my mind. There's some things I don't like to carry—cattle, for instance. They can dirty up the hold of a ship to the point where it takes weeks to get it clean again. Well, my friend, he says to me that there wouldn't be no cargo involved at all. It was just some people as wanted passage to the mainland. I says that it wouldn't hurt none to talk with them, and so he takes me into this room in the back of the tavern where four people was sitting at a table—two men, a woman, and a little boy. One of the men was dressed in expensive clothes—a nobleman of some kind, I think— but it was the other one as did all the talking."

"Was there anything unusual about that one?" Silk prompted.

"I was just getting to that. He was wearing ordinary clothes, but that wasn't what caught my attention. At first I thought he was blind—because of his eyes, you understand—but it seems that he can see well enough, even though his eyes don't have no color at all. I had a ship's cook one time, and one of his eyes was the same way. Foul-tempered sort he was, and a real poor excuse for a cook. Well sir, this man with the funny eyes, he says that he and his friends had to get to Peldane in a hurry, but that they sort of wanted it kept quiet that they was going there. Then he asks me if I knows of a place outside of the town of Selda where I could put them on the beach with no one the wiser, and I says that I did." He pulled his nose slyly. "Just about any man as owns a ship knows of a few places like that—customs people being what they are an' all. I sort of had my suspicions up by now. People who want to end a voyage on a lonely beach someplace are usually up to no good. Now, I figure that what a man does is his own concern, but if he gets me mixed up in it, it starts being my business real quick. I can get into trouble enough on my own without no help from others." He paused and took a long drink from his tankard and wiped his mouth with the back of his hand.

"Like I say, I had my suspicions about these people by now and I was just about to tell them that I wasn't really interested in the proposition, but then the woman, she says something I didn't hear to the one as was doing the talking. She was wearing a kind of long cloak or robe of some kind made out of black satin. She kept the hood of it up the whole time, so I never saw her face, but she was keeping a real tight grip on the little boy. Anyhow, the one with the white eyes, he pulls out a purse and spills it out on the table, and that purse was full of gold, my friends, more than I'd make in a dozen voyages along these coasts. That put a whole new light on the situation, let me tell you. Well sir, to make it short, we struck the bargain right then and there, and I asks them when they wanted to leave, and the fellow as was doing the talking, he says they'd come down to my ship just as soon as it gets dark. I saw right off that my suspicions wasn't too far off the mark. You don't find very many as is honest who want

to sail out of a harbor in the dark of night, but we'd already
struck our bargain, and I had his purse tucked under my belt,
so it was too late to back out. We sailed that very night and
got to the coast of Peldane on the next afternoon."

"Tell them about the fog," Silk said intently.

"I was just about to, your Highness," Kadian said. "That
coast down there is sunk in fog almost all spring, and the day
we got there wasn't no exception. It was thicker than a wool
cloak, but the people in Selda, they're used to it, so they
always lights beacons on the city walls to guide ships into their
harbor on foggy days. I took my bearings on those beacons
and I didn't have no trouble finding the beach I wanted. We
hove to a few hundred yards offshore, and I sent my passengers toward the beach in a small boat with my bo'sun in charge.
We hung a lantern from the mainmast to guide him back
through the fog, and I put some men to banging on pots and
pans to help him find the way. Anyhow, after some time
passed, we could hear the sound of the oarlocks out there in
the fog near the beach, and we knowed the bo'sun's coming
back. And then, all of a sudden, I seen the light of a fire
coming through the fog all sort of misty, like. I heard some
screaming, and then everything got quiet. We waited for a
bit, but the bo'sun, he never came back. I didn't like the
smell of things, so I ordered the anchor up, and we sort of
eased on back out to sea. I don't know what happened and
I wasn't going to stay around to find out. There was things
going on that made me real nervous."

"Oh?" Beldin said, "such as what?"

"Well sir, one time in the main cabin, this woman as the
white-eyed man and the aristocrat had with them, she reached
out to take hold of the little boy, him acting kind of restless
and all, and I seen her hand. Now, it might have been bad
light in the cabin or some such—I don't spend all that much
on lamp oil or candles. But—and strike me blind if I'm

wrong—it seemed to me that there was sparkles under the skin of her hand."

"Sparkles?" Belgarath asked him.

"Yes, sir. I seen it with my own eyes, and they was moving—all these little tiny sparkles moving around in her flesh, almost like fireflies on a summer's evening."

"As if all the starry universe were contained therein?" Beldin asked intently, quoting from the obscure passage in the Ashabine Oracles.

"Now that you put it that way, that's exactly how it was," Kadian agreed. "I knowed right off that these wasn't no ordinary folks and, after I seen that fire in the fog, I didn't really want to stay around to find out just how *un*-ordinary they was."

"That might just have saved your life, Captain," Belgarath told him. "Have you ever heard of Zandramas?"

"The witch? Everybody's heard of her."

"I think she was your glittering passenger, and Zandramas is a firm believer in the old notion that dead people can't tell stories. So far as we know, she's drowned three ships and fed several people to the lions. I expect it was only the fog that saved you. If she'd have been able to see you, you wouldn't be here now."

Captain Kadian swallowed hard.

"Do you need any more?" Silk asked.

"No," Belgarath replied. "I think that covers everything." He looked at the captain. "We thank you, Kadian. Can you sketch us a map of the beach where you dropped off these passengers of yours?"

"I can indeed," Kadian replied bleakly. "Is it in your mind to chase down the witch?"

"We were sort of thinking along those lines, yes."

"When you burn her, throw on a few logs of wood in memory of my bo'sun and his oarsmen."

"You have my word on that, Captain," Garion told him.

"Green logs," Kadian added. "They don't burn so fast."

"We'll keep that in mind."

Silk stood up and handed the captain a leather pouch.

Kadian bounced it on his palm a few times, and it gave forth a jingling sound. "You're very generous, your Highness," he said, also rising to his feet. "Is there pen and ink handy? I'll draw you that chart."

"Right over on that table," Silk said, pointing.

The captain nodded and crossed the room.

"Where's Aunt Pol?" Garion asked, "and the others?"

"They're changing clothes," Silk replied. "I sent word to our ship just as soon as one of Vetter's men came back and told us that they'd found Captain Kadian. She's waiting in the harbor for us right now." He looked closely at Garion. "Aren't you feeling well?" he asked. "You're looking a little pale."

"I got a message that had some bad news in it."

Silk gave Belgarath a puzzled look.

"We found the Ashabine Oracles," the old man explained tersely. "Torak left a message for Garion on the last page. It wasn't very pleasant. We can talk about it once we get on board ship."

Captain Kadian came back holding a sheet of parchment. "This is Selda," he said, pointing at his drawing. "There's a headland to the south, and the beach I was telling you about is just south of that. I can't tell you exactly where the witch landed because of the fog, but this place marked with the **X** should be fairly close."

"Thanks again, Captain," Silk said.

"My pleasure, your Highness, and good hunting." Kadian turned and left the room with the rolling gait of a man who spends little time on shore.

It was only a few moments later when Polgara and the others joined them. Ce'Nedra and Velvet were both wearing plain gray dresses much like the one Polgara always wore when she was traveling. Gray, Garion noticed, was not a good color for

Ce'Nedra. It made her skin look very pale, and the only touch of color about her was her flaming wealth of copper-colored hair.

Durnik and the other men—except for Toth, who still wore only his unbleached blanket and loincloth—were dressed in the same nondescript brown that Silk wore.

"Well, father?" Polgara asked as she entered, "did you find what we wanted?"

He nodded. "Why don't we talk about that after we get on board ship, though? We've done what we came to do in Melcena and we can talk while our ship's moving." He led the way out and down the stairs.

It was a silvery evening. The full moon had risen early and it filled the streets of Melcena with its pale light. Candles glowed golden in the windows of the houses they passed, and hundreds of lanterns winked from the rigging of the ships anchored in the harbor. Garion rode in silence, his melancholy thoughts still on the dreadful communication Torak had left for him thousands of years ago.

They boarded their ship quickly and went immediately below to the cramped cabin beneath the aft deck.

"All right," Belgarath said to them after Durnik had closed the door, "we found the Oracles and we also found the place where the Sardion was kept until just about the time of the battle of Vo Mimbre."

"That was a profitable trip, wasn't it?" Silk noted. "Is Senji really as old as they say?"

Beldin grunted. "Older."

"Wouldn't that mean that he's a sorcerer?" Ce'Nedra asked. Perhaps it was the somber gray dress, but she seemed a bit disconsolate as she sat on an ornately carved bench under a swinging oil lamp.

Belgarath nodded. "He's not very good at it, but he does have the ability, yes."

"Who was his instructor?" Polgara wanted to know. She sat

down beside Ce'Nedra and laid one arm affectionately across the little queen's shoulders.

"Nobody," Belgarath said with a certain disgust. "Would you believe that he just stumbled over it on his own?"

"Did you look into that?"

"Yes. Beldin's got a theory. He can explain it to you later. At any rate, the Sardion was brought to the university here several thousand years ago. They kept it in a museum. I don't think anybody knew what it really was. Then, about five hundred years ago, one of the scholars stole it and took it around the southern tip of Gandahar and sailed off in the general direction of the Dalasian Protectorates. Nobody knows for sure what happened to it after that. Anyway, Senji had an unmutilated copy of the Ashabine Oracles."

"What did it say?" Velvet asked intently.

"A great deal. We found out why Zandramas abducted Geran."

"As a sacrifice?" she said.

"Only in an obscure sense of the word. If the Dark Prophecy wins out, Geran is going to be the new God of Angarak."

"My baby?" Ce'Nedra exclaimed.

"He won't be your baby any more, I'm afraid," the old man told her bleakly. "He'll be Torak."

"Or worse," Beldin added. "He'll have the Orb in one hand and the Sardion in the other. He'll have dominion over everything that exists, and I don't think he'll be a kindly God."

"We have to stop her!" Ce'Nedra cried. "We can't let this happen!"

"I think that's the general idea, your Majesty," Sadi told her.

"What else did it say, father?" Polgara asked.

"It said something about Zandramas that's a little obscure. For some reason her body's being gradually taken over by some kind of light. The sea captain who carried her to Selda caught a glimpse of her hand and he said that there are moving

168

lights under her skin. The Oracles said it was going to happen."

"What does it mean?" Durnik asked.

"I haven't got the faintest idea," Belgarath admitted. He looked at Garion and moved his fingers slightly. —*I don't think we need to tell Ce'Nedra what the book said about her, do you?*—

Garion shook his head.

"Anyway, we're going to have to go to Kell."

"Kell?" Polgara's voice was startled. "What for?"

"The location of the place we're looking for is in the copy of the Mallorean Gospels the seers keep there. If we go to Kell, we can get to this meeting place before Zandramas does."

"That might be a nice change," Silk said. "I'm getting a little tired of tagging along behind her."

"But we'll lose the trail," Ce'Nedra protested.

"Little girl," Beldin said to her gruffly, "if we know where Zandramas is going, we won't *need* the trail. We can just go directly to the Place Which Is No More and wait for her to show up."

Polgara's arm curled more tightly about Ce'Nedra's shoulders in a protective fashion. "Be gentle with her, uncle. She was brave enough to kiss you at the archduke's house, and I'd imagine that was quite a shock to her sensibilities."

"Very funny, Pol." The ugly hunchback dropped heavily into a chair and scratched vigorously at one armpit.

"Was there anything else, father?" Polgara asked.

"Torak wrote something to Garion," Belgarath replied. "It was fairly bleak, but it appears that even he knew how bad things would get if Zandramas succeeds. He told Garion to stop her at all costs."

"I was going to do that anyway," Garion said quietly. "I didn't need any suggestions from Torak."

"What are we going to be up against in Peldane?" Belgarath asked Silk.

"More of what we ran into in Voresebo and Rengel, I'd imagine."

"What's the fastest way to get to Kell?" Durnik asked.

"It's in the Protectorate of Likandia," Silk replied, "and the shortest way there is right straight across Peldane and Darshiva and then down through the mountains."

"What about Gandahar?" Sadi asked. "We could avoid all that unpleasantness if we sailed south and went through there." Somehow Sadi looked peculiar in hose and a belted tunic. Once he had discarded his iridescent robe, he seemed more like an ordinary man and less like a eunuch. His scalp, however, was freshly shaved.

Silk shook his head. "It's all jungle down in Gandahar, Sadi," he said. "You have to chop your way through."

"Jungles aren't all that bad, Kheldar."

"They are if you're in a hurry."

"Could you send for those soldiers of yours?" Velvet asked.

"It's possible, I suppose," Silk answered, "but I'm not sure they'd be all that much help. Vetter says that Darshiva's crawling with Grolims and Zandramas' troops, and Peldane's been in chaos for years. My troops are good, but not that good." He looked at Belgarath. "I'm afraid you're going to get more burrs in your fur, old friend."

"Are we just going to ignore the trail, then," Garion asked, "and make straight for Kell?"

Belgarath tugged at one earlobe. "I've got a suspicion that the trail is going to lead in the general direction of Kell anyway," he said. "Zandramas read the Ashabine Oracles, too, you know, and she knows that Kell's the only place where she can get the information she needs."

"Will Cyradis let her look at the Gospels?" Durnik asked.

"Probably. Cyradis is still neutral and she's not likely to show any favoritism."

Garion rose to his feet. "I think I'll go up on deck, Grandfather," he said. "I've got some thinking to do, and sea air helps to clear my head."

The lights of Melcena twinkled low on the horizon behind them, and the moon laid a silvery path across the surface of the sea. The ship's captain stood at the tiller on the aft deck, his hands steady and sure.

"Isn't it a little hard to know which way you're going at night?" Garion asked him.

"Not at all," the captain replied. He pointed up toward the night sky. "Seasons come and go, but the stars never change."

"Well," Garion said, "we can hope, I guess." Then he walked forward to stand in the bow of the ship.

The night breeze that blew down the strait between Melcena and the mainland was erratic, and the sails first bellied and then fell slack, their booming sounding like a funeral drum. That sound fitted Garion's mood. For a long time he stood toying with the end of a knotted rope and looking out over the moon-touched waves, not so much thinking as simply registering the sights and sounds and smells around him.

He knew she was there. It was not merely the fragrance he had known since his earliest childhood, but also the calm sense of her presence. With a peculiar kind of abstraction he sought back through his memories. He had, it seemed, always known exactly where she was. Even on the darkest of nights he could have started from sleep in a strange room in some forgotten town and pointed unerringly to the place where she was. The captain of this ship was guided by the lights in the sky, but the star that had led Garion for his entire life was not some far-distant glimmer on the velvet throat of night. It was much closer, and much more constant.

"What's troubling you, Garion?" she asked, laying a gentle hand on his shoulder.

"I could hear his voice, Aunt Pol—Torak's voice. He hated

171

me thousands of years before I was even born. He even knew my name."

"Garion," she said very calmly, "the universe knew your name before that moon up there was spun out of the emptiness. Whole constellations have been waiting for you since the beginning of time."

"I didn't want them to, Aunt Pol."

"There are those of us who aren't given that option, Garion. There are things that have to be done and certain people who have to do them. It's as simple as that."

He smiled rather sadly at her flawless face and gently touched the snowy white lock at her brow. Then, for the last time in his life, he asked the question that had been on his lips since he was a tiny boy. "Why me, Aunt Pol? Why me?"

"Can you possibly think of anyone else you'd trust to deal with these matters, Garion?"

He had not really been prepared for that question. It came at him in stark simplicity. Now at last he fully understood. "No," he sighed, "I suppose not. Somehow it seems a little unfair, though. I wasn't even consulted."

"Neither was I, Garion," she answered. "But we didn't have to be consulted, did we? The knowledge of what we have to do is born in us." She put her arms around him and drew him close. "I'm so very proud of you, my Garion," she said.

He laughed a bit wryly. "I suppose I didn't turn out too badly after all," he conceded. "I can get my shoes on the right feet at least."

"And you have no idea how long that took to explain to you," she replied with a light laugh. "You were a good boy, Garion, but you'd never listen. Even Rundorig would listen. He didn't usually understand, but at least he'd listen."

"I miss him sometimes. Him and Doroon and Zubrette."

Garion paused. "Did they ever get married? Rundorig and Zubrette, I mean?"

"Oh, yes. Years and years ago, and Zubrette is up to her waist in children—five or so. I used to get a message every autumn, and I'd have to go back to Faldor's farm to deliver her newest baby."

"You did that?" He was amazed.

"I certainly wouldn't have let anyone else do it. Zubrette and I disagreed about certain things, but I'm still very fond of her."

"Is she happy?"

"I think she is, yes. Rundorig's easy to manage, and she has all those children to keep her mind occupied." She looked at him critically. "Are you a little less moody now?" she asked.

"I feel better," he replied. "I always feel better when you're around."

"That's nice."

He remembered something. "Did Grandfather get a chance to tell you what the Oracles said about Ce'Nedra?"

"Yes," she said. "I'll keep an eye on her. Why don't we go below now? The next few weeks might be hectic, so let's get all the sleep we can while we have the chance."

The coast of Peldane was engulfed in fog just as Captain Kadian had predicted, but the beacon fires burning on the walls of Selda provided reference points, and they were able to feel their way carefully along the coast until the ship's captain estimated that they were near the beach shown on Kadian's chart.

"There's a fishing village about a mile south of here, your Highness," the captain advised Silk. "It's deserted now, because of all the troubles in the area, but there's a dock there—or at least there was the last time I sailed past this coast. We should be able to unload your horses there."

"Excellent, Captain," Silk replied.

They crept along through the fog until they reached the deserted village and its shaky-looking dock. As soon as Chretienne reached the shore, Garion saddled him, then mounted and rode slowly back along the beach with Iron-grip's sword resting on the pommel of his saddle. After he had gone perhaps a mile and a half, he felt the familiar pull. He turned and rode back.

The others had also saddled their horses and led them to the edge of the fog-shrouded fishermen's village. Their ship was moving slowly out to sea, a dim shape in the fog with red and green lanterns marking her port and starboard sides and with a lone sailor astride her bowsprit blowing a melancholy foghorn to warn other ships away.

Garion dismounted and led his big gray stallion to where the others waited.

"Did you find it?" Ce'Nedra asked intently in a hushed little voice. Garion had noticed that for some reason, fog always made people speak quietly.

"Yes," he replied. Then he looked at his grandfather. "Well?" he asked. "Do we just ignore the trail and take the shortest route to Kell or what?"

Belgarath scratched at his beard and looked first at Beldin, then at Polgara. "What do you think?" he asked them.

"The trail was going inland, wasn't it?" Beldin asked Garion.

Garion nodded.

"Then we don't have to make the decision yet," the hunchback said. "As long as Zandramas is going in the same direction we want to go, we can keep on following her. If she changes direction later on, then we can decide."

"It makes sense, father," Polgara agreed.

"All right, we'll do it that way, then." The old man looked around. "This fog should hide us just as well as darkness would. Let's go pick up the trail, and then Garion, Pol, and

I can scout on ahead." He squinted up into the murky sky.
"Can anybody make a guess about the time?"

"It's about midafternoon, Belgarath," Durnik told him
after a momentary consultation with Toth.

"Let's go find out which way she's going, then."

They rode along the beach, following Chretienne's tracks
until they reached the spot where Garion's sword swung in
his hand to point inland.

"We should be able to gain some time on her," Sadi noted.

"Why's that?" Silk asked him.

"She came ashore in a small boat," the eunuch replied, "so
she didn't have horses."

"That's no real problem for her, Sadi," Polgara told him.
"She's a Grolim, and she can communicate with her underlings over long distances. I'm sure she was on horseback within
an hour of the time her foot touched the sand."

The eunuch sighed. "I forget about that from time to
time," he admitted. "It's very convenient for us to have that
advantage, but not nearly so convenient when the other side
has it, too."

Belgarath swung down from his horse. "Come along, Garion. You, too, Pol. We might as well get started." He looked
over at Durnik. "We'll stay in close touch," he told the smith.
"This fog could make things a little tricky."

"Right," Durnik agreed.

Garion took Polgara's arm to help her through the soft sand
and followed his grandfather up the beach to the line of driftwood at the high-water mark.

"This should do it," the old man decided. "Let's make
the change here, and then Garion and I can scout on ahead.
Pol, try to keep the others more or less in sight. I don't want
them straying."

"Yes, father," she said even as she began to shimmer and
change.

Garion formed the image in his mind, pulled in his will,

and once again felt that curious melting sensation. He looked himself over carefully as he always did. On one occasion he'd made the change in a hurry and had forgotten his tail. A tail does not mean very much to a two-legged animal, but it is distinctly necessary for a four-legged one.

"Stop admiring yourself," he heard Belgarath's voice in the silences of his mind. "We've got work to do."

"I was just making sure that I had everything, Grandfather."

"Let's go. You won't be able to see very much in the fog, so use your nose."

Polgara was perched sedately on a bone-white limb jutting up from a driftwood log. She was meticulously preening her snowy feathers with her hooked beak.

Belgarath and Garion effortlessly hurdled over the driftwood and loped off into the fog. "It's going to be a wet day," Garion noted soundlessly as he ran alongside the great silver wolf.

"Your fur won't melt."

"I know, but my paws get cold when they're wet."

"I'll have Durnik make you some little booties."

"That would be absolutely ridiculous, Grandfather," Garion said indignantly. Even though he had only recently made the change, the wolf's enormous sense of decorum and propriety had already begun to permeate his consciousness.

"There are some people just ahead," Belgarath said, sniffing at the air. "Tell your aunt."

They separated and moved off into the tall, fog-wet marsh grass. "Aunt Pol." Garion cast the words into the foggy silence around him.

"Yes, dear?"

"Tell Durnik and the others to rein in. There are some strangers up ahead."

"All right, Garion. Be careful."

Garion slunk low to the ground through the wet grass, setting each paw down carefully.

"Will it never lift?" he heard a voice somewhere off to his left demand irritably.

"The local people say that it's always foggy around here in the spring," another voice replied.

"It's not spring."

"It is here. We're south of the line. The seasons are reversed."

"That's a stupid sort of thing."

"It wasn't my idea. Talk to the Gods if you want to register a complaint."

There was a long silence. "Have the Hounds found anything yet?" the first voice asked.

"It's very hard to sniff out a trail after three days—even for the Hounds—and all the wet from this fog isn't making it any easier."

Garion froze. "Grandfather!" he hurled the thought into the fog.

"Don't shout."

"There are two men talking just up ahead. They have some of the Hounds with them. I think they're trying to find the trail, too."

"Pol." The old man's thought seemed to crackle. "Come up here."

"Yes, father."

It was no more than a few minutes, but it seemed like hours. Then in the murky fog overhead, Garion heard the single stroke of soft wings.

"There are some men over there to the left," Belgarath's voice reported. "I think they might be Grolims. Have a look, but be careful."

"All right," she replied. There was another soft wing beat in the fog. Again there was that interminable wait.

Then her voice came back quite clearly. "You're right, father," she said. "They're Chandim."

A muttered oath came out of the stillness. "Urvon," Belgarath's voice said.

"And probably Nahaz as well," Polgara added.

"This complicates things," the old man said. "Let's go back and talk with the others. We might have to make the decision sooner than Beldin thought."

CHAPTER TEN

They gathered not far from the driftwood-littered beach. The fog had slipped imperceptibly from white to gray as evening settled slowly over this misty coast.

"That's it, then," Beldin said after Belgarath had told them what lay ahead. "If the Chandim and the Hounds are out there trying to sniff out Zandramas' trail the same as we are, we're bound to run into them sooner or later."

"We've dealt with them before," Silk objected.

"I'll grant that," Beldin replied, "but why risk that sort of thing if we don't have to? The trail of Zandramas isn't really important to us now. What we really need to do at this point is to get to Kell."

Belgarath was pacing up and down. "Beldin's right," he said. "There's no point in taking risks over something that doesn't really matter any more."

"But we're so close," Ce'Nedra protested.

"If we start running into Chandim—and Hounds—we won't *stay* very close," Beldin told her.

Sadi had put on a western-style traveler's cloak and had turned the hood up to ward off the dampness of the fog. The covering of his shaved scalp peculiarly altered his appearance. "What's Zandramas likely to do when she finds out that the Chandim are trailing her?" he asked.

"She'll put every Grolim and every soldier she can lay her hands on in their path," Polgara replied.

"And they'll just bring in more force to counter that. won't they?"

"That's the logical assumption," Durnik agreed.

"That sort of means that things are going to come to a head here fairly soon, wouldn't you say—even if neither side would particularly have chosen this place for a major confrontation?"

"What are you getting at, Sadi?" Silk asked him.

"If Urvon and Zandramas are concentrating on each other, they won't really pay that much attention to us, will they? About all we have to do is get out of this general vicinity, and then we should be able to make straight for Kell without much in the way of interference."

"What lies to the south of us?" Beldin asked Silk.

"Nothing major." Silk shrugged. "At least not until you get to Gandahar."

Beldin nodded. "But we've got a city just to the north of here, don't we?"

"Selda," Silk supplied.

"Urvon's probably there already, but if we go south, we should be able to avoid him—and Zandramas as well. Sadi's right. They'll be so busy with each other they won't have time to look for us."

"Anybody want to add anything?" Belgarath asked them.

"A fire maybe?" Durnik said.

"I don't quite follow you."

"We've got all this fog," Durnik explained, "and night's coming on. The Chandim are out there ahead of us, and we need something to distract their attention while we slip around them. There's all that driftwood along the upper edge of the beach. A bonfire on a foggy night lights up the whole sky. You can see it for miles. If we build a few fires, the Chandim are going to think that something serious is going on behind them and they'll all rush back to investigate. That ought to clear the way for us."

Beldin grinned and clapped a gnarled hand on the smith's shoulder. "You made a good choice, Pol," he chortled. "This is a rare fellow here."

"Yes," she murmured. "I saw that almost immediately."

They rode back along the beach to the abandoned fishing village. "Do you want me to do it, Grandfather?" Garion offered. "Set fire to the driftwood, I mean?"

"No," the old man replied, "I'll take care of it. You and Pol take the others on down along the shoreline. I'll catch up in a bit."

"Do you want these?" Durnik asked, offering the old man his flint and steel.

Belgarath shook his head. "I'll do it the other way," he said. "I want to give the Chandim some noise to listen to, as well as the fire to watch. That should get their undivided attention." He strode off into the fog, heading back up the beach.

"Come along, Garion," Polgara said, pushing back the hood of her cloak. "We'll scout ahead again. I think we'll want to move fairly fast."

The two of them walked a short distance down the beach and made the change once more. "Keep your mind awake as well as your ears and nose," Polgara's voice silently instructed.

"With this fog, the Chandim will probably be watching with their thoughts rather than their eyes."

"Yes, Aunt Pol," he replied, loping toward the upper end of the beach. Sand was different underfoot than grass or turf. It gave slightly under his paws and it slowed him a bit. He decided that he did not really like running in sand. He ran along for a couple of miles without any encounters, then he heard and felt a shockingly loud surge coming from somewhere behind him. He flinched and glanced back over his shoulder. The fog was illuminated by a sooty orange glow. There was another surge that sounded almost like a detonation, then another, and another.

"Tacky, father," he heard Polgara say disapprovingly. "Why are you being so ostentatious?"

"I just wanted to be sure they heard me, is all," the old man replied.

"They probably heard you in Mal Zeth. Are you coming back now?"

"Let me start a few more fires first. The Chandim have a limited attention span. Besides, the smoke should confuse the Hounds' sense of smell."

There were several more detonations.

"That should do it." Belgarath's thought had a note of self-satisfaction in it.

About twenty minutes later, the great silver wolf came out of the fog like a ghost. "Oh, there you are," Belgarath said to Garion in the way of wolves. "Let's spread out a bit and move right along. Durnik and the others are right behind us."

"Did the Chandim go back to the beach to see what was happening?"

"Oh, yes." Belgarath's tongue lolled out in the wolf's version of a grin. "They were definitely curious. There were quite a few of them. Shall we go?"

They ran along for about another hour before Garion's nostrils caught the scent of a horse and rider coming from somewhere ahead. He loped on through the fog, ranging back and forth until he pinpointed the man's location. Then he ran forward.

It was a solitary Temple Guardsman who was galloping northward toward the towering fires Belgarath had ignited. Garion rushed him, snarling terribly. The Guardsman's horse squealed in panic, rearing up onto his hind legs and dumping his startled rider into a bleached pile of driftwood. The horse fled, and the Guardsman groaned as he lay tangled up in the white logs and branches half-buried in the sand.

"Trouble?" Belgarath's thought came out of the fog.

"A Guardsman," Garion replied. "He fell off his horse. I think he may have broken some things."

"Was he alone?"

"Yes, Grandfather. Where are you?"

"Just a ways ahead of you. There are some woods up here. This looks like as good a place as any to turn west. I don't think we need to go all the way down to Gandahar."

"I'll tell Aunt Pol to pass the word to Durnik."

The woods were quite extensive, and there was very little undergrowth. At one point, Garion passed the embers of a campfire still glowing in the foggy dark. The campsite, however, was deserted, and there were signs that whoever had been there had departed in some haste. The track of churned loam on the forest floor indicated that the people had galloped off toward the fires on the beach.

Garion ran on.

Near the edge of the woods, a faint breeze carried a sharp canine reek. Garion stopped. "Grandfather," he sent his thought out urgently, "I smell a dog up ahead."

"Only one?"

"I think so." He crept forward, his ears and nose alert. "I can only smell one," he reported.

"Stay put. I'll be right there."

Garion dropped to his haunches and waited. A few moments later, the silver wolf joined him.

"Is he moving around at all?" Belgarath asked.

"No, Grandfather. He seems to be just sitting in one place. Do you think we can slip around him?"

"You and I could, but I don't think that Durnik and the others would be able to. The Hounds can hear and smell almost as well as wolves can."

"Can we frighten him off?"

"I doubt it. He's bigger than we are. Even if we did, he'd just go for help—and we definitely don't want a pack of the Hounds on our trail. We're going to have to kill him."

"Grandfather!" Garion gasped. For some reason, the thought of deliberately killing another canine profoundly shocked him.

"I know," Belgarath agreed. "The notion's repugnant, but we don't have any choice. He's blocking our way out of this area, and we have to be clear of here by daylight. Now listen carefully. The Hounds are big, but they're not very agile. They particularly aren't very good at turning around in a hurry. I'll confront him head-on. You run in behind him and hamstring him. You know how to do that?"

That knowledge was instinctive in wolves, and Garion found, almost with surprise, that he knew precisely what to do. "Yes," he replied. The speech of wolves is limited in its emotional range, so he could not indicate how uncomfortable this impending encounter made him.

"All right," Belgarath continued, "once you cut his hamstrings, get back out of the range of his teeth. He'll try to turn on you. That's instinctive, so he won't be able to stop himself. That's when I'll take his throat."

Garion shuddered at the deliberateness of the plan. Belgarath was proposing not a fight, but a cold-blooded killing. "Let's get it over with, Grandfather," he said unhappily.

"Don't whine, Garion," Belgarath's thought came to him. "He'll hear you."

"I don't like this," Garion thought back.

"Neither do I, but it's the only thing we can do. Let's go."

They crept among the fog-dimmed tree trunks with the smell of the Hound growing stronger in their nostrils. It was not a pleasant smell, since dogs will eat carrion, while wolves will not. Then Garion saw the Hound outlined black against the fog beyond the edge of the trees. Belgarath paused, indicating that he also saw their intended victim. Then the two wolves separated and moved in the slow, deliberate pace of the hunt, setting each paw carefully and noiselessly down on the damp forest loam.

It was over in a shockingly short time. The Hound screamed once when Garion's fangs ripped the tendons of his hind legs, but the scream died into a hideous rattling gurgle as Belgarath's jaws closed on his throat. The huge black body twitched a few times with its front paws scratching convulsively at the dirt. Then it shuddered and went limp. The dead Hound blurred peculiarly, and then there was a Grolim lying on the ground before them with his throat torn out.

"I didn't know they did that," Garion said, fighting down a surge of revulsion.

"Sometimes they do." Then Belgarath sent out his thought. "It's clear now, Pol. Tell Durnik to bring them on through."

As dawn turned the fog opalescent, they took shelter in a ruined village. There had been a wall around it, and part of it was still standing. The houses had been made of stone. Some were still more or less intact—except for the roofs. Others had been tumbled into the narrow streets. In places, smoke still rose from the shattered debris.

"I think we can risk a fire," Durnik suggested, looking at the smoke.

Polgara looked around. "A hot breakfast wouldn't hurt,"

she agreed. "It might be some time before we get another chance for one. Over there, I think," she added, "in what's left of that house."

"In just a moment, Durnik," Belgarath said. "I'll need you to translate for me." He looked at Toth. "I assume you know how to get to Kell from here?" he asked the huge mute.

Toth shifted the unbleached wool blanket he wore draped over one shoulder and nodded.

"In Melcena, we heard that Kell has been sealed off," the old man continued. "Will they let us through?"

Toth made a series of those obscure gestures.

"He says that there won't be any problem—as long as Cyradis is still at Kell," Durnik translated. "She'll instruct the other seers to let us through."

"She's there, then?" Belgarath asked.

The gestures came more rapidly.

"I didn't quite follow that," Durnik told his friend.

Toth gestured again, slower this time.

Durnik frowned. "This is a little complicated, Belgarath," he said. "As closely as I can make out what he says, she's there and yet not there at the same time—sort of the way she was when we saw Zandramas that time. But she's also there and not there in several other places as well—and in several different times."

"That's a neat trick," Beldin said. "Did he tell you where these other places and times are?"

"No. I think he'd rather not."

"We can respect that," Belgarath said.

"It doesn't diminish the curiosity, though," Beldin said. He brushed a few twigs out of his beard, then pointed at the sky. "I'm going up there," he added. "I think we ought to know how far this fog extends and what we're likely to run into once we get past it." He stopped, spread his arms, shimmered, and swooped away.

Durnik led the way into the ruined house and built a small

fire in the fireplace while Silk and Sadi prowled through the shattered village. After a short while they returned with a very thin Melcene in the brown robe of a bureaucrat. "He was hiding in a cellar," Silk reported.

The bureaucrat was trembling visibly, and his eyes were wild.

"What's your name?" Belgarath asked him.

The Melcene stared at the old man as if he didn't understand.

"I think he's had a bad time lately," Silk said. "We weren't able to get a word out of him."

"Can you give him something to calm his nerves?" Belgarath asked Sadi.

"I was just about to suggest that myself, Ancient One." Sadi went to his red leather case and took out a small glass vial filled with amber liquid. He took a tin cup from the table and poured some water into it. Then he carefully measured a few drops of the amber liquid into the water and swirled it around. "Why don't you drink this?" he said, handing the trembling Melcene the cup.

The fellow seized the cup gratefully and drained it in several noisy gulps.

"Give it a few moments to take effect," Sadi said quietly to Belgarath.

They watched the terrified man until his trembling subsided. "Are you feeling any better now, friend?" Sadi asked him.

"Y-yes," the thin fellow replied. He drew in a long shuddering breath. "Thank you," he said. "Have you any food? I'm very hungry."

Polgara gave him some bread and cheese. "This should tide you over until breakfast," she said.

"Thank you, Lady." He hungrily took the food and began to wolf it down.

"You look as if you've been through quite a lot lately," Silk said.

"And none of it pleasant," the bureaucrat told him.

"What did you say your name was?"

"Nabros. I'm with the Bureau of Roads."

"How long have you been in Peldane?"

"It seems like forever, but I suppose it's only been twenty years or so."

"What's going on here?" The rat-faced man gestured around at the shattered houses.

"Absolute chaos," Nabros replied. "Things have been in an upheaval for several years now, but last month Zandramas annexed Peldane."

"How did she do that? I'd heard that she was somewhere in the western part of the continent."

"So had I. Maybe she just got word back to her generals. Nobody's seen her for several years now."

"You seem to be fairly well informed, Nabros," Silk suggested.

Nabros shrugged. "It goes with being a member of the bureaucracy." He smiled a bit wanly. "Sometimes I think we spend more time gossiping than we do working."

"What have you heard about Zandramas lately?" Belgarath asked.

"Well," the fellow replied, rubbing at his unshaven cheek, "just before I fled the bureau offices in Selda, a friend of mine from the Bureau of Commerce came by. He said that there's supposed to be a coronation of some kind in Hemil—that's the capital of Darshiva, you know. My friend told me that they're going to crown some archduke from Melcena as Emperor of Mallorea."

"Mallorea's already got an emperor," Velvet objected.

"I think that may be part of the idea. My friend from Commerce is a fairly shrewd fellow, and he was speculating a bit after he told me what they were planning. Kal Zakath's been in Cthol Murgos for years now, but he recently returned to Mal Zeth. Most of his army is still in the west, however, so he can't put great masses of troops in the field. My friends seemed to think that Zandramas ordered this coronation in order to infuriate the Emperor to the point that he'll do something rash. It's my guess that she hopes to lure him out of Mal Zeth so her forces can fall on him. If she succeeds in killing him, this archduke from Melcena will actually *be* the emperor."

"What's the point of that?" Silk asked him.

"You've heard of Urvon, haven't you?"

"The Disciple?"

"That's the one. He's been sitting for centuries in Mal Yaska, but what's been going on in this part of the world has finally lured him out. It's because of Zandramas, you see. She's a direct challenge to him. Anyway, he marched across Karanda gathering up an enormous army. The Karands even believe he has demons aiding him. That's nonsense, of course, but Karands will believe anything. That's why Zandramas—or her people—have to get control of the imperial throne. She needs to bring the Mallorean army back from Cthol Murgos to match Urvon's forces. Otherwise, he'll destroy everything she's worked for." The suddenly talkative bureaucrat sighed deeply, and his head began to nod.

"I think he'll sleep now," Sadi murmured to Belgarath.

"That's all right," the old man replied. "I've got what I need."

"Not quite yet," Polgara said crisply from her cook-fire. "There are some things that I need as well." She carefully stepped across the littered floor of the half-ruined house and lightly touched one hand to the dozing bureaucrat's face. His eyes opened, and he looked at her a bit blankly. "How much do you know about Zandramas?" she asked him. "I think I'd like to hear the full story—if you know it. How did she gain so much power?"

"That's a long story, Lady."

"We have time."

The thin Melcene rubbed at his eyes and stifled a yawn. "Let me see," he said, half to himself, "where did it all start?" He sighed. "I came here to Peldane about twenty years ago. I was young and very enthusiastic. It was my first post, and I wanted very much to make good. Peldane's not such a bad place, really. We had Grolims here, naturally, but they were a long way from Urvon and Mal Yaska, and they didn't take their religion very seriously. Torak had been dormant for five hundred years, and Urvon wasn't interested in what was going on out here in the hinterlands.

"Over in Darshiva, though, things were different. There had been some kind of a schism in the Temple in Hemil, the capital, and it ended up in a bloodbath." He smiled faintly. "One of the few times Grolims have ever put their knives to good use, I suppose. The upshot of the affair was that a new archpriest gained control of the Temple—a man named Naradas."

"Yes," Polgara said. "We've heard of him."

"I've never actually seen him, but I'm told he has very strange eyes. Anyway, among his followers there was a young Grolim priestess named Zandramas. She must have been about sixteen then, and very beautiful, I've heard. Naradas reintroduced the old forms of worship, and the altar in the Temple at Hemil ran with blood." He shuddered. "It seems that the young priestess was the most enthusiastic participant in the Grolim rite of sacrifice—either out of an excess of fanaticism, or innate cruelty, or because she knew that this was the best way to attract the eye of the new archpriest. There are rumors that she attracted his eye in other ways as well. She'd unearthed a very obscure passage in the *Book of Torak* that seemed to say that the rite of sacrifice should be performed unclad. They say that Zandramas has a striking figure, and I guess the combination of blood and her nakedness com-

190

pletely inflamed Naradas. I've heard that things used to happen in the sanctum of the Temple during the rite that cannot
be described in the presence of ladies."

"I think we can skip over that part, Nabros," Polgara told
him primly, glancing at Eriond.

"Anyhow," Nabros continued, "all Grolims *claim* to be sorcerers, but from what I gather, the ones in Darshiva weren't
very skilled. Naradas could manage a few things, but most of
his followers resorted to charlatanism—sleight of hand and
other forms of trickery, you understand.

"At any rate, not long after Naradas had consolidated his
position, word reached us here that Torak had been killed.
Naradas and his underlings went into absolute despair, but
something rather profound seems to have happened to Zandramas. She walked out of the Temple at Hemil in a kind of
a daze. My friend from the Bureau of Commerce was there
at the time and he saw her. He said that her eyes were glazed
and that she had an expression of inhuman ecstasy on her
face. When she reached the edge of the city, she stripped off
her clothes and ran naked into the forest. We all assumed
that she'd gone completely mad and that we'd seen the last
of her.

"Once in a while, though, travelers would report having
seen her in that wilderness near the border of Likandia. Sometimes, she'd run away from them, and other times, she'd stop
them and speak to them in a language no one could understand. They listened, though—perhaps because she still
hadn't managed to find any clothes.

"Then one day after a few years, she showed up at the
gates of Hemil. She was wearing a black Grolim robe made
of satin, and she seemed to be totally in control of herself.
She went to the Temple and sought out Naradas. The archpriest had given himself wholly over to the grossest kind of
debauchery in his despair, but after he and Zandramas spoke
together privately, he seems to have had a reconversion of

some kind. Since that time, he's been the follower. He'll do anything Zandramas tells him to do.

"Zandramas spent a short time in the Temple, then she began to move about in Darshiva. At first she spoke only with Grolims, but in time she went out and talked with ordinary people as well. She always told them the same thing—that a new God of Angarak was coming. After a time, word of what she was doing got back to Mal Yaska, and Urvon sent some very powerful Grolims to Darshiva to stop her. I'm not sure what happened to her out there in that wilderness, but whatever it was seems to have filled her with enormous power. When Urvon's Grolims tried to stop her from preaching, she simply obliterated them."

"Obliterated?" Belgarath exclaimed in astonishment.

"That's about the only word I can use. Some of them she consumed with fire. Others were blasted to bits by bolts of lightning that shot down out of a cloudless sky. Once, she opened the earth, dropped five of them into a pit, and then closed the earth on them again. Urvon began to take her very seriously at that point, I guess. He sent more and more Grolims to Darshiva, but she destroyed them all. The Darshivan Grolims who chose to follow her were given *real* powers, so they didn't have to resort to to trickery any more."

"And the ones who didn't?" Polgara asked.

"None of them survived. I understand that a few of them tried deception—pretending to accept her message—but I guess she could see right through them and took appropriate steps. It probably wasn't really necessary, though. She spoke as if inspired, and no one could resist her message. Before long, all of Darshiva—Grolims and secular people alike—groveled at her feet.

"She moved north from Darshiva into Rengel and Voresebo, preaching as she went and converting whole multitudes. The archpriest Naradas followed her blindly and he was also enormously eloquent and appears to have only slightly less power than she does. For some reason, she never came across the River Magan into Peldane—until recently."

"All right," Polgara said, "she converted Rengel and Voresebo. Then what?"

"I really can't say." Nabros shrugged. "About three years ago, both she and Naradas disappeared. I think they went off to the west someplace, but I don't know for sure. About the last thing she told the crowds before she left was that she was going to be the bride of this new God she's been talking about. Then, a month ago, her forces came across the Magan and invaded Peldane. That's about all I know, really."

Polgara stepped back. "Thank you, Nabros," she said gently. "Why don't you see if you can get some sleep now? I'll save some breakfast for you."

He sighed, and his eyelids began to droop. "Thank you, Lady," he said drowsily, and a moment later he was fast asleep. Polgara gently covered him with a blanket.

Belgarath motioned to them, and they all went back over to the fire again. "It's all beginning to fit together now, isn't it?" he said. "When Torak died, the Dark Spirit took over Zandramas and made her the Child of Dark. That's what that business in the wilderness was all about."

Ce'Nedra had been muttering to herself under her breath. Her eyes were dangerous and her face angry. "You'd better do something about this, old man," she said threateningly to Belgarath.

"About what?" He looked a little baffled.

"You heard what that man said. He told us that Zandramas plans to be the bride of this new God."

"Yes," he said mildly, "I heard him."

"You're not going to let something like that happen, are you?"

"I hadn't planned to, no. What's got you so upset, Ce'Nedra?"

Her eyes flashed. "I will *not* have Zandramas for a daughter-in-law," she declared hotly, "no matter what happens."

He stared at her for a moment, then he began to laugh.

CHAPTER ELEVEN

By midafternoon the wan dish of the sun had begun to burn through the pervading mist, and Beldin returned. "The fog's completely cleared away about a league west of here," he told them.

"Are there any signs of movement out there?" Belgarath asked him.

"Some," Beldin replied. "A few detachments of troops that are all headed north. Otherwise it's as empty as a merchant's soul. Sorry, Kheldar, it's just an old expression."

"That's all right, Beldin," Silk forgave him grandly. "These little slips of the tongue are common in the very elderly."

Beldin gave him a hard look and then continued. "The villages up ahead all seem to be deserted and mostly in ruins. I'd say that the villagers have fled." He glanced at the sleeping Melcene. "Who's your guest?" he asked.

"He's with the Bureau of Roads," Belgarath replied. "Silk found him hiding in a cellar."

"Is he really all that sleepy?"

"Sadi gave him something to calm his nerves."

"I'd say it worked pretty good. He looks very calm."

"Would you like something to eat, uncle?" Polgara asked.

"Thanks all the same, Pol, but I had a fat rabbit an hour or so ago." He looked back at Belgarath. "I think we'll still want to travel at night," he advised. "You don't have whole regiments out there, but there are enough to give us trouble if they happen to surprise us."

"Any idea of whose troops they are?"

"I didn't see any Guardsmen or Karands. I'd guess that they belong to Zandramas—or to the King of Peldane. Whoever they are, they're going north toward that battle that's about to begin."

"All right," Belgarath said, "we'll travel at night, then— at least until we get past the soldiers."

They moved along at a fair rate of speed that night. They had passed the woods, and the watchfires of the soldiers encamped on the plain made them easy to avoid. Then, just before dawn, Belgarath and Garion stopped atop a low hill and looked down at a camp that seemed quite a bit larger than those they had passed earlier. "About a battalion, Grandfather," Garion surmised. "I think we've got a problem here. The country around here's awfully flat. This is the only hill we've seen for miles, and there isn't very much cover. No matter how we try to hide, their scouts are going to see us. It might be safer if we turned around and went back a ways."

Belgarath laid back his ears in irritation. "Let's go back and

196

warn the others," he growled. He rose to his feet and led Garion back the way they had come.

"There's no point in taking chances, father," Polgara said after she had drifted in on silent wings. "The country was more broken a few miles back. We can go back there and find shelter."

"Were the cooks making breakfast?" Sadi asked.

"Yes," Garion replied. "I could smell it—some kind of porridge and bacon."

"They're not likely to move or send out scouts until after they eat, are they?"

"No," Garion told him. "Troops get very surly if you make them start marching before you feed them."

"And were the sentries all wearing the standard military cloak—the ones that look more or less like these?" He plucked at the front of his traveler's cloak.

"The ones I saw were," Garion said.

"Why don't we pay them a visit, Prince Kheldar?" The eunuch suggested.

"What have you got in mind?" Silk asked suspiciously.

"Porridge is so bland, don't you think? I have a number of things in my case that can spice it up just a bit. We can walk through the encampment like a pair of sentries who've just been relieved and go directly to the cook-fires for a bite of breakfast. I shouldn't have much trouble seasoning the kettles with certain condiments."

Silk grinned at him.

"No poison," Belgarath said firmly.

"I hadn't considered poison, Ancient One," Sadi protested mildly. "Not out of any sense of morality, mind you. It's just that soldiers tend to grow suspicious when their messmates turn black in the face and topple over. I have something much more pleasant in mind. The soldiers will all be deliriously happy for a short while, then they'll fall asleep."

"For how long?" Silk asked.

"Several days," Sadi shrugged. "A week at the very most."

Silk whistled. "Is it dangerous at all?"

"Only if one has a weak heart. I've used it on myself on occasion—when I was particularly tired. Shall we go, then?"

"Teaming those two together may have been a moral blunder," Belgarath mused as the two rogues walked off in the darkness toward the twinkling watchfires.

It was about an hour later when the little Drasnian and the eunuch returned. "It's safe now," Sadi reported. "We can go on through their camp. There's a low range of hills a league or so farther on where we can take shelter until night."

"Any trouble at all?" Velvet asked.

"Not a bit," Silk smirked. "Sadi's very good at that sort of thing."

"Practice, my dear Kheldar," the eunuch said deprecatingly. "I've poisoned a fair number of people in my time." He grinned mirthlessly. "Once I gave a banquet for a group of my enemies. Not a single one of them saw me season the soup course, and Nyissans are very observant when it comes to that sort of thing."

"Didn't they get suspicious when you didn't eat any soup?" Velvet asked curiously.

"But I did, Liselle. I'd spent an entire week dosing myself with the antidote." He shuddered. "Vile-tasting stuff, as I recall. The poison itself was quite tasty. A number of my guests even complimented me on the soup before they left." He sighed. "Those were the good old days," he mourned.

"I think we can reminisce later on," Belgarath said. "Let's see if we can reach those hills before the sun gets much higher."

The soldiers' encampment was silent, except for an occasional snore. The troops were all smiling happily as they slept.

The following night was cloudy, and the air smelled strongly of incipient rain. Garion and Belgarath had no trouble finding the encampments of the soldiers in their path, and a few overheard snatches of conversation revealed the fact that these troops were members of the royal army of Peldane, and further that they were approaching the impending battle with a great deal of reluctance. About morning, Garion and his grandfather trotted back to rejoin the others with Polgara ghosting just above them on silent wings.

"A sound is still a sound," Durnik was saying stubbornly to Beldin. The two were riding side by side.

"But if there's nobody to hear it, how can we call it a sound?" Beldin argued.

Belgarath shook himself into his own form. "The noise in the woods again, Beldin?" he said in a tone of profoundest disgust.

The hunchback shrugged. "You've got to start somewhere."

"Can't you think of anything new? After we argued the question for a thousand years, I thought you might have gotten tired of it."

"What's this?" Polgara asked, walking through the tall grass to join them in the shadowless light of dawn.

"Beldin and Durnik are discussing a very tired old philosophical question." Belgarath snorted. "If there's a noise in the woods, and there's nobody around to hear it, is it really a noise?"

"Of course it is," she replied calmly.

"How did you reach that conclusion?" Beldin demanded.

"Because there's no such thing as an empty place, uncle. There are always creatures around—wild animals, mice, insects, birds—and they can all hear."

"But what if there weren't? What if the woods are truly empty?"

"Why waste your time talking about an impossibility?"

He stared at her in frustration.

"Not only that," Ce'Nedra added just a bit smugly, "you're

talking about woods, so there are trees there. Trees can hear, too, you know."

He glared at her. "Why are you all taking sides against me?"

"Because you're wrong, uncle." Polgara smiled.

"Wrong, Polgara?" He spluttered. *"Me?"*

"It happens to everybody once in a while. Why don't we all have some breakfast?"

The sun rose while they were eating, and Belgarath looked up, squinting into the morning rays. "We haven't seen any soldiers since midnight," he said, "and all we've seen so far are troops of the army of Peldane. They're not really anything to worry about, so I think it's safe to ride on a little farther this morning." He looked at Silk. "How far is it to the border of Darshiva?"

"Not really all that far, but we haven't been making very good time. It's spring, so the nights are getting shorter, and we lose time when we have to circle around those troops." He frowned. "We might have a bit of a problem at the border, though. We're going to have to cross the River Magan, and if everyone has fled the area, we could have some trouble finding a boat."

"Is the Magan really as big as they say?" Sadi asked.

"It's the biggest river in the world. It runs for a thousand leagues and more, and it's so wide that you can't see the far shore."

Durnik rose to his feet. "I want to check over the horses before we go any farther," he said. "We've been riding them in the dark, and that's always a little dangerous. We don't want any of them pulling up lame."

Eriond and Toth also rose, and the three of them went through the tall grass to the place where the horses were picketed.

"I'll go on ahead," Beldin said. "Even if the troops are Peldanes, we still don't need any surprises." He changed form

200

and flew off toward the west, spiraling up into the cloudless morning sky.

Garion stretched his legs out in front of him and leaned back on his elbows.

"You must be tired," Ce'Nedra said, sitting beside him and touching his face tenderly.

"Wolves don't really get that tired," he told her. "I get the feeling that I could run for a week if I really had to."

"Well, you don't have to, so don't even consider it."

"Yes, dear."

Sadi had risen to his feet with his red leather case in his hands. "As long as we're stopped, I think I'll find something to feed Zith," he said. A small frown touched his brow. "You know, Liselle," he said to Velvet, "I think you were right back in Zamad. She definitely looks as if she's gained a few ounces."

"Put her on a diet," the blond girl suggested.

"I'm not sure about that." He smiled. "It's very hard to explain to a snake why you're starving her, and I wouldn't want her to get cross with me."

They rode out not long afterward, following Toth's gestured directions.

"He says that we can probably find a village south of the big town on the river," Durnik told them.

"Ferra," Silk supplied.

"I suppose so. I haven't looked at a map for a while. Anyway, he says that there are quite a few villages on this side where we might be able to hire a boat to get us across to Darshiva."

"That's assuming that they aren't all deserted," Silk added.

Durnik shrugged. "We'll never know until we get there."

It was a warm morning, and they rode across the rolling grasslands of southern Peldane under cloudless skies. About midmorning, Eriond rode forward and fell in beside Garion. "Do you think Polgara would mind if you and I took a little gallop?" he asked. "Maybe to that hill over there?" He pointed at a large knoll off to the north.

"She probably would," Garion said, "unless we can come up with a good reason."

"You don't think she'd accept the idea that Horse and Chretienne need to run once in a while?"

"Eriond, you've known her for a long time. Do you really think she'd listen if we tried to tell her that?"

Eriond sighed. "No, I suppose not."

Garion squinted at the hilltop. "We really ought to keep an eye out to the north, though," he said thoughtfully. "That's where the trouble's going to break out. We sort of need to know what's happening up there, don't we? That hilltop would be a perfect place to have a look."

"That's very true, Belgarion."

"It's not as if we'd actually be lying to her."

"I wouldn't dream of lying to her."

"Of course not. Neither would I."

The two young men grinned at each other. "I'll tell Belgarath where we're going," Garion said. "We'll let him explain it to her."

"He's the perfect one to do it," Eriond agreed.

Garion dropped back and touched his half-dozing grandfather's shoulder. "Eriond and I are going to ride over to that hill," he said. "I want to see if there are any signs that the fighting's started yet."

"What? Oh, good idea." Belgarath yawned and closed his eyes again.

Garion motioned to Eriond, and the two of them trotted off into the tall grass at the side of the trail.

"Garion," Polgara called, "where are you going?"

"Grandfather can explain it, Aunt Pol," he shouted back. "We'll catch up again in just a bit." He looked at Eriond. "Now let's get out of earshot in a hurry."

They went north, first at a gallop and then at a dead run

be a broken nose and some missing teeth, but when you start getting armies involved, people get killed."

"Are you and Zakath going to have a war, then?"

It was a troubling question, and Garion wasn't sure he knew the answer. "I don't really know," he admitted.

"He wants to rule the world," Eriond pointed out, "and you don't want him to. Isn't that the sort of thing that starts a war?"

"It's awfully hard to say," Garion replied sadly. "Maybe if we hadn't left Mal Zeth when we did, I might have been able to bring him around. But we had to leave, so I lost the chance." He sighed. "I think it's finally going to be up to him. Maybe he's changed enough so that he'll abandon the whole idea—but then again, maybe he hasn't. You can never tell with a man like Zakath. I *hope* he's given up the notion. I don't want a war—not with anybody; but I'm not going to bow to him, either. The world wasn't meant to be ruled by one man—and certainly not by somebody like Zakath."

"But you like him, don't you?"

"Yes, I do. I wish I could have met him before Taur Urgas ruined his life." He paused, and his face grew set. "Now there's a man I'd have rather cheerfully gone to war with. He contaminated the whole world just by living in it."

"But it wasn't really his fault. He was insane, and that excuses him."

"You're a very forgiving young man, Eriond."

"Isn't it easier to forgive than to hate? Until we learn how to forgive, that sort of thing is going to keep on happening." He pointed at the tall pillars of smoke rising to the north. "Hate is a sterile thing, Belgarion."

"I know." Garion sighed. "I hated Torak, but in the end I guess I forgave him—more out of pity than anything else. I still had to kill him, though."

"What do you think the world would be like if people didn't kill each other any more?"

with the grass whipping at their horses' legs. The chestnut and the gray matched stride for stride, plunging along with their heads thrust far forward and their hooves pounding on the thick turf. Garion leaned forward in his saddle, surrendering to the flow and surge of Chretienne's muscles. Both he and Eriond were laughing with delight when they reined in on the hilltop.

"That was good," Garion said, swinging down from his saddle. "We don't get the chance to do that very often any more, do we?"

"Not often enough," Eriond agreed, also dismounting. "You managed to arrange it very diplomatically, Belgarion."

"Of course. Diplomacy's what kings do best."

"Do you think we fooled her?"

"Us?" Garion laughed. "Fool Aunt Pol? Be serious, Eriond."

"I suppose you're right." Eriond made a wry face. "She'll probably scold us, won't she?"

"Inevitably, but the ride was worth a scolding, wasn't it?"

Eriond smiled. Then he looked around, and his smile faded. "Belgarion," he said sadly, pointing to the north.

Garion looked. Tall columns of black smoke rose along the horizon. "It looks as if it's started," he said bleakly.

"Yes." Eriond sighed. "Why do they have to do that?"

Garion crossed his arms on Chretienne's saddle and leaned his chin pensively on them. "Pride, I suppose," he replied, "and the hunger for power. Revenge, too, sometimes. I guess. Once in Arendia, Lelldorin said that very often it's because people just don't know how to stop it, once it's started."

"But it's all so senseless."

"Of course it is. Arends aren't the only stupid people on earth. Any time you have two people who both want the same thing badly enough, you're going to have a fight. If the two people have enough followers, they call it a war. If a couple of ordinary men have that kind of disagreement, there might

"Nicer, probably."

"Why don't we fix it that way then?"

"You and I?" Garion laughed. "All by ourselves?"

"Why not?"

"Because it's impossible, Eriond."

"I thought you and Belgarath had settled the issue of impossible a long time ago."

Garion laughed again. "Yes, I suppose we did. All right, let's drop impossible. Would you accept extremely difficult instead?"

"Nothing that's really worthwhile should be easy, Belgarion. If it's easy, we don't value it; but I'm certain we'll be able to find an answer." He said it with such shining confidence in his face that for a moment Garion actually believed that the wild notion might indeed be feasible.

Then he looked out at the ugly columns of smoke again, and the hope died. "I suppose we should go back and let the others know what's happening out there," he said.

It was about noon when Beldin returned. "There's another detachment of troops about a mile ahead," he told Belgarath. "A dozen or so."

"Are they going toward that battle to the north?"

"No, I'd say this particular group is running away from it. They look as if they were fairly well mauled recently."

"Could you tell which side they're on?"

"That doesn't really matter, Belgarath. A man gives up his allegiances when he deserts."

"Sometimes you're so clever you make me sick."

"Why don't you have Pol mix you up something to cure it?"

"How long has that been going on?" Velvet asked Polgara.

"Which was that, dear?"

"That constant wrangling between those two?"

Polgara closed her eyes and sighed. "You wouldn't believe

it, Liselle. Sometimes I think it started at about the beginning of time."

The soldiers they encountered were wary, even frightened. They stood their ground, however, with their hands on their weapons. Silk made a quick motion to Garion, and the two of them rode forward at an unthreatening walk.

"Good day, gentlemen," Silk greeted them conversationally. "What in the world is happening around here?"

"You mean you haven't heard?" a wiry fellow with a bloody bandage around his head asked.

"I haven't found anybody to tell me," Silk replied. "What happened to all the people who used to live in this part of Peldane? We haven't seen a soul in the last four days."

"They all fled," the bandaged man told him. "The ones who were still alive did, at any rate."

"What were they fleeing from?"

"Zandramas," the fellow replied with a shudder. "Her army marched into Peldane about a month ago. We tried to stop them, but they had Grolims with them, and ordinary troops can't do much against Grolims."

"That's the truth, certainly. What's all that smoke up to the north?"

"There's a big battle going on." The soldier sat down on the ground and began to unwind the bloodstained bandage from around his head.

"It's not like any battle *I've* ever seen," another soldier supplied. His left arm was in a sling, and he looked as if he had just spent several days lying in the mud. "I've been in a few wars, but nothing like this. When you're a soldier, you takes your chances—swords and arrows and spears and the like, y'know—but when they starts throwing horrors at me, I begins to feel it's time to find another line of work."

"Horrors?" Silk asked him.

"They's got demons with 'em, friend—both sides of 'em

206

has—monstrous big demons with snaky arms and fangs and claws and suchlike."

"You're not serious!"

"I seen 'em with my own eyes. You ever seen a man get et alive? Makes your hair stand on end, it does."

"I don't quite follow this," Silk confessed. "Who's involved in this battle? I mean, ordinary armies don't keep tame demons with them to help with the fighting."

"That's the honest truth," the muddy man agreed. "A ordinary soldier's likely to leave the service if they expect him to march alongside something that looks at him as if he was something to eat. I never did get the straight of it, though." He looked at the man with the wounded head. "Did you ever find out who was fighting, corporal?"

The corporal was wrapping a clean bandage around his head. "The captain told us before he got killed," he said.

"Maybe you'd better start at the beginning," Silk said. "I'm a little confused about this."

"Like I told you," the corporal said, "about a month ago the Darshivans and their Grolims invaded Peldane. Me and my men are in the Royal Army of Peldane, so we tried to hold them back. We slowed them some on the east bank of the Magan, but then the Grolims come at us, and we had to retreat. Then we heard that there was another army coming down out of the north—Karands and soldiers in armor and more Grolims. We figured that we was really in for it at that point, but as it turns out, this new army isn't connected with the Darshivans. It seems that it's working for some High Grolim from way off to the west. Well, this Grolim, he sets up along the coast and don't come inland at all. It's like he's waiting for something. We had our hands full with the Darshivans, so we wasn't too interested in what it was he was waiting for. We was doing a lot of what our officers called 'maneuvering'—which is officer talk for running away."

"I take it that the Grolim finally decided to come inland after all," Silk observed.

"He surely did, friend. He surely did. It was just a few days ago when he struck inland just as straight as a tight string. Either he knew exactly where he was going or he was following something, I don't know exactly which. Anyway, the Darshivans, they stopped chasing us and rushed in to try to block his way, and that's when he called in the demons Vurk here was talking about. At first, the demons charged right through the Darshivans, but then their Grolims—or maybe it was Zandramas herself—they conjured up *their* demons, and that's when the big fight commenced. The demons, they went at each other for all they was worth and they trampled over anybody unlucky enough to get in the way. There we was, caught right in the middle of it all and getting trampled on by first one set of demons and then the other. That's when me and Vurk and these others put our heads together and decided to find out what the weather's like in Gandahar."

"Hot this time of year," Silk told him.

"Not near as hot as it is north of here, friend. You ever see a demon breathe fire? I seen one of them armored soldiers get roasted alive right inside his chain mail. Then the demon picked him out of his armor piece by piece and et him while he was still smoking." The corporal knotted the ends of his fresh bandage. "That ought to hold it," he said, rising to his feet again. He looked up into the noon sky, squinting slightly. "We can make some more miles before the sun goes down, Vurk," he said to his muddy friend. "Get the men ready to march. If that battle starts to spread out, we could get caught in the middle of it again, and none of us want that."

"I'll do 'er, corporal," Vurk replied.

The corporal looked at Silk again, his eyes narrowed appraisingly. "You and your friends are welcome to come along," he offered. "A few men on horseback might be a help in case we run into trouble."

"Thanks all the same, corporal," Silk declined, "but I think we'll ride over to the Magan and see if we can find a boat. We could be at the mouth of the river in a week or so."

"I'd advise riding hard, then, my friend. Demons can run awful fast when they're hungry."

Silk nodded. "Good luck in Gandahar, corporal," he added.

"I think I'll stop being a corporal," the fellow said ruefully. "The pay wasn't bad, but the work's getting dangerouser and dangerouser, and all the pay in the world won't do a man much good once he takes up residence inside a demon." He turned to his friend. "Let's move out, Vurk," he ordered.

Silk wheeled his horse and rode back to where the others were waiting, Garion close behind him.

"It's more or less what we thought," the little man reported, dismounting. "The battle up north is between Urvon and Zandramas, and both sides have demons now."

"She went *that* far?" Polgara asked incredulously.

"She didn't really have that much choice, Polgara," Silk told her. "Nahaz was leading his hordes of demons into the ranks of her troops, and her army was being decimated. She had to do something to stop him. Being captured by a demon is no joke—not even for the Child of Dark."

"All right," Durnik said soberly, "what do we do now?"

"The corporal in charge of those troops made an interesting suggestion," Silk told him.

"Oh? What was that?"

"He recommended that we get out of Peldane as fast as we possibly can."

"Corporals usually have good sense," Durnik noted. "Why don't we follow his advice?"

"I was hoping someone would say that," Silk agreed.

CHAPTER TWELVE

Vella was feeling melancholy. It was an unusual emotion for her, but she found that she rather liked it. There was much to be said for sweet, languorous sadness. She went with quiet dignity through the stately, marble-clad corridors of the palace in Boktor, and everyone gave way to her pensive expression. She chose not to consider the fact that her daggers may have played a certain part in this universal respect. In point of fact, Vella had not drawn a dagger on anyone for almost a week now—the last having been a slightly overfamiliar serving man who had mistaken her bluff camaraderie for an offer of a more intimate friendship. But she had not hurt him very much, and he had forgiven her almost before the bleeding had stopped.

Her destination that early morning was the sitting room of the Queen of Drasnia. In many ways Queen Porenn baffled Vella. She was petite and imperturbable. She carried no daggers and seldom raised her voice, but all of Drasnia and the other Alorn kingdoms held her in universal regard. Vella herself, not knowing exactly why, had acceded to the tiny queen's suggestion that she should customarily garb herself in gowns of lavender satin. A gown is a cumbersome thing that tangles up one's legs and confines one's bosom. Always before, Vella had preferred black leather trousers, boots, and a leather vest. The garb was comfortable and utilitarian. It was sturdy, and yet it provided opportunities for Vella to display her attributes to those whom she wished to impress. Then, on special occasions, she had customarily donned an easily discardable wool dress and a fine diaphanous undergown of rose-colored Mallorean silk that clung to her as she danced. Satin, on the other hand, rustled disturbingly, but felt good against her skin, and it made Vella uncomfortably aware of the fact that there was more to being a woman than a couple pair of daggers and a willingness to use them.

She tapped lightly on Porenn's door.

"Yes?" Porenn's voice came to her.

Did the woman never sleep?

"It's me, Porenn—Vella."

"Come in, child."

Vella set her teeth. She was not, after all, a child. She had been abroad in the world since her twelfth birthday. She had been sold—and bought—a half-dozen times, and she had been married for a brief, deliriously happy year to a lean Nadrak trapper named Tekk, whom she had loved to distraction. Porenn, however, seemed to prefer to look upon her as some half-gentled colt in sore need of training. In spite of herself, that thought softened Vella's resentment. The little blond

Queen of Drasnia had in some strange way become the mother she had never known, and thoughts of daggers and of being bought and sold slid away under the influence of that wise, gentle voice.

"Good morning, Vella," Porenn said as the Nadrak girl entered her room. "Would you like some tea?" Although the queen always wore black in public, her dressing gown that morning was of the palest rose, and she looked somehow very vulnerable in that soft color.

"Hullo, Porenn," Vella said. "No tea, thanks." She flung herself into a chair beside the blond queen's divan.

"Don't flop, Vella," Porenn told her. "Ladies don't flop."

"I'm not a lady."

"Not yet, perhaps, but I'm working on it."

"Why are you wasting your time on me, Porenn?"

"Nothing worthwhile is ever a waste of time."

"Me? Worthwhile?"

"More than you could possibly know. You're early this morning. Is something troubling you?"

"I haven't been able to sleep. I've been having the strangest dreams lately."

"Don't let dreams bother you, child. Dreams are sometimes the past, sometimes the future, but mostly they're only that—dreams."

"Please don't call me 'child,' Porenn," Vella objected. "I think if we got right down to it, I'm almost as old as you are."

"In years, perhaps, but years aren't the only way to measure time."

There was a discreet rap at the door.

"Yes?" Porenn replied.

"It's me, your Majesty," a familiar voice said.

"Come in, Margrave Khendon," the queen said.

Javelin had not changed since Vella had last seen him. He was still bone-thin and aristocratic and had a sardonically amused twist to his lips. He wore, as was his custom, a pearl-gray doublet and tight-fitting black hose. His skinny shanks were not shown to any particular advantage by the latter. He bowed rather extravagantly. "Your Majesty," he greeted the queen, "and my Lady Vella."

"Don't be insulting, Javelin," Vella retorted. "I don't have a title, so don't 'my Lady' me."

"Haven't you told her yet?" Javelin mildly asked the queen.

"I'm saving it for her birthday."

"What's this?" Vella demanded.

"Be patient, dear," Porenn told her. "You'll find out about your title all in due time."

"I don't need a Drasnian title."

"Everybody needs a title, dear—even if it's only 'ma'am.'"

"Has she always been like this?" Vella bluntly asked the Chief of Drasnian Intelligence.

"She was a little more ingenuous when she still had her baby teeth," Javelin replied urbanely, "but she got to be more fun when she developed her fangs."

"Be nice, Khendon," Porenn told him. "How was Rak Urga?"

"Ugly—but then, most Murgo cities are."

"And how is King Urgit?"

"Newly married, your Majesty, and a little distracted by the novelty of it."

Porenn made a face. "I didn't send a gift," she fretted.

"I took the liberty of attending to that, your Majesty," Javelin said. "A rather nice silver service I picked up in Tol Honeth—at a bargain price, of course. I have this limited budget, you understand."

She gave him a long, unfriendly look.

"I left the bill with your chamberlain," he added with not even the faintest trace of embarrassment.

"How are the negotiations going?"

"Surprisingly well, my queen. The King of the Murgos

seems not to have yet succumbed to the hereditary disorder of the House of Urga. He's very shrewd, actually."

"I somehow thought he might be," Porenn replied just a bit smugly.

"You're keeping secrets, Porenn," Javelin accused.

"Yes. Women do that from time to time. Are the Mallorean agents in the Drojim keeping abreast of things?"

"Oh, yes." Javelin smiled. "Sometimes we have to be a little obvious in order to make sure that they're getting the point, but they're more or less fully aware of the progress of the negotiations. We seem to be making them a bit apprehensive."

"You made good time on your return voyage."

Javelin shuddered slightly. "King Anheg put a ship at our disposal. Her captain is that pirate Greldik. I made the mistake of telling him I was in a hurry. The passage through the Bore was ghastly."

There was another polite knock on the door.

"Yes?" Porenn answered.

A servant opened the door. "The Nadrak Yarblek is here again, your Majesty," he reported.

"Show him in, please."

Yarblek had a tight look on his face that Vella recognized all too well. Her owner was in many respects a transparent man. He pulled off his shabby fur cap. "Good morning, Porenn," he said without ceremony, tossing the cap into a corner. "Have you got anything to drink? I've been in the saddle for five days and I'm perishing of thirst."

"Over there." Porenn pointed at a sideboard near the window.

Yarblek grunted, crossed the room, and filled a large goblet from a crystal decanter. He took a long drink. "Javelin," he said then, "have you got any people in Yar Nadrak?"

"A few," Javelin admitted cautiously.

"You'd better have them keep an eye on Drosta. He's up to something."

"He's always up to something."

"That's no lie, but this might be a little more serious. He's reopened lines of communication with Mal Zeth. He and Zakath haven't been on speaking terms since he changed sides at Thull Mardu, but now they're talking again. I don't like the smell of it."

"Are you sure? None of my people have reported it."

"They're probably in the palace, then. Drosta doesn't conduct serious business there. Have them go to a riverside tavern in the thieves' quarter. It's called the One-Eyed Dog. Drosta goes there to amuse himself. The emissary from Mal Zeth's been meeting with him in an upstairs room there—that's when Drosta can drag himself away from the girls."

"I'll put some people on it right away. Could you get any idea at all of what they're discussing?"

Yarblek shook his head and dropped wearily into a chair. "Drosta's ordered his guards to keep me out of the place." He looked at Vella. "You're looking a little pecky this morning," he observed. "Did you drink too much last night?"

"I almost never get drunk any more," she told him.

"I knew it was a mistake to leave you here in Boktor," he said glumly. "Porenn's a corrupting influence. Did you get over your irritation with me yet?"

"I suppose so. It's not really your fault that you're stupid."

"Thanks." He looked her up and down appraisingly. "I like the dress," he told her. "It makes you look more like a woman, for a change."

"Did you ever have any doubts, Yarblek?" she asked him archly.

Adiss, the Chief Eunuch in the palace of Eternal Salmissra, received the summons early that morning and he approached the throne room with fear and trembling. The queen had been in a peculiar mood of late, and Adiss painfully remembered the fate of his predecessor. He entered the dimly lit throne room and prostrated himself before the dais.

"The Chief Eunuch approaches the throne," the adoring chorus intoned in unison. Even though he himself had been until recently a member of that chorus, Adiss found their mouthing of the obvious irritating.

The queen dozed on her divan, her mottled coils moving restlessly with the dry hiss of scales rubbing against each other. She opened her soulless serpent's eyes and looked at him, her forked tongue flickering. "Well?" she said peevishly in the dusty whisper that always chilled his blood.

"Y-you summoned me, Divine Salmissra," he faltered.

"I'm aware of that, you idiot. Do not irritate me, Adiss. I'm on the verge of going into molt, and that always makes me short-tempered. I asked you to find out what the Alorns are up to. I am waiting for your report."

"I haven't been able to find out very much, my Queen."

"That is not the answer I wanted to hear, Adiss," she told him dangerously. "Is it possible that the duties of your office are beyond your capabilities?"

Adiss began to tremble violently. "I-I've sent for Droblek, your Majesty—the Drasnian Port Authority here in Sthiss Tor. I thought he might be able to shed some light on the situation."

"Perhaps so." Her tone was distant, and she gazed at her reflection in the mirror. "Summon the Tolnedran Ambassador as well. Whatever the Alorns are doing in Cthol Murgos also involves Varana."

"Forgive me, Divine Salmissra," Adiss said, feeling a trifle confused, "but why should the activities of the Alorns and Tolnedrans concern us?"

She swung her head about slowly, her sinuous neck weaving in the air. "Are you a total incompetent, Adiss?" she asked him. "We may not like it, but Nyissa is a part of the world, and we must always know what our neighbors are doing—and why." She paused, her tongue nervously tasting the air. "There is a game of some kind afoot, and I want to find out exactly what it is before I decide whether or not to become involved in it." She paused again. "Have you ever found out what happened to that one-eyed fellow, Issus?"

"Yes, your Majesty. He was recruited by Drasnian intelligence. At last report, he was in Rak Urga with the Alorn negotiators."

"How very curious. I think this entire business is reaching the point where I must have detailed information—and very, very soon. Do not fail me, Adiss. Your position is not all that secure, you know. Now you may kiss me." She lowered her head, and he stumbled to the dais to touch his cringing lips to her cold forehead.

"Very well, Adiss," she said. "Leave now." And she went back to gazing at her reflection in the mirror.

King Nathel of Mishrak ac Thull was a slack-lipped, dull-eyed young man with lank, mud-colored hair and a profound lack of anything even remotely resembling intelligence. His royal robes were spotted and wrinkled, and his crown did not fit him. It rested atop his ears and quite often slid down over his eyes.

Agachak, the cadaverous Hierarch of Rak Urgo, could not stand the young King of the Thulls, but he forced himself to be civil to him during their current discussions. Civility was not one of Agachak's strong points. He much preferred peremptory commands backed up by threats of dreadful retribution for failure to comply, but a careful assessment of Nathel's personality had persuaded him that the young Thull would collapse on the spot if he were suddenly given any kind of threat or ultimatum. And so it was that Agachak was forced to rely on cajolery and wheedling instead.

"The prophecy clearly states, your Majesty," he tried

again, "that whichever king accompanies me to the place of the meeting will become Overking of all of Angarak."

"Does that mean I get Cthol Murgos and Gar og Nadrak, too?" Nathel asked, a faint glimmer coming into his uncomprehending eyes.

"Absolutely, your Majesty," Agachak assured him, "and Mallorea as well."

"Won't that make Kal Zakath unhappy with me? I wouldn't want him to feel that way. He had my father flogged once, did you know that? He was going to crucify him, but there weren't any trees around."

"Yes, I'd heard about that, but you don't have to worry. Zakath would have to genuflect to you."

"Zakath genuflect—to me?" Nathel laughed. It was a sound frighteningly devoid of thought.

"He would have no choice, your Majesty. If he were to refuse, the New God would blast him to atoms on the spot."

"What's an atom?"

Agachak ground his teeth. "A very small piece, your Majesty," he explained.

"I wouldn't mind making Urgit and Drosta bow to me," Nathel confessed, "but I don't know about Zakath. Urgit and Drosta think they're so smart. I'd like to take them down a peg or two. Zakath, though—I don't know about that." His eyes brightened again. "That means I'd get all the gold in Cthol Murgos and Gar og Nadrak, doesn't it? And I could make them dig it out of the ground for me, too." His crown slipped down over his eyes again, and he tilted his head back so that he could peer out from under its rim.

"And you'd get all the gold in Mallorea, too, and the jewels, and the silks and carpets—and they'd even give you your own elephant to ride."

"What's an elephant?"

"It's a very large animal, your Majesty."

"Bigger than a horse, even?"

"Much bigger. Besides, you'd also get Tolnedra and you know how much money they've got. You'd be the king of the world."

"Even bigger than an ox? I've seen some awful big oxes sometimes."

"Ten times as big."

Nathel smiled happily. "I bet that would make people sit up and take notice."

"Absolutely, your Majesty."

"What is it I have to do again?"

"You must go with me to the Place Which Is No More."

"That's the part I don't understand. How can we go there if it's not there any more?"

"The prophecy will reveal that to us in time, your Majesty."

"Oh. I see. Have you got any idea about where it is?"

"The clues I've been getting indicate that it's somewhere in Mallorea."

Nathel's face suddenly fell. "Now that's a real shame," he said petulantly.

"I don't quite—"

"I'd really like to go with you, Agachak. Truly I would—what with all the gold and carpets and silks and stuff—and making Urgit and Drosta and maybe even Zakath bow down to me and all, but I just can't."

"I don't understand. Why not?"

"I'm not allowed to leave home. My mother'd punish me something awful if I did. You know how that goes. I couldn't even think of going as far away as Mallorea."

"But you're the king."

"That doesn't change a thing. I still do what mother says. She tells everybody that I'm the best boy ever when it comes to that."

Agachak resisted a powerful urge to change this half-wit into a toad or perhaps a jellyfish. "Why don't I talk with your mother?" he suggested. "I'm sure I can persuade her to give you her permission."

"Why, that's a real, real good idea, Agachak. If mother says it's all right, I'll go with you quick as lightning."

"Good," Agachak said, turning.

"Oh, Agachak?" Nathel's voice sounded puzzled.

"Yes?"

"What's a prophecy?"

They had gathered at Vo Mandor, far from the watchful eyes of their kings, to discuss something that was very private and very urgent. It was also just a trifle on the disobedient side, and there is a very ugly word men use to describe those who disobey their kings.

Barak was there, and also Hettar, Mandorallen, and Lelldorin. Relg had just arrived from Maragor, and Barak's son Unrak sat on a high-backed bench by the window.

The Earl of Trellheim cleared his throat by way of calling them to order. They had gathered in the tower of Mandorallen's keep, and the golden autumn sunlight streamed in through the arched window. Barak was huge and resplendent in a green velvet doublet. His red beard was combed, and his hair was braided. "All right," he rumbled, "let's get started. Mandorallen, are you sure the stairway leading up here is guarded? I wouldn't want anybody to overhear us."

"Of a certainty, my Lord of Trellheim," the great knight replied earnestly. "I vouchsafe it upon my life to thee." Mandorallen wore mail and his silver-trimmed blue surcoat.

"A simple yes would have been enough, Mandorallen." Barak sighed. "Now," he continued briskly, "we've been forbidden to ride along with Garion and the others, right?"

"That's what Cyradis said at Rheon," Hettar replied softly. He wore his usual black horsehide, and his scalplock was caught in a silver ring. He lounged in a chair with his long legs thrust far out in front of him.

"All right, then," Barak continued. "We can't go with them, *but* there's nothing to stop us from going to Mallorea on business of our own, is there?"

"What kind of business?" Lelldorin asked blankly.

"We'll think of something. I've got a ship. We'll run on down to Tol Honeth and load her with a cargo of some kind. Then we'll go to Mallorea and do some trading."

"How do you plan to get the *Seabird* across to the Sea of the East?" Hettar asked. "That could be a long portage, don't you think?"

Barak winked broadly. "I've got a map," he said. "We can sail around the southern end of Cthol Murgos and right on into the eastern sea. From there to Mallorea is nothing at all."

"I thought the Murgos were very secretive about maps of their coastline," Lelldorin said, a frown creasing his open young face.

"They are," Barak grinned, "but Javelin's been in Rak Urga and he managed to steal one."

"How did you get it away from Javelin?" Hettar asked. "He's even more secretive than the Murgos."

"He sailed back to Boktor aboard Greldik's ship. Javelin's not a good sailor, so he wasn't feeling very well. Greldik pinched the map and had his cartographer make a copy. Javelin never even knew he'd been robbed."

"Thy plan is excellent, my Lord," Mandorallen said gravely, "but methinks I detect a flaw."

"Oh?"

"As all the world knows, Mallorea is a vast continent, thousands of leagues across and even more thousands from the south to the polar ice of the far north. It could well take us our lifetimes to locate our friends, for I perceive that to be the thrust of thy proposal."

Barak slyly laid one finger aside his nose. "I was just coming to that," he said. "When we were in Boktor, I got Yarblek drunk. He's shrewd enough when he's sober, but once you get a half keg of ale into him, he gets talkative. I asked him a few questions about the operation of the business he and Silk are running in Mallorea, and I got some very useful answers. It seems that the two of them have offices in every major city in Mallorea, and those offices keep in constant touch with each other. No matter what else he's doing, Silk's going to keep an eye on his business interests. Every time he gets near one of those offices, he'll find some excuse to stop by to see how many millions he's made in the past week."

"That's Silk, all right," Hettar agreed.

"All we have to do is drop anchor in some Mallorean seaport and look up the little thief's office. His people will know approximately where he is, and where Silk is, you're going to find the others."

"My Lord," Mandorallen apologized, "I have wronged thee. Canst thou forgive me for underestimating thy shrewdness?"

"Perfectly all right, Mandorallen," Barak replied magnanimously.

"But," Lelldorin protested, "we're still forbidden to join Garion and the others."

"Truly," Mandorallen agreed. "We may not approach them lest we doom their quest to failure."

"I think I've worked that part out, too," the big man said. "We can't ride along with them, but Cyradis didn't say anything about how far we have to stay away from them, did she? All we're going to be doing is minding our own business—a league or so away—or maybe a mile. We'll be close enough so that if they get into any kind of trouble, we'll be able to lend a hand and then be on our way again. There's nothing wrong with that, is there?"

Mandorallen's face came suddenly alight. "'Tis a duty, my Lord," he exclaimed, "a moral obligation. The Gods look with great disfavor upon those who fail to come to the aid of travelers in peril."

"Somehow I knew you'd see it that way," Barak said, slapping his friend on the shoulder with one huge hand.

"Sophistry," Relg said with a note of finality in his harsh voice. The Ulgo zealot now wore a tunic that looked very much like the one Durnik customarily wore. His once-pale skin was now sun-browned, and he no longer wore a cloth across his eyes. The years of working out of doors near the house he had built for Taiba and their horde of children had gradually accustomed his skin and eyes to sunlight.

"What do you mean, sophistry?" Barak protested.

"Just what I said, Barak. The Gods look at our intent, not our clever excuses. You want to go to Mallorea to aid Belgarion—we all do—but don't try to fool the Gods with these trumped-up stories."

They all stared at the zealot helplessly.

"But it was such a good plan," Barak said plaintively.

"Very good," Relg agreed, "but it's disobedient, and disobedience of the Gods—and of prophecy—is sin."

"Sin again, Relg?" Barak said in disgust. "I thought you'd gotten over that."

"Not entirely, no."

Barak's son Unrak, who at fourteen was already as big as a grown man, rose to his feet. He wore a mail shirt and had a sword belted at his side. His hair was flaming red, and his downy beard had already begun to cover his cheeks. "Let's see if I've got this right," he said. Unrak's voice no longer cracked and warbled, but had settled into a resonant baritone. "We have to obey the prophecy, is that it?"

"To the letter," Relg said firmly.

"Then I *have* to go to Mallorea," Unrak said.

"That went by a little fast," his father said to him.

"It's not really all that complicated, father. I'm the hereditary protector of the heir to the Rivan Throne, aren't I?"

"He's got a point there," Hettar said. "Go ahead, Unrak. Tell us what you've got in mind."

"Well," the young man said, blushing slightly under the scrutiny of his elders, "if Prince Geran's in Mallorea and in danger, I have to go there. The prophecy says so. Now, I don't know where he is, so I'm going to have to follow King Belgarion until he finds his son so that I can protect him."

Barak grinned broadly at his son.

"But," Unrak added, "I'm a little inexperienced at this protection business, so I might need a little guidance. Do you suppose, father, that I might be able to persuade you and your friends to come with me? Just to keep me from making any mistakes, you understand."

Hettar rose and shook Barak's hand. "Congratulations," he said simply.

"Well, Relg," Barak said, "does that satisfy your sense of propriety?"

Relg considered it. "Why yes," he said, "as a matter of fact, I think it does." Then he grinned the first grin Barak had ever seen on his harsh face. "When do we leave?" he asked.

His Imperial Majesty, Kal Zakath of Mallorea, stood at a window in a high tower in Maga Renn, looking out at the broad expanse of the great River Magan. A huge armada of river craft of all sizes dotted the surface of the river upstream of the city and moved down in orderly progression to the wharves where the imperial regiments waited to embark.

"Have you had any further news?" the Emperor asked.

"Things are a bit chaotic down there, your Imperial Majesty," Brador, the brown-robed Chief of the Bureau of Internal Affairs, reported, "but it appears that the major confrontation between Urvon and Zandramas is going to take place in Peldane. Urvon has been moving down from the north, and Zandramas annexed Peldane last month to put a buffer between him and Darshiva. She's been rushing her forces into Peldane to meet him."

"What's your assessment, Atesca?" Zakath asked.

General Atesca rose and went to the map hanging on the wall. He studied it for a moment, then stabbed one blunt finger at it. "Here, your Majesty," he said, "the town of Ferra. We move down in force and occupy that place. It's a logical forward base of operations. The River Magan is about fifteen miles wide at that point, and it shouldn't be too difficult to interdict any further movement across it from Darshiva. That will eliminate Zandramas' reinforcements. Urvon will have numerical superiority when they meet, and he'll crush her army. He'll take casualties, though. Both sides are fanatics, and they'll fight to the death. After he wipes out Zandramas' army, he'll stop to lick his wounds. That's when we should hit him. He'll be weakened, and his troops will be exhausted. Ours will be fresh. The outcome ought to be fairly predictable. Then we can cross the Magan and mop up in Darshiva."

"Excellent, Atesca," Zakath said, a faint smile touching his cold lips. "There's a certain ironic charm to your plan. First we have Urvon eliminate Zandramas for us, then we eliminate him. I like the idea of having the Disciple of Torak do my dirty work for me."

"With your Majesty's permission, I'd like to lead the forward elements and oversee the occupation of Ferra," the general said. "Zandramas will almost have to counterattack, since we'll have cut her army in two. We'll need to fortify the town. I'll also need to put out patrols on the river to keep her from trying to slip her troops into Peldane around our flanks. It's a fairly crucial part of the operation, and I'd like to supervise it myself."

"By all means, Atesca," Zakath gave his consent. "I wouldn't really trust anyone else to do it anyway."

Atesca bowed. "Your Majesty is very kind," he said.

"If I may, your Imperial Majesty," Brador said, "we're getting some disturbing reports from Cthol Murgos. Our agents there report that there are some fairly serious negotiations going on between Urgit and the Alorns."

"The Murgos and the Alorns?" Zakath asked incredulously. "They've hated each other for eons."

"Perhaps they've found a common cause," Brador suggested delicately.

"Me, you mean?"

"It does seem logical, your Majesty."

"We have to put a stop to that. I think we'll have to attack the Alorns. Give them something close to home to worry about so they won't have time for any adventures in Cthol Murgos."

Atesca cleared his throat. "May I speak bluntly, your Majesty?" he asked.

"I've never heard you speak any other way, Atesca. What's on your mind?"

"Only an idiot tries to fight a war on two fronts, and only a madman tries to fight one on three. You have this war here in Peldane, another in Cthol Murgos, and now you're contemplating a third in Aloria. I advise against it in the strongest possible terms."

Zakath smiled wryly. "You're a brave man, Atesca," he said. "I can't recall the last time somebody called me an idiot and a madman in the same breath."

"I trust your Majesty will forgive my candor, but that's my honest opinion of the matter."

"That's all right, Atesca." Zakath waved one hand as if brushing it aside. "You're here to advise me, not to flatter me, and your plain language definitely got my attention. Very well, we'll hold off on going to war with the Alorns until we finish up here. I'll go as far as idiocy; lunacy is something else. The world had enough of that with Taur Urgas." He began to pace up and down. "Curse you, Belgarion!" he burst out suddenly. "What *are* you up to?"

"Uh—your Majesty," Brador interposed diffidently, "Belgarion isn't in the West. He was seen just last week in Melcena."

"What's he doing in Melcena?"

"We weren't able to determine that, your Majesty. It's

226

fairly certain that he left the islands, however. We think that he's somewhere in this general vicinity."

"Adding to the confusion, no doubt. Keep an eye out for him, Atesca. I really want to have a long talk with that young man. He stalks through the world like a natural disaster."

"I'll make a point of trying to locate him for your Majesty," Atesca replied. "Now, with your Majesty's permission, I'd like to go supervise the loading of the troops."

"How long is it going to take you to get to Ferra?"

"Perhaps three or four days, your Majesty. I'll put the troops to manning the oars."

"They won't like that."

"They don't have to like it, your Majesty."

"All right, go ahead. I'll be along a few days behind you."

Atesca saluted and turned to go.

"Oh, by the way, Atesca," Zakath said as an afterthought, "why don't you take a kitten on your way out?" He pointed at a number of prowling, half-grown cats on the far side of the room. His own mackerel-striped tabby was perched high on the mantlepiece with a slightly harried expression on her face.

"Ah . . ." Atesca hesitated. "I'm overwhelmed with gratitude, your Majesty, but cat fur makes my eyes swell shut, and I think I'll need my eyes during the next few weeks."

Zakath sighed. "I understand, Atesca," he said. "That will be all."

The general bowed and left the room.

Zakath considered it. "Well," he said, "if he won't take a kitten, I suppose we'll have to give him a field marshal's baton instead—but *only* if this campaign of his is successful, you understand."

"Perfectly, your Majesty," Brador murmured.

The coronation of the Archduke Otrath as Emperor of Mallorea went off quite smoothly. Otrath, of course, was an unmitigated ass and he had to be led by the hand through the ceremony. When it was over, Zandramas installed him on an ornate throne in the palace at Hemil and left instructions that he be flattered and fawned over. Then she quietly left.

Prince Geran was in the simple room Zandramas had chosen for herself in the temple. A middle-aged Grolim priestess had been watching over him. "He's been very good this morning, Holy Zandramas," the priestess advised.

"Good, bad—what difference does it make?" Zandramas shrugged. "You can go now."

"Yes, Holy Priestess." The middle-aged woman genuflected and left the room.

Prince Geran looked at Zandramas with a grave expression on his little face.

"You're quiet this morning, your Highness," Zandramas said ironically.

The child's expression did not change. Though they had been together for over a year, Geran had never shown the slightest sign of affection for her and, perhaps even more disturbing, he had never shown fear either. He held up one of his toys. "Ball," he said.

"Yes," she replied, "I suppose so." Then, perhaps because his penetrating gaze disturbed her, she crossed the room to stand before her mirror. She pushed back her hood and gazed intently at her reflection. It had not touched her face yet. That was something at least. She looked with distaste at the whirling, sparkling lights beneath the skin of her hands. Then, quite deliberately, she opened the front of her robe and gazed at her nude reflection. It was spreading, there could be no question about that. Her breasts and belly were also underlaid with those selfsame whirling points of light.

Geran had come silently up to stand beside her. "Stars," he said, pointing at the mirror.

"Just go play, Geran," the Child of Dark told him, closing her robe.

CHAPTER THIRTEEN

As they rode west that afternoon, they could see a heavy, dark purple cloudbank building up ahead of them, rising higher and higher and blotting out the blue of the sky. Finally Durnik rode forward. "Toth says that we'd better find shelter," he told Belgarath. "These spring storms in this part of the world are savage."

Belgarath shrugged. "I've been rained on before."

"He says that the storm won't last long," Durnik said, "but it's going to be very intense. It should blow through by morning. I really think we should listen to him, Belgarath. It's not only the rain and wind. He says that there's usually hail as well, and the hailstones can be as big as apples."

Belgarath peered toward the blue-black clouds towering up into the western sky with lightning bolts staggering down from their centers. "All right," he decided. "We wouldn't be able to go much farther today anyway. Does he know of any shelter nearby?"

"There's a farm village a league or so ahead," Durnik told him. "If it's like the others we've passed, there won't be anybody there. We ought to be able to find a house with enough roof left to keep the hailstones off our heads."

"Let's aim for there then. That storm's moving fast. I'll call in Beldin and have him take a look." He lifted his face, and Garion could feel his thought reaching out.

They rode at a gallop into a mounting wind that whipped their cloaks about them and carried with it an unpleasant chill and vagrant spatters of cold rain.

When they crested the hill above the deserted village, they could see the storm front advancing like a wall across the open plain.

"It's going to be close," Belgarath shouted above the wind. "Let's make a run for it."

They plunged down the hill through wildly tossing grass and then across a broad belt of plowed ground that encircled the village. The place was walled, but the gate was off its hinges, and many houses showed signs of recent fires. They clattered along a rubble-littered street with the wind screaming at them. Garion heard a loud pop. Then another. Then several more in a growing staccato. "Here comes the hail!" he shouted.

Velvet suddenly cried out and clutched at her shoulder. Silk, almost without thinking, it seemed, pulled his horse in beside hers and flipped his cloak over her, tenting it protectively with his arm.

Beldin stood in the dooryard of a relatively intact house. "In here!" he called urgently. "The stable doors are open! Get the horses inside!"

They swung out of their saddles and quickly led their mounts into a cavernlike stable. Then they pushed the doors shut and dashed across the yard to the house.

"Did you check the village for people?" Belgarath asked the hunchbacked sorcerer as they entered.

"There's nobody here," Beldin told him, "unless there's another bureaucrat hiding in a cellar somewhere."

The banging sound outside grew louder until it became a steady roar. Garion looked out the door. Great chunks of ice were streaking out of the sky and smashing themselves to bits on the cobblestones. The chill grew more intense moment by moment. "I think we made it just in time," he said.

"Close the door, Garion," Polgara told him, "and let's get a fire going."

The room into which they had come showed signs of a hasty departure. The table and the chairs had been overturned, and there were broken dishes on the floor. Durnik looked around and picked up a stub of candle from the corner. He righted the table, set the candle on a piece of broken plate, and reached for his flint, steel, and tinder.

Toth went to the window and opened it. Then he reached out, pulled the shutters closed, and latched them.

Durnik's candle guttered a bit, then its flame grew steady, casting a golden glow through the room. The smith went to the fireplace. Despite the litter on the floor and the disarray of the furniture, the room was pleasant. The walls had been whitewashed, and the overhead beams were dark and had been neatly adzed square. The fireplace was large and it had an arched opening. A number of pothooks jutted from its back wall, and a pile of firewood was neatly stacked beside it. It was a friendly kind of place.

"All right, gentlemen," Polgara said to them. "Let's not just stand there. The furniture needs to be put right, and the floor needs to be swept. We'll need more candles, and I'll want to check the sleeping quarters."

231

The fire Durnik had built was catching hold. He gave it a critical look; satisfied, he rose to his feet. "I'd better see to the horses," he said. "Do you want the packs in here, Pol?"

"Just the food and the cooking things for now, dear. But don't you think you should wait until the hail lets up?"

"There's a sort of covered walkway along the side of the house," he replied. "I'd guess that the people who built the place knew about this sort of weather." He went out with Toth and Eriond close behind him.

Garion crossed the room to where Velvet sat on a rude bench with her hand laid protectively over her right shoulder. Her face was pale, and her brow was dewed with sweat.

"Are you all right?" he asked her.

"It surprised me, that's all," she replied. "It's nice of you to ask, though."

"Nice my foot!" He was suddenly angry. "You're like a sister to me, Liselle, and if you let yourself get hurt, I'll take it as a personal insult."

"Yes, your Majesty," she said, her smile suddenly lighting up the room.

"Don't play with me, Velvet. Don't try to be brave. If you're hurt, say so."

"It's only a little bruise, Belgarion," she protested. Her large brown eyes conveyed a world of sincerity, mostly feigned.

"I'll spank you," he threatened.

"Now, that's an interesting notion." She laughed.

He didn't even think about it. He simply leaned forward and kissed her on the forehead.

She looked a little surprised. "Why, your majesty," she said in mock alarm. "What if Ce'Nedra had seen you do that?"

"Ce'Nedra can cope with it. She loves you as much as I do. I'll have Aunt Pol look at that shoulder."

"It's really fine, Belgarion."

"Do you want to argue about that with Aunt Pol?"

She thought about it. "No," she said, "I don't really think so. Why don't you send Kheldar over to hold my hand?"

"Anything else?"

"You could kiss me again, if you'd like."

With a certain clinical detachment, Polgara opened the front of Velvet's gray dress and carefully examined the large purple bruise on the blond girl's shoulder. Velvet blushed and modestly covered her more salient features.

"I don't think anything's broken," Polgara said, gently probing the bruised shoulder. "It's going to be very painful, though."

"I noticed that almost immediately," Velvet said, wincing.

"All right, Sadi," Polgara said briskly, "I need a good analgesic. What would you suggest?"

"I have oret, Lady Polgara," the eunuch answered.

She thought about it. "No," she said. "Oret would incapacitate her for the next two days. Do you have any miseth?"

He looked a bit startled. "Lady Polgara," he protested. "Miseth is an excellent painkiller, but—" He looked at the suffering Velvet. "There are those side effects, you know."

"We can control her if necessary."

"What side effects?" Silk demanded, hovering protectively over the blond girl.

"It tends to rouse a certain—ah, shall we say—ardor," Sadi replied delicately. "In Nyissa it's widely used for that purpose."

"Oh," Silk said, flushing slightly.

"One drop," Polgara said. "No. Make that two."

"*Two?*" Sadi exclaimed.

"I want it to last until the pain subsides."

"Two drops will do that, all right," Sadi said, "but you'll have to confine her until it wears off."

"I'll keep her asleep if I need to."

Dubiously, Sadi opened his red case and removed a vial of

deep purple liquid. "This is against my better judgment, Lady Polgara," he said.

"Trust me."

"It always makes me nervous when somebody says that," Belgarath said to Beldin.

"A lot of things make you nervous. We can't go anywhere until the girl's better. Pol knows what she's doing."

"Maybe," Belgarath replied.

Sadi carefully measured two drops of the purple medication into a cup of water and stirred the mixture with his finger. Then he rather carefully dried his hand on a piece of cloth. He handed the cup to Velvet. "Drink it slowly," he instructed. "You'll begin to feel very strange almost immediately."

"Strange?" she asked suspiciously.

"We can talk about it later. All you need to know now is that it's going to make the pain go away."

Velvet sipped at the cup. "It doesn't taste bad," she observed.

"Of course not," the eunuch replied, "and you'll find that it tastes better and better as you get toward the bottom of the cup."

Velvet continued to take small sips of the liquid. Her face grew flushed. "My," she said, "isn't it warm in here all of a sudden?"

Silk sat down on the bench beside her. "Is it helping at all?" he asked.

"Hmm?"

"How's the shoulder?"

"Did you see my bruise, Kheldar?" She pulled her dress open to show it to him. She showed him—and everyone else in the room—other things as well. "Oops," she said absently, not bothering to cover herself.

"I think you'd better take those steps you mentioned, Lady

Polgara," Sadi said. "The situation is likely to get out of hand any minute now."

Polgara nodded and put one hand briefly on Velvet's brow. Garion felt a light surge.

"Suddenly I feel so very drowsy," Velvet said. "Is the medicine doing that?"

"In a manner of speaking," Polgara replied.

Velvet's head drooped forward, and she laid it on Silk's shoulder.

"Bring her along, Silk," Polgara told the little man. "Let's find a bed for her."

Silk picked the sleeping girl up and carried her from the room with Polgara close beside him.

"Does that stuff always have that effect?" Ce'Nedra asked Sadi.

"Miseth? Oh yes. It could arouse a stick."

"And does it work on men, too?"

"Gender makes no difference, your Majesty."

"How very interesting." She gave Garion a sly, sidelong glance. "Don't lose that little bottle, Sadi," she said.

"Never mind," Garion told her.

It took them perhaps a quarter of an hour to tidy up the room. Polgara was smiling when she and Silk returned. "She'll sleep now," she said. "I looked into the other rooms, too. The woman of the house appears to have been a very neat sort of person," she said. "This is the only room that was seriously disturbed when the family left." She set her candle down and smoothed the front of her gray dress with a satisfied expression. "The house will do very nicely, uncle," she told Beldin.

"I'm glad you approve," he replied. He was sprawled on a high-backed bench by the window and was carefully retying the thong that held his ragged left sleeve in place.

"How far are we from the river?" Belgarath asked him.

"It's still a ways—a good day's hard riding at least. I can't

235

be much more exact than that. When the wind came up, it almost blew off my feathers."

"Is the country on up ahead still empty?"

"It's hard to be sure. I was up fairly high, and if there are any people out there, they'd all have taken cover from this storm."

"We'll have to have a look in the morning." Belgarath leaned back in his chair and stretched his feet out toward the hearth. "That fire was a good idea," he said. "There's a definite chill in the air."

"That happens sometimes when you pile three or four inches of ice on the ground," Beldin told him. The ugly little man squinted thoughtfully. "If this sort of storm is a regular afternoon occurrence around here, we'll need to cross the Magan during the morning hours," he noted. "Getting caught in a hailstorm in an open boat isn't my idea of fun."

"Now you stop that!" Sadi said sharply to Zith's earthenware bottle.

"What's the trouble?" Ce'Nedra asked.

"She was making a funny little noise," Sadi replied. "I wanted to see if she was all right, and she hissed at me."

"She does that every now and then, doesn't she?"

"This was a bit different. She was actually warning me to stay away from her."

"Could she be ill?"

"I wouldn't think so. She's a fairly young snake, and I've been very careful about what I feed her."

"Perhaps she needs a tonic." Ce'Nedra looked questioningly at Polgara.

Polgara laughed helplessly. "I'm sorry, Ce'Nedra," she said, "but I have no experience with the illnesses of reptiles."

"Do you suppose we could talk about something else?" Silk asked plaintively. "Zith is a nice enough little animal, I suppose, but she's still a snake."

Ce'Nedra whirled on him, her eyes suddenly flashing.

"How can you say that?" she snapped angrily. "She's saved all our lives twice—once in Rak Urga when she nipped that Grolim, Sorchak, and again at Ashaba when she bit Harakan. Without her, we wouldn't be here. You might show at least a little bit of gratitude."

"Well . . ." he said a little uncertainly. "You could be right, I suppose, but hang it all, Ce'Nedra, I can't abide snakes."

"I don't even think of her as a snake."

"Ce'Nedra," he said patiently, "she's long and skinny, she wriggles, she doesn't have any arms or legs, and she's poisonous. By definition, she's a snake."

"You're prejudiced," she accused.

"Well—yes, I suppose you could say that."

"I'm bitterly disappointed in you, Prince Kheldar. She's a sweet, loving, brave little creature, and you're insulting her."

He looked at her for a moment, then rose to his feet and bowed floridly to the earthenware bottle. "I'm dreadfully sorry, dear Zith," he apologized. "I can't think what came over me. Can you possibly find it in your cold little green heart to forgive me?"

Zith hissed at him, a hiss ending in a curious grunt.

"She says to leave her alone," Sadi told him.

"Can you really understand what she's saying?"

"In a general sort of way, yes. Snakes have a very limited vocabulary, so it's not all that difficult to pick up a few phrases here and there." The eunuch frowned. "She's been swearing a great deal lately, though, and that's not like her. She's usually a very ladylike little snake."

"I can't believe I'm actually involved in this conversation," Silk said, shaking his head and going off down the hall toward the back of the house.

Durnik returned with Toth and Eriond. They were carrying the packs containing Polgara's utensils and the food. Polgara looked critically at the fireplace and its facilities. "We've been eating some rather sketchy meals lately," she noted. "We have a fairly adequate kitchen here, so why don't we take advantage of it?" She opened the food pack and rummaged through it. "I wish I had something besides travel rations to work with," she said half to herself.

"There's a hen roost out back, Pol," Beldin told her helpfully.

She smiled at him. "Durnik, dear," she said in an almost dreamy tone of voice.

"I'll see to it at once, Pol. Three, maybe?"

"Make it four. Then we'll be able to carry some cold chicken with us when we leave. Ce'Nedra, go with him and gather up all the eggs you can find."

Ce'Nedra stared at her in astonishment. "I've never gathered eggs before, Lady Polgara," she protested.

"It's not hard, dear. Just be careful not to break them, that's all."

"But—"

"I thought I'd make a cheese omelette for breakfast."

Ce'Nedra's eyes brightened. "I'll get a basket," she said quickly.

"Splendid idea, dear. Uncle, are there any other interesting things about this place?"

"There's a brewhouse at the back of the building." he shrugged. "I didn't have time to look into it."

Belgarath rose to his feet. "Why don't we do that right now?" he suggested.

"People in farm villages don't make very good beer, Belgarath."

"Maybe this one's an exception. We'll never know until we try it, will we?"

"You've got a point there."

The two old sorcerers went off toward the back of the house while Eriond piled more wood on the fire.

Ce'Nedra returned, frowning and a little angry. "They

won't give me their eggs, Lady Polgara," she complained. "They're sitting on them."

"You have to reach under them and take the eggs, dear."

"Won't that make them angry?"

"Are you afraid of a chicken?"

The little queen's eyes hardened, and she left the room purposefully.

A root cellar behind the house yielded a store of vegetables, and Belgarath and Beldin brought a cask of beer in from the brewhouse. While the chickens were roasting, Polgara rummaged through the canisters and bins in the kitchen. She found flour and a number of other staples, and she rolled up her sleeves in a businesslike way, mixed up a large batch of dough, and began to knead it on a well-scrubbed cutting board near the fire. "We can have some biscuits tonight, I think," she said, "and I'll bake some fresh bread in the morning."

The supper was the best Garion had eaten in months. There had been banquets and adequate meals in inns and the like, but there was a certain indefinable quality to his Aunt Pol's cooking that no other cook in the world could hope to match. After he had eaten more perhaps than was really good for him, he pushed his plate away with a sigh and leaned back in his chair.

"I'm glad you decided to leave some for the rest of us," Ce'Nedra said in a slightly snippy tone.

"Are you cross with me for some reason?" he asked her.

"No, I suppose not, Garion. I'm just a little irritated, that's all."

"Why?"

"A chicken bit me." She pointed at the remains of a roasted hen lying on a large platter. "That one," she added. She reached out, wrenched a drumstick off the chicken and bit into it rather savagely with her small white teeth. "There," she said in a vengeful tone. "How do you like it?"

Garion knew his wife, so he knew better than to laugh.

After supper, they all lingered at the table in a kind of happy contentment as the storm outside abated.

Then there was a light, almost diffident rap on the door. Garion sprang to his feet, reaching over his shoulder for his sword.

"I don't mean to disturb you," a querulous old voice came from the other side of the door. "I just wanted to be sure you have everything you need."

Belgarath rose from his chair, went to the door, and opened it.

"Holy Belgarath," the man outside said with a bow of the profoundest respect. He was very old, with snowy white hair and a thin, lined face.

He was also a Grolim.

Belgarath stared at him warily. "You know me?" he asked.

"Of course. I know you all. I've been waiting for you. May I come in?"

Wordlessly, Belgarath stepped aside for him, and the aged Grolim tottered into the room, aided by a twisted cane. He bowed to Polgara. "Lady Polgara," he murmured. Then he turned to Garion. "Your Majesty," he said, "may I beg your forgiveness?"

"Why?" Garion replied. "You've never done anything to me."

"Yes I have, your Majesty. When I heard about what had happened in the City of Endless Night, I hated you. Can you forgive that?"

"There's nothing to forgive. It was only natural for you to feel that way. You've had a change of heart, I take it?"

"It was changed for me, King Belgarion. The New God of Angarak will be a kindlier, gentler God than was Torak. I live now only to serve that God and I abide against the day of his coming."

"Sit down, my friend," Belgarath told him. "I assume you've had a religious experience of some kind?"

The old Grolim sank into a chair with a beatific smile on his lined face. "My heart has been touched, Holy Belgarath," he said simply. "I had devoted all of my life to the service of Torak in the temple in this village. I grieved more than you can know when I learned of His death, for I served Him without question. Now I have removed His likeness from the Temple wall and I decorate the altar with flowers instead of the blood of sacrificial victims. Bitterly I repent the times when I myself held the knife during the rite of sacrifice."

"And what was it that so changed you?" Polgara asked him.

"It was a voice that spoke to me in the silences of my soul, Lady Polgara, a voice that filled me with such joy that it seemed that all the world was bathed in light."

"And what did the voice say to you?"

The old priest reached inside his black robe and withdrew a parchment sheet. "I took great care to inscribe the words exactly as the voice spoke them to me," he said, "for such was the instruction I received. A man may misconstrue what he is told, or change it if it is not to his liking or if he fails to understand." He smiled gently. "What I have written is for the benefit of others, though, for the words are engraved upon my heart far more indelibly than upon this sheet." He lifted the parchment and read from it in a quavering voice. "'Behold:'" he read, "'In the days which shall follow the meeting of the Child of Light and the Child of Dark in the City of Endless Night shall a great despair fall over the Priests of the Dark God, for He shall have been laid low and shall come no more among His people. But lift up thine heart, for thy despair is but the night which shall be banished by the rising of a new sun. For verily I say to thee, Angarak shall have a new birth with the coming of her true God—He who was purposed to lead her since the Beginning of Days. For lo, the Dark God was born out of nothingness in the instant of the EVENT which divided all creation, and it was not He who was foreordained to guide and protect Angarak. In the last meeting of the Child of Dark and the Child of Light shall the *true* God of Angarak be revealed, and ye shall render up unto Him your hearts and your devotion.

"'And the course which Angarak shall follow shall be determined by the CHOICE, and once the CHOICE is made, it may not be unmade and shall prevail eternally for good or for ill. For harken, *two* shall stand in the Place Which Is No More, but only one shall be chosen. And the Child of Light and the Child of Dark shall surrender up the burden of the spirits which guide them to the two who shall stand in expectation of the CHOICE. And should the CHOICE fall to the one hand, the world shall be drowned in darkness, but should it fall to the other hand, shall all be bathed in light, and that which was ordained since before the beginning of time shall come to pass.

"'Abide in hope, therefore, and treat thy fellow creatures kindly and with love, for this is pleasing to the true God, and should He prevail and be chosen, He shall bless thee and shall lay but a gentle yoke upon thee.'" The old Grolim lowered the sheet and bowed his head prayerfully. "Thus spoke the voice which filled my heart with joy and banished my despair," he said simply.

"We're grateful that you shared this with us," Belgarath told him. "Might we offer you something to eat?"

The Grolim shook his head. "I do not eat meat anymore," he said. "I would not offend my God. I have cast away my dagger and will shed no more blood for all the days of my life." He rose to his feet. "I will leave you now," he said. "I came but to reveal to you the words the voice spoke to me, and to assure you that one at least in all of Angarak shall pray for your success."

"We thank you," Belgarath said sincerely. He went to the door and held it open for the gentle old man.

"That was fairly specific, wasn't it?" Beldin said after the

Grolim had left. "It's the first time I heard a prophecy that got straight to the point."

"You mean to say that he's really a prophet?" Silk asked.

"Of course he is. It's an almost classic case. He had all the symptoms—the ecstasy, the radical change of personality, all of it."

"There's something wrong here, though," Belgarath said, frowning. "I've spent eons reading prophecies, and what he said didn't have the same tone as any that I've ever come across—either ours or the others." He looked at Garion. "Can you get in touch with your friend?" he asked. "I need to talk with him."

"I can try," Garion replied. "He doesn't always come when I call, though."

"See if you can reach him. Tell him that it's important."

"I'll see what I can do, Grandfather." Garion sat down and closed his eyes. *"Are you in there?"* he asked.

"Please don't shout, Garion," the voice responded in a pained tone. *"It hurts my ears."*

"Sorry," Garion apologized. *"I didn't realize I was talking so loud. Grandfather wants to talk with you."*

"All right. Open your eyes, Garion. I can't see when they're closed."

As had happened occasionally in the past, Garion felt himself shunted off into some quiet corner of his mind, and the dry voice took over. *"All right, Belgarath,"* it said through Garion's lips. *"What is it this time?"*

"I've got a couple of questions," the old man replied.

"There's nothing new about that. You've always got questions."

"Did you hear what the Grolim said?"

"Naturally."

"Was it you? I mean, were you the voice that came to him?"

"No, as a matter of fact, I wasn't."

"Then it was the other spirit?"

"No. It wasn't him either."

243

"Then who was it?"

"Sometimes I can't believe that Aldur chose you as his first disciple. Are your brains packed in wool?"

"You don't have to be insulting." Belgarath sounded a bit injured, but Beldin laughed an ugly, cackling kind of laugh.

"All right," the voice sighed, *"I'll go through it carefully. Try not to miss too much. My counterpart and I came into existence when Destiny was divided. Have you got that part?"*

"I knew that already."

"And you even managed to remember it? Amazing."

"Thanks," Belgarath said in a flat tone.

"I'm working with Garion's vocabulary. He's a peasant, so he can be a little blunt sometimes. Now, doesn't it seem logical that when Destiny is reunited, there should be a new *voice? My counterpart and I will have served our purpose, so there won't be any further need for us. Millions of years of enmity between us have warped our perceptions a bit."*

Belgarath looked startled at that.

"Think, old man," the voice told him. *"I'm not suited to deal with a united universe. I've got too many old grudges. The new voice can start out fresh without any preconceptions. It's better that way, believe me."*

"I think I'm going to miss you."

"Don't get sentimental on me, Belgarath. I don't think I could bear that."

"Wait a minute. This new voice will come into existence after the meeting, right?"

"At the instant of the meeting, actually."

"Then how did it speak to the old Grolim, if it's not in existence yet?"

"Time doesn't really mean that much to us, Belgarath. We can move backward and forward in it without any particular difficulty."

"You mean the voice was speaking to him from the future?"

"Obviously." Garion felt a faint, ironic smile cross his lips. *"How do you know I'm not speaking to you from the past?"*

Belgarath blinked.

"Now we've got you," Beldin said triumphantly. *"We're going to win, aren't we?"*

"We can hope so, but there's no guarantee."

"The voice that spoke to the Grolim represents a kindlier God, doesn't it?"

"Yes."

"If the Child of Dark wins, the New God isn't going to be very kindly, is he?"

"No."

"Then the simple fact that the voice came to him from out of the future—after the choice—indicates that the Child of Light is going to win, doesn't it?"

The Voice sighed. *"Why do you always have to complicate things, Beldin? The Voice that spoke to the Grolim is the* possibility *of the new spirit. It's simply reaching back in time to make certain preparations so that things will be ready in the eventuality that it comes out on top. The Choice still hasn't been made yet, you know."*

"Even the possibility *of existence has that kind of power?"*

"Possibility has enormous power, Beldin—sometimes even more than actuality."

"And the possibility of the other spirit could be making its own preparations as well, couldn't it?"

"I wouldn't be at all surprised. You have an enormous grasp of the obvious."

"Then we're right back where we started from. We're still going to have two spirits wrestling across time and the universe for dominance."

"No. The Choice will eliminate one of the possibilities once and for all."

"I don't understand," Beldin confessed.

"I didn't think you would."

"What preparations was this new voice making?" Polgara asked suddenly.

"The Grolim who came to you here will be the prophet and the

first Disciple of the New God—assuming that the Child of Light is chosen, of course."

"A Grolim?"

"The decision wasn't mine to make. The new God will be a God of Angarak, though, so it does make sense, I suppose."

"That might take a bit of getting adjusted to."

"You have as many prejudices as I do, Polgara," the Voice laughed, "but I think in the long run, you're more adaptable—and certainly more so than these two stubborn old men are. You'll come to accept it in time. Now, if there aren't any more questions, I still have some things to attend to—in another part of time."

And then the voice was gone.

CHAPTER FOURTEEN

The sun was just going down, staining the purple cloudbank to the west with a jaundiced yellow as it broke through an opening in the approaching storm. Garion crested a long hill and looked down into the next valley. There was a complex of buildings there, a complex so familiar that he dropped onto his haunches and stared at it in amazement for a moment. Then he rose on all fours again and moved cautiously through the tall grass toward the farmstead. He saw no smoke, and the large gate was open, but he didn't see any point in taking chances. Farmers have an automatic aversion to wolves, and Garion did not particularly want to dodge arrows shot at him from concealment.

He stopped at the edge of the cleared area surrounding the farm, dropped to his belly in the grass, and looked at the farm for quite some time. It seemed to be deserted. He ran forward and slunk cautiously through the open gate. The compound was quite nearly as large as Faldor's farm, half a world away.

He slipped through an open shed door and stood inside with one forepaw slightly raised as his nose and ears intently sought for any evidence that he was not alone. The farmstead was silent, save for the complaining moan of an udder-heavy cow lowing to be milked in the barn across the central yard. The smells of people were here, of course, but they were all many days old.

Garion slipped out of the shed and trotted cautiously from door to door, opening each in turn by twisting the handle with his jaws. The place in many respects was so strikingly familiar that it brought him a sharp pang of a homesickness he thought he had long since put behind him. The storage rooms were all almost the same as at Faldor's. The smithy was so like Durnik's that Garion could almost hear the steely ring of his friend's hammer on the anvil. He was quite certain that he could close his eyes and pad unerringly across the yard to the kitchen.

Methodically, he entered each room around the lower floor of the farmstead, then scrambled up the stairs leading to the gallery with his toenails scratching at the wooden steps.

All was deserted.

He returned to the yard and poked an inquiring nose into the barn. The cow bawled in panic, and Garion backed out through the door to avoid causing her further distress.

"Aunt Pol," he sent his thought out.

"Yes, dear?"

"There's nobody here, and it's a perfect place."

"Perfect is an extravagant word, Garion."

"Wait until you see it."

A few moments later, Belgarath trotted through the gateway, sniffed, looked around, and blurred into his own form. "It's like coming home, isn't it?" He grinned.

"I thought so myself," Garion replied.

Beldin came spiraling in. "It's about a league to the river," he said even as he changed. "If we move right along, we can make it by dark."

"Let's stay here instead," Belgarath said. "The river banks might be patrolled, and there's no point in creeping around in the dark if we don't have to."

The hunchback shrugged. "It's up to you."

Then Polgara, as pale and silent as a ghost, drifted over the wall, settled on the tailgate of a two-wheeled cart in the center of the yard, and resumed her own form. "Oh, my," she murmured, stepping down and looking around. "You were right, Garion. It *is* perfect." She folded her cloak across her arm and crossed the yard to the kitchen door.

About five minutes later, Durnik led the others into the yard. He also looked around, then suddenly laughed. "You'd almost expect Faldor himself to come out that door," he said. "How's it possible for two places so far apart to look so much alike?"

"It's the most practical design for a farm, Durnik," Belgarath told him, "and sooner or later, practical people the world over are going to arrive at it. Can you do something about that cow? We won't get much sleep if she bawls all night long."

"I'll milk her right away." The smith slid down from his saddle and led his horse toward the barn.

Belgarath looked after him with an affectionate expression. "We may have to drag him away from here in the morning," he noted.

"Where's Polgara?" Silk asked, looking around as he helped Velvet down from her horse.

"Where else?" Belgarath pointed toward the kitchen. "Get-

249

ting her out of there may be even harder than dragging Durnik out of the smithy."

Velvet looked around with a slightly dreamy expression on her face. The drug Sadi had given her the previous night had not yet entirely worn off, and Garion surmised that Polgara was keeping her under rigid control. "Very nice," she said, leaning involuntarily toward Silk. "Sort of homey."

Silk's expression was wary, like that of a man about ready to bolt.

They ate well again that evening, sitting around a long table in the beamed kitchen with the golden light of wax candles filling the room and winking back from the polished copper bottoms of kettles hung on the wall. The room was snug and warm, even though the storm which had been building up all afternoon raged outside, filling the night with thunder and wind and driving rain.

Garion felt oddly at peace, a peace he had not known for more than a year now, and he accepted this time of renewal gratefully, knowing that it would strengthen him in the climactic months ahead.

"Oh, my goodness!" Sadi exclaimed. After he had finished eating, the eunuch had taken his red case to the far end of the kitchen and had been trying to coax Zith from her little home with a saucer of fresh, warm milk.

"What is it, Sadi?" Velvet said, seeming to shake off the effects of the drug and Polgara's insistence that she remain calm.

"Zith had a little surprise for us," Sadi replied in a delighted tone. "Several little surprises, in fact."

Velvet went curiously to his side. "Oh," she said with a little catch in her voice, "aren't they adorable?"

"What is it?" Polgara asked.

"Our dear little Zith is a mother," Velvet said.

The rest of them rose and went to the other end of the room to look at the new arrivals. Like their mother, they were all bright green with the characteristic red stripe running from nose to tail. There were five of them, and they were no larger than angleworms. They all had their chins on the edge of the saucer and they were lapping up warm milk with their forked little tongues, purring all the while. Zith hovered over them protectively, somehow managing to look demure.

"That would explain why she's been so bad-tempered lately," Sadi said. "Why didn't you tell me, Zith? I could have helped you with the delivery."

"I'm not sure I'd want to be a midwife to a snake," Silk said. "Besides, I thought reptiles laid eggs."

"Most of them do," Sadi admitted. "Some kinds are live-bearers, though. Zith happens to be one of those kinds."

"And here I thought she was just getting fat," Velvet said, "and all the time she was pregnant."

Durnik was frowning. "Something doesn't quite fit here," he said. "Isn't Nyissa the only place where her species is found?"

"Yes," Sadi said, "and they're very rare even in Nyissa."

"Then how . . ." Durnik flushed slightly. "What I'm getting at is, how did this happen? We've been away from Nyissa for a long time. Where did she meet the father?"

Sadi blinked. "That's true, isn't it? This is impossible. Zith, what have you been up to?"

The little green snake ignored him.

"It's really not such a mystery, Sadi," Eriond told him, smiling slightly. "Don't you remember what Cyradis said to Zith at Ashaba?"

"Something about something being delayed. I didn't really pay that much attention. We were in the middle of something fairly distracting at the moment, if I remember right."

"She said, 'Be tranquil, little sister, for the purpose of all thy days is now accomplished, and that which was delayed may now come to pass.' This is what she was talking about. This is what was delayed."

251

"You know," Beldin said to Belgarath, "I think he's right. This isn't the first time the prophecy's tampered with things in order to get the job done. That business about the 'purpose of all her days' simply means that Zith was born for one thing—to bite Harakan. Once she'd done that, things went back to normal again." Then the hunchback looked at Eriond. "How is it that you remembered exactly what she said? We were all fairly excited there in Urvon's throne room."

"I always try to remember what people say," Eriond replied. "It may not always make sense at the time they say it, but sooner or later it always seems to fit together."

"This is a strange boy, Belgarath," Beldin said.

"We've noticed that on occasion."

"Is it really possible?" Sadi asked the old sorcerer. "That sort of intervention, I mean?"

"That's the wrong question to ask my grandfather." Garion laughed. "He doesn't believe that anything's impossible."

Silk was standing a safe distance away from Zith and her new brood. His eyebrow was raised slightly. "Congratulations, Zith," he said finally to the little green mother. Then he looked sternly at the others. "This is all very nice, I suppose," he added, "but if anybody calls them little nippers, I'll just scream."

They had bathed and gone to bed, but Ce'Nedra was restless, and she tossed and turned. Suddenly she sat up. "I wonder if that milk's still warm," she murmured. She tossed back the blanket and padded on little bare feet to the door. "Do you want some, too?" she asked Garion.

"No, thanks all the same, dear."

"It would help you sleep."

"I'm not the one who's having trouble sleeping."

She stuck her tongue out at him and went out into the hallway.

When she returned a few moments later with her glass of milk, she was stifling a naughty little giggle.

"What's so funny?" he asked her.

"I saw Silk."

"So?"

"He didn't see me, but I saw him. He was going into a bedroom."

"He can go in and out of his bedroom if he wants to."

She giggled again and hopped into bed. "That's the point, Garion," she said. "It wasn't *his* bedroom."

"Oh." Garion coughed in embarrassment. "Drink your milk."

"I listened at the door for a moment," she said. "Don't you want to hear what they were saying?"

"Not particularly, no."

She told him anyway.

The rain had passed on through, although there were still rumbles of thunder far to the west, and jagged sheets of lightning raked the western horizon. Garion awoke suddenly and sat upright in bed. There was a different kind of rumble outside, and it was occasionally accompanied by a shrill bellowing noise. He slipped softly out of bed and went out onto the balcony that encircled the farmyard. A long line of torches was slowly moving out there in the darkness, perhaps a half mile to the west. Garion peered out through the tag end of the storm, then began to form up the image of the wolf in his mind. This was definitely something that needed to be investigated.

The torches moved at a peculiarly slow pace; as Garion loped closer to them, he noticed that they seemed much higher than they would have been if the torchbearers were mounted on horses. The slow rumbling sound and the peculiar bellowing continued. Then he stopped beside a bramble thicket and sat down on his haunches to watch and listen. A long line of huge grey beasts was plodding through the night in a northeasterly direction. Garion had seen the image, at least, of an elephant on the Isle of Verkat in Cthol Murgos when his Aunt Pol had routed the mad hermit in the forest. An image of an elephant is one thing, however, but the reality is quite something else. They were enormous, far larger than any animal Garion had ever seen, and there was a kind of ponderous implacability about their steady pace. Their foreheads and flanks were covered with skirts of chain mail, and Garion shuddered inwardly at the thought of such vast weight, though the elephants moved as if the mail were as insubstantial as cobwebs. Their sail-like ears swayed as they walked, and their pendulous trunks drooped down before them. Occasionally, one of them would curl his trunk up, touching it to his forehead, and give vent to a shattering trumpet sound.

Men in crude body armor were mounted on the huge, plodding beasts. One, bearing a torch, sat cross-legged atop each huge neck. Those riding behind were armed with javelins, slings, and short-limbed bows. At the head of the column, riding astride the neck of a beast fully a yard taller than the ones in his wake, was a man wearing the black robe of a Grolim.

Garion rose and slunk closer, his careful paws making no sound in the rain-wet grass. Although he was certain that the elephants could easily catch his scent, he reasoned that beasts so large would pay little attention to a predator who posed no real threat to them. In the presence of such immensity, he felt small, even flealike. He did not particularly like the feeling. His own bulk approached two hundred pounds, but an elephant's weight was measured in tons, not in pounds.

He ranged on silent paws along the column, maintaining a distance of perhaps fifty yards and keeping his nose and eyes alert. His attention was concentrated on the black-robed Grolim astride the neck of the lead animal.

The elephants moved on, and Garion trotted alongside the column, maintaining his distance.

Then there appeared in the track ahead of the lead elephant a figure robed in shiny black satin that gleamed in the torchlight. The column halted, and Garion slunk closer.

The satin-robed figure pushed back her hood with a hand that seemed filled with swirling light. At Ashaba and again in Zamad, Garion had briefly seen the face of his son's abductor, but the confrontations with the Darshivan sorceress had been so charged with danger and dread that he had not really had time to let the features of the Child of Dark register on his memory. Now, slinking still closer, he looked upon her torch-lit face.

Her features were regular, even beautiful. Her hair was a lustrous black, and her skin was very nearly as pale as that of Garion's cousin Adara. The similarity ended there, however. Zandramas was a Grolim, and her dark eyes had that peculiar angularity common to all Angaraks, her nose was slightly aquiline, and her forehead was broad and unlined. Her chin was pointed, which made her face seem oddly triangular.

"I have been awaiting thee, Naradas," she said in her harshly accented voice. "Where hast thou been?"

"Forgive me, mistress," the Grolim astride the neck of the massive lead bull apologized. "The herdsmen were farther south than we had been told." He pushed back his hood. His face was cruel, and his white eyes gleamed in the flickering torchlight. "How fares the struggle with the Disciple's minions?"

"Not well, Naradas," she replied. "His Guardsmen and his Chandim and the rabble out of Karanda outnumber our forces."

"I have a regiment of elephant cavalry behind me, mistress," Naradas informed her. "They will turn the tide of battle. The grass of central Peldane will be well watered with the blood of Urvon's Guardsmen, Chandim, and Karands. We will roll them back and make Darshiva secure once and for all."

"I care nothing for Darshiva, Naradas. I seek the world, and the fate of one small principality on the eastern edge of Mallorea is a matter of sublime indifference to me. Let it stand or let it fall. I care not. It hath served its purpose, and now I am weary of it. How long will it take you to deliver your beasts to the field of battle?"

"Two days at most, mistress."

"Do so then. Put them under the command of my generals and then follow me to Kell. I will return to Hemil and gather up Otrath and Belgarion's brat. We will await thee in the shadow of the holy mountain of the seers."

"Is it true that Urvon brought the Demon Lord Nahaz and his hordes with him, mistress?"

"He did, but that no longer concerns us. Demons are not so difficult to raise, and Nahaz is not the only Demon Lord in Hell. Lord Mordja consented to aid us with *his* hordes. There hath long been enmity between Mordja and Nahaz. They do war upon each other now with no concern for ordinary forces."

"Mistress!" Naradas exclaimed. "Surely you would not consort with such creatures!"

"I would consort with the King of Hell himself in order to triumph in the Place Which Is No More. Mordja hath feigned flight and hath lured Nahaz away from the battlefield. Take thy beasts there so that they may destroy Urvon's hosts. Nahaz and his minions shall not be there to delay thee. Then come with all possible speed to Kell."

"I shall, mistress," Naradas promised submissively.

A slow rage had been building up in Garion. His son's abductor was no more than seconds away from him, and he knew that there was no way she could gather in her will before his fangs were into her flesh, and then it would be too late. He curled his lips back from his dreadful teeth and slunk closer, one step at a time, his hackles erect and his belly low to the ground. He thirsted for blood, and his hatred burned like a fire in his brain. Quivering in awful anticipation, he bunched his muscles, and a low, rumbling growl filled his throat.

It was that sound that ultimately brought him to his senses. The thought that had seared his brain was the thought of a wolf, and it considered nothing beyond the immediate moment. If Zandramas indeed stood no more than a few bounds away, he could rend her flesh and scatter her blood in the tall grass beside the track upon which she stood before the echo of her shrieks had returned from nearby hillsides. But if the figure standing before white-eyed Naradas was but an insubstantial projection, he would clash his curved fangs on nothingness, and the Sorceress of Darshiva would escape his vengeance once again, even as she had at Ashaba.

It was perhaps the thought burning in his brain that alerted her; or perhaps, as Polgara had done so often, she had merely sampled the surrounding region with her mind and had located the others. Whatever it was, the sorceress suddenly hissed in alarm. "Danger!" she snapped to her white-eyed underling. Then she smiled a cruel, mirthless smile. "But I have a form immune to Alorn sorcery." She tensed herself, then blurred, and then the immense shape of the dragon appeared before the suddenly terrified elephants. She spread the vast sails of her wings and launched herself into the damp night air, filling the darkness with her shrieking bellow and her sooty red fire.

"Aunt Pol!" Garion's thought flew out. "The dragon's coming!"

"What?" her answering thought came back.

"Zandramas has changed form! She's flying toward you!"

"Come back here!" she commanded crisply. "Now!"

He spun, his claws digging into the damp turf, and ran toward the farmstead as fast as he could. Behind him he could hear the shrill, panicky trumpeting of the elephants, and overhead the shrieking bellow of the vast dragon. He ran on desperately, knowing that Zandramas was immune to whatever countermeasures Polgara and the others might try, and that only the flaming sword of Iron-grip could drive her away.

It was not far, though the seconds seemed like hours as he bunched and stretched in the running gait of the wolf. Ahead of him he could see the dragon's fiery breath illuminating the storm clouds roiling overhead, a fire eerily accompanied by pale blue lightning that danced in jerky streaks down from the clouds. Then she folded her huge wings and plummeted down toward the farmstead with billows of fire preceding her.

Between bounds, Garion changed and ran on toward the gate with the sword of Iron-grip flaming in the air above his head.

At the last instant, the dragon extended her vast pinions and settled into the farmyard, still belching fire and smoke. She swung her snakelike neck around, sending incandescent billows of flame into the wooden structures surrounding the yard. The seasoned wood began to char and smoke, and here and there small blue flames began to flicker their way up the sides of the door frames.

Garion rushed into the yard, his burning sword aloft. Grimly, he began to flail at the dragon with it. "You may be immune to sorcery, Zandramas!" he shouted at her, "but you're *not* immune to this!"

She shrieked, engulfing him in a sheet of flame, but he ignored it and continued to lash her with the blue flame of the Orb and the sword. Finally, unable to bear his relentless strokes any longer, she hurled herself into the air, flapping her great wings frantically. She clawed at the air and finally managed to clear the second-story roof of the farmstead. Then she settled to earth again and continued to bathe the structure in flame.

Garion dashed out through the gateway, fully intending to confront her again. But then he stopped. The dragon was not alone. Glowing with her peculiar nimbus, the blue wolf faced the altered form of the Sorceress of Darshiva. Then, even as Polgara had once expanded into immensity in Sthiss Tor to face the God Issa and as Garion himself had done in the City of Endless Night when he had come at last to his fated meeting with Torak, the blue wolf swelled into vastness.

The meeting of the two was the sort of thing nightmares are made of. The dragon fought with flame, and the wolf with her terrible fangs. Since the wolf was insubstantial—except for her teeth—the dragon's flame had no effect; and though the teeth of the wolf were very sharp, they could not penetrate the dragon's scaly hide. Back and forth they raged in titanic but inconclusive struggle. Then Garion thought he detected something. The light was not good. The sky overhead was still obscured by the last tattered clouds of the evening's storm, and the sullen flickers of lightning seemed to obscure more than they revealed, but it appeared that each time the wolf lunged, the dragon flinched visibly. Then it came to him. Though the wolf's teeth could not injure the dragon, her blue nimbus could. It seemed in some way to be akin to the glow of the Orb and the fire of Iron-grip's sword. Somehow the blue glow surrounding Poledra, when she assumed the shape of the wolf, partook of the power of the Orb, and Garion had discovered that even in the form of the invincible dragon, Zandramas feared the Orb and anything connected with it. Her flinching became more visible, and Poledra pressed her advantage with savage, snarling lunges. Then, suddenly, they both stopped. A wordless agreement seemed to pass between them and each blurred back into her natural form. Their eyes flashing with implacable hatred, Zandramas and Poledra faced each other as two women.

"I've warned you about this, Zandramas," Poledra said in a deadly voice. "Each time you try to thwart the purpose of the Destiny which controls us all, I will block you."

"And I have told thee, Poledra, that I do not fear thee," the sorceress retorted.

"Fine, then," Poledra almost purred. "Let us summon the seeress of Kell and let her make the choice here and now and based upon the outcome of *this* meeting."

"Thou art not the Child of Light, Poledra. Thou hast no part in the ordained meeting."

"I can stand in Belgarion's stead, if need be," Poledra replied, "for the meeting between you and him is not the meeting upon which the fate of creation hinges. In that last meeting you will no longer be the Child of Dark, and he will no longer be the Child of Light. Others are destined to take up those burdens, so let the meeting between you and me come now and in this place."

"Thou wilt turn all to chaos, Poledra," Zandramas screamed.

"Not *all*, I think. You have far more to lose than I. Belgarion is the Child of Light and he will go from here to the Place Which Is No More. You are the Child of Dark, but if we have our meeting here and now, and if you are the one to fall, who will assume your burden? Urvon, perhaps, or Agachak? Or some other? You, however, will not be the exalted one, and I think that thought might be more than you can bear. Consider it, Zandramas, and then choose."

The two stood facing each other with the last flickers of lightning from the evening's storm playing luridly among the clouds to the west, bathing their faces in an eerie light.

"Well, Zandramas?"

"We will surely meet, Poledra, and all shall be decided— but not here. This is not the place of my choosing." Then the Child of Dark shimmered and vanished, and Garion heard and felt the rushing surge of her translocation.

CHAPTER FIFTEEN

She walked toward him with a stately, unhurried step, her golden eyes a mystery. "Put your sword away, Garion," she told him. "There's no need for it now."

"Yes, Grandmother." He reached back over his shoulder and inserted the tip of his blade into the sheath and let it slide home of its own weight.

"You heard, I suppose?"

"Yes, Grandmother."

"Then you understand?"

"Not entirely, no."

"I'm sure you will in time. Let's go inside. I need to talk with my husband and my daughter."

"All right." Garion was not entirely sure about the proprieties and he was just a bit unsure of what his reaction might be should he attempt to assist her, only to discover that she had no substance. Good manners, however, dictated that a gentleman help a lady across uneven ground, and so he set his teeth, reached out, and took her elbow.

She was as solid as he was. That made him feel better.

"Thank you, Garion." She smiled a bit whimsically at him. "Did you really think your hand would pass right through me?"

He flushed. "You knew what I was thinking."

"Of course." She laughed a low, warm laugh. "It's not really all that miraculous, Garion. You're a wolf in your other form, and wolves are very open about their thoughts. You were speaking them out loud in a hundred little moves and gestures you weren't even aware you were making."

"I didn't know that."

"There's a great deal of charm about it. Puppies do it all the time."

"Thanks," he said drily as the two of them passed through the gateway into the yard of the farmstead.

Durnik and Toth were extinguishing the last flickers of flame from the scorched wall of a first-floor shed with buckets full of water carried to them by Silk, Eriond, and Sadi. The dragon had not had enough time to ignite the structures fully with her searing breath, and so none of the fires were very serious.

Polgara crossed the yard gravely with Ce'Nedra and Velvet close behind her. "Mother," she said simply.

"You're looking well, Polgara," the tawny-haired woman replied as if they had spoken together only last week. "Married life agrees with you."

"I rather like it." Polgara smiled.

"I rather thought you might. Is *he* around? I need to talk with him as well as with you."

"He's in one of the upstairs rooms. You know how he feels about these meetings."

"Would you fetch him for me, Garion? I have only so much time, and there are things he has to know. He's going to have to put his feelings aside this time."

"Right away, Grandmother." He turned and went quickly up the wooden steps to the second floor gallery and the door his Aunt Pol had indicated.

Belgarath sat on a rumpled cot. His elbows were on his knees, and his face was buried in his hands.

"Grandfather," Garion said gently.

"What?"

"She wants to talk with you."

Belgarath lifted his face. His expression was one of mute suffering.

"I'm sorry, Grandfather, but she says it's very important."

Belgarath set his jaw, then sighed in resignation. "All right," he said, rising to his feet. "Let's go, then."

As the two of them started down the steps, they saw Durnik bowing a bit awkwardly to Poledra. "Ma'am," the smith was saying. Garion suddenly realized that this was probably the first time the two had been formally introduced.

"So stiff and proper, Durnik?" she replied. She reached out and lightly touched his face with one hand. Then she embraced him. "You've made my daughter very happy, Durnik," she told him. "Thank you." Then she turned and looked directly at Belgarath. "Well?" she said. There was a challenge in her voice.

"You haven't changed a bit," he said in a voice thick with emotion.

"Oh, I've changed all right," she replied wryly, "in ways not even you could imagine."

"It doesn't show."

"It's nice of you to say so. Did you hear the little exchange between the witch and me?"

He nodded. "You were taking chances, Poledra. What if she'd taken up your challenge?"

"Wolves enjoy taking chances." She shrugged. "It adds a certain zest to their lives. It really wasn't all that risky, though. Zandramas is the Child of Dark, and the Dark Spirit is gradually taking over her body as well as her soul; it's not going to gamble at this particular time. It takes too long to train replacements, and there's not that much time left before the final meeting. All right, let's get down to business. Zandramas has her Angarak King now."

Belgarath nodded. "We'd heard about that."

"You always were good at ferreting out secrets. The coronation ceremony was fairly grotesque. Zandramas followed the ancient Angarak ritual. Torak was supposed to be present, but she worked her way around that. It involved a certain amount of fakery, but the image of Him she conjured up was convincing enough to deceive the gullible." Poledra smiled. "It certainly persuaded Archduke Otrath," she added. "He fainted on three separate occasions during the ceremony. I think the oaf actually believes that he really *is* the emperor now—a delusion Kal Zakath's headsman will relieve him of shortly if Otrath is unlucky enough to fall into his cousin's hands. At any rate, Zandramas has only one more major task."

"Oh?" Belgarath said. "What's that?"

"The same as yours. She has to find out where the meeting's supposed to take place. Don't dally on your way to Kell. You've still got a long way to go. Time's getting short, and you have to get across the Magan before Zakath gets here."

"Zakath?" He sounded startled.

"You mean you didn't know? He moved his army into place around Maga Renn some weeks back. He sent out advance elements a few days ago, and he left Maga Renn with the bulk of his army just yesterday. He plans to blockade the river from the northern end of the Dalasian Mountains to the jungles of Gandahar. If he gets that blockade in place, you might

have some difficulty getting across the river." Then she
looked at Beldin. "You haven't changed much, my crooked
friend," she noted.

"Did you expect me to, Poledra?" He grinned at her.

"I thought you might at least have changed that disrepu-
table old tunic—or that it might have rotted off your back by
now."

"I patch it from time to time." he shrugged. "Then I replace the patches when they wear out. It's a comfortable tunic
and it fits me. The original is probably only a memory, though.
Is there anything else you think we need to know? Or are we
going to stand around discussing my wardrobe?"

She laughed. "I've missed you," she told him. "Oh, one
of the hierarchs of Cthol Murgos has landed at Finda on the
west coast of the Dalasian Protectorates."

"Which one?"

"Agachak."

"Does he have an Angarak King with him?" Silk asked
eagerly.

"Yes."

"Urgit—the King of the Murgos?"

She shook her head. "No. Apparently Urgit defied Agachak
and refused to make the journey."

"Urgit defied Agachak? Are you sure? Urgit's afraid of his
own shadow."

"Not any more, it seems. Your brother's changed quite a
bit since you last saw him, Kheldar. His new wife may have
had something to do with that. She's a very determined young
woman, and she's making him over to fit her conception of
him."

"That's terribly depressing," Silk mourned.

"Agachak brought the new king of the Thulls instead—a
cretin named Nathel." Poledra looked at her husband. "Be
very careful when you get to Dalasia," she told him. "Zandramas, Urvon, and Agachak will all be converging on you.

265

They hate each other, but they all know that you're the common enemy. They may decide to put aside their feelings in order to join forces against you."

"When you add Zakath and the whole Mallorean army to that, the Place Which Is No More might be just a little crowded when we get there," Silk observed wryly.

"Numbers will mean absolutely nothing in that place, Kheldar. There will only be three who matter there—the Child of Light, the Child of Dark, and the Seeress of Kell, who will make the choice." She looked at Eriond then. "Do you know what it is you have to do?" she asked him.

"Yes," he replied simply. "It's not such a difficult thing, really."

"Perhaps not," Poledra told him, "but you're the only one who can do it."

"I'll be ready when the time comes, Poledra."

Then the tawny-haired woman looked again at Belgarath. "Now I think it's finally time for you and me to have that little talk you've been avoiding since our daughters were born," she said very firmly.

The old man started.

"In private," she added. "Come with me."

"Yes, Poledra," he replied meekly.

Purposefully she walked toward the gate of the farmstead with Belgarath trailing behind her like a schoolboy anticipating a scolding—or worse.

"At last," Polgara sighed with relief.

"What's going on, Lady Polgara?" Ce'Nedra asked in a baffled little voice.

"My mother and father are going to be reconciled," Polgara replied happily. "My mother died—or perhaps didn't—when my sister Beldaran and I were born. My father always blamed himself because he wasn't there to help her. He and Bear-shoulders and the others had gone to Cthol Mishrak to steal the Orb back from Torak. Mother never blamed him because she knew how important what they were doing was. Father doesn't forgive himself that easily, however, and he's been punishing himself about it for all these centuries. Mother's finally gotten tired of it, so she's going to take steps to correct the situation.''

"Oh," Ce'Nedra said with that odd little catch in her voice. "That's just beautiful." Her eyes filled with sudden tears.

Wordlessly, Velvet drew a flimsy little bit of a handkerchief from her sleeve, dabbed at her own eyes, then passed it to Ce'Nedra.

It was perhaps an hour later when Belgarath returned. He was alone, but there was a gentle smile on his face and a youthful twinkle in his eye. No one saw fit to ask him any questions. "What time of night would you say it is?" he asked Durnik.

The smith squinted up at the sky where the last remnants of cloud were being swept off to the east by the prevailing wind to reveal the stars. "I'd guess about two hours until first light, Belgarath," he replied. "The breeze has come up, and it sort of smells like morning."

"I don't think we'll get any more sleep tonight," the old man said. "Why don't we load the packs and saddle the horses while Pol fixes some of those eggs for breakfast?"

Polgara looked at him with a slightly raised eyebrow.

"You weren't planning to let us leave without feeding us first, were you, Pol?" he asked her roguishly.

"No, father," she said, "as a matter of fact, I wasn't."

"I didn't think so." Then he laughed and threw his arms about her. "Oh, my Pol," he said exuberantly.

Ce'Nedra's eyes filled with tears again, and Velvet reached for her handkerchief once more.

"Between them, they're going to wear that little thing out," Silk noted clinically.

"That's all right," Garion replied. "I've got a couple of spares in my pack." Then he remembered something.

267

"Grandfather," he said, "in all the excitement, I almost forgot something. Before she changed into the dragon, I heard Zandramas talking with Naradas."

"Oh?"

"He's been in Gandahar and he's taking a regiment of elephant cavalry to the battlefield."

"That won't matter very much to the demons."

"The demons aren't there any more. Zandramas raised another Demon Lord—Mordja, his name is—and he's managed to lure Nahaz away from the battlefield. They've gone off someplace else to fight."

Belgarath scratched at one bearded cheek. "Just how good is that elephant cavalry out of Gandahar?" he asked Silk.

"Pretty close to invincible," Silk replied. "They drape them in chain mail, and they trample wide paths through opposing armies. If the demons have left the field, Urvon's army hasn't got a chance."

"There are too many people involved in this race anyway," Belgarath grunted. "Let's get across the Magan and leave all these armies to their own devices."

They ate breakfast and rode out from the farmstead as the first light of dawn began to creep slowly up out of the eastern horizon. Oddly, Garion felt no particular weariness despite a night significantly short on sleep. A great deal had happened since the sun had gone down, and he had much to think about.

The sun had risen when they reached the great River Magan. Then, following Toth's gestured directions, they rode slowly southward, looking for a village where they might find a boat large enough to carry them across to Darshiva. The day was warm, and the grass and trees had all been washed clean by the previous night's storm.

They came to a small settlement of mud-smeared shacks standing on stilts, with rickety docks thrusting out into the river. A lone fisherman sat at the end of one of the docks negligently holding a long cane pole.

"Talk to him, Durnik," Belgarath said. "See if he knows where we can hire a boat."

The smith nodded and reined his horse around. On an impulse, Garion followed him. They dismounted at the landward end of the dock and walked out toward the fisherman.

He was a stumpy-looking little fellow, dressed in a homespun tunic and with muddy, baglike shoes on his feet. His bare legs were laced with knotty, purple veins, and they were not very clean. His face was tanned, and he was not so much bearded as unshaven.

"Any luck?" Durnik asked him.

"See fer yerself," the fisherman said, pointing at the wooden tub at his side. He did not turn, but rather kept his eyes intently on the floating red stick to which his line was attached and which dangled his baited hook down into the murky water of the river. The tub was half-full of water, and several foot-long trout swam in circles in it. The fish had angry-looking eyes and jutting lower jaws.

Durnik squatted down beside the fisherman, his hands on his knees. "Nice-looking fish," he observed.

"A fish is a fish." The stumpy fellow shrugged. "They look better on the plate than they do in the tub."

"That's why we catch them," Durnik agreed. "What are you using for bait?"

"Tried angleworms earlier," the fellow replied laconically. "Didn't seem to interest 'em, so I switched over to fish roe."

"I don't think I've ever tried that," Durnik admitted. "How does it work?"

"Caught them five in the last half hour. Sometimes it makes 'em so excited, you got to go behind a tree to bait your hook to keep 'em from chasin' you right up onto the bank."

"I'll have to try it," Durnik said, eyeing the water wistfully. "Have you got any idea of where we might be able to hire a boat? We've got to go across the river."

The fisherman turned and stared at the smith incredu-

lously. "To the Darshiva side?" he exclaimed. "Man, are you
out of your mind?"

"Is there some trouble over there?"

"Trouble? That don't even *begin* to describe what's hap-
penin' over there. You ever hear tell of what they call a
demon?"

"A few times."

"You ever seen one?"

"Once, I think."

"There's no *think* about it, friend. If you seen one, you'd
know." The fellow shuddered. "They're just plain awful.
Well, sir, the whole of Darshiva's just crawlin' with 'em.
There's this Grolim, he come down from the north with a
whole pack of 'em snappin' an' growlin' at his heels. Then
there's this other Grolim—a woman, if you can believe that—
Zandramas, her name is, an' she stepped back an' cast a spell
an' hauled some of her own out of wherever it is they come
from, an' them demons is fightin' each other over there in
Darshiva."

"We'd heard that there was fighting to the north of here
in Peldane."

"Those are just ordinary troops, and what they're fightin'
is an ordinary war with swords an' axes an' burnin' pitch an'
all. The demons, they all went across the river lookin' fer
fresh ground to tear up an' fresh people to eat. They do that,
y' know—demons I mean. They eat folks—alive, most of the
time."

"I'm afraid we still have to go over there," Durnik told
him.

"I hope yer a good swimmer then. Yer gonna have no luck
at all findin' a boat. Ever'body from here jumped on anythin'
as would float an' headed downriver t'ward Gandahar. Guess
they figgered them wild elephants down there was a whole
lot preferable to demons."

"I think you're getting a bite," Durnik said politely, pointing at the floating stick on the stumpy man's line. The stick was submerging and popping back to the surface again.

The fisherman jerked his pole straight up into the air and then swore. "Missed 'im," he said.

"You can't catch them all," Durnik said philosophically.

"You can sure try, though." The fellow laughed, pulling in his line and rebaiting his hook with a dripping gobbet of fish roe he took from an earthenware bowl at his side.

"I'd try under the dock, myself," Durnik advised. "Trout always seem to like shade."

"That's the good thing about usin' fish roe fer bait," the fisherman said sagely. "They kin smell it, an' they'll go fer it even if they gotta climb a fence to get there." He cast his line out again and absently wiped his hand on the front of his tunic.

"How is it that you stayed behind?" Durnik asked. "I mean, if there's so much trouble around here, why didn't you go to Gandahar with the other people who left here?"

"I never lost nothin' in Gandahar. Them folks is all crazy down there. They spend all their time chasin' elephants. I mean, what y' gonna do with a elephant once y' catch 'im? An' the fish down there aren't worth the bait. Besides, this is the first time I've had this dock all to myself in the last five years. Most of the time I can't even get my line in the water, there's so many out here."

"Well," Durnik said, rising to his feet a little regretfully, "I suppose we'd better push on. We're going to have to find a boat somewhere."

"I'd sure advise stayin' away from the Darshiva side, friend," the fisherman said seriously. "You'd be better off t' cut yerself a pole an' sit right here with me until all the trouble blows over."

"I certainly wish I could," Durnik sighed. "Good luck, friend."

"Just bein' here with my line in the water is the best luck

in the world." The fellow shrugged, turning his eyes back to the floating stick on his line. "If you go over to the Darshiva side, try not t' get et by demons."

"I'll make a special point of it," Durnik promised.

As Garion and his friend walked back along the rickety dock to where their horses were tethered, Durnik smiled. "They talk differently in this part of the world, don't they?"

"Yes," Garion agreed, remembering the gabby old man and his pig in the wayside tavern above the plains of Voresebo.

"I sort of like it, though," Durnik admitted. "It's kind of free and relaxed and easy, somehow."

"I wouldn't necessarily try to imitate it, though, if I were you," Garion advised. "Aunt Pol might wash your mouth out with soap if you did."

"Oh," Durnik smiled, "I don't think she'd really do that, Garion."

Garion shrugged. "She's your wife—and it's your mouth."

Belgarath was waiting for them atop the grassy hill rising above the village on the riverbank. "Well?" he asked.

"The fish are biting," Durnik told him seriously.

Belgarath stared at him for a moment, then rolled his eyes heavenward and groaned. "I meant in Darshiva," he said from between clenched teeth.

"I couldn't really say for sure about that, Belgarath, but if they're biting on this side, it only stands to reason that they'd be biting over there, too, doesn't it?" Durnik's face was very sincere, and his tone was earnest.

Belgarath turned and stamped away, muttering to himself.

When they rejoined the others, Garion briefly repeated the information he and Durnik had gleaned from the solitary man at the end of the dock.

"That puts a whole new complexion on things, doesn't it?" Silk said. "Now what?"

"If you don't mind a suggestion, Ancient One," Sadi said to Belgarath. "I think we might be wise to follow the example of the villagers Belgarion mentioned and go on downriver to Gandahar and find a boat there. It might take us a little longer, but we'll avoid the demons."

Toth shook his head. The huge mute's usually impassive face had a worried frown on it. He made a quick series of those obscure gestures to Durnik.

"He says we don't have time," the smith translated.

"Is there some kind of special time when we have to get to Kell?" Silk asked.

Toth gestured again, his big hands moving rapidly.

"He says that Kell has been sealed off from the rest of Dalasia," Durnik told them. "Cyradis has made arrangements for us to get through, but once she leaves, the other seers will seal it off again."

"Leaves?" Belgarath said with some surprise. "Where's she going?"

Durnik looked inquiringly at Toth, and the mute gestured some more.

"Oh," Durnik said, "I see." He turned back to Belgarath. "She needs to go to the place of the meeting soon. She has to be there when it happens so that she can make the choice."

"Couldn't she just travel with us?" Velvet asked.

Toth shook his head again, and his gestures became more emphatic.

"I'm not sure I got all that," Durnik confessed. "Tell me if I make any mistakes." He turned once more. "He says that something's supposed to happen before we get to Kell, but if it doesn't, she'll have to travel alone."

"Did he say what this something is going to be?" Polgara asked her husband.

"The way I understand it, he doesn't know, Pol."

"Does he know *where* it's going to happen?" Belgarath asked intently.

Toth spread his hands.

"That young lady's really beginning to irritate me." The old man looked at Beldin. "What do you think?"

"I don't see that we have much choice, Belgarath. If this event's supposed to happen in Darshiva and we avoid the place, it might not happen at all, and the whole business could hinge on that."

"All right," Belgarath said. "We go to Darshiva then. We've dodged demons before. The main thing right now is to get across the river before Zakath gets here."

"We're going to need a boat," Durnik said.

"I'll go see if I can find one," Beldin said, crouching and spreading his arms.

"You don't have to be too selective," Belgarath said. "Anything that floats should do it."

"I'll keep that in mind," Beldin replied and soared away.

Part Three

DARSHIVA

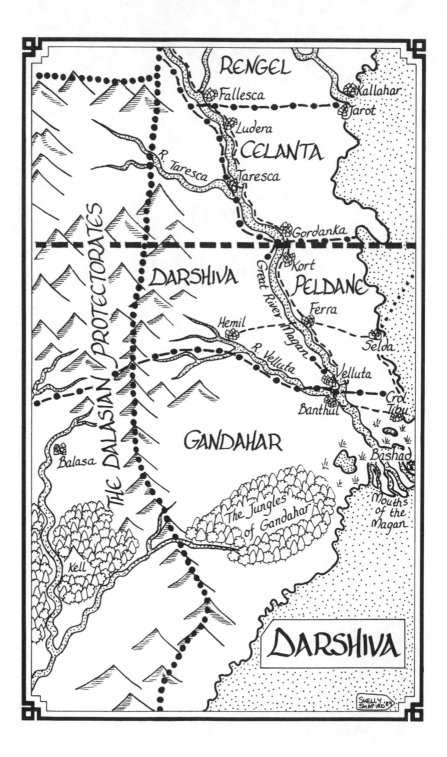

RENGEL

Fallesca
Kallahar
Jarot

Ludera

R. Taresca
CELANTA

Taresca

Gordanka

THE DALASIAN PROTECTORATES

DARSHIVA

Kort
PELDANE

Great River Magan

Ferra

Hemil
Selda

R. Velluta
Velluta

Banthul
Crol Tibu

GANDAHAR

Balasa
Bashad

The Jungles
of Gandahar
Mouths
of the
Magan

Kell

DARSHIVA

SHELLY
SHAPIRO '89

CHAPTER SIXTEEN

It was not really a boat. In point of fact, it was a river barge, and its long, trailing rope gave evidence that it had broken its moorings somewhere upriver and had drifted downstream with the current. It would serve, however. The only real drawback Garion could see was the fact that it was lying in about eight feet of water with its starboard bow staved in.

"What do you think, Belgarath?" Beldin asked.

"A boat that's already been sunk once doesn't inspire much confidence," the old man said.

"How would you like to try swimming? There's not even a raft for ten miles in either direction."

Durnik stood squinting down into the cloudy water of the river. "It might be all right," he said.

"Durnik," Silk objected, "it's got a big hole in the front of it."

"I can fix that—provided it hasn't been down there long enough to start rotting." He pulled off his rust-colored tunic and his boots. "Well," he said, "there's one way to find out." He waded out into the river, sank beneath the surface, and swam down to the wreck. He went hand over hand down one side, stopping every few feet to dig at the wood with his knife. After what seemed an eternity, he came up for air.

"Well?" Belgarath called to him.

"That side seems all right," Durnik replied. "Let me check the other." He dove down again through the greenish water and went up along the other side. He came up briefly, then went back down to look over the interior of the barge. Then he inspected the gaping hole in the bow. He was breathing hard when he came back up. "It's sound," he reported as he came dripping out of the river, "and whatever it ran into didn't damage anything major. I think I can fix it well enough to get us across the river. We'll have to unload it first, though."

"Oh?" Silk's nose twitched with curiosity. "What kind of cargo was it carrying?"

"Beans," Durnik replied, "bags of them. Most of the bags burst when the beans swelled up, though."

Silk groaned.

"Maybe they belonged to someone else, Kheldar," Velvet said consolingly.

"Are you trying to be funny?"

"I'll help you, Durnik," Garion offered, starting to pull off his plain tunic.

"Ah . . ." Durnik hesitated. "Thanks all the same, Garion, but I've seen you swim. You'd better stay on the bank. Toth and I can manage."

"How do you plan to get it out of the water?" Sadi asked.

"We have all these horses." Durnik shrugged. "Once we swing it around, they should be able to pull it up on the bank."

"Why swing it around?"

"Because the hole's in the bow. We want the water to drain out as we pull it up onto the beach. A whole herd of horses couldn't move it if we left it full of water."

"Oh. I guess I didn't think of that."

Toth laid aside his staff, pulled off the blanket he wore across one shoulder, and waded out into the river.

Eriond started to remove his tunic.

"Where do you think you're going, young man?" Polgara asked him.

"I'm going to help unload the boat, Polgara," he replied earnestly. "I swim very well. I've had lots of practice, remember?" Then he, too, waded out into the water.

"I'm not sure I caught the significance of that," Velvet admitted.

Polgara sighed ruefully. "When he was a little boy, he lived with Durnik and me in the Vale. There was a river nearby, and he used to fall into it regularly."

"Oh. That explains it, I guess."

"All right," Belgarath said crisply. "They're going to need lumber to patch that hole. We passed a shed about a half mile upstream. Let's go back and tear it apart."

It was well after sundown by the time Durnik got the foundered barge up onto the beach. For once, nature cooperated, and there was no hailstorm that evening. They built a fire on the beach to provide light, and the smith, Toth, and Eriond got down to work.

Silk walked mournfully around the barge. "It's mine, all right," he sighed.

"You keep well-equipped barges, Silk," Durnik said, carefully measuring a board. "This one had everything I need right in the bow—nails, a barrel of tar, and even a fairly good saw. We'll have it afloat before morning."

"I'm glad you approve," Silk said sourly. He made a wry face. "This is unnatural," he complained.

"What's the problem, Kheldar?" Velvet asked him.

"Usually, when I want a boat, I steal one. Using one of my own seems immoral somehow."

She laughed gaily and patted his cheek. "Poor, poor dear," she said. "It must be terrible to be burdened with so delicate a conscience."

"All right, ladies," Polgara said then, "let's see to supper."

While Durnik, Toth, and Eriond worked on the patch and Polgara, Ce'Nedra, and Velvet prepared supper, Garion and the others fetched more lumber and began to fashion crude oars. They continued to work, even as they ate. Somehow, everything seemed right to Garion. All his friends were around him and they were all busy. Although the repairing of the boat was of vital importance, the simple chores involved seemed almost mundane, and Garion could lose himself in the tasks at hand with no sense of the urgency which had attended the things he had been forced to do lately. It was almost soothing.

After the ladies had finished with supper, they carried canvas buckets of water from the river and heated the water with hot rocks. Then they retired behind a screen of tenting to bathe.

About midnight, Garion went down to the water's edge to dip his sore hands into the river. Ce'Nedra sat not far away, idly letting handfuls of sand trickle out from between her fingers. "Why don't you see if you can get some sleep, Ce'Nedra?" Garion asked her.

"I can stay awake as long as you can," she replied.

"I'm sure you can, but why?"

"Don't patronize me, Garion. I'm not a child."

"You know," he said slyly, "I've noticed that myself on any number of occasions."

"Garion!" she gasped, and then she suddenly blushed.

He laughed, rose to his feet, and went over and kissed her soundly. "Go get some sleep, dear," he told her.

"What are you doing over there?" she asked, looking up the beach to where the others still worked.

"We're making oars. If we just push that barge out into the river, the current's going to take us all the way down into Gandahar."

"Oh. All right then. Have a pleasant night." She stretched and yawned. "Why don't you get me a blanket before you go back to building oars?"

It took Durnik and Toth most of the night to nail a rough, tar-smeared patch over the hole in the bow, while the others fashioned crude oars fixed on long poles. Several hours before daylight, fog began to rise in misty tendrils from the surface of the river. After Durnik had liberally applied hot tar to the inside and the outside of the patch, he stepped back and critically examined his handiwork.

"I think it's going to leak," Silk predicted.

"All boats leak." Durnik shrugged. "We can bail the water out."

It took a great deal of effort and some fairly exotic rigging to get the barge back into the river again. Durnik leaped aboard and went forward with a torch to examine the patch. "A little trickle is all," he said with some satisfaction. "It's nothing we can't keep ahead of."

The fog grew steadily thicker as they loaded their packs aboard the barge. It was spring in this part of the world, and frogs sang lustily of love in the rushes at the river's edge just upstream. It was a pleasant, drowsy sound. Durnik scouted several hundred yards downstream and found a shallow bank where the current had cut away the soil. He fashioned a ramp from the remaining lumber. They towed the barge down to the cut bank and loaded the horses on board.

"Let's wait until we have a little more light," the smith

suggested. "Fog's bad enough, but when you add darkness to it, it's almost impossible to see where you're going. Rowing this thing isn't going to be so enjoyable that we need to paddle around in circles just for the entertainment of it."

"Couldn't we rig a sail of some sort?" Silk asked hopefully.

"Easily," Durnik replied. He wet one finger with his tongue and held it up. "I'll do that just as soon as you work out a way to make the wind blow."

Silk's face fell.

"While you're doing that, I need to go talk with Ce'Nedra." He went back up the beach and gently shook Garion's sleeping wife awake.

"You know? Sometimes he has a very warped sense of humor," Silk observed.

When the first light of day began to tinge the misty eastern horizon, they pushed out into the fog and took their places at the oars.

"I don't want to seem critical, Goodman," Sadi said to Durnik, who stood in the stern with his hands gripping the tiller, "but I've seen a lot of fog in Nyissa, and, once it's fully daylight, you won't have the faintest idea of where the sun is. How do you plan to keep your course?"

"Ce'Nedra's taking care of that," the smith replied, pointing toward the bow.

The Rivan Queen was leaning over the portside intently watching a floating piece of wood attached to a long cord.

"What's she doing?" Sadi asked, sounding a bit perplexed.

"She's watching the current. We'll be quartering it, but as long as that cord stays at the same angle from the boat, we'll be right on course. I put a mark on the rail to show her what the angle ought to be."

"You think of everything, don't you?" Sadi said, continuing to pull his oar.

"I try. You can usually avoid problems if you think your way completely through a job."

Ce'Nedra raised one arm and pointed imperiously to starboard. She seemed to be taking her job very seriously. Durnik obediently moved the tiller.

Once the eastern shore of the great river vanished in the fog, it seemed to Garion that time had stopped entirely. There was no real sense of motion, though he bent his back over his oar with monotonous regularity.

"Tiresome, isn't it?" Silk said.

"Rowing always is," Garion replied.

Silk looked around, then spoke quietly. "Do you notice a change in Durnik?" he asked.

"No. Not really."

"What I'm getting at is that usually he's so self-effacing that you almost forget that he's around, but back there on the beach, he just sort of took charge."

"He's always been like that, Silk. When we're doing something he doesn't know all that much about, he just follows along and keeps his eyes open; but when we come to something he knows about, he steps in and does what has to be done." Garion smiled affectionately back over his shoulder at his old friend. Then he looked slyly at Silk. "He also learns very fast. By now, he's probably at least as good a spy as you are, and he watched you very closely while you were manipulating the bean market back there in Melcena. If he ever decides to go into business, I think you and Yarblek had better start keeping a close count of your tail feathers."

Silk looked a bit worried. "He wouldn't really do that, would he?"

"He might. You never really know about Durnik, do you?"

As the sun rose higher, the fog diffused its light, and the world around them became a monochrome—white fog and black water with no hint at all that they were making any progress or, if they were, that it was in the right direction. Garion felt a bit strange, knowing that they were entirely at Ce'Nedra's mercy. It was only her eyes on that cord lightly lying across an angled mark on the rail that kept them on course. He loved her, but he knew that she was sometimes flighty, and her judgment was not always the best. Her insistent little gestures to port or to starboard, however, showed no sign of hesitancy or lack of certainty, and Durnik obeyed them implicitly. Garion sighed and kept on rowing.

About midmorning, the fog began to thin, and Beldin drew in his oar. "Can you manage here without me?" he asked Belgarath. "I think we ought to know just exactly what we're running into. There's all sorts of unpleasantness going on in Darshiva, and I don't think we'll want to come ashore right in the middle of it."

"And you're getting tired of rowing, right?" the old man replied sarcastically.

"I could row all the way around the world if I wanted to," the gnarled-looking little hunchback replied, flexing his oak-stump arms, "but this might be more important. Do you really want to beach this tub and find Nahaz waiting for you on the sand?"

"Do whatever you think is right."

"I always do, Belgarath—even if it makes you unhappy sometimes." The grimy little gnome went forward toward the bow. "Excuse me, me little darlin'," he said to Ce'Nedra in an exaggerated brogue, "but I must be off now."

"I need you at that oar," she objected. "How can I keep the course if everybody runs away?"

"I'm sure y' kin manage, me little darlin'," he said, patting her cheek; then, leaving a ghostly laugh behind him, he disappeared into the fog.

"You come back here!" she shouted after him, but he was already gone.

There was the faintest touch of a breeze then. Garion could feel it brushing across the back of his sweaty neck as he rowed. The fog eddied and swirled slightly, thinning even more.

And then there were looming black shapes all around them.

"Garion!" Ce'Nedra exclaimed.

A number of triumphant shouts came out of the rapidly dissipating fog. They were surrounded by ships that moved purposefully to block them.

"Do we make a run for it?" Silk asked in a tense, hoarse whisper.

Belgarath looked at the ships moving to surround them, his eyes like flint. "Run?" he said. "In this tub? Don't be ridiculous."

A boat had moved directly in front of them, and, as they drifted closer, Garion could see the oarsmen. "Mallorean soldiers," he noted quietly. "Zakath's army."

Belgarath muttered a few choice oaths. "Let's sit tight for a bit. They may not know who we are. Silk, see if you can talk us out of this."

The little man rose and went to the bow of their barge. "We're certainly glad to see imperial troops in this region, Captain," he said to the officer commanding the boat blocking their path. "Maybe you can put a stop to all the insanity that's been going on around here."

"I'll need your name," the officer replied.

"Of course," Silk said, slapping his forehead. "How stupid of me. My name is Vetter. I work for Prince Kheldar. Perhaps you've heard of him?"

"The name's familiar. Where are you going?"

"Actually, we're bound for Balasa down in the Dalasian Protectorates. Prince Kheldar has interests there—that's assuming we can make our way across Darshiva. Things are in turmoil there." He paused. "I wonder, Captain, do you suppose you could spare us a few soldiers to act as an escort? I'm authorized to pay quite handsomely."

"We'll see," the officer said.

Then an even larger ship emerged from the fog and moved alongside their patched and leaky vessel. A familiar face looked over the rail. "It's been quite some time, hasn't it,

King Belgarion?" General Atesca said in a pleasant, conversational tone. "We really ought to try to stay in touch." Atesca wore his customary scarlet cloak and a burnished steel helmet embossed with gold.

Garion's heart sank. Subterfuge was quite out of the question now. "You knew we were out here," he said accusingly.

"Of course. I had people watching you on the Peldane side." The red-clad general sounded a bit smug about that.

"I felt no presence," Polgara declared, pulling her blue cloak about her.

"I'd have been very surprised if you had, my Lady," Atesca replied. "The men who were watching you are imbeciles. Their minds are as vacant as the minds of mushrooms." He looked distastefully out across the river. "You have no idea of how long it took me to explain to them what they were supposed to do. Every army has a few men like that. We try to weed them out, but even gross stupidity has its uses, I suppose."

"You're very clever, General Atesca," she said in a tight voice.

"No, Lady Polgara," he disagreed. "I'm just a plain soldier. No officer is more clever than his intelligence service. Brador's the clever one. He's been gathering information about your peculiar gifts from various Grolims since the battle of Thull Mardu. Grolims pay very close attention to your exploits, my Lady, and over the years they've amassed a great deal of information about your abilities. As I understand it—although I'm certainly no expert—the more acute a mind is, the more easily you can detect its presence. That's why I sent those human turnips out to watch you." He looked critically at their boat. "That's really a wretched thing, you know. Are you keeping it afloat by sorcery?"

"No," Durnik told him in a flat, angry tone of voice, "by skill."

"I bow to your skill, Goodman Durnik," Atesca said a bit

extravagantly. "You could probably work out a way to make a rock float—if you really wanted to." He paused and looked at Belgarath. "I assume we're going to be civilized about this, Ancient One?" he asked.

"I'm willing to listen," Belgarath replied warily.

"His Imperial Majesty feels a strong need to discuss certain matters with you and your companions, Holy Belgarath," Atesca said, "and I think I should advise you that you're paddling this wreck of yours directly into the middle of a hornet's nest. Sensible people are avoiding Darshiva right now."

"I've never pretended to be sensible."

Atesca laughed ruefully. "I haven't either," he admitted. "At the moment, I'm trying to map out a military campaign to invade that most insensible region. May I offer you gentlemen—and your ladies—the hospitality of my ship?" He paused. "I think I'll have to insist," he added regretfully. "Orders, you understand. Besides, we might want to pool our information while we await the arrival of his Imperial Majesty."

"Is Zakath coming here?" Garion asked.

"I doubt that he's more than a day behind me, your Majesty," Atesca replied, "and he's aflame with the desire to have a long, long talk with you."

—*What do we do, Grandfather?*—Garion's fingers asked.

—*I don't think we've got much choice at the moment. Beldin's out there somewhere. I'll let him know what's happening. He'll come up with something.*—"All right, General," he said aloud. "I was getting a little tired of rowing anyway."—*Pass the word to the others*—He motioned to Garion.—*Let's seem to go along—at least until we get to the Darshiva side.*—

Atesca's ship, while not opulent, was comfortable. They gathered in the forward cabin, a room littered with maps and various-sized bits and pieces of parchment. As always, General Atesca was polite, but firm. "Have you had breakfast yet?" he inquired.

"We were a little rushed," Belgarath told him.

"I'll send word to the cook, then," Atesca said. He went to the door and spoke with one of the red-garbed guards posted outside. Then he came back. "While we're waiting, why don't we share that information I was talking about? I'd heard that you were going to Ashaba when you left Mal Zeth. Then you suddenly surface in Melcena, and now you're half-way across the Magan to Darshiva. You people certainly move around."

—He already knows what we're doing.—Silk's fingers said to Belgarath.—*There's no point in trying to hide it.*—

"Please, Prince Kheldar," Atesca said in a pained tone, "don't do that. It's very impolite, you know."

Silk laughed. "Either your eyes are very sharp, General, or advancing age is making my fingers clumsy. In point of fact, I was merely suggesting to Belgarath that we'd made no secret of our reason for coming to Mallorea. Kal Zakath knew why we were here, so there's no point in being coy about it." He gave Belgarath an inquiring look, and the old man nodded. Silk's face grew serious, even bleak. "We went to Ashaba in pursuit of Zandramas—and King Belgarion's son. Then we followed her across Karanda and on down to Jarot in northern Celanta. Her trail led to Melcena, so we followed her there. Then we came back to the continent."

"And you're still on her trail?" Atesca asked intently.

"More or less," Silk lied smoothly. Then he sidestepped the issue. "We discovered at Ashaba that Urvon is totally mad now. I'm sure Kal Zakath will be interested in that. Anyhow, Urvon's under the control of a Demon Lord named Nahaz. Zandramas has raised another Demon Lord named Mordja, and the two are fighting each other in Darshiva. I'd think a long time before I invaded that region, General. Nahaz and Mordja might prefer not to be interrupted."

"What happened to Mengha?" Atesca asked suddenly. "I thought he was the one who was raising demons."

Silk smiled wryly. "Mengha was actually a Chandim priest named Harakan. He was Urvon's underling for centuries."

"Was?"

"I'm afraid he's no longer with us. He met a little green snake named Zith and he lost interest in things shortly after that."

Atesca threw back his head and laughed. "I'd heard about your pet, your Excellency," he said to Sadi. "Do you suppose she'd accept a medal—Heroine of the Empire or something?"

"I don't think she'd really be interested, General Atesca," Sadi replied coolly. "Besides, if somebody tried to pin a medal to her, she might misunderstand."

"You've got a point there," Atesca said. He looked around a little nervously. "You *do* have her confined, don't you?"

"Of course, General," Velvet assured him with a dimpled smile. "At the moment, she's taking care of her babies. They're absolutely adorable. Why don't you show them to the General, Sadi?"

"Ah . . ." Atesca hesitated. "Some other time, perhaps."

"All right, General Atesca," Belgarath said, "we've told you what we've been doing. Now I think it's time for you to share a bit of information with us."

"We haven't really made a secret of our activities either, Ancient Belgarath. The Emperor's forces moved out of Mal Zeth, and we used Maga Renn as a staging area. I was instructed to lead the advance elements of the army down the Magan and to occupy Ferra. The idea was to cut off Zandramas' reinforcements out of Darshiva so that Urvon's army could annihilate the troops she had in Peldane. Then we planned to fall on Urvon—heavily. After that, we were going to cross the river and deal with whatever force Zandramas had left."

289

"Good plan," Silk said.

"Unfortunately, it didn't work. We've got Darshiva cut off, but one of Zandramas' underlings went down into Gandahar and hired a sizable body of elephant cavalry." Atesca frowned. "I think I'll speak with his Imperial Majesty about that. I don't really object to mercenaries, but the elephant herders of Gandahar are just a bit unselective when it comes to hiring themselves out. At any rate, there was a battle in central Peldane yesterday, and elephants did what elephants usually do. Urvon's army fled, but instead of running back toward Celanta, they outflanked the elephants and the rest of the Darshivan army, and they're driving straight toward the Magan. If they get across into Darshiva, I'll have my work cut out for me. I'll have demons and Grolims and Chandim and Hounds and elephants and Karands and the whole army of Darshiva to deal with." He sighed mournfully. "This is not, I'm afraid, going to be the short, easy campaign I'd anticipated."

"Why not just let Urvon and Zandramas fight it out?" Silk suggested.

"Policy, Prince Kheldar. The Emperor does not want to appear timid—or powerless—and he most certainly doesn't want any army in Mallorea except his own to win any kind of a victory. It sets a bad precedent and it might give others certain ideas. Mallorea is not as monolithic a society as it might appear from the outside. Overwhelming imperial force is the only thing that holds us together."

"I approve of the reasoning," Silk agreed. "Stability is good for business."

"Speaking of that," Atesca said. "One of these days you and I are going to have to have a long talk about beans."

"Are you buying or selling, General Atesca?" Silk asked impudently.

"Let's get down to cases, gentlemen," Polgara said.

"General Atesca, what are the Emperor's plans concerning us?"

"That's for him to decide, my Lady," Atesca replied. "His Majesty doesn't always confide in me. He was, however, quite distressed about the way you chose to abuse his hospitality in Mal Zeth."

"He knew where we were going," Garion said flatly, "and why."

"That's likely to be one of the things he'll want to discuss with your Majesty. It's possible that the two of you might be able to work out an accommodation of some kind."

"Possible, but not very probable."

"That's up to his Imperial Majesty, isn't it?"

The fog had lifted, but the sky over Darshiva was heavily overcast. As Garion stood in the bow of Atesca's ship, he caught a scent that was hauntingly familiar. It was a compound of damp rust, stagnant water, and the musty smell of fungus. He peered ahead and saw a forest composed of dead white snags. His heart sank.

Atesca quietly joined him. "I hope your Majesty isn't offended with me," he said. "I seem to be making a habit of apprehending you and your friends."

"You're only following orders, General," Garion said shortly. "My quarrel is with your Emperor, not with you."

"You're a very tolerant man, your Majesty."

"Not really, General, but I don't waste my time holding grudges against people who are only doing what they're told to do."

Atesca looked toward the Darshivan shore, less than a mile away. "I expect that overcast will burn off by noon," he said, smoothly changing the subject.

"I wouldn't count on it, Atesca," Garion said somberly. "Did you ever visit Cthol Mishrak?"

"Military people don't have much reason to visit uninhabited ruins, your Majesty."

"Cthol Mishrak wasn't uninhabited," Garion told him. "The Chandim were there, and the Hounds, and other things I can't even put names to."

"Religious fanatics," Atesca shrugged. "They do things for strange reasons. I'm told it was an unhealthy sort of place."

Garion pointed at the Darshivan shore. "You're looking at another one, I'm afraid. I know that Melcenes are almost as skeptical as Tolnedrans, so I don't know how much you'll believe of what I'm going to tell you. Do you smell that peculiar odor in the air?"

Atesca sniffed, then wrinkled his nose. "Not very pleasant, is it?"

"Cthol Mishrak smelled exactly the same way. I'd guess that the cloud cover over Darshiva has been there for a dozen years at least."

"I find that a bit hard to accept."

"Look at those trees." Garion pointed at the snags. "What do you think it would take to kill a whole forest?"

"Some kind of disease, I suppose."

"No, General. Seedlings would have sprouted by now, and there's not even any undergrowth there. The trees died from lack of sunlight. The only thing growing out there now is fungus. It rains from time to time, and the rain water collects in pools. The sun doesn't come out to evaporate the water, so it just lies there and stagnates. That's a part of what you're smelling."

"I seem to smell rust, too. Where's that coming from?"

"I really don't know. At Cthol Mishrak it came from the ruins of Torak's iron tower. Darshiva's shrouded in perpetual gloom because it's the home of the Child of Dark."

"I've heard the term before. Who is this Child of Dark?"

"Zandramas—at least for the time being. Are you really sure you want to land your troops there?"

292

"I have my orders, King Belgarion. My troops are well trained. They'll build a fortified enclave on that shore whether the sun shines or not. Then we'll wait for the Emperor. He has a number of decisions to make—not the least of which is what he's going to do about you."

CHAPTER SEVENTEEN

They waited on board Atesca's ship while the soldiers went ashore and began to build the enclave. The Mallorean troops were quite nearly as efficient as the legions of Imperial Tolnedra, and in a very short period of time, they had cleared several acres of ground and erected a neat, orderly city of tents. It was surrounded on the inland side by breastworks, catapults, and a deep ditch bristling with sharpened stakes. A palisade of sharpened poles lined the river's edge, and a number of floating docks extended out into the water.

It was midafternoon when Garion and the others disembarked and were escorted to a large, guarded pavilion in the center of the enclave and politely, but firmly, asked to remain inside.

"Have you been able to contact Beldin?" Silk asked Belgarath in a whisper.

The old man nodded. "He's working on something."

"I hope he doesn't take too long," the little man said. "I expect that once Zakath gets here, he'll decide that we need slightly more secure quarters—probably a place involving stout walls and locked doors." He made a sour face. "I hate jails."

"Don't you think you're exaggerating, Prince Kheldar?" Ce'Nedra asked. "Zakath's always behaved like a perfect gentleman."

"Oh, of course," he replied with heavy sarcasm. "Why don't you tell that to all those Murgos he crucified on the plains of Hagga? He can be polite when it doesn't inconvenience him too much, but we've seriously irritated him. If we're not gone by the time he gets here, I expect he'll show us just how irritated he really is."

"You're wrong, Prince Kheldar," Eriond said gravely. "He just doesn't know what he's supposed to do yet, that's all."

"What's that supposed to mean?"

"Back in Cthol Murgos, Cyradis told him that he was going to come to a crossroads in his life. This is it, I think. Once he makes the right choice, we can be friends again."

"Just like that?"

"More or less, yes."

"Polgara, would you please make him stop that?"

The tent was familiar. It was a Mallorean officer's pavilion with the usual red carpeting, and furniture which could be easily disassembled. They had been housed in this same kind of pavilion many times in the past. Garion looked around without much interest, then he sprawled on a bench.

"What's the matter, Garion?" Ce'Nedra asked, coming over to sit beside him.

"Isn't it obvious? Why don't they just leave us alone?"

"I think you worry too much," she told him. She reached out and touched his forehead with one little finger. "Your friend in there isn't going to let anything happen that's not supposed to happen, so stop brooding about this. We're supposed to go to Kell, and Zakath couldn't stop us, even if he brought his whole army back from Cthol Murgos and piled them in our path."

"You're taking this all awfully calmly."

"I have to believe, Garion," she replied with a little sigh. "If I didn't, I'd go insane." She leaned forward and kissed him. "Now get that grumpy look off your face. You're starting to look exactly like Belgarath."

"Of course I am. He's my grandfather, after all."

"The resemblance shouldn't start to show up for several thousand years yet, though," she said tartly.

Two soldiers brought them a supper consisting of standard military rations. Silk opened one of the metal pots and looked inside. He sighed. "I was afraid of that."

"What's the trouble, Kheldar?" Sadi asked him.

"Beans," Silk replied, pointing at the pot.

"I thought you liked beans."

"Not to eat, I don't."

Because they had not slept the previous night, they retired early. Garion tossed restlessly for a while and then finally dropped off.

The following morning they all slept late, and Garion emerged from the curtained-off compartment he shared with Ce'Nedra to find Silk pacing up and down restlessly. "Finally," the little man said with some relief. "I thought everybody was going to sleep till noon."

"What's your problem?" Garion asked him.

"I need somebody to talk to, that's all."

"Lonesome?"

"No. Edgy. Zakath's probably going to show up today. Do you suppose we ought to wake Belgarath?"

"Why?"

"To find out if Beldin's come up with a way to get us out of here, naturally."

"You worry too much."

"My, aren't *we* complacent this morning?" Silk snapped.

"Not really, but there's not much point in chewing off all our fingernails over something that's out of our hands, is there?"

"Garion, why don't you go back to bed?"

"I thought you were lonesome."

"Not that lonesome."

"Has Atesca come by this morning?"

"No. He's probably fairly busy. He's going to have some sort of campaign mapped out by the time Zakath gets here." The little man flung himself into one of the folding chairs. "No matter what Beldin comes up with, we're very likely to have at least a regiment hot on our heels when we ride out of here," he predicted, "and I hate being chased."

"We've had people chasing us ever since the night we left Faldor's farm. You should be used to it by now."

"Oh, I am, Garion. I still don't like it, though."

Perhaps an hour or so later, the others began to wake up, and not long after that, the same red-garbed soldiers brought them breakfast. The two men were the only people they had seen since they had been confined in the pavilion.

They spent the rest of the morning in desultory conversation. By unspoken agreement, no one mentioned their present situation.

About noon, General Atesca entered the tent. "His Imperial Majesty will arrive shortly," he announced. "His ships are approaching the docks."

"Thank you, General," Belgarath replied.

Atesca bowed stiffly and went back out.

Polgara rose to her feet. "Come along, ladies," she said to Ce'Nedra and Velvet. "Let's go make ourselves presentable."

Sadi looked down at his plain tunic and hose. "Hardly suitable for an imperial audience," he said. "Do you think we ought to change?"

"Why bother?" Belgarath shrugged. "Let's not give Zakath the impression that we take him seriously."

"Don't we?"

"Maybe, but we don't need to let him know about it."

Not much later, the Emperor of Mallorea entered with General Atesca and the Chief of the Bureau of Internal Affairs. As was his custom, Zakath wore a plain linen robe, but he had a scarlet military cape draped across his shoulders. His eyes were once again melancholy, and his pallid lips expressionless. "Good day, your Majesty," he said to Garion in a flat, emotionless tone. "You've been well, I trust?"

"Tolerably, your Majesty," Garion replied. If Zakath wanted formality, Garion would give him formality.

"Your extensive travels must have been fatiguing," Zakath said in that same flat tone, "particularly for the ladies. I'll see to it that your return journey to Mal Zeth is made in easy stages."

"Your Majesty is very kind, but we're not going back to Mal Zeth."

"You're wrong, Belgarion. You *are* going back to Mal Zeth."

"Sorry. I've got a pressing engagement elsewhere."

"I'll convey your regrets to Zandramas when I see her."

"I'm sure she'd be overjoyed to hear that I'm not coming."

"Not for very long, she won't. I fully intend to have her burned as a witch."

"Good luck, your Majesty, but I don't think you'll find that she's very combustible."

"Aren't you gentlemen being just a little silly?" Polgara asked then. She had changed into a blue dress and she sat at a table, calmly mending a pair of Eriond's socks.

"Silly?" Zakath snapped, his eyes suddenly flashing.

"You're still friends and you both know it. Now stop behaving like a couple of schoolboys."

"I think you go too far, Lady Polgara," Zakath told her in a frigid tone.

"Really?" she replied. "I thought I'd described the situation rather accurately. You're not going to put Garion in chains, and he's not going to turn you into a radish, so stop trying to bully each other."

"I think we can continue this discussion some other time," Zakath said curtly. He bowed slightly to Polgara and left the tent.

"Wasn't that perhaps a trifle abrupt, Lady Polgara?" Sadi asked her.

"I don't think so," she replied. "It cut through a lot of nonsense." She carefully folded the socks she had been mending. "Eriond, I think it's time for you to trim your toenails again. You're cutting your way out of your socks faster than I can mend them."

"He's gone back to being the way he was before, hasn't he?" Garion said sadly. "Zakath, I mean."

"Not entirely," Polgara disagreed. "Most of that was a pose to conceal his real feelings." She looked at Belgarath. "Well, father, has Uncle Beldin come up with anything yet?"

"He was working on something this morning. I can't talk to him right now because he's chasing a rabbit. We'll get back in touch after he finishes his lunch."

"Can't he concentrate on business?"

"Oh, come now, Pol. I've known you to go out of your way for a fat rabbit on occasion."

"You don't!" Ce'Nedra gasped to Polgara, her eyes wide with sudden horror.

"I really don't think you'd understand, dear," Polgara told her. "Why don't you bring me your gray dress? I noticed a rip in the hem and I've already got my sewing box out."

They waited out the remainder of the afternoon; after supper, they sat around talking quietly.

Silk squinted toward the door of the tent, beyond which the guards were posted. "Any luck with Beldin yet?" he whispered to Belgarath.

"He's working on something—something fairly exotic, I'd imagine, knowing Beldin. He's still hammering out the details. He'll tell me the whole thing once he gets it put together."

"Wouldn't it be better if the two of you worked on it together?"

"He knows what he has to do. I'd just get in his way if I tried to stick my oar in, too." The old man stretched and yawned. Then he stood up. "I don't know about the rest of you," he said, "but I think I'll go to bed."

The next morning, Garion rose quietly, dressed, and slipped out of the curtained-off chamber, leaving Ce'Nedra still asleep.

Durnik and Toth were seated at the table in the main part of the pavilion with Belgarath.

"Don't ask me how he did it," Belgarath was saying. "All he told me was that Cyradis agreed to come here when Toth summoned her."

Durnik and Toth exchanged a few gestures. "He says he can do that," the smith translated. "Do you want her to come here now?"

Belgarath shook his head. "No, let's wait until Zakath is in here with us. I know how much it tires her to project her image over long distances." He made a face. "Beldin suggests that we let the conversation get to a climax before we send for her. Beldin has urges in the direction of melodrama sometimes. We've all talked to him about it over the years, but he backslides from time to time. Good morning, Garion."

Garion nodded briefly to each of them, then sat at the table.

300

"What's Cyradis going to be able to do that we can't?" he asked.

"I'm not sure," Belgarath replied. "We all know that she has a peculiar effect on Zakath, though. He tends to lose his grip on things every time he sees her. Beldin wouldn't tell me exactly what he's got in mind, but he sounded disgustingly pleased with himself. Do you feel up to some theatricality this morning?"

"Not really, but I suppose I can manage something."

"You're supposed to goad Zakath a little—not too much, mind, but push him into making some threats. That's when we're supposed to call Cyradis. Don't be too obvious about it. Sort of lead him into it gradually." The old man looked at Toth. "Keep your eyes on me when Garion and Zakath start arguing," he instructed. "I'll cover my mouth and cough. That's when we'll need your mistress."

Toth nodded.

"Are we going to tell the others?" Garion asked.

Belgarath squinted. "No," he decided. "Their reactions might be more natural if they don't know what's going on."

Durnik smiled slightly. "I'd say that Beldin isn't the only one with a flair for the dramatic."

"I used to be a professional storyteller, Durnik," Belgarath reminded him. "I can play an audience like a lute."

After the others had awakened and breakfast had been served, General Atesca came into the tent. "His Imperial Majesty instructs that you make ready. You'll be departing for Mal Zeth within the hour."

Garion moved quickly to head that off. "Tell his Imperial Majesty that we're not going anyplace until we finish the conversation we started yesterday."

Atesca looked momentarily startled, then recovered. "People do not speak so to the Emperor, your Majesty," he declared.

"He might find it refreshing, then."

Atesca drew himself up. "The Emperor is otherwise oc-cupied at the moment."

Garion leaned back in his chair and crossed his legs. "We'll wait," he said flatly. "That will be all, General."

Atesca's face grew tight, then he bowed stiffly, turned, and went out without another word.

"Garion!" Ce'Nedra gasped, "We're at Zakath's mercy, and you were being deliberately rude."

"He hasn't been overly polite to me." Garion shrugged. "I told him we weren't going back to Mal Zeth, and he ignored me. It appears that sometimes it takes a bit to get his attention."

Polgara was looking narrowly at Garion. Then she turned to Belgarath. "What are you two up to, father?" she asked.

He winked at her, but did not reply.

It took Kal Zakath approximately two minutes to arrive. He burst into the tent with his eyes wild and his face beet-red. "What do you mean?" he almost screamed at Garion.

"What do you mean, what do I mean?"

"I gave you an imperial command!"

"So? I'm not one of your subjects."

"This is intolerable!"

"You'll get used to it. You should know by now that I always do what I set out to do. I thought I'd made that point when we left Mal Zeth. I told you we were going to Ashaba, and that's exactly what we did."

With some effort, the Emperor got himself under control. "I was trying to protect you and your friends, you idiot," he said from between clenched teeth. "You were riding directly into Mengha's path."

"We didn't have any particular problem with Mengha."

"Atesca told me that you'd killed him. I didn't get the details, though." Zakath seemed to have recovered his com-posure to some degree.

"Actually, I'm not the one who did it. Margravine Liselle killed him."

Zakath looked with one raised eyebrow at the dimpled Velvet.

"His Majesty is perhaps overgenerous," she murmured with a little curtsy. "I had some help."

"Help? From whom?"

"Zith, actually. Mengha was very surprised."

"Will someone *please* tell me what happened without all this clever repartee?"

"It was really fairly simple, your Majesty," Silk said smoothly. "We were having a little disagreement with the Chandim and some others in Torak's old throne room at Ashaba. Mengha was shouting orders to his men, and Liselle pulled Zith out of her bodice and threw the little green darling right into his face. Zith nipped him a few times, he stiffened up like a plank, and he was dead before he hit the floor."

"You don't actually carry that snake down the front of your dress, do you?" Zakath asked Velvet incredulously. "How can you?"

"It took a bit of getting used to," she admitted, placing one modest hand on her bodice.

"It didn't *really* happen that way, did it?"

"Prince Kheldar's description of what took place was fairly accurate, your Imperial Majesty," Sadi assured him. "Zith was very put out. I think she was asleep when the Margravine threw her at Mengha, and being awakened suddenly always makes her cross."

"As it turns out, Zakath," Belgarath said, "Mengha was really one of the Chandim and Urvon's chief underling."

"Yes, so Atesca told me. That puts Urvon behind what was going on in Karanda, doesn't it?"

"Only marginally," Belgarath replied. "Urvon isn't sane enough to be behind much of anything. He's completely under the domination of a Demon Lord named Nahaz, and consorting with demons usually unhinges a man's mind. Urvon's totally convinced that he's a God now."

"If he's that mad, who's running his campaign here? Atesca said that his outflanking of the Darshivan army and their elephant cavalry was a stroke of tactical genius."

"It's my guess that Nahaz is more or less in command, and Demon Lords pay very little attention to casualties. They also have ways of making people run very fast."

"I've never gone to war with a Demon Lord before," Zakath mused. "What's his objective?"

"The Sardion," Garion replied. "Everybody wants to get his hands on it—me included."

"To raise a new God over Angarak?"

"That's its purpose, I suppose."

"I don't think I'd like that. You liberated us from Torak, and I don't propose to see his replacement enthroned at either Mal Zeth or Mal Yaska. Angarak doesn't need a God. It has me. Who's your candidate?"

"I don't know yet. They haven't told me."

"What am I going to do with you, Belgarion?" Zakath sighed.

"You're going to let us go so we can do what we're supposed to do. You might not like the idea of a New God, but I think you'll find my choice a lot preferable to anything Zandramas or Urvon or Agachak might come up with."

"Agachak?"

"The Hierarch of Rak Urga. He's here in Mallorea as well."

"I'll deal with him, too, then. That still leaves you, I'm afraid."

"I just told you what to do about me."

A faint smile touched Zakath's lips. "I don't think I really like your proposal. You're a little undependable."

"What's your goal in all this?" Belgarath asked him.

"I'm going to restore order in Mallorea, even if I have to depopulate whole districts to do it. Since this Sardion is the thing that's got everyone so agitated, I'd guess that my best course would be to find it and destroy it."

"Good," Garion said, rising to his feet. "Let's go, then."

"Oh, no, your Majesty." Zakath's tone was once again coldly imperial. "I don't trust you any more. I made that mistake once already. I can eliminate at least one of the people trying to reach the Sardion by sending you and your friends back to Mal Zeth under heavy guard. Then I can concentrate on looking for the Sardion myself."

"Where do you plan to start looking?" Garion asked him bluntly. The conversation, he decided, had moved around to the point where the goading Belgarath had suggested seemed to be in order. "You don't even know what you're looking for and you haven't got the faintest idea of where to start. You're just floundering around."

"I don't think I care for that, Belgarion."

"That's too bad. The truth is sometimes painful, isn't it?"

"And I suppose you do know where it is?"

"I can find out."

"If you can, so can I, and I'm sure you'll give me a few clues."

"Not a chance."

"You'll grow more cooperative once I put a few of your friends on the rack. I'll even let you watch."

"You'd better hire an expendable torturer, then. Haven't you realized yet just what I'm capable of? And all this time I thought you were intelligent."

"I think that's quite enough, Belgarion," Zakath snapped. "Make ready. You're leaving for Mal Zeth; and to make sure you behave yourself, I'm going to separate all of you people. That should give me plenty of hostages in the event you decide to do something rash. I think that covers everything. This conversation is concluded."

Belgarath covered his mouth with one hand and coughed. Toth nodded and lowered his head.

Zakath stepped back in startled amazement as a shimmering apparition suddenly appeared directly in front of him. He glared at Garion. "Is this some kind of trick?" he demanded.

"No tricks, Zakath," Garion replied. "She has some things to tell you. I suggest that you listen."

"Wilt thou hear my words, Zakath?" the glowing form of the blindfolded Seeress of Kell asked him.

Zakath's face was still taut with suspicion. "What is it, Cyradis?" he asked bluntly.

"My time with thee must needs be short, Emperor of Mallorea. I spoke to thee once concerning a crossroad in thy life. Thou hast reached that point now. Put aside thine imperious manner and submit willingly to the task which I must lay upon thee. Thou hast spoken here of hostages."

He drew himself up. "A custom, Cyradis," he told her. "It's a simple means of insuring good behavior."

"Dost thou indeed feel so feeble that thou must threaten the innocent to impose thy will upon others?" Her tone was lightly touched with scorn.

"Feeble? Me?"

"Why else wouldst thou choose so cowardly a course? But hear me well, Kal Zakath, for thy life hangs in the balance. In the instant that thou dost raise thy hand against the Child of Light or any of his companions, thy heart shall burst, and thou shalt die between two breaths."

"So be it then. I rule in Mallorea, and to change or falter because of any threat—even yours—is to become as nothing in my own eyes, and I will not do that."

"Then shalt thou surely die, and in thy death shall thy mighty empire crumble into dust." She said it with a dreadful finality.

He stared at her, his pale face growing even more livid.

"Thou wilt not hear my warnings, Emperor of Mallorea, so I will make thee an offer instead. If thou dost require a hostage, *I* will be thy hostage. The Child of Light doth know that should I depart from this life 'ere my task is complete, his quest will surely fail. What better restraint canst thou place upon him?"

"I will not threaten you, Holy Seeress," he said, sounding a bit less sure of himself.

"And why not, mighty Zakath?"

"It would not be appropriate," he said shortly. "Was that all you had to say to me? I have certain duties to attend to."

"They are of no moment. Thine only true duties are to me and to the task which I shall lay upon thee. The completion of that task is the purpose of thy life. It was for that and for that only that thou wast born. Shouldst thou refuse it, thou wilt not live to see another winter."

"That's the second time you've threatened my life since you arrived, Cyradis. Do you hate me so much?"

"I do not hate thee, Zakath, and I made no threats. I merely revealed unto thee that which fate has in store for thee. Wilt thou accept thy task?"

"Not until I know a little more about it."

"Very well, then. I will reveal unto thee the first part of thy task. Thou must come to me at Kell, where I shall submit to thee. I shall be thy hostage, but thou art also surely mine. Come thou then to Kell with the Child of Light and his other chosen companions; for, as hath been foretold since the beginning of days, thou art of their company."

"But—"

She held up one slim hand. "Leave behind thee thy retinue and thine army and thy symbols of power. They will be of no use to thee." She paused. "Or art thou fearful, O mighty Zakath, to go about in thy vast realm without thy soldiers clustered about thee to compel the stubborn knee to bend and to coerce the rebellious to submit to thy will?"

Zakath flushed angrily. "I fear nothing, Holy Seeress," he replied in a cold voice, "not even death."

"Death is a small thing, Kal Zakath. Methinks it is *life*

307

which thou dost fear. As I have said, thou art my hostage, and I command thee to come to me at Kell and there to take up thy burden."

The Emperor of Mallorea began to tremble. Garion knew this man and he knew that Zakath would normally reject Cyradis' imperious command instantly, but he appeared seized by some overpowering compulsion. His trembling grew more violent, and his pale face broke out in a sweat.

Cyradis, despite her blindfolded eyes, seemed to be aware of the turmoil which had seized her "hostage." "Thy choice is well made, Kal Zakath," she declared. "Thou wilt submit to me willingly—or with reluctance—but thou *must* submit, for it is thy destiny." She drew herself up. "Speak now, Emperor of Mallorea, for thy fate requires thine acceptance of it. Wilt thou come to me at Kell?"

He seemed to choke on it. "I will come," he croaked.

"So be it then. Take thy foreordained place at Belgarion's side and come to the Holy City. There shall I instruct thee further in thy task and tell thee why it is not merely thy life which doth hinge upon it, but the life of all this world." She turned slightly so that her blindfolded eyes seemed to be looking at Garion. "Bring him to me, Child of Light," she told him, "for all of this is a part of what must come to pass ere the final meeting."

She stretched out her hand to Toth in a gesture of longing. And then she vanished.

"And now we are twelve," Sadi murmured.

The most recent recruit to their company, however, stood ashen-faced in the center of the tent, and Garion was astonished to see unshed tears standing in the eyes of the Emperor of Mallorea.

CHAPTER EIGHTEEN

"The Empty One," Eriond said with a slight note of satisfaction in his voice. "It's almost complete now."

"I don't quite follow you," Sadi confessed.

"Cyradis came to us at Rheon," the young man explained. "She told us who would come with us to the Place Which Is No More. I've been wondering who the Empty One would be. Now I know."

"And how did she describe me?" the eunuch asked.

"Are you really sure you want to know?"

"I have a certain curiosity about it, yes."

"She called you the Man Who Is No Man."

Sadi winced. "That's direct enough, isn't it?"

"You did ask."

Sadi sighed. "It's all right, Eriond," he said. "The procedure took place when I was a baby, so I've never known what it might be like to be different. Actually, I find all this interest in that particular function slightly amusing. Mine is a much less complicated way of life."

"Why did they do it to you?"

Sadi shrugged, rubbing his hand over his shaved scalp. "My mother was poor," he replied. "It was the only gift she could give me."

"Gift?"

"It gave me the chance for employment in Queen Salmissra's palace. Otherwise, I'd have probably been a street beggar like the rest of my family."

"Are you all right?" Garion asked the ashen-faced Zakath.

"Just leave me alone, Garion," Zakath muttered.

"Why don't you let me deal with it, dear?" Polgara suggested to Garion. "This is very difficult for him."

"I can understand that. It didn't come too easily for me, either."

"And we broke it to you gently. Cyradis didn't have time to be gentle. I'll talk with him."

"All right, Aunt Pol." Garion walked away and left her alone with the shaken Zakath. This particular turn of events gave him some misgivings. Although he liked the Mallorean Emperor personally, he could foresee any number of difficulties arising from the inclusion of this man in their party. Quite often in the past, their very survival had depended entirely upon the absolute oneness of purpose of every member of the group, and Zakath's motives were never really clear.

"Garion," the voice in his mind said wearily, *"don't tamper with things you don't understand. Zakath has to go with you, so you might as well get used to the idea."*

"But—"

310

"No buts. Just do it."

Garion muttered a few oaths under his breath.

"And don't swear at me, either."

"This is an absurdity!" Zakath burst out, slumping into a chair.

"No," Polgara disagreed. "You just have to get used to looking at the world in a different way, that's all. For most people, that's not necessary. You're a member of a very select group now, and different rules apply."

"Rules have *never* applied to me, Lady Polgara. I make my own rules."

"Not anymore."

"Why me?" Zakath demanded.

"That's always the first question they ask," Belgarath said drily to Silk.

"Has anybody ever answered it?"

"Not to my knowledge, no."

"We can instruct you as we go along," Polgara assured Zakath. "The only important thing right now is whether or not you intend to honor your commitment to Cyradis."

"Of course I do. I gave my word. I don't like it, but I don't have any choice. How can she possibly manipulate me the way she does?"

"She has very strange powers."

"She does it by sorcery, you mean?"

"No. By truth."

"Did you understand any of that gibberish she was speaking?"

"Some of it, but certainly not all. I told you that we look at the world in a different way. The seers look at it in yet another. No one who does not share their vision can fully understand it."

Zakath stared at the floor. "I suddenly feel very helpless," he admitted, "and I don't like the feeling. I've been rather effectively dethroned, you know. This morning I was the Emperor of the largest nation on earth; this afternoon, I'm going to be a vagabond."

"You might find it refreshing," Silk told him lightly.

"Shut up, Kheldar," Zakath said almost absently. He looked back at Polgara. "You know something rather peculiar?"

"What's that?"

"Even if I hadn't given my word, I'd still have to go to Kell. It's almost like a compulsion. I feel as if I'm being driven, and my driver is a blindfolded girl who's hardly more than a child."

"There are rewards," she told him.

"Such as what?"

"Who knows? Happiness, perhaps."

He laughed ironically. "Happiness has never been a driving ambition of mine, Lady Polgara, not for a long time now."

"You may have to accept it anyway." She smiled. "We aren't allowed to choose our rewards any more than we are our tasks. Those decisions are made for us."

"Are *you* happy?"

"Why, yes, as a matter of fact, I am."

He sighed.

"And why so great a sigh, Kal Zakath?"

He held up his thumb and forefinger spread an inch or so apart. "I was that close to becoming the master of the entire world."

"Why would you want to be?"

He shrugged. "No one's ever done it before, and power has its satisfactions."

"You'll find other satisfactions, I'm sure," she smiled, laying one hand on his shoulder.

"It's settled?" Belgarath asked the Mallorean.

"Nothing is ever really settled, Belgarath," Zakath replied. "Not until we're in our graves; but yes, I'll go to Kell with you."

"Why don't you send for Atesca, then? You'll need to tell him where you're going, so he can at least cover our rear. I don't like having people sneak up behind me. Has Urvon made it across the Magan as yet?"

"That's very hard to say. Have you looked outside today, Belgarath?"

"The tent door is guarded, and Atesca's soldiers don't encourage sight-seeing."

"The fog's so thick you could walk on it. Urvon could be anyplace out there."

Polgara rose and quickly crossed to the tent flap. She opened it, and one of the guards outside said something to her sharply.

"Oh, don't be silly," she told him. Then she took several deep breaths and closed the flap. "It's not natural, father," she said soberly. "It doesn't smell right."

"Grolims?"

"I think so, yes. Probably Chandim trying to conceal Urvon's forces from Atesca's patrol boats. They should be able to cross the Magan without much difficulty."

"Once they get across, the trip to Kell might just turn into a horse race."

"I'll talk to Atesca," Zakath said. "He might be able to delay them a bit." He looked speculatively at the old man. "I know why I'm going to Kell," he said, "but why are *you*?"

"I have to read the Mallorean Gospels to find out what our ultimate destination is."

"You mean you don't know?"

"Not yet, no. I know what it's called, though. They keep calling it the Place Which Is No More."

"Belgarath, that's pure gibberish."

"I didn't come up with the name, so don't blame me."

"Why didn't you say something back at Mal Zeth? I have a copy of the Gospels in my library."

"In the first place, I didn't know about it when I was at

Mal Zeth. I only found out recently. In the second place, your copy wouldn't have done me any good. They're all different, I'm told, and the only one that contains the passage I need is at Kell."

"It all sounds very complicated."

"It is. These things usually are."

Zakath went to the door of the tent and spoke briefly with one of the guards posted there. Then he came back. "I've sent for Atesca and Brador," he said. He smiled a bit ruefully. "I wouldn't be surprised if they objected rather violently to this whole thing."

"Don't give them time to object," Garion advised.

"They're both Melcenes, Garion," Zakath pointed out. "Melcenes object to things out of habit." He frowned. "Speaking of that, why did you go to Melcena? Wasn't it a bit out of your way?"

"We were following Zandramas," Garion replied.

"Why did *she* go there?"

"She had to pick up your cousin, Archduke Otrath."

"That silly ass? What for?"

"She took him to Hemil and crowned him Emperor of Mallorea."

"She did *what?*" Zakath's eyes bulged.

"She needs an Angarak king with her when she gets to the Place Which Is No More. As I understand it, the coronation ceremony had a certain validity."

"Not after I get my hands on Otrath, it won't!" Zakath's face was scarlet with anger.

"There was another reason for our going to Melcena—although we didn't know it at the time," Belgarath said. "There was an unmutilated copy of the Ashabine Oracles there. I had to read that in order to find out that our next step is the trip to Kell. I'm following a trail that was laid down for me thousands of years ago."

Atesca and Brador entered. "You sent for us, your Majesty?" Atesca said with a crisp salute.

"Yes," Zakath replied. He looked at the two of them speculatively. "Please listen carefully," he instructed, "and try not to argue with me." Oddly he said it not so much in the tone of imperial command, but rather as a man appealing to two old friends. "There's been a change of plans," he went on. "Certain information has come into my possession, and it's absolutely imperative that we not interfere with Belgarion and his friends. Their mission is vital to the security of Mallorea."

Brador's eyes came alight with curiosity. "Shouldn't I perhaps be briefed on this matter, your Imperial Majesty?" he asked. "State security is my responsibility, after all."

"Ah—no, Brador," Zakath said regretfully, "I'm afraid not. It might require too great an adjustment in your thinking. You're not ready for that. As a matter of fact, I'm not sure I am, either. At any rate, Belgarion and these others absolutely *must* go to Dalasia." He paused. "Oh, one other thing," he added. "I'll be going with them."

Atesca stared incredulously at his Emperor. Then, with some effort, he got himself under control. "I'll notify the commander of the Imperial Guard, your Majesty," he said stiffly. "They'll be ready to leave within the hour."

"Don't bother," Zakath told him. "They won't be going with us. I'll be going with Belgarion alone."

"Alone?" Atesca exclaimed. "Your Majesty, that's unheard of."

Zakath smiled wanly. "You see," he said to Garion. "What did I tell you?"

"General," Belgarath said to Atesca, "Kal Zakath is simply following orders. I'm sure you can understand that. He was told not to bring any troops along. Troops wouldn't do him any good where we're going anyway."

"Orders?" Atesca said in amazement. "Who has the authority to give his Majesty orders?"

"It's a long story, Atesca," the old man told him, "and we're pressed for time."

"Ah—your Imperial Majesty," Brador said diffidently, "if you're going to Dalasia, that means you'll have to cross the whole of Darshiva. Might I remind you that Darshiva is hostile territory at the moment? Is it wise to risk the imperial person under such circumstances? Might not an escort at least as far as the border be prudent?"

Zakath looked at Belgarath.

The old man shook his head. "Let's just do it the way we were told to," he said.

"Sorry, Brador," Zakath said. "We can't take an escort with us. I think I'll need some armor, though, and a sword."

"Your Majesty has not held a sword for years," Atesca objected.

"Belgarion can give me some instruction." Zakath shrugged. "I'm sure I'll pick it up again. Now then, Urvon's going to cross the Magan. I have it on very good authority that there won't be very much we can do to stop him. I imagine that the Darshivan Army won't be very far behind him, and they have elephant cavalry with them. I want you to keep all those people off my back. Delay Urvon long enough for the Darshivans to catch up with him. After that, they can annihilate each other, for all I care. Once those two armies are fully engaged, pull back your forces. Don't get any more of my soldiers killed than you absolutely have to."

Atesca frowned. "Then the policy we discussed at Maga Renn is no longer in force?" he asked.

Zakath shrugged. "Policy changes from time to time," he said. "At this point, I'm militantly indifferent about who wins an unimportant battle in this corner of the world. That may give you some idea of just how vital Belgarion's mission is." He looked at Garion. "Does that cover everything?"

"Except for the demons," Garion replied. "They're here in Darshiva, too."

Zakath frowned. "I'd forgotten about them. They'll come to Urvon's aid, won't they?"

"Nahaz will," Belgarath told him. "Mordja will help the Darshivans."

"You're going a little fast for me."

"When Urvon showed up with Nahaz in tow, Zandramas raised a Demon Lord of her own," the old man explained. "She went a little far afield for him, actually. Mordja is Lord over the demons in Morindland. He and Nahaz are evenly matched, and they've hated each other for all eternity."

"Then it still appears to be a stalemate. Both sides have an army and they both have demons."

"Demons are grossly unselective in their choice of victims, Zakath," Polgara said. "They'll kill anything that moves, and your own army's here in Darshiva."

"I hadn't thought of that," he conceded. He looked around. "Any suggestions?"

Belgarath and Polgara exchanged a long look. "I suppose it's worth a try," the old sorcerer shrugged. "He's not fond of Angaraks, but He's even less fond of demons. I think we'll have better luck with Him if we go outside the camp, though."

"Exactly who are we talking about?" Zakath asked curiously.

"Aldur," Belgarath replied. He scratched at his cheek. "Would it be safe to tell Him that you'd be very reluctant to go with us if your army was in danger?" he asked.

"I think you could say that, yes." Zakath's eyes widened. "Are you trying to say you can actually summon a God?" he asked incredulously.

"I'm not sure if summon is exactly the right word. We can talk with Him, though. We'll see what He says."

"You're not really going to try subterfuge, are you, father?" Polgara asked the old man.

317

"Aldur knows what I'm doing," he replied. "I couldn't deceive Him if I tried. Zakath's reluctance just gives us a starting point for the conversation. Aldur's reasonable, but He's always liked a good argument. You should know that, Pol. He helped to educate you, after all. Let's see if we can talk with Him."

"Would it be all right if I came along?" Eriond asked. "I need to talk with Him, too."

Belgarath looked a bit surprised at that. He looked for a moment as if he were about to refuse, but then he seemed to change his mind. "Suit yourself," he shrugged. "Atesca, could you have your guards escort us as far as that ditch around the outside of the camp? We'll go on from there alone."

Atesca spoke with the guards at the door of the tent, and the three were allowed to leave without challenge.

"I'd give a great deal to witness this meeting," Brador murmured. "Have you ever seen Aldur, Prince Kheldar?"

"A couple of times, yes," Silk replied in an offhand manner. "Once in the Vale and then again at Cthol Mishrak when He and the other Gods came to claim the body of Torak after Garion killed Him."

"I'd imagine that He took a certain satisfaction in that," Zakath said. "Aldur and Torak were sworn enemies."

"No," Garion disagreed sadly. "No one took any pleasure in the death of Torak. He and Aldur were brothers. I think UL grieved the most, though. Torak was His son, after all."

"There seem to be some fairly huge gaps in Angarak theology," Zakath mused. "I don't think the Grolims even admit the existence of UL."

"They would if they ever saw Him," Silk said.

"Is He really that impressive-looking?" Brador asked.

"It's not so much the way He looks." Silk shrugged. "It's the sense of His presence. It's overwhelming."

"He was very nice to *me*," Ce'Nedra objected.

"Everybody's nice to you, Ce'Nedra," Silk told her. "You have that effect on people."

"Most of the time," Garion corrected.

"I suppose we'd better start packing," Durnik suggested. "I think Belgarath's going to want to leave just as soon as he gets back." He looked at Atesca. "Do you suppose we could get a few things from your stores?" he asked. "It's a long way to Kell, and I don't think we'll be able to pick up much in the way of supplies here in Darshiva."

"Of course, Goodman Durnik," the general replied.

"I'll make out a list of the things we'll need, then."

As Durnik sat down at the table to draw up his list, Atesca gave Silk a penetrating look. "We never did get the chance to talk about your recent venture in the commodities market, did we, your Highness?" he said.

"Are you considering a second career, Atesca?" Zakath asked him.

"Hardly, your Majesty. I'm quite happy as a soldier. Prince Kheldar recently did a bit of speculation in this year's bean crop. The Bureau of Military Procurement went into a state of anguished consternation when they found out his asking price."

Brador suddenly chuckled. "Good for you, Kheldar," he said.

"That's a peculiar attitude, Brador," Zakath reproved him. "How would you like it if I took Prince Kheldar's excess profits out of your budget?"

"Actually, your Majesty, Kheldar's venture didn't cost your treasury a thing. The members of the Bureau of Military Procurement are the greatest unhanged scoundrels in the empire. Some years ago, while you were busy in Cthol Murgos, they sent you a rather innocuous-looking document having to do with standardizing the prices of all the items they purchase for the army."

"I remember it—vaguely. Their argument seemed to be that it would provide a basis for long-range planning."

"That was on the surface, your Majesty. In actuality, fixing those prices provided them with a golden opportunity to line their own pockets. They could buy at below the fixed price, sell to the army at the legal rate, and keep the difference for themselves."

"What is the fixed rate on beans?"

"Ten half-crowns per hundredweight, your Majesty."

"That doesn't seem unreasonable."

"When they're buying at three half-crowns?"

Zakath stared at him.

Brador held up one hand. "However," he said, "by law, they *have* to sell to the army at ten—no matter what price they have to pay, so they have to make up the difference out of their own pockets. That might account for the anguish General Atesca mentioned."

Zakath suddenly grinned a wolfish sort of grin. "What price were you asking, Kheldar?" he asked.

"I sold out to the Melcene Consortium at fifteen." The little man shrugged, buffing his nails on the front of his tunic. "I'd imagine that they added a few points to that—reasonable profit, you understand."

"And you controlled the entire bean crop?"

"I certainly tried."

"I feel fairly sure that your Majesty will receive several letters of resignation from members of the Bureau," Brador said. "I'd advise not accepting them until *after* all accounts are settled."

"I'll keep that in mind, Brador." Zakath looked speculatively at Silk. "Tell me, Kheldar," he said, "how much would you take to suspend operations here in Mallorea?"

"I don't really believe your Majesty's treasury has that much money," Silk replied blandly. "Besides, I've become a sort of necessity. The Mallorean economy was stagnant until I got here. You could almost say that I'm working for you."

"Did that make any sense?" Zakath asked Brador.

"Yes, your Majesty," Brador sighed. "In a peculiar way, it

does. Our tax revenues have been rising steadily since Kheldar and his scruffy-looking partner began doing business here in the empire. If we were to expel him, it's entirely possible that the economy would collapse."

"Then I'm at his mercy?"

"To some degree, yes, your Majesty."

Zakath sighed mournfully. "I wish I hadn't gotten out of bed this morning," he said.

Both Belgarath and Polgara looked troubled when they returned with Eriond close behind them. The blond young man, however, looked as unconcerned as always.

"What did He say?" Garion asked.

"He didn't like it too much," Belgarath said, "but He finally agreed. General Atesca, how many troops do you have here in Darshiva?"

"Several hundred thousand. They're in enclaves like this one up and down the east bank of the Magan. The bulk of our forces are across the river in Peldane. We can summon them on short notice."

"Leave them where they are. Once you've delayed Urvon long enough to allow the Darshivan army to catch up with him, withdraw all your men to this enclave."

"It's hardly big enough for that many men, Ancient One," Atesca pointed out.

"You'd better expand it, then. Aldur has agreed to protect this enclave. He didn't say anything about any of the others. Bring your men here. He'll keep the demons away."

"How?" Brador asked curiously.

"Demons can't bear the presence of a God. Neither Nahaz nor Mordja will come within ten leagues of this place."

"He's actually going to be here?"

"Only in a rather peculiar sense of the word. Once the enclave is expanded, that ditch of yours is going to be filled with a kind of blue light. Tell your men to stay out of it. Aldur's still not fond of Angaraks, and peculiar things might

321

happen to any soldier who strays into that light." The old man suddenly grinned at Zakath. "You might find it interesting to know that your whole army here in Darshiva will be at least nominally subject to Aldur for a while," he said. "He's never had an army before, so it's a little hard to say what he might decide to do with one."

"Is your grandfather always like this?" Zakath asked Garion.

"Usually, yes." Garion stood up, moving his fingers slightly. Then he crossed to the far side of the tent. Belgarath followed him. "What happened out there, Grandfather?" Garion whispered.

Belgarath shrugged. "We talked with Aldur, and He promised to protect Zakath's army."

Garion shook his head. "No," he said, "something else happened, too. Both you and Aunt Pol were looking very strange when you came back—and why did Eriond go with you?"

"It's a long story," the old man replied evasively.

"I've got time. I think I'd better know what's going on."

"No, as a matter of fact, you'd better not. Aldur was quite emphatic about that. If you know what's happening, it might interfere with what you have to do."

"I thought we'd exhausted that tired old excuse a long time ago. I'm grown now. You don't have to try to keep me stupid."

"I'll tell you what, Garion. Since you're the Child of Light, why don't you go talk with Aldur yourself? He might even decide to tell you, but that's up to Him. He told me to keep my mouth shut, and I'm not going to disobey my Master, whether you like it or not." And he turned and went back to rejoin the others.

CHAPTER NINETEEN

"I still don't understand why I have to look so shabby," Zakath said as he reentered the pavilion. He wore a battered breastplate over a mail shirt and a rust-splotched helmet devoid of any kind of decoration. A patched brown cloak was draped over his shoulders, and a plain, leather-bound sword hung at his side.

"Explain it to him, Silk," Belgarath said. "You're the expert at this sort of thing."

"It's really not all that complicated," Silk told the Emperor. "It's fairly standard practice for travelers to hire a few mercenary soldiers to act as armed guards. Mercenaries don't usu-

323

ally spend all that much time taking care of their equipment, so we had to make you look a bit down at the heels. All you and Garion have to do is wear armor and ride in front looking dangerous."

A faint smile touched the Mallorean's pallid features. "I didn't think anonymity would require such pains."

Silk grinned at him. "Actually, it's harder to be anonymous than it is to be a grand duke. Now, please don't be offended, Zakath, but we're all going to forget we know how to say 'your Majesty.' Someone might make a slip at the wrong time."

"That's perfectly all right, Kheldar," Zakath replied. "All the 'Majesties' grate on my ears sometimes anyway."

Silk looked closely at their newest recruit's face. "You really ought to spend more time outside, you know. You're as pale as a sheet."

"I can take care of that, Silk," Polgara said. "I'll mix up something to make him look suitably weather-beaten."

"Oh, one other thing," Silk added. "Your face is on every coin in Mallorea, isn't it?"

"You should know. You've got most of them, haven't you?"

"Well, I've picked up a few here and there," Silk said modestly. "Let's cover up that famous face with whiskers. Stop shaving."

"Kheldar, I haven't shaved my own face since my beard sprouted. I wouldn't even know how to hold a razor."

"You let somebody else near your throat with a razor? Isn't that a trifle imprudent?"

"Does that more or less cover everything?" Belgarath asked the little Drasnian.

"That covers the basics," Silk replied. "I can coach him on the finer details as we go along."

"All right, then." The old man looked around at them. "We're likely to encounter people out there. Some of them might be hostile, but most of them will probably just be trying to stay out of harm's way, so they won't bother a group of ordinary travelers." He looked directly at Zakath. "Silk should be able to talk us out of most situations, but if we get into any serious confrontations, I want you to fall back a bit and let the rest of us handle things. You're out of practice with your weapons, and I didn't go to all the trouble of finding you to lose you in some meaningless skirmish."

"I can still carry my own weight, Belgarath."

"I'm sure you can, but let's not risk it right at first. Cyradis might be very unhappy if we don't have you with us in one piece when we get to Kell."

Zakath shrugged, walked over, and sat on the bench beside Garion. The Rivan King was dressed in his mail shirt and he was sliding the snug-fitting leather sleeve over the hilt of Iron-grip's sword. Zakath was actually grinning, and the unaccustomed expression made him look ten years younger. Garion was uncomfortably reminded of Lelldorin. "I think you're actually enjoying this, aren't you?" he asked.

"For some reason, I feel almost like a young man again," Zakath replied. "Is it always like this—subterfuge and a little danger and this wild sense of exhilaration?"

"More or less," Garion replied. "Sometimes there's more than just a little danger, though."

"I can live with that. My life's been tediously secure so far."

"Even when Naradas poisoned you back in Cthol Murgos?"

"I was too sick to know what was going on," Zakath said. "I envy you, Garion. You've had a wildly exciting life." He frowned slightly. "Something rather peculiar is happening to me," he confessed. "Ever since I agreed to meet Cyradis at Kell, I've felt as if some vast weight had been lifted off me. The whole world looks fresh and new now. I have absolutely no control over my life, and yet I'm as happy as a fish in deep water. It's irrational, but I can't help it."

Garion looked rather closely at him. "Don't misunderstand," he said. "I'm not deliberately trying to be mystical about this, but you're probably happy because you're doing what you're supposed to do. It happens to all of us. It's a part of that different way of looking at things Aunt Pol mentioned earlier, and it's one of the rewards she talked about."

"That's a little obscure for me," Zakath admitted.

"Give it some time," Garion told him. "It comes to you gradually."

General Atesca entered the tent with Brador close behind him. "The horses are ready, your Majesty," he reported in a neutral tone. Garion could tell by Atesca's expression that he still strongly disapproved of this whole business. The General turned to Durnik. "I've added a few more pack animals, Goodman," he said. "Yours were fairly well loaded down."

"Thank you, General," Durnik replied.

"I'm going to be out of touch, Atesca," Zakath said, "so I'm leaving you in charge here. I'll try to get word to you from time to time, but there may be long periods when you won't hear from me."

"Yes, your Majesty," Atesca replied.

"You know what to do, though. Let Brador handle civil matters, and you deal with the military situation. Get the troops back here to this enclave as soon as Urvon and the Darshivans are engaged. And keep in touch with Mal Zeth." He tugged a large signet ring off his finger. "Use this if you need to seal any official documents."

"Such documents require your Majesty's signature," Atesca reminded him.

"Brador can forge it. He writes my name better than I do myself."

"Your Majesty!" Brador protested.

"Don't play innocent with me, Brador. I've known about your experiments in penmanship. Take care of my cat while I'm gone, and see if you can find homes for the rest of those kittens."

"Yes, your Majesty."

"Anything else that needs my attention before I leave?"

"Ah—one thing, your Majesty," Atesca said. "A disciplinary matter."

"Can't you take care of it?" Zakath asked a bit irritably. He was obviously impatient to be off.

"I can, your Majesty," Atesca said, "but you've sort of placed the man under your personal protection, so I thought I'd consult with you before I took action."

"Whom am I protecting?" Zakath looked puzzled.

"It's a corporal from the Mal Zeth garrison, your Majesty—a man named Actas. He was drunk on duty."

"Actas? I don't recall—"

"It was that corporal who'd been demoted just before we arrived in Mal Zeth," Ce'Nedra reminded him. "The one whose wife was making such a scene in that side street."

"Oh, yes," Zakath said. "Now I remember. Drunk, you say? He's not supposed to drink any more."

"I doubt if he could drink any more, your Majesty," Atesca said with a faint smile, "at least not right now. He's as drunk as a lord."

"Is he nearby?"

"Just outside, your Majesty."

Zakath sighed. "I guess you'd better bring him in," he said. He looked at Belgarath. "This should only take a moment or two," he apologized.

Garion remembered the scrawny corporal as soon as the fellow staggered into the tent. The corporal tried to come to attention, without much success. Then he attempted to bang his breastplate in a salute, but hit himself in the nose with his fist instead. "Yer Imperrl Majeshy," he slurred.

"What am I going to do with you, Actas," Zakath said wearily.

"I've made a beash of myshelf, yer Majeshy," Actas confessed, "an absholute beash."

"Yes," Zakath agreed, "you have." He turned his head

away. "Please don't breathe on me, Actas. Your mouth smells like a reopened grave. Take him out and sober him up, Atesca."

"I'll personally throw him in the river, your Majesty." Atesca was trying to suppress a grin.

"You're enjoying this, aren't you?"

"Me, your Majesty?"

Zakath's eyes narrowed slyly. "Well, Ce'Nedra?" he said. "He's your responsibility, too. What do we do with him?"

She waved one little hand negligently. "Hang him," she said in an indifferent tone. She looked more closely at her hand. "Great Nedra!" she exclaimed. "I've broken another fingernail!"

Corporal Actas' eyes were bulging and his mouth was suddenly agape. Trembling violently, he fell to his knees. "Please, your Majesty," he begged, suddenly cold sober. "Please!"

Zakath squinted at the Rivan Queen, who sat mourning the broken nail. "Take him outside, Atesca," he said. "I'll give you orders for his final disposition in a moment."

Atesca saluted and hauled the blubbering Actas to his feet.

"You weren't really serious, were you, Ce'Nedra?" Zakath asked after the two men had left.

"Oh, of course not," she said. "I'm not a monster, Zakath. Clean him up and send him back to his wife." She tapped one finger thoughtfully on her chin. "*But* erect a gibbet in the street in front of his house. Give him something to think about the next time he gets thirsty."

"You actually *married* this woman?" Zakath exclaimed to Garion.

"It was sort of arranged by our families," Garion replied with aplomb. "We didn't have much to say about it."

"Now, be nice, Garion," Ce'Nedra said with unruffled calm.

They mounted their horses outside the pavilion and rode

through the camp to the drawbridge spanning the deep, stake-studded ditch that formed a part of the outer fortifications. When they reached the far side of the ditch, Zakath let out an explosive breath of relief.

"What is it?" Garion asked him.

"I was half afraid that somebody might have found a way to keep me there." He glanced a bit apprehensively back over his shoulder. "Do you think we could possibly gallop for a ways?" he asked. "I'd hate to have them catch up with me."

Garion began to have misgivings at that point. "Are you sure you're all right?" he asked suspiciously.

"I've never felt better—or more free—in my entire life," Zakath declared.

"I was afraid of that," Garion muttered.

"What?"

"Just keep moving at a canter, Zakath. There's something I need to discuss with Belgarath. I'll be right back." He reined Chretienne in and rode back to where his grandfather and his aunt rode side by side, deep in conversation. "He's absolutely out of control," he told them. "What's happened to him?"

"It's the first time in his entire life that he hasn't had the weight of half the world on his shoulders, Garion," Polgara replied calmly. "He'll settle down. Just give him a day or so."

"Do we have a day or so? He's acting exactly the way Lelldorin would—or maybe even Mandorallen. Can we afford that?"

"Talk to him," Belgarath suggested. "Just keep talking. Recite the *Book of Alorn* to him if you have to."

"But I don't know the *Book of Alorn*, Grandfather," Garion objected.

"Yes, you do. It's in your blood. You could have recited it letter-perfect in your cradle. Now get back up there before he gets completely out of hand."

Garion swore and rode back to rejoin Zakath.

"Trouble?" Silk asked him.

"I don't want to talk about it."

Beldin was waiting for them around the next bend in the road. "Well," the grotesque little hunchback said. "It seems to have worked, but why did you bring him along?"

"Cyradis persuaded him to come with us," Belgarath replied. "What gave you the idea of going to her?"

"It was worth a try. Pol told me about a few of the things she said to him back in Cthol Murgos. She seems to have some sort of interest in him. I didn't really think he was supposed to join us, though. What did she say to him?"

"She told him that he'd die if he didn't come with us."

"I imagine that got his attention. Hello, Zakath."

"Do we know each other?"

"I know you—by sight, anyway. I've seen you parading through the streets of Mal Zeth a few times."

"This is my brother Beldin," Belgarath introduced the misshapen dwarf.

"I didn't know you had any brothers."

"The relationship's a bit obscure, but we serve the same Master, so that makes us brothers in a peculiar sort of way. There used to be seven of us, but there are only four of us left now."

Zakath frowned slightly. "Your name rings a bell, Master Beldin," he said. "Aren't you the one whose picture is posted on every tree for six leagues in any direction from Mal Yaska?"

"I believe that's me, all right. I make Urvon a little nervous. He seems to think that I want to split him up the middle."

"Do you?"

"I've thought about it a time or two. I think what I'd really like to do, though, is yank out his guts, hang them on a thorn-bush, and invite in some vultures. I'm sure he'd find watching them eat very entertaining."

Zakath blanched slightly.

"Vultures have to eat, too." The hunchback shrugged. "Oh, speaking of eating, Pol, do you have anything decent around? All I've had in the last few days was a very scrawny rat and a nest full of crow's eggs. I don't think there's a rabbit or a pigeon left in the whole of Darshiva."

"This is a very unusual fellow," Zakath said to Garion.

"He gets more unusual the more you get to know him." Garion smiled slightly. "He frightened Urvon almost into sanity at Ashaba."

"He was exaggerating, wasn't he—about the vultures, I mean?"

"Probably not. He fully intends to gut Torak's last Disciple like a butchered hog."

Zakath's eyes grew bright. "You think he might want some help?" he asked eagerly.

"Were any of your ancestors possibly Arendish?" Garion asked suspiciously.

"I don't understand the question."

"Never mind." Garion sighed.

Beldin squatted in the dirt at the roadside, tearing at the carcass of a cold roast chicken. "You burnt it, Pol," he accused.

"I didn't cook it, uncle," she replied primly.

"Why not? Did you forget how?"

"I have a wonderful recipe for boiled dwarf," she told him. "I'm almost sure I could find someone willing to eat that sort of thing."

"You're losing your edge again, Pol," he said, wiping his greasy fingers on the front of his ragged tunic. "Your mind's getting as flabby as your bottom."

Garion restrained Zakath with one hand when the Mallorean Emperor's face grew outraged. "It's a personal thing," he cautioned. "I wouldn't interfere. They've been insulting each other for thousands of years. It's a peculiar kind of love, I think."

"Love?"

"Listen," Garion suggested. "You might learn something.

331

Alorns aren't like Angaraks. We don't bow very often and we sometimes hide our feelings with jokes."

"Polgara is an Alorn?" Zakath sounded surprised.

"Use your eyes, man. Her hair's dark, I'll grant you, but her twin sister was as blond as a wheat field. Look at her cheekbones and her jaw. I rule a kingdom of Alorns and I know what they look like. She and Liselle could be sisters."

"Now that you mention it, they *do* look a bit alike, don't they? How is it I never saw that before?"

"You hired Brador to be your eyes," Garion replied, shifting his mail shirt. "I don't trust other peoples' eyes all that much."

"Is Beldin an Alorn, too?"

"Nobody knows what Beldin is. He's so deformed that you can't put a name to him."

"Poor fellow."

"Don't waste your pity on Beldin," Garion replied. "He's six thousand years old and he could turn you into a frog if he felt like it. He can make it snow or rain, and he's far, far smarter than Belgarath."

"But he's so grubby," Zakath said, eyeing the filthy dwarf.

"He's grubby because he doesn't care," Garion said. "This is the form he uses to go among us. It's ugly, so he doesn't waste time on it. His other form is so magnificent it would blind you."

"Other form?"

"It's a peculiarity of ours. Sometimes a human form isn't practical for some of the things we have to do. Beldin likes to fly, so he spends most of his time as a blue-banded hawk."

"I'm a falconer, Garion. I don't believe there is such a bird."

"Tell *him* that." Garion pointed at the ugly dwarf ripping the chicken apart with his teeth by the roadside.

"You could have cut it up first, uncle," Polgara said.

"Why?" He took another huge bite.

"It's more polite."

"Pol, I taught you how to fly and how to hunt. Don't you try to teach me how to eat."

"I don't think 'eat' is the right word, uncle. You're not an eater; you're a ravener."

"We all do it our own way, Pol." He belched. "You do it with a silver fork off a porcelain plate, and I do it with my talons and beak in a ditch beside the road. It all gets to the same place no matter how you do it." He raked a patch of burned skin off the chicken leg he was holding in one hand. "This isn't too bad," he conceded, "at least not after you get down to the real meat."

"Anything up ahead?" Belgarath asked him.

"A few troops, some terrified civilians, and a Grolim now and then. That's about it."

"Any demons?"

"I didn't see any. Of course that doesn't mean they're not lurking around somewhere. You know how it is with demons. Are you going to travel at night again?"

Belgarath thought about it. "I don't think so," he decided. "It takes too long to do it that way, and time's running out on us. Let's just make a run for it."

"Suit yourself." Beldin discarded the remains of the chicken and stood up. "I'll keep an eye out up ahead and let you know when you're about to run into trouble." The hunchback bent, spread his arms, and soared up into the murky sky.

"Torak's teeth!" Zakath exclaimed. "He *is* a blue-banded hawk!"

"He invented it himself," Belgarath said. "He didn't like the regular colors. Let's move along."

Although it was nearly summer, there was a dreary chill hanging over Darshiva. Garion could not be certain if it was the result of the prevailing overcast or if it derived from some other, more ominous, source. The white snags of dead trees lined the road, and the air was thick with the reek of fungus, decay, and stagnant water. They passed long-deserted villages tumbled now into ruins. A roadside temple seemed to huddle mournfully with fungus creeping up its walls like some loathesome disease. Its doors gaped open, and the polished steel mask of the face of Torak, which should have surmounted them, was gone. Belgarath reined in his horse and dismounted. "I'll be right back," he said. He went up the steps of the temple and looked inside. Then he turned and came back. "I thought they might have done that," he said.

"Done what, father?" Aunt Pol asked him.

"They've taken Torak's face down from the wall behind the altar. There's a blank mask there now. They're waiting to see what the New God looks like."

They took shelter for the night beside the half-tumbled wall of a ruined village. They built no fire and traded off standing watch. At first light the next morning, they pushed on. The countryside grew more bleak and foreboding with each passing mile.

About midmorning, Beldin swooped in, flared his wings, and settled to earth. He shimmered into his own form and stood waiting for them. "There are some troops blocking the road about a mile ahead," he announced.

"Any chance of getting around them?" Belgarath asked.

"I doubt it. The country's pretty flat there, and all the vegetation's been dead for years."

"How many are there?" Silk asked.

"Fifteen or so. They've got a Grolim with them."

"Any idea which side they're on?" Belgarath said.

"They're not that distinctive."

"Do you want me to see if I can talk our way past them?" Silk offered.

Belgarath looked at Beldin. "Are they deliberately blocking the road, or are they just camped on it?"

"They've built a barricade out of dead logs."

"That answers that, then. Talk isn't going to do us any good." He mulled it over.

"We could wait until dark and then slip around them," Velvet suggested.

"We'd lose a whole day that way," Belgarath replied. "I don't see any help for it. We're going to have to go through them. Try not to kill any more of them than you absolutely have to."

"That gets right to the point, doesn't it?" Zakath said wryly to Garion.

"There's no sense in trying to surprise them, I suppose?" Belgarath asked Beldin.

The dwarf shook his head. "They'll see you coming for at least a half a mile." He went to the side of the road, wrenched a half-rotten stump out of the ground, and pounded it against a rock until all the decayed wood had been knocked loose. The gnarled taproot made a fearsome-looking cudgel.

"Well, I guess we'd better go have a look," Belgarath said bleakly.

They rode on to the crest of the hill and looked down the road toward the barricade and the troops standing behind it. Zakath peered at them. "Darshivans," he said.

"How can you tell from this distance?" Silk asked him.

"By the shape of their helmets." The Mallorean narrowed his eyes. "Darshivan soldiers are not notoriously brave and they get very little in the way of training. Do you think there might be some way we can lure them out from behind that barricade?"

Garion looked down at the soldiers crouched behind their logs. "I'd say they've been told not to let anybody past," he said. "What if we charge them and then at the last minute swing out and around them? They'll run for their horses. Then we turn around and charge back at them. They'll be confused and milling around, and we'll be able to pin them up against their own barricade. It shouldn't be too hard to put a fair number of them on the ground. The rest should run at that point."

"That's not a bad plan, Garion. You're quite a tactician. Have you had any formal military training?"

"No. I just picked it up."

In a land of brittle, dead trees, a lance was quite out of the question, so Garion strapped his shield to his left arm and drew his sword.

"All right," Belgarath said, "let's give it a try. It might hold down the casualties."

"One other thing," Silk added. "I think we should make a special point of not letting any of them get on a horse. A man on foot can't go for help very fast. If we run off their horses, we can be out of the area before they can bring in reinforcements."

"I'll take care of that," Belgarath said. "All right. Let's go."

They urged their horses into a gallop and charged down the road toward the barricade, brandishing their weapons. As they pounded down the hill, Garion saw Zakath pulling a curious-looking leather half-glove clad with steel onto his right hand.

Just before they reached the barricade and the alarmed soldiers standing behind it, they veered sharply to the left, then galloped around the obstruction and back onto the road.

"After them!" a black-robed Grolim screamed at the startled troops. "Don't let them escape!"

Garion rode on past the soldiers' picketed horses, then wheeled Chretienne around. He charged back with the others close on his heels and rode full into the face of the confused Darshivans. He did not really want to kill any of them, so he laid about him with the flat of the blade rather than the edge. He put three of them down as he crashed through their ranks; behind him he could hear the sound of blows and cries of pain. The Grolim rose before him, and he could feel the black-robed man drawing in his will. He did not falter, but simply rode the priest down. Then he wheeled again. Toth was laying about him with his heavy staff, and Durnik was busily caving in helmets with the butt of his axe. Zakath, however, was leaned far over in his saddle. He had no weapon in his hand but rather was smashing his metal-clad fist into the faces of the Darshivan soldiers. The glove appeared to be quite effective.

Then, from where the soldiers' horses were picketed, there came a blood-curdling howl. The great silver wolf was snapping and snarling at the horses. They lunged back in panic, the picket rope snapped, and they fled.

"Let's go!" Garion shouted to his friends, and they galloped once again through the center of the Darshivans and on down the road to rejoin Polgara, Ce'Nedra, Velvet, and Eriond. Belgarath loped after them, then changed into his own form and walked back to his horse.

"It seems to have worked more or less the way we'd planned," Zakath noted. He was panting, and his forehead was dewed with sweat. "I seem to be a bit out of condition, though," he added.

"Too much sitting down," Silk said. "What's that thing you've got on your hand?"

"It's called a cestus," the Mallorean replied, pulling it off. "I'm a little rusty with my sword, so I thought this might work just as well—particularly since Belgarath wanted to keep down the fatalities."

"Did we kill anybody?" Durnik asked.

"Two," Sadi admitted. He held up his small dagger. "It's a little hard to unpoison a knife."

"And one other," Silk told the smith. "He was running up behind you with a spear, so I threw a knife at him."

"It couldn't be helped," Belgarath said, "Now let's get out of here."

They continued at a gallop for several miles, then slowed back to a canter again.

They took shelter that night in a sizable stand of dead trees. Durnik and Toth dug a shallow pit and built a small fire in it. After the tents were pitched, Garion and Zakath walked to the edge of the trees to keep watch on the road.

"Is it always like this?" Zakath asked quietly.

"Like what?"

"All this sneaking and hiding?"

"Usually. Belgarath tries to avoid trouble whenever he can. He doesn't like to risk people in random skirmishes. Most of the time we're able to avoid the kind of thing that happened this morning. Silk—and Sadi, too, for that matter—have lied us out of some very tight spots." He smiled faintly. "Up in Voresebo, Silk bribed our way past a group of soldiers with a pouchful of brass Mallorean half-pennies."

"But they're virtually worthless."

"That's what Silk said, but we were quite a ways past the soldiers before they opened the pouch."

Then they heard a chilling howl.

"A wolf?" Zakath asked. "Belgarath again?"

"No. That wasn't a wolf. Let's go back. I think Urvon's managed to outflank General Atesca."

"What makes you think so?"

"That was a Hound."

CHAPTER TWENTY

They walked carefully through the forest of dead snags, avoiding as best they could the litter of fallen limbs and twigs on the ground. The faint glow from Durnik's sunken fire guided them, and Garion knew it would serve as a dim beacon for the Hounds as well. Zakath's euphoria seemed to have evaporated. His expression now was wary, and he walked with his hand on his sword hilt.

They entered the small clearing where the others were seated around the fire pit. "There's a Hound out there," Garion said quietly. "It howled once."

"Could you make out what it was saying?" Belgarath asked, his voice tense.

"I don't speak its language, Grandfather. It seemed to be some kind of a call, though."

"Probably to the rest of the pack," the old man grunted. "The Hounds don't hunt alone very often."

"The glow from our fire is fairly visible," Garion pointed out.

"I'll take care of that right away," Durnik said, starting to shovel dirt into the fire pit.

"Could you pinpoint the Hound's location at all?" Belgarath asked.

"It was some distance away," Garion replied. "I think it's out there on the road."

"Following our trail?" Silk asked.

"It's following something. I could pick up that much."

"If the Hound is following us, I can divert it with some of that powder I used back at Ashaba," Sadi suggested.

"What do you think?" Belgarath asked Beldin.

The dwarf squatted on the ground, absently scratching an obscure diagram in the dirt with a broken stick. "It wouldn't work," he said finally. "The Hounds aren't entirely dogs, so they're not going to just blindly follow the one in the lead. Once they pinpoint our location, they'll spread out and come at us from all sides. We're going to have to come up with something else."

"Fairly soon, I'd think," Silk added, looking around nervously.

Polgara removed her blue cloak and handed it to Durnik. "I'll deal with it," she said calmly.

"What have you got in mind, Pol?" Belgarath asked suspiciously.

"I haven't decided yet, Old Wolf. Maybe I'll just make it up as I go along—the way you do sometimes." She drew herself up, and the air around her shimmered with an odd luminescence. She was winging her way off among the dead white trees even before the light had faded.

"I hate it when she does that," Belgarath muttered.

"You do it all the time," Beldin said.

"That's different."

Zakath was staring at the ghostly shape of the disappearing white owl. "That's uncanny," he shuddered. Then he looked at Garion. "I can't say that I understand all this concern," he confessed. "You people—at least some of you—are sorcerers. Can't you just . . . ?" He left it hanging.

"No," Garion shook his head.

"Why not?"

"It makes too much noise. Not the sort of noise ordinary people can hear—but we can hear it, and so can the Grolims. If we tried to do it that way, we'd have every Grolim in this part of Darshiva down our necks. Sorcery's an overrated thing, Zakath. I'll grant you we can do things that other people can't, but there are so many restrictions on us that sometimes it's not worth the trouble—unless you're in a hurry."

"I didn't know that," Zakath admitted. "Are the Hounds as big as they say they are?"

"Probably even bigger," Silk replied. "They're about the size of small horses."

"You're a droll fellow, Kheldar," Zakath said, "so I think I'd have to see that to believe it."

"You'd better hope that you don't get that close."

Belgarath looked narrowly at the Mallorean. "You don't believe in very much, do you?" he asked.

"What I can see." Zakath shrugged. "I've had most of the belief washed out of me over the years."

"That could prove to be a problem," the old man said, scratching at his cheek. "A time might come when we'll have to do something in a hurry and we won't have time for explanations—and *you* won't have time to stand around gaping in astonishment. I think this might be a good time to fill you in on a few things."

"I'll listen to you," Zakath said. "I don't promise to believe everything you say, though. Go ahead."

"I'll let Garion do it. I want to keep in touch with Pol. Why don't you two go back to the edge of the woods and keep watch? Garion can fill you in there. Try not to be skeptical just on principle."

"We'll see," Zakath replied.

During the next hour, as Garion and Zakath crouched behind a fallen tree at the edge of the woods, the Emperor of Mallorea had his credulity stretched to the limits. Garion spoke in a half whisper even as he kept his eyes and ears alert. He began by briefly sketching in the *Book of Alorn*, then went on to a few salient points from the Mrin Codex. Then, so far as he knew it, he described the early life of Belgarath the sorcerer. And then he got down to business. He explained the possibilities and the limitations of the Will and the Word, covering such matters as projections, translocation, shape-change, and so on. He covered the mysterious sound that accompanies the use of what common people call sorcery, the exhaustion that comes over a sorcerer after its use, and the single absolute prohibition—that of unmaking. "That's what happened to Ctuchik," he concluded. "He was so afraid of what would happen if I got my hands on the Orb that he forgot he was stepping over the line when he tried to destroy it."

Out in the darkness, the Hound howled again, and there was an answering howl from a different direction. "They're getting closer," Garion whispered. "I hope Aunt Pol hurries."

Zakath, however, was still mulling over the things Garion had told him. "Are you trying to tell me that it was the Orb that killed Ctuchik and not Belgarath?" he whispered.

"No. It wasn't the Orb. It was the universe. Do you really want to get into theology?"

"I'm even more skeptical in that direction."

"That's the one thing you can't afford, Zakath," Garion

said seriously. "You *have* to believe. Otherwise, we'll fail, and, if we fail, the world fails—forever."

The Hound howled again, even closer this time.

"Keep your voice down," Garion warned in a tense whisper. "The Hounds have very sharp ears."

"I'm not afraid of a dog, Garion, no matter how big it is."

"That could be a mistake. Being afraid is one of the things that keeps us alive. All right. As closely as I understand it, this is the way it went. UL created the universe."

"I thought it was just spun out of nothingness."

"It was, but UL was the spinner. Then he joined his thought with the awareness of the universe, and the Seven Gods were born."

"The Grolims say it was Torak who made everything."

"That's what Torak wanted them to believe. That's one of the reasons I had to kill him. He thought he owned the universe and that he was more powerful than UL. He was wrong, and nobody owns the universe. She owns herself, and she makes the rules."

"*She?*"

"Of course. She's the mother of everything—you, me, that rock, and even this dead tree we're hiding behind. We're all related, I suppose, and the universe won't permit unmaking." Garion pulled off his helmet and scratched at his sweaty hair. He sighed. "I'm awfully sorry, Zakath. I know this is coming at you very fast, but we don't have time for subtlety. For some reason, we're caught up in this—you and I." He smiled wryly. "We're both woefully unsuited for the task, I'm afraid, but our mother needs us. Are you up to it?"

"I'm up to most things, I suppose," Zakath replied in an indifferent tone. "Regardless of what Cyradis said back there, I don't really expect to come out of this alive anyway."

"Are you sure you're not Arendish?" Garion asked suspiciously. "The whole idea is to live, Zakath, not to die. Dying defeats the purpose. Don't do it. I might need you later on.

The voice told me that you're supposed to be a part of this. I think we're walking directly into the ultimate horror. You might have to hold me up when we get there."

"Voice?"

"It's in here," Garion tapped his forehead. "I'll explain that later. You've got enough to think about for now."

"You hear voices? There's a name for people who hear voices, you know."

Garion smiled. "I'm not really crazy, Zakath," he said. "I get a little distracted once in a while, but I've still got a fairly firm grip on reality."

There was a sudden, shocking sound that echoed through Garion's head like an explosion.

"What was that?" Zakath exclaimed.

"You heard it, too?" Garion was amazed. "You shouldn't have been able to hear it!"

"It shook the earth, Garion. Look there." Zakath pointed off toward the north where a huge pillar of fire was soaring up toward the murky, starless sky. "What is it?"

"Aunt Pol did something. She's *never* that clumsy. Listen!"

The baying of the Hound, which had been coming closer and closer as they had been speaking, had broken off into a series of pained yelps. "It probably hurt his ears," Garion said. "I know it hurt mine."

The Hound took up his baying again, and his howls were soon joined by others. The sound began to fade off toward the north and the boiling column of fire.

"Let's go back," Garion said. "I don't think we need to keep watch here any more."

Belgarath and Beldin were both pale and shaken, and even Durnik seemed awed.

"She hasn't done anything that noisy since she was about sixteen," Beldin said, blinking in astonishment. He looked suspiciously at Durnik. "Have you gone and got her pregnant?"

344

Even in the faint light from the overcast sky Garion could see his friend blushing furiously.

"What would that have to do with it?" Belgarath asked.

"It's only a theory of mine," Beldin said. "I can't prove it, because Polgara's the only sorceress I know right now, and she's never been in that condition."

"I'm sure you'll get around to explaining it—eventually."

"It's not that complicated, Belgarath. A woman's body gets a little confused when she's carrying a child. It does some peculiar things to her emotions and her thought processes. Focusing the Will takes control and concentration. A pregnant woman might just lose her grip on that sort of thing. You see—" He went on at some length to describe the physical, emotional, and intellectual changes involved in pregnancy. He spoke in matter-of-fact, even graphic, terms. After a moment, Ce'Nedra and Velvet withdrew, firmly taking Eriond with them. A moment later, Durnik joined them.

"Did you work this out all by yourself?" Belgarath asked.

"It gave me something to speculate about while I was watching the cave where Zedar had hidden Torak."

"It took you five hundred years, then?"

"I wanted to be sure I'd covered all the possibilities." Beldin shrugged.

"Why didn't you just ask Pol? She could have told you immediately."

Beldin blinked. "I never thought of that," he admitted.

Belgarath walked away, shaking his head.

Some time later, they heard a sudden, screeching bellow coming from the west through the murky sky.

"Everybody get down!" Belgarath hissed. "And keep quiet!"

"What is it?" Zakath exclaimed.

"Be still!" Beldin snapped. "She'll hear you!"

From overhead there came the flap of vast wings and a sooty

345

orange billow of fire. Then the huge beast flew on, screeching and belching out flames.

"What was it?" Zakath repeated.

"Zandramas," Garion whispered. "Keep your voice down. She might come back."

They waited.

"She seems to be going toward all the noise Pol kicked up," Belgarath said in a low voice.

"At least she's not looking for us," Silk said with some relief.

"Not yet, anyway."

"That wasn't actually a dragon, was it?" Zakath asked the old man.

"No, not really. Garion was right. It was Zandramas. That's her other form."

"Isn't it just a bit ostentatious?"

"Zandramas seems to have urges in that direction. She can only go for so long without doing something spectacular. It might have something to do with the fact that she's a woman."

"I heard that, Belgarath," Ce'Nedra's voice came threateningly from the far side of the clearing.

"Maybe it didn't come out exactly the way I'd intended," he half apologized.

The snowy owl came drifting through the forest of dead trees. She hovered for a moment near the fire, then shimmered back into her own form.

"What did you do out there, Pol?" Belgarath asked her.

"I found a dormant volcano," she replied, taking her cloak from Durnik and wrapping it around her shoulders. "I reignited it. Did the Hounds go off to investigate?"

"Almost immediately," Garion assured her.

"So did Zandramas," Silk added.

"Yes, I saw her." She smiled faintly. "It worked out rather well, actually. When she gets there, she'll probably find the Hounds slinking around and decide to do something about them. I don't think they'll be bothering us any more, and I'm sure Zandramas would be filled with chagrin if she found out that she's helping us."

"Were you that clumsy on purpose, Pol?" Beldin asked her.

"Of course. I wanted to make enough noise to draw off the Hounds—and any Grolims who might be in the area. Zandramas was just a bonus. Could you build up the fire again, dear?" she said to Durnik. "I think it's safe now to start thinking about supper."

They broke camp early the next morning. Polgara's volcano was still belching smoke and ash high into the air, where they mingled with the pervading overcast to cause a sullen kind of gloom. The murky air reeked of sulfur.

"Flying in that isn't going to be very enjoyable," Beldin said sourly.

"We need to know what's ahead," Belgarath told him.

"I know that," Beldin replied. "I'm not stupid, you know. I was just making an observation." He bent slightly, changed form, and drove himself into the air with powerful strokes of his wings.

"I'd pay a fortune to have a hawk like that," Zakath said wistfully.

"You might have trouble training him," Belgarath said. "He's not the most tractable bird in the world."

"And the first time you tried to hood him, he'd probably rip off one of your fingers," Polgara added.

It was nearly noon when Beldin returned, flying hard. "Get ready!" he shouted almost before he had completed the change. "Temple Guardsmen—about ten—just over that rise! They're coming this way and they've got a Hound with them!"

Garion reached for his sword, and he heard Zakath's blade come whistling out of its sheath. "No!" he said sharply to the Mallorean. "Stay out of it!"

"Not a chance," Zakath replied.

"I'll take care of the dog," Sadi said, reaching into the pouch at his belt for some of the powder he had used so effectively in Karanda.

They spread out with their weapons in their hands as Eriond led the women to the rear.

The Hound came over the hill first, and it stopped when it saw them. Then it wheeled and loped back.

"That's it," Belgarath said. "They know we're here now."

The Guardsmen came over the top of the hill at a rolling trot. Garion noticed that they weren't carrying lances, but each mail-clad man held a sword and wore a shield. They paused for a moment to assess the situation, then they charged. The Hound came first, running smoothly and with his lips peeled back from his teeth in a fearful snarl. Sadi spurred forward to meet him, holding a fistful of the powder. When the Hound reared up on his hind legs to drag the eunuch from his saddle, Sadi coolly hurled the powder full into the animal's face. The Hound shook his massive head, trying to clear his eyes. Then he sneezed once. His eyes grew wide, and his snarl turned into a terrified whimper. He shrieked suddenly, a dreadful, half-human sound. Then he turned and fled, howling in terror.

"Let's go!" Garion barked, and he charged toward the oncoming Guardsmen. These were more serious opponents than the Darshivan soldiers had been, so the choices in dealing with them were greatly reduced. One, somewhat larger than his fellows and astride a heavy-bodied warhorse, was leading the charge, and Garion cut him out of his saddle with a single stroke of Iron-grip's great sword.

Garion heard the sound of steel on steel off to his left, but he dared not take his eyes off the still-charging Guardsmen. He chopped two more from their saddles, and Chretienne crashed into the horse of a third, sending the rider and his mount tumbling. Then Garion was through the ranks of their enemies, and he wheeled around.

Zakath was being hard pressed by two mailed men. He had, it appeared, already felled a third; but then the other two had come at him, one from either side. Garion kicked at Chretienne's flanks, intending to go to his friend's aid, but Toth was already there. With one huge hand he plucked one of Zakath's attackers from his saddle and hurled him headfirst at a large boulder at the side of the road. Zakath turned on his other enemy, deftly parried a couple of strokes, then smoothly ran the man through.

Silk's daggers were already doing their deadly work. One Guardsman was aimlessly riding around in a circle, doubled over in his saddle and clutching at the dagger hilt protruding from his stomach. The acrobatic little Drasnian then leaped from his horse and landed behind the saddle of a confused Guardsman. With a wide sweep of his arm, Silk drove a dagger into the side of the man's neck. Blood gushed from the Guardsman's mouth as he fell to the ground.

The remaining two armored men tried to flee, but Durnik and Beldin were already on them, clubbing at them with cudgel and axe. They tumbled senselessly from their horses and lay twitching in the dirt of the road.

"Are you all right?" Garion asked Zakath.

"I'm fine, Garion." The Mallorean was breathing hard, though.

"Your training seems to be coming back to you."

"I had a certain amount of incentive." Zakath looked critically at the bodies littering the road. "When this is all over, I think I'll order this organization disbanded," he said. "The notion of private armies offends me for some reason."

"Did any of them get away?" Silk asked, looking around.

"Not a one," Durnik told him.

"Good. We wouldn't want somebody going for help." Silk frowned. "What were they doing this far south?" he asked.

"Probably trying to stir up enough trouble to draw the Darshivan troops away from Urvon's main body," Belgarath replied. "I think we'll have to be alert from now on. This whole area could be crawling with soldiers at any time now." He looked at Beldin. "Why don't you have a look around?" he said. "See if you can find out what Urvon's up to and where the Darshivans are. We don't want to get caught between them."

"It's going to take a while," the hunchback replied. "Darshiva's a fairly large place."

"You'd better get started, then, hadn't you?"

They took shelter that night in the ruins of another village. Belgarath and Garion scouted the surrounding region, but found it to be deserted. The following morning, the two wolves ranged out ahead of the rest of the party, but again they encountered no one.

It was almost evening when Beldin returned. "Urvon out-flanked your army," he told Zakath. "He's got at least one general who knows what he's doing. His troops are in the Dalasian Mountains now, and they're coming south at a forced march. Atesca had to stay near the coast to meet the Darshivans and their elephants."

"Did you see Urvon?" Belgarath asked him.

Beldin cackled an ugly little laugh. "Oh, yes. He's absolutely mad now. He's got two dozen soldiers carrying him on a throne and he's doing parlor tricks to demonstrate his divinity. I doubt if he could focus enough of his will right now to wilt a flower."

"Is Nahaz with him?"

Beldin nodded. "Right beside him, whispering in his ear. I'd say he needs to keep a tight grip on his plaything. If Urvon starts giving the wrong orders, his army could wind up wandering around in those mountains for a generation."

Belgarath frowned. "This doesn't exactly fit," he said. "Every bit of information we picked up pointed to the probability that Nahaz and Mordja were concentrating on each other."

"Maybe they've already had it out," the hunchback shrugged, "and Mordja lost."

"I doubt it. That sort of thing would have made a lot of noise, and we'd have heard it."

"Who knows why demons do anything?" Beldin scowled, scratching at his matted hair. "Let's face it, Belgarath," he said. "Zandramas knows that she has to go to Kell, and so does Nahaz. I think this is turning into a race. We're all trying to be the first one to get to Cyradis."

"I get the feeling that I'm overlooking something," Belgarath said. "Something important."

"You'll think of it. It might take you a couple of months, but you'll think of it."

Belgarath ignored that.

The heavy pall of smoke and ash began to subside as evening drew on, but the prevailing gloom of thick overcast remained. Darshiva was still a land of dead trees, fungus, and stagnant water. Increasingly, that last became a problem. The supplies of water they had carried with them from the Mallorean camp on the shores of the Magan had long since been exhausted. As night fell, the others continued along the road, and Belgarath and Garion ranged ahead as wolves again, searching this time not so much for trouble as for fresh water. Their sharp noses easily detected the stale reek of long-standing pools, and they passed them without slowing.

It was in a blasted forest of long-dead trees that Garion encountered another wolf. She was gaunt and bedraggled, and she limped painfully on her left front paw. She looked at him warily, baring her teeth in warning.

He sat down on his haunches to show his peaceable intent.

"What is it you do here?" she asked him in the language of wolves.

"I am going from one place to another place," he replied politely. "I have no intention to hunt in the place which is yours. I seek only clean water to drink."

"Clean water comes from the ground on the other side of that high place." She glanced toward a hill deeper in the forest. "Drink your fill."

"I have others with me as well," he told her.

"Your pack?" She came cautiously closer to him and sniffed. "You have the scent of the man-things about you," she accused.

"Some of those in my pack are man-things," he admitted. "Where is your pack?"

"Gone," she told him. "When there were no longer creatures to hunt in this place, they went into the mountains." She licked at her injured foot. "I could not follow."

"Where is your mate?"

"He no longer runs or hunts. I visit his bones sometimes." She said it with such simple dignity that a lump caught in Garion's throat.

"How do you hunt with that hurt in your paw?"

"I lie in wait for unwary things. All are very small. I have not eaten my fill for many seasons."

"Grandfather," Garion sent his thought out. "I need you."

"Trouble?" the old man's thought came back.

"Not that kind. Oh, I found water, by the way, but don't come in here running. You'll frighten her."

"Her?"

"You'll understand when you get here."

"To whom were you speaking?" she asked.

"You heard?" He was startled.

"No, but your manner was that of one who was speaking."

"We can talk of that after some time has passed. My pack-leader is coming to this place. He must make the decisions."

"That is only proper." She lay down on her belly and continued to lick at her paw.

"How did you come to be hurt?"

"The man-things conceal things beneath the leaves. I

stepped on one of those things, and it bit my paw. Its jaws were very strong."

Belgarath came trotting through the dead forest. He stopped and dropped to his haunches, his tongue lolling out.

The she-wolf laid her muzzle submissively on the ground in a gesture of respect.

"What's the problem?" Belgarath's thought came to Garion.

"She caught her foot in a trap. Her pack left her behind, and her mate died. She's crippled and starving."

"It happens sometimes."

"I'm not going to leave her behind to die."

Belgarath gave him a long, steady look. "No," he replied. "I don't imagine you would—and I'd think less of you if you did." He approached the she-wolf. "How is it with you, little sister?" he asked in the language of wolves, sniffing at her.

"Not well, revered leader," she sighed. "I will not hunt much longer, I think."

"You will join my pack, and we will see to your hurt. We will bring you such meat as you require. Where are your young? I can smell them on your fur."

Garion gave a startled little whine.

"There is but one remaining," the she-wolf replied, "and he is very weak."

"Take us to him. We will make him strong again."

"As you decide, revered leader," she said with automatic obedience.

"Pol," Belgarath sent out his thought. "Come here. Take your mother's form." The note of command in his voice was incisive and far more wolflike than human.

There was a startled silence. "Yes, father," Polgara replied. When she arrived a few moments later, Garion recognized her from the characteristic white streak above her left brow. "What is it, father?" she asked.

"Our little sister here is hurt," he replied. "It's her left front paw. Can you fix it?"

353

She approached the she-wolf and sniffed at the paw. "It's ulcerated," she said with her thought. "Nothing seems to be broken. Several days with a poultice ought to do it."

"Fix it, then. She also has a puppy. We'll need to find him as well."

She looked at him, a question in her golden eyes.

"She and her puppy are joining our pack. They'll be going with us." Then he sent his thought to her. "It's Garion's idea, actually. He refuses to leave her behind."

"It's very noble, but is it practical?"

"Probably not, but it's his decision. He thinks it's the right thing to do, and I more or less agree with him. You're going to have to explain some things to her, though. She doesn't have much reason to trust man, and I don't want her to go into a panic when the others catch up with us." He turned to the she-wolf. "Everything will be well again, little sister," he told her. "Now, let us go find your young one."

CHAPTER TWENTY-ONE

The half-grown pup was so emaciated that it could not stand, so Polgara resorted to the simple expedient of picking it up by the scruff of its neck between her jaws and carrying it out of the den.

"Go meet the others," she instructed Garion. "Don't let them get too close until I've had time to talk with our little sister here. Bring back food, though. Put as much as you can carry in a sack and come right back."

"Yes, Aunt Pol." He loped back toward the road, changed into his own form, and waited for his friends.

"We've got a little bit of a problem," he told them when

they arrived. "We've found an injured female just up ahead in those woods. She's starving, and she has a young one as well."

"A baby?" Ce'Nedra exclaimed.

"Not exactly," he said, going to one of the food packs and beginning to load a stout canvas bag with meat and cheese.

"But you just said—"

"It's a puppy, Ce'Nedra. The female is a she-wolf."

"*What?*"

"It's a wolf. She got her paw caught in a trap. She can't run, so she can't hunt. She'll be coming with us—at least until her paw heals."

"But—"

"No buts. She's coming with us. Durnik, can you work out some way we can carry her without having the horses go wild?"

"I'll think of something," the smith replied.

"Under the circumstances, don't you think this altruism might be misplaced?" Sadi asked mildly.

"No," Garion said, tying the top of the sack shut, "I don't. There's a hill in the middle of those woods. Stay on this side of it until we can persuade her that we don't mean to harm her. There's water there, but it's too close to her den. We'll have to wait a bit before we can water the horses."

"What's got you so angry?" Silk asked him.

"If I had the time, I'd look up the man who set that trap and break his leg—in several places. I've got to go back now. She and the puppy are very hungry." He slung the sack over his shoulder and stalked off. His anger was, he knew, irrational, and there had not really been any excuse for being surly with Ce'Nedra and the others, but he could not have helped himself. The wolf's calm acceptance of death and her mourning for her lost mate had torn at his heart, and anger kept the tears out of his eyes.

The sack was awkward to carry, once he had changed form, and it kept throwing him off balance, but he stumbled on with his head high to keep his burden from dragging on the ground.

Polgara and Belgarath were talking with the she-wolf when he reached the den again. The injured wolf had a skeptical expression in her eyes as she listened.

"She can't accept it," Polgara said.

"Does she think you're lying?" Garion asked, dropping the sack.

"Wolves don't understand the meaning of that word. She thinks we're mistaken. We're going to have to show her. She met you first, so she might trust you a little more. Change back. You'll need your hands to untie the knot in that sack, anyway."

"All right." He drew his own image in his imagination and changed.

"How remarkable," the she-wolf said in amazement.

Belgarath looked at her sharply. "Why did you say that?" he asked her.

"Did you not find it so?"

"I am accustomed to it. Why did you choose those particular words?"

"They came to me. I am no pack-leader, and I have no need to choose my word with care in order to protect my dignity."

Garion had opened the sack and he laid meat and cheese on the ground in front of her. She began to eat ravenously. He knelt beside the starving pup and began to feed him, being careful to keep his fingers away from the needle-sharp teeth.

"A little bit at a time," Polgara cautioned. "Don't make him sick."

When the she-wolf had eaten her fill, she limped to the spring which came bubbling out from between two rocks and drank. Garion picked up the puppy and carried him to the spring so that he could also drink.

357

"You are not like the other man-things," the she-wolf observed.

"No," he agreed. "Not entirely."

"Are you mated?" she asked.

"Yes."

"To a wolf or to one of the shes of the man-things?"

"To one of the shes of this kind." He tapped his own chest.

"Ah. And does she hunt with you?"

"Our shes do not usually hunt."

"What useless things they must be." The wolf sniffed disdainfully.

"Not altogether."

"Durnik and the others are coming," Polgara said. Then she looked at the she-wolf. "The others of our pack are coming to this place, little sister," she said. "They are the man-things of which I spoke. Do not be afraid of them, for they are like this one." She pointed her nose at Garion. "Our leader here and I will now also change our forms. The presence of wolves alarms the beasts we have with us, and they must drink from your water. If it please you, will you go with this one who fed you, so that our beasts may drink?"

"It shall be as you say," the she-wolf replied.

Garion led the limping wolf away from the spring, carrying the now drowsy puppy in his arms. The puppy raised his muzzle, licked Garion's face once, and then fell asleep.

Durnik and Toth set up their camp near the spring, while Eriond and Silk watered the horses and then took them back to picket them in the woods.

After a while, Garion led the now wary she-wolf toward the fire. "It is time for you to meet the other members of our pack," he told her, "for they are now your pack-mates as well."

"This is not a natural thing," she said nervously as she limped along at his side.

"They will not harm you," he assured her. Then he spoke to the others. "Please stand very still," he told them. "She'll want to smell each of you so that she can recognize you later. Don't try to touch her and, when you speak, do it quietly. She's very nervous right now." He led the wolf around the fire, allowing her to sniff at each of his companions.

"What's her name?" Ce'Nedra asked as the she-wolf sniffed at her little hand.

"Wolves don't need names."

"We have to call her *something*, Garion. May I hold the puppy?"

"I think she'd rather you didn't just yet. Let her get used to you first."

"This one is your mate," the she-wolf said. "I can smell your scent on her."

"Yes," Garion agreed.

"She's very small. I see now why she can't hunt. Is she fully grown?"

"Yes, she is."

"Has she had her first litter yet?"

"Yes."

"How many puppies?"

"One."

"One only?" The wolf sniffed. "I have had as many as six. You should have chosen a larger mate. I'm sure she was the runt of her litter."

"What's she saying?" Ce'Nedra asked.

"It wouldn't translate," Garion lied.

After the wolf had grown a little more at ease, Polgara boiled a number of herbs in a small pot, mixed them with a paste of soap and sugar, and applied the poultice to the wolf's injured paw. Then she wrapped the paw in a clean white cloth. "Try not to lick this or chew it off, little sister," she instructed. "It will not taste good and it needs to stay where it is to heal your hurt."

"One is grateful," the wolf replied. She looked into the dancing flames of the fire. "That is a comforting thing, is it not?" she observed.

"We find it so," Polgara said.

"You man-things are very clever with your forepaws."

"They're useful," Polgara agreed. She took the sleeping puppy from Garion's arms and nestled him beside his mother.

"I will sleep now," the wolf decided. She laid her muzzle protectively on her puppy's flank and closed her eyes.

Durnik motioned to Garion and led him aside. "I think I've come up with a way to bring her along without frightening the horses," he said. "I can make a sort of sled for her to ride in. I'll put a long enough towrope on it to keep her smell away from them, and I'll cover her and her puppy with an old horse blanket. She might make them a little jumpy at first, but they'll get used to her." The smith looked gravely at his friend. "Why are we doing this, Garion?" he asked.

"I couldn't bear the thought of just leaving the two of them here. They'd have both died before the week was out."

"You're a good man," Durnik said simply, putting his hand on Garion's shoulder. "You're decent as well as brave."

"I'm a Sendar." Garion shrugged. "We're all like that."

"But you're not actually a Sendar, you know."

"That's how I was raised, and that's all that matters, isn't it?"

The sled Durnik contrived for the wolf and her puppy the next morning had wide-set runners and was built low to the ground so there was little chance of its overturning. "It might be better if it had wheels," he admitted, "but I don't have any wheels to work with, and it would take too long to make some."

"I'll ransack the next village we come to," Silk told him. "Maybe I can find a cart of some kind."

They rode out, slowly at first until they saw that the sled

ran smoothly on the damp earth of the road, and then they moved on at their usual canter.

Silk was checking a map as he rode along. "There's a fair-sized town just up ahead," he told Belgarath. "I think we could use some up-to-date information about now, don't you?"

"Why is it that you absolutely *have* to go into every town we pass?" Belgarath asked him.

"I'm a city dweller, Belgarath," the little man replied in an offhand manner. "I get edgy if I can't walk on cobblestones every so often. Besides, we need supplies. Garion's wolf eats a great deal. Why don't the rest of you go out in a wide circle around the place, and we'll catch up with you on the other side?"

"We?" Garion asked him.

"You're coming along, aren't you?"

Garion sighed. "I guess so," he said. "You always seem to get into trouble if we let you go off alone."

"Trouble?" Silk said innocently. "Me?"

Zakath rubbed at his stubbled chin. "I'll come, too," he said. "I don't look that much like the coins any more." He glared briefly at Belgarath. "How can you stand this?" he demanded, scratching vigorously at his face. "The itching is about to drive me wild."

"You get used to it," Belgarath told him. "I wouldn't feel right if my face didn't itch."

The place appeared to be a market town that had at some time in the past been fortified. It crouched atop a hill and it was surrounded by a thick stone wall with watchtowers at each corner. The pervading overcast that seemed to cover all of Darshiva made the town look gray and dismal. The gate was unguarded, and Silk, Garion, and Zakath clattered on through into what appeared to be a deserted street.

"Let's see if we can find somebody," Silk said. "If not, we can at least ransack a few shops for the food we'll need."

"Don't you ever pay for anything, Kheldar?" Zakath asked with some asperity.

"Not if I don't have to. No honest merchant ever passes up an opportunity to steal. Let's push on, shall we?"

"This is a very corrupt little man; do you know that?" Zakath said to Garion.

"We've noticed that from time to time."

They rounded a corner and saw a group of men in canvas smocks loading a wagon under the direction of a sweating fat man.

Silk reined in his horse. "Where are all the people, friend?" he called to the fat man.

"Gone. Fled to either Gandahar or Dalasia."

"Fled? What for?"

"Where have you been, man? Urvon's coming."

"Really? I hadn't heard that."

"Everybody in Darshiva knows it."

"Zandramas will stop him," Silk said confidently.

"Zandramas isn't here." The fat man suddenly bawled at one of his workers. "Be careful with that box!" he shouted. "The things in there are breakable!"

Silk led the others closer. "Where did she go? Zandramas, I mean?"

"Who knows? Who cares? There's been nothing but trouble in Darshiva ever since she gained control of the country." The fat man mopped at his face with a soiled kerchief.

"You'd better not let the Grolims hear you talking like that."

"Grolims," the fat man snorted. "They were the first ones to run. Urvon's army uses Darshivan Grolims for firewood."

"Why would Zandramas leave when her country's being invaded?"

"Who knows why she does anything?" The fat fellow looked around nervously, then spoke in a quiet voice. "Just between you and me, friend, I think she's mad. She held

362

some kind of ceremony at Hemil. She stuck a crown on the head of some archduke from Melcena and said that he's the Emperor of Mallorea. He'll be a head shorter when Kal Zakath catches up with him, I'll wager."

"I'd like to put some money on the same proposition," Zakath agreed quietly.

"Then she gave a speech in the temple at Hemil," the fat man went on. "She said that the day is at hand." He sneered. "Grolims of every stripe have been saying that the day is at hand for as long as I can remember. Every one of them seems to be talking about a different day, though. Anyway, she came through here a few days ago and told us all that she was going to the place where the New God of Angarak will be chosen. She held up her hand and said, 'And this is a sign to you that I shall prevail.' It gave me quite a turn at first, let me tell you. There were swirling lights under her skin. I thought for a while that there was really something significant about it, but my friend, the apothecary who keeps the shop next to mine, he told me that she's a sorceress and she can make people see anything she wants them to see. That explains it, I guess."

"Did she say anything else?" Silk asked him intently.

"Only that this New God of hers will appear before the summer is gone."

"Let's hope she's right," Silk said. "That might put an end to all this turmoil."

"I doubt it," the fat man said moodily. "I think we're in for a long siege of trouble."

"Was she alone?" Garion asked him.

"No. She had her bogus emperor with her and that white-eyed Grolim from the temple at Hemil—the one who follows her around like a tame ape."

"Anyone else?"

"Only a little boy. I don't know where she picked him up. Just before she left, she told us that the army of Urvon the

Disciple was coming and she ordered the whole populace to go out and block his path. Then she left, going that way." He pointed off toward the west. "Well, my friends and I, we all sort of looked at each other for a while, and then everybody grabbed up whatever he could carry and bolted. We're not stupid enough to throw ourselves in the path of an advancing army, no matter who orders us to."

"How is it that you stayed behind?" Silk asked him curiously.

"This is my shop," the fat man replied in a plaintive tone. "I've worked all my life to build it up. I wasn't going to run off and let the riffraff from the gutters loot it. Now they're all gone, so it's safe for me to make a run for it with whatever I can salvage. A lot of what I'll have to leave behind won't keep anyway, so I'm not losing very much."

"Oh," Silk said, his pointed nose twitching with interest. "What is it you deal in, friend?"

"General merchandise." The fat man looked critically at his workmen. "Stack those boxes closer together!" he shouted. "There's still a lot left to go in that wagon!"

"What sort of general merchandise?" Silk pressed.

"Household goods, tools, bolts of cloth, foodstuffs—that sort of thing."

"Well, now," Silk said, his nose twitching even more violently. "Maybe you and I can do some business. My friends and I have a long way to go, and we're running a little short of supplies. You mentioned foodstuffs. What sort of foodstuffs?"

The merchant's eyes narrowed. "Bread, cheese, butter, dried fruit, hams. I've even got a fresh side of beef. I warn you, though, those things are going to cost you very dearly. Food's scarce in this part of Darshiva."

"Oh," Silk said blandly, "I don't think they'll cost all that much—unless you plan to wait here to greet Urvon when he arrives."

The merchant stared at him in consternation.

"You see, my friend," Silk continued, "you have to leave—and very soon, I think. That wagon of yours won't carry everything you've got in your shop, and your team isn't going to be able to move very fast—not the way you're loading the wagon. My friends and I have fast horses, though, so we can afford to wait a little longer. After you leave, we might just browse through your shop for the things we need."

The merchant's face went suddenly very pale. "That's robbery," he gasped.

"Why, yes," Silk admitted blandly, "I believe some people do call it that." He paused for a moment to allow the merchant time to understand the situation fully. The fat man's face grew anguished. Then Silk sighed. "Unfortunately, I'm cursed with a delicate conscience. I can't bear the thought of cheating an honest man—unless I absolutely have to." He lifted a pouch from his belt, opened it, and peered inside. "I seem to have eight or ten silver half-crowns in here," he said. "What would you say to five of them for everything my friends and I can carry?"

"That's outrageous!" the merchant spluttered.

With some show of regret, Silk closed the pouch and tucked it back under his belt. "I guess we'll just have to wait, then. Do you think you and your men will be much longer?"

"You're robbing me!" the merchant wailed.

"No, not really. The way I see it, what we have here is a buyer's market. That's my offer, friend—five silver half-crowns. Take it or leave it. We'll wait over there across the street while you decide." He turned his horse and led Garion and Zakath toward a large house on the other side of the street.

Zakath was trying very hard to stifle a laugh as they dismounted.

"We're not quite done yet," Silk muttered. "It needs just one more little touch." He went up to the locked door of the house, reached into his boot, and took out a long, pointed needle. He probed at the lock for a moment, and it snapped open with a solid-sounding *click*. "We'll need a table and three chairs," he told them. "Bring them out and set them up in front of the house. I'll rummage around and find the other things we'll need." He went into the house.

Garion and Zakath went into the kitchen and carried out a fair-sized table. Then they went back for chairs.

"What's he up to?" Zakath asked with a look of bafflement on his face.

"He's playing," Garion said with a certain disgust. "He does that from time to time during his business dealings."

They carried out the chairs and found Silk waiting for them. Several bottles of wine and four goblets sat on the table. "All right, gentlemen," the little Drasnian said. "Seat yourselves and have some wine. I'll be right back. I want to check something I saw at the side of the house." He went around the corner and came back after a few minutes with a broad smirk on his face. He sat, poured himself a goblet of wine, leaned back in his chair, and put his feet up on the table with the air of a man planning to make a long stay of it. "I give him about five minutes," he said.

"Who?" Garion asked.

"The merchant." Silk shrugged. "He'll only be able to watch us sitting here for so long and then he'll start to see things my way."

"You're a cruel, cruel man, Prince Kheldar." Zakath laughed.

"Business is business," Silk replied, taking a sip of his wine. "This really isn't bad, you know," he said, holding up his goblet to admire the color of the wine.

"What were you doing around at the side?" Garion asked him.

"There's a carriage house there—with a large lock on the door. You don't flee a town and lock a door unless there's something valuable behind it, do you? Besides, locked doors always pique my curiosity."

"So? What was inside?"

"Rather a nice little cabriolet, actually."

"What's a cabriolet?"

"A two-wheeled carriage."

"And you're going to steal it."

"Of course. I told the merchant over there that we'd take only what we could carry. I didn't tell him how we were going to carry it. Besides, Durnik wanted wheels to make something to carry your wolf in. That little carriage could save him all the trouble of building things. Friends should always help their friends, right?"

As Silk had predicted, the merchant could only bear watching the three of them lounging at the table across from his shop for just so long. As his men finished loading the wagon, he came across the street. "All right," he said sullenly, "five half-crowns—but only so much as you can carry, mind."

"Trust me," Silk told him, counting out the coins on the table. "Would you care for a glass of wine? It's really quite good."

The merchant snatched up the coins and turned without answering.

"We'll lock up for you when we leave," Silk called after him.

The fat man did not look back.

After the merchant and his men had ridden off down the street, Silk led his horse around to the side of the house while Garion and Zakath crossed the street to plunder the fat man's shop.

The little two-wheeled carriage had a folding top and a large leather-covered box across its back. Silk's saddle horse looked a bit uncomfortable between the shafts of the carriage, and the sense of being followed by the wheeled thing definitely made him nervous.

The box across the back of the cabriolet held an astonishing amount of supplies. They filled it with cheeses, rolls of butter, hams, slabs of bacon, and several bags of beans. Then they filled up the empty spaces with loaves of bread. When Garion picked up a large bag of meal, however, Silk firmly shook his head. "No," he said adamantly.

"Why not?"

"You know what Polgara makes with ground meal. I'm not deliberately going to volunteer to eat gruel for breakfast every morning for the next month. Let's get that side of beef instead."

"We won't be able to eat all that before it goes bad," Garion objected.

"We have these two new mouths to feed, remember? I've seen your wolf and her puppy eat. The meat won't have time to go bad, believe me."

They rode out of town with Silk idly lounging in the seat of the little carriage with the reins held negligently in his left hand. In his right, he held a wine bottle. "Now this is more like it," he said happily, taking a long drink.

"I'm glad you're enjoying yourself," Garion said a little tartly.

"Oh, I am," Silk replied. "But after all, Garion, fair is fair. I stole it, so I get to ride in it."

CHAPTER TWENTY-TWO

The others were clustered in the yard of an abandoned farmstead a league or so beyond the town. "I see you've been busy," Belgarath observed as Silk drove the little carriage up and stopped.

"We needed something to carry the supplies in," Silk replied glibly.

"Of course."

"I hope you were able to find something beside beans," Sadi said. "Soldiers' rations tend to grow monotonous after a while."

"Silk swindled a shopkeeper," Garion said, opening the

leather-covered box at the back of the carriage. "We did rather well, actually."

"*Swindled?*" Silk protested.

"Didn't you?" Garion moved the side of beef so that Polgara could look into the box.

"Well—I suppose so," Silk admitted, "but swindled is such an awkward way to sum up."

"It's perfectly all right, Prince Kheldar." Polgara almost purred as she took a mental inventory of the items in the box. "To be honest with you, I don't care how you came by all this."

He bowed. "My pleasure, Polgara," he said grandly.

"Yes," she said absently, "I'm sure you enjoyed it."

"What did you find out?" Beldin asked Garion.

"Well, for one thing, Zandramas is ahead of us again," Garion replied. "She went through here a few days ago. She knows that Urvon's army is coming down through the mountains. He might be moving a little faster than we thought, though, because she's ordering the civilian population to delay him. They're more or less ignoring her."

"Wise decision." Beldin grunted. "Anything else?"

"She told them that this is all going to be settled before the summer's over."

"That agrees with what Cyradis told us at Ashaba," Belgarath said. "All right, then. We all know when the meeting's going to happen. The only thing that's left to find out is *where*."

"That's why we're all in such a hurry to get to Kell," Beldin said. "Cyradis is sitting on that information like a mother hen on a clutch of eggs."

"What *is* it?" Belgarath burst out irritably.

"What's what?"

"I'm missing something. It's something important and it's something you told me."

"I've told you lots of things, Belgarath. You don't usually listen, though."

"This was a while back. It seems to me we were sitting in my tower, talking."

"We've done that from time to time over the last several thousand years."

"No. This was more recent. Eriond was there and he was just a boy."

"That would put it at about ten years or so ago, then."

"Right."

"What were we doing ten years ago?"

Belgarath began to pace up and down, scowling. "I'd been helping Durnik. We were making Poledra's cottage livable. You'd been here in Mallorea."

Beldin scratched reflectively at his stomach. "I think I remember the time. We were sharing a cask of ale you'd stolen from the twins, and Eriond was scrubbing the floor."

"What were you telling me?"

Beldin shrugged. "I'd just come back from Mallorea. I was describing conditions here and telling you about the Sardion—although we didn't know very much about it at that point."

"No," Belgarath shook his head. "That wasn't it. You said something about Kell."

Beldin frowned, thinking back. "It must not have been very important, because neither of us seems to be able to remember it."

"It seems to me it was just something you said in passing."

"I say a lot of things in passing. They help to fill up the blank spaces in a conversation. Are you certain it was all that important?"

Belgarath nodded. "I'm sure of it."

"All right. Let's see if we can track it down."

"Won't this wait, father?" Polgara asked.

"No, Pol. I don't think so. We're right on the edge of it, and I don't want to lose it again."

"Let's see," Beldin said, his ugly face creased with thought. "I came in, and you and Eriond were cleaning. You offered me some of the ale you'd stolen from the twins. You asked me what I'd been doing since Belgarion's wedding, and I told you I'd been keeping an eye on the Angaraks."

"Yes," Belgarath agreed. "I remember that part."

"I told you that the Murgos were in general despair about the death of Taur Urgas, and that the western Grolims had gone to pieces over the death of Torak."

"Then you told me about Zakath's campaign in Cthol Murgos and about how he'd added the Kal to his name."

"That actually wasn't my idea," Zakath said with a slightly pained look. "Brador came up with it—as a means of unifying Mallorean society." He made a wry face. "It didn't really work all that well, I guess."

"Things do seem a bit disorganized here," Silk agreed.

"What did we talk about then?" Belgarath asked.

"Well," Beldin replied, "as I remember it, we told Eriond the story of Vo Mimbre, and then you asked me what was going on in Mallorea. I told you that things were all pretty much the same—that the bureaucracy's the glue that holds everything together, that there were plots and intrigues in Melcena and Mal Zeth, that Karanda and Darshiva and Gandahar were on the verge of open rebellion, and that the Grolims—" He stopped, his eyes suddenly going very wide.

"Are still afraid to go near Kell!" Belgarath completed it in a shout of triumph. "That's it!"

Beldin smacked his forehead with his open palm. "How could I have been so stupid?" he exclaimed. Then he fell over on his back, howling with laughter and kicking at the ground in sheer delight. "We've got her, Belgarath!" he roared. "We've got them all—Zandramas, Urvon, even Agachak! They *can't* go to Kell!"

Belgarath was also laughing uproariously. "How did we miss it?"

"Father," Polgara said ominously. "This is beginning to make me cross. Will one of you please explain all this hysteria?"

Beldin and Belgarath were capering hand in hand in a grotesque little dance of glee.

"Will you two stop that?" Polgara snapped.

"Oh, this is just too rare, Pol," Beldin gasped, catching her in a bear hug.

"Don't do that! Just talk!"

"All right, Pol," he said, wiping the tears of mirth from his eyes. "Kell is the holy place of the Dals. It's the center of their whole culture."

"Yes, uncle. I know that."

"When the Angaraks overran Dalasia, the Grolims came in to erase the Dalasian religion and to replace it with the worship of Torak—the same way they did in Karanda. When they found out the significance of Kell, they moved to destroy it. The Dals had to prevent that, so they put their wizards to work on the problem. The wizards laid curses on the entire region around Kell." He frowned. "Maybe curses isn't the right word," he admitted. "Enchantments might be closer, but it amounts to the same thing. Anyway, since the Grolims were the real danger to Kell, the enchantments were directed at them. Any Grolim who tries to approach Kell is struck blind."

"Why didn't you tell us about this earlier?" she asked him tartly.

"I've never really paid that much attention to it. I probably even forgot about it. I don't bother to go into Dalasia because the Dals are all mystics, and mysticism has always irritated me. The seers all talk in riddles, and necromancy seems like a waste of time to me. I wasn't even sure if the enchantments really worked. Grolims are very gullible sometimes. A suggestion of a curse would probably work just as well as a real one."

"You know," Belgarath mused, "I think the reason we missed it was because we've been concentrating on the fact that Urvon, Zandramas, and Agachak are all sorcerers. We kept overlooking the fact that they're also Grolims."

"Is this curse—or whatever you call it—aimed specifically at the Grolims," Garion asked, "or would it affect us, too?"

Beldin scratched at his beard. "It's a good question, Belgarath," he said. "That's not the sort of thing you'd want to risk lightly."

"Senji!" Belgarath snapped his fingers.

"I didn't quite follow that."

"Senji went to Kell, remember? And even as inept as he is, he's still a sorcerer."

"That's it, then," Beldin grinned. "*We* can go to Kell, and *they* can't. They'll have to follow us for a change."

"What about the demons?" Durnik asked soberly. "Nahaz is already marching toward Kell, and as far as we know, Zandramas has Mordja with her. Would they be able to go to Kell? What I'm getting at is that even if Urvon and Zandramas can't go there, couldn't they just send the demons instead to get the information for them?"

Beldin shook his head. "It wouldn't do them any good. Cyradis won't let a demon anywhere near her copy of the Mallorean Gospels. No matter what other faults they have, the seers refuse to have anything to do with the agents of chaos."

"Could she prevent either of the demons from just taking what they want, though?" Durnik looked worried. "Let's face it, Beldin. A demon is a fairly awful thing."

"She can take care of herself," Beldin replied. "Don't worry about Cyradis."

"Master Beldin," Zakath objected, "she's little more than a child, and with her eyes bound like that, she's utterly helpless."

Beldin laughed coarsely. "Helpless? Cyradis? Man, are you

out of your mind? She could probably stop the sun if she needed to. We can't even begin to make guesses about how much power she has."

"I don't understand." Zakath looked baffled.

"Cyradis is the focus of all the power of her race, Zakath," Polgara explained. "Not only the power of the Dals who are presently alive, but also that of all of them who have ever lived."

"Or who might live in the future, for all we know," Belgarath added.

"That's an interesting idea," Beldin said. "We might want to discuss it someday. Anyway," he continued to Zakath, "Cyradis can do just about anything she has to do to make sure the final meeting takes place at the correct time and the correct place. Demons aren't a part of that meeting, so she'll probably just ignore them; and if they get too troublesome, she'll just send them back where they came from."

"Can you do that?"

Beldin shook his head.

"But she can?"

"I think so, yes."

"I'm having a little trouble with all this," Silk admitted. "If none of the Grolims can go to Kell without going blind, and if the demons aren't going to find out anything, even if they do go there, why are they all running toward it? What good's it going to do them?"

"They're putting themselves into a position where they can follow us when we come out," Belgarath replied. "They know we *can* go there and that we'll find out where the meeting is going to take place. They probably plan to tag along behind when we leave."

"That's going to make it very nervous when we leave Kell, isn't it? We'll have half the Grolims in the world right behind us."

"Everything will work out, Silk," Belgarath replied confidently.

"Fatalism does not fill me with confidence at this point, old man," Silk said acidly.

Belgarath's expression became almost beatific. "Trust me," he said.

Silk glared at him, threw his arms in the air, and then stamped away, swearing under his breath.

"You know, I've been wanting to do that to him for years," the old man chuckled, his blue eyes twinkling. "I think it was actually worth the wait. All right. Let's get things together again and move on."

They transferred some of the supplies from the box across the back of the little carriage to the packhorses, and then Durnik stood considering the vehicle thoughtfully. "It's not going to work," he said.

"What's wrong with it?" Silk asked him a bit defensively.

"The horse has to be hitched between those shafts. If we put the wolf on the seat, she'll be right behind him. He'll bolt at that point. Nothing could stop him."

"I suppose I didn't think of that," Silk said glumly.

"It's the smell of the wolf that sends horses into such a panic, isn't it?" Velvet asked.

"That and the snapping and snarling," Durnik replied.

"Belgarion can persuade her not to snap and snarl."

"What about the smell?" Silk asked.

"I'll take care of that." She went to one of the packs and removed a small glass bottle. "I expect you to buy me some more of this, Prince Kheldar," she said firmly. "You stole the wrong kind of carriage, so it's up to you to replace what I have to use to smooth over your blunder."

"What is it?" he asked suspiciously.

"Perfume, Kheldar, and it's dreadfully expensive." She looked at Garion, her smile dimpling her cheeks. "I'll need you to translate for me," she said. "I wouldn't want the wolf to misunderstand when I start to sprinkle this on her."

"Of course."

When the two of them returned from the sledlike contraption the wolf and her puppy were riding in, they found Ce'Nedra firmly ensconced on the front seat of the smart little carriage. "This will do very nicely, Prince Kheldar," she said brightly. "Thank you ever so much."

"But—"

"Was there something?" she asked, her eyes wide.

Silk's expression grew surly, and he wandered away muttering to himself.

"His morning has taken a turn for the worse, hasn't it?" Zakath observed to Garion.

"He's doing all right," Garion replied. "He got all the entertainment out of cheating that merchant and stealing the carriage. He gets unbearable if he has too many successes in a row. Ce'Nedra and Liselle usually manage to let the air out of him, though."

"You mean they cooked all that up between them?"

"They didn't have to. They've been doing it for so long now that they don't even have to discuss it any more."

"Do you think Liselle's perfume will work?"

"There's one way to find out," Garion said.

They transferred the injured wolf from the sled to the front seat of the two-wheeled carriage and dabbed some perfume on the bridge of the horse's nose. Then they stepped back and looked closely at the horse while Ce'Nedra held the reins tightly. The horse looked a bit suspicious, but did not panic. Garion went back for the puppy and deposited him in Ce'Nedra's lap. She smiled, patted the she-wolf on the head, and shook the reins gently.

"That's really unfair," Silk complained to Garion as they all moved out in the Rivan Queen's wake.

"Did you want to share that seat with the she-wolf?" Garion asked him.

Silk frowned. "I hadn't thought of that, I guess," he admitted. "She wouldn't really bite me, though, would she?"

"I don't think so, but then, you never know with wolves."

"I think I'll stay where I am, then."

"That might be a good idea."

"Aren't you just a little worried about Ce'Nedra? That wolf could eat her in two bites."

"No. She won't do that. She knows that Ce'Nedra's my mate and she sort of likes me."

"Ce'Nedra's your wife." Silk shrugged. "If the wolf bites her in two, I suppose Polgara could put her back together again."

As they started out, a thought came to Garion. He rode forward and fell in beside Zakath. "You're the Emperor of Mallorea, right?"

"How nice of you to notice finally," Zakath replied dryly.

"Then how is it that you didn't know about that curse Beldin was talking about?"

"As you may have noticed, Garion, I pay very little attention to the Grolims. I knew that most of them wouldn't go there, but I thought it was just a superstition of some kind."

"A good ruler tries to know everything he can about his kingdom," Garion said, then realized how priggish that sounded. "Sorry, Zakath," he apologized. "That didn't come out exactly the way I'd intended it to."

"Garion," Zakath said patiently, "your kingdom's a small island. I'd imagine you know most of your subjects personally."

"Well, a lot of them—by sight, anyway."

"I thought you might. You know their problems, their dreams, and their hopes, and you take a personal interest in them."

"Well, yes, I suppose I do."

"You're a good king—probably one of the best in the world—but it's very easy to be a good king when your kingdom is so small. You've seen my empire, though—part of it anyway—and I'm sure you have at least some idea of how many people live here. It would be utterly impossible for me to be a good king. That's why I'm an emperor instead."

"And a God?" Garion asked slyly.

"No. I'll leave that particular delusion to Urvon and Zandramas. People's wits seem to slip a bit when they aspire to divinity, and, believe me, I need all my wits about me. I found that out after I'd wasted half my life trying to destroy Taur Urgas."

"Garion, dear," Ce'Nedra called from the carriage.

"Yes?"

"Could you come back here a moment? The wolf is whimpering a little, and I don't know how to ask her what the trouble is."

"I'll be right back," Garion said to Zakath, turning Chretienne around and trotting back to the carriage.

Ce'Nedra sat in the carriage with the wolf pup in her lap. The little creature lay blissfully on his back with all four paws in the air while she scratched his furry tummy.

The she-wolf lay on the seat beside her. The wolf's ears were twitching and her eyes were mournful.

"Are you in pain?" Garion asked her.

"Does this she of yours always talk this much?" she whined.

It was impossible to lie, and evasion was almost as much out of the question. "Yes," he admitted.

"Can you make her stop?"

"I can try." He looked at Ce'Nedra. "The wolf is very tired," he told her. "She wants to go to sleep."

"I'm not stopping her."

"You've been talking to her," he pointed out gently.

"I was only trying to make friends with her, Garion."

379

"You're already friends. She likes you. Now let her go to sleep."

Ce'Nedra pouted. "I won't bother her," she said, sounding a bit injured. "I'll talk to the puppy instead."

"He's tired, too."

"How can they be so tired in the daytime?"

"Wolves usually hunt at night. This is their normal sleeping time."

"Oh. I didn't know that. All right, Garion. Tell her that I'll be quiet while they sleep."

"Little sister," he said to the wolf, "she promises not to talk to you if your eyes are closed."

The wolf gave him a puzzled look.

"She will think you're sleeping."

The wolf managed to look shocked. "Is it possible in the language of the man-things to say that which is not truth?"

"Sometimes."

"How remarkable. Very well," she said. "If it is the rule of the pack, I will do this. It is, however, very unnatural."

"Yes. I know."

"I will close my eyes," the wolf said. "I will keep them closed all day if it will keep her from chattering at me." She let out a long sigh and closed her eyes.

"Is she asleep?" Ce'Nedra whispered.

"I think so," Garion whispered back. Then he turned and rode back to the head of the column.

The countryside grew more hilly and broken as they rode west. Although the overcast continued to be as heavy as before, there appeared to be some hint of light along the western horizon as afternoon progressed.

They clattered across a stone bridge that arched over a tumbling stream. "It smells clean, Belgarath," Durnik said. "I think it's coming down out of the mountains."

Belgarath squinted up the gully from which the stream emerged. "Why don't you have a look?" he suggested. "See

if there's a place to make camp. Good water has been hard
to find, so let's not pass any up.''

"I was thinking the same thing myself." Then the smith
and his towering mute friend rode off upstream.

They set up camp for the night several hundred yards up
the gully where a bend in the stream had opened out a kind
of curved gravel bench. After they had watered the horses and
set up the tents, Polgara began cooking supper. She cut steaks
from the side of beef and made a thick soup of dried peas,
seasoned with chunks of ham. Then she set a large loaf of
dark peasant bread near the fire to warm, humming to herself
all the while. As always, cooking seemed to satisfy some deep-
seated need in her.

The supper which came from her fire that evening was of
near-banquet proportions, and evening was settling in as they
finished eating and leaned back contentedly.

"Very good, Pol." Beldin belched. "I guess you haven't
lost your touch after all."

"Thank you, uncle." She smiled. Then she looked at Eriond. "Don't get too comfortable," she told him. "At least
not until you've finished helping with the dishes."

Eriond sighed and took a bucket down to the stream for
water.

"That used to be my job," Garion told Zakath. "I'm glad
there's someone younger along this time."

"Isn't that women's work?"

"Would you like to tell *her* that?"

"Ah—now that you mention it, perhaps not."

"You learn very fast, Zakath."

"I don't believe I've ever washed a dish—not in my entire
life."

"I've washed enough for both of us, and I wouldn't say
that too loudly. She might decide that it's time for you to learn
how." Garion gave Polgara a speculative sidelong glance.
"Let's go feed the wolf and her puppy," he suggested. "Idle-

ness in others irritates Aunt Pol for some reason, and she can almost always think of things for people to do."

"Garion, dear," Polgara said sweetly as they rose. "After the dishes are done, we'll need water for bathing."

"Yes, Aunt Pol," he said automatically. "You see?" he muttered to the Emperor of Mallorea, "I knew we hadn't moved quite fast enough."

"Do you always do what she asks? And does she mean me, too?"

Garion sighed. "Yes," he replied, "on both counts."

They rose early the next morning, and Beldin soared off to scout on ahead while the rest ate breakfast, struck camp, and saddled their horses. The damp, sullen chill which had hovered over this desolate countryside was now edged with a drier kind of cold as the prevailing wind swept down from the summits of the Dalasian mountains. Garion pulled his cloak about him and rode on. They had gone only a league or so when Beldin spiraled down out of the overcast sky. "I think you'd better turn south," he advised. "Urvon's just ahead, and his whole army's right behind him."

Belgarath swore.

"There's more," the hunchback told him. "The Darshivans managed to get past Atesca—or through him. They're coming up from behind. The elephants are leading the march. We're right between two armies here."

"How far ahead of us is Urvon?" Belgarath asked him.

"Six or eight leagues. He's in the foothills of the mountains."

"And how far behind us are the elephants?"

"About five leagues. It looks to me as if they're going to try to cut Urvon's column off. There's no help for it, Belgarath. We're going to have to run. We have to get out of the middle of this before the fighting starts."

"Is Atesca pursuing Zandramas' army?" Zakath asked intently.

"No. I think he followed your orders and pulled back to that enclave on the bank of the Magan."

Belgarath was still swearing. "How did Urvon get this far south so fast?" he muttered.

"He's killing his troops by the score," Beldin replied. "He's making them run, and Nahaz has demons whipping them along."

"I guess we don't have any choice," Belgarath said. "We'll have to go south. Toth, will you be able to lead us to Kell if we go into the mountains down near the border of Gandahar?"

The big mute nodded, then gestured to Durnik.

"It's going to be more difficult, though," the smith translated. "The mountains are very rugged down there, and there's still a lot of snow at the higher elevations."

"We'll lose a lot of time, Grandfather," Garion said.

"Not as much as we'll lose if we get caught in the middle of a battle. All right. Let's go south."

"In a moment, father," Polgara said. "Ce'Nedra," she called, "come up here."

Ce'Nedra shook her reins and drove her carriage up to where they stood.

Polgara quickly explained the situation to her. "Now then," she said, "we need to know exactly what they're doing and what they're planning to do—both armies. I think it's time for you to use my sister's amulet."

"Why didn't I think of that?" Belgarath said, sounding a bit embarrassed.

"You were too busy trying to remember all the swearwords you've ever heard," Beldin suggested.

"Can you do that and drive the carriage at the same time?" Polgara asked the little queen.

"I can try, Lady Polgara." Ce'Nedra sounded a little dubious. She lifted the sleeping puppy out of her lap and laid him beside his mother.

"Let's move out," Belgarath said.

They turned off the road and jolted across an open field through long-dead grass. After they had gone a short distance, Ce'Nedra called to Polgara. "It's not working, Lady Polgara," she said. "I need both hands on the reins on this rough ground."

They reined in.

"It's not that big a problem," Velvet said. "I'll lead the carriage horse, and Ce'Nedra can concentrate on what she's doing."

"It's a little dangerous, Liselle," Belgarath objected. "If that carriage horse shies, he'll jerk you out of the saddle and the carriage will run right over you."

"Have you ever seen me fall off a horse, Ancient One? Don't worry, I'll be perfectly fine." She rode over to the carriage horse and took hold of his reins. They started out slowly and then gradually picked up speed. Polgara rode beside the carriage, and Ce'Nedra, a little frown of concentration on her face, kept her hand on the amulet chained about her throat.

"Anything?" Polgara asked.

"I'm hearing a lot of random conversation, Lady Polgara," the little queen replied. "There are great numbers of people out there. Wait a minute," she said, "I think I've pinpointed Nahaz. That's not the sort of voice you forget." She frowned. "I think he's talking to Urvon's generals. They've had the Hounds out, so they know the elephants are coming."

"Will you be able to come back to them?" Belgarath asked her.

"I think so. Once I find somebody, I can usually locate him again fairly quickly."

"Good. See if you can find out if the Darshivan generals know that Urvon's just ahead of them. If there's going to be a battle, I want to know exactly where it's going to happen."

Ce'Nedra turned slightly, her amulet clenched tightly in her fist. She closed her eyes. After a moment, she opened them. "I *do* wish they'd be still," she fretted.

"Who?" Silk asked her.

"The elephant herders. They babble worse than old women. Wait. There they are. I've got them now." She listened for a few moments as the carriage jolted along over the rough ground. "The Darshivan officers are very worried," she reported. "They know that Urvon's army is somewhere in the mountains, but they don't know his exact location. None of their scouts came back to report."

"The Hounds are probably seeing to that," Silk said.

"What are the Darshivans planning?" Belgarath asked.

"They're undecided. They're going to push on cautiously and send out more scouts."

"All right. Now see if you can go back to Nahaz."

"I'll try." She closed her eyes again. "Oh, that's revolting!" she exclaimed after a moment.

"What is it, dear?" Polgara asked her.

"The Karands have found a narrow gorge. They're going to lure the elephants into it and then roll boulders and burning bushes down on them from the top." She listened for a few moments longer. "Once they've eliminated the elephants, the whole army is going to charge down out of the foothills and attack the rest of the Darshivans."

"Is Urvon there?" Beldin asked, his eyes intent.

"No. He's off to the side someplace. He's raving."

"I think you'd better go find that gorge," Belgarath told the dwarf. "That's where the battle's going to be, and I want to be sure it's behind us and not on up ahead somewhere."

"Right," Beldin agreed, crouching and spreading his arms. "Keep in touch," he suggested even as he began to change form.

They rode along at a careful walk, and Garion buckled on his shield.

"Do you really think that's going to help if we run into an entire army?" Zakath asked him.

"It may not help much, but it won't hurt."

Belgarath rode now with his face lifted toward the murky sky. Garion could feel the old man's thought reaching out.

"Not so loud, father," Polgara cautioned. "We've got Grolims all around us."

"Good," he replied. "None of them will be able to tell who's making the noise. They'll all think it's just another Grolim."

They rode on slowly with all of them watching the old sorcerer. "North!" he exploded finally. "Beldin's found the gorge where the ambush is. It's behind us. A little hard riding now and we'll be completely clear of both armies."

"Why don't we just sort of step right along, then?" Silk suggested.

CHAPTER TWENTY-THREE

They galloped south through the desolate countryside of western Darshiva with Velvet once again leading Ce'Nedra's horse. The little queen clung to the side of the carriage with one hand and kept the other on her amulet. "The Darshivans still don't know that Urvon's waiting in ambush for them," she called.

"I'd imagine they'll find out before too long," Silk called back.

"How far is it to the border of Gandahar?" Garion asked Zakath.

"I'd guess about twenty leagues."

"Grandfather," Garion said, "do we really have to go that far south?"

"Probably not," the old man replied. "Beldin's on up ahead. As soon as we're well past Urvon's scouts, he'll lead us up into the mountains. I don't have any particular urge to explore Gandahar, do you?"

"Not really, no."

They rode on.

The overcast grew perceptibly thicker, and Garion felt the first drops of a chill rain striking his face.

They crested a hill, and Belgarath rose in his stirrups the better to see what lay ahead. "There," he said, pointing. "He's circling."

Garion peered out across the shallow valley on the far side of the hill. A solitary bird, hardly more than a minuscule black speck in the distance, swung almost lazily in the air. They plunged down the hill, and the bird veered and flew off toward the west with slow strokes of his wings. They turned and followed.

The intermittent rain turned to a chilly drizzle, obscuring the surrounding countryside with its filmy haze.

"Don't you just love to ride in the rain?" Silk said with heavy irony.

"Under the circumstances, yes," Sadi replied. "Rain's not quite as good as fog, but it does cut down the visibility, and there are all manner of people looking for us."

"You've got a point there," Silk admitted, pulling his cloak tighter about him.

The terrain grew increasingly rugged with outcroppings of weathered stone jutting up out of the ground. After about a half-hour of hard riding, Beldin led them into a shallow gully. They rode on, and the gully walls grew progressively steeper and higher. Soon they were riding up a narrow, rocky ravine.

It was midafternoon by now, and they were all thoroughly soaked. Garion wiped his face and peered ahead. The sky to

the west appeared to be growing lighter, giving promise of
clearing. He had perhaps not even been aware of how much
the prevailing gloom hanging over Darshiva had depressed
him. He urged Chretienne into a run. Somehow he seemed
to feel that once they reached the sunlight again, they would
be safe.

He rounded a bend in the ravine and saw Beldin standing
in the trail ahead of them. The dwarf's matted hair hung in
scraggly wet strands about his shoulders, and his beard was
dripping. "You'd better slow down," he growled at them. "I
could hear you coming for a mile, and we're not alone in these
foothills."

Regretfully, Garion reined Chretienne in.

"Exactly where does this ravine lead?" Belgarath asked the
hunchback.

"It twists and turns a lot, but eventually it opens out onto
a ridge top. The ridge runs north and south. If we follow it
north, we'll come to the main caravan route. That's the fastest
way down into Dalasia."

"Everybody else knows that, too."

"That's all right. We'll be at least a day ahead of them.
They still have a battle to fight."

"Are you going to scout ahead again?"

"Not until the rain lets up. My feathers are wet. It'd take
a derrick to get me off the ground again. Oh, one other thing.
When we get to that ridge, we're going to have to be careful.
A couple leagues north, it runs just a few miles above the spot
where Nahaz has his ambush set up."

"Your choice of a route leaves a lot to be desired," Belgarath
said. "If someone down there happens to look up, we'll have
half of Urvon's army all over us."

"Not unless they can fly. An earthquake went through here
a few thousand years ago and it sliced off the side of that
ridge. It's a very steep cliff now."

"How high?"

"High enough—a thousand feet or so."

"How far is it to the caravan route?"

"About fifteen leagues from the place where we'll come out on the ridge."

"North of Urvon's army, then?"

"Quite a bit north, yes."

"Why did Nahaz pass it by? Why didn't he just turn west?"

"He probably didn't want the Darshivans and their elephants coming up behind him. Besides, he's a demon. I'd guess he just couldn't bring himself to pass up the chance for a mass slaughter."

"Maybe. Do you think the battle's going to start this afternoon?"

"I doubt it. Elephants don't move all that fast, and the Darshivans are moving cautiously. They'll stop for the night soon. First thing tomorrow morning, though, things are going to start getting noisy."

"Maybe we can get past the place where the ambush is set up during the night."

"I wouldn't advise it. You won't be able to light any torches, and that cliff's a sheer drop. If you ride off the edge of it, you'll bounce all the way back to the Magan."

Belgarath grunted. "Are you sure you can't fly?"

"Not a chance. Right now you couldn't get me into the air with a catapult."

"Why don't you change into a duck?"

"Why don't you mind your own business?"

"All right, Garion," Belgarath said with some resignation, "I guess it's up to us, then." He slid down out of his saddle and walked on up the ravine. Garion sighed, dismounted, and followed him.

They ranged out ahead, searching the soggy terrain with their ears and noses. It was almost evening when the walls of the ravine began to fan out, and they could see the line of the ridge top ahead. They reached it and loped north through the gradually diminishing drizzle.

"Grandfather," Garion said, "I think that's a cave over there." He pointed with his muzzle at an opening in the rock.

"Let's look."

The opening of the cave was narrow, not much more than a wide crack, and the cavern did not open up noticeably inside. It was deep, however, running far back into the rock. It seemed more like a long corridor than a room.

"What do you think?" Garion asked as the two of them stood at the entrance peering back into the darkness.

"It's a place to get in out of the weather, and it's a good place to hide for the night. Go get the others, and I'll see if I can get a fire started."

Garion turned and loped back down the ridge. The rain was definitely slacking off now, but the wind was coming up, and it was getting colder.

The others were coming warily up out of the ravine when Garion reached them.

"Another cave?" Silk said plaintively when Garion told them what he and Belgarath had found.

"I'll hold your hand, Kheldar," Velvet offered.

"I appreciate the gesture, Liselle, but I don't think it's going to help very much. I loathe caves."

"Someday you'll have to tell me why."

"No. I don't think so. I don't like to talk about it. I don't even like to think about it."

Garion led them to the narrow track atop the ridge. Ce'Nedra's carriage jolted over the rocky ground. The smug look that had come over her face when she had expropriated the vehicle had evaporated, and she rode with resignation, wincing at every bump.

"That's not much of a cave," Beldin said critically when they reached the opening in the rock.

"Feel free to sleep outside," Belgarath told him.

391

"We're going to have to put blinders on the horses to get them inside," Durnik noted. "They'll take one look at that opening and flatly refuse even to try it."

"I feel much the same way myself," Silk said. "Sometimes it's surprising just how intelligent horses really are."

"We're not going to be able to get the carriage inside," Sadi said.

"We can cover it with tent canvas and sprinkle dirt over it," Durnik said. "It won't be really visible—at least not in the dark."

"Let's get started," Belgarath said. "I think we want to be inside before it gets much darker."

It took the better part of half an hour to get the balky horses into the narrow cave. Then Durnik covered the entrance with tent canvas and went back outside to help Eriond and Toth conceal the carriage.

The she-wolf had limped into the cave, followed by her frolicsome pup. Now that he was being fed regularly, the previously listless animal had turned playful. His mother, too, Garion noted, had begun to fill out again, and her fur was glossy and less matted. "An excellent den," she observed. "Will we hunt from here?"

"No, little sister," Polgara replied, stirring the small pot of simmering herbs on the fire. "We have things that must be done in another place. Let me have a look at your hurt."

Obediently, the wolf lay down by the fire and extended her injured paw. Polgara gently unwrapped it and examined the ulcers. "Much better," she said. "It's nearly healed. Does it still cause you pain?"

"Pain is to be endured," the wolf replied indifferently. "It is of no moment."

"The amount of pain, however, tells us how much longer it will be until the hurt is gone."

"That is true," the wolf admitted. "I have observed the

same thing myself in times past. The pain is less now. The hurt is going away, I think."

Polgara bathed the injured paw in the pungent juice from her pot, then mixed the pulped herbs with soap and sugar again, packed it over the wound, and replaced the bandage. "We will not have to do this again, little sister," she told her patient. "The hurt is nearly gone."

"I am grateful," the wolf said simply. "Will I be able to walk when it grows light again? The thing which runs on round feet is most uncomfortable to sit in, and the she who makes it run talks much."

"Sit in it one more time while it is light," Polgara advised. "Give the hurt that much more time to go away."

The wolf sighed and laid her chin on her paws.

They carried water from a nearby spring, and Polgara cooked supper. After they had eaten, Belgarath rose to his feet. "Let's have a look around," he said to Garion. "I want to get an idea of what we're dealing with."

Garion nodded and stood up. The two of them went outside the cave, carrying Silk's supper out to him. The little man had volunteered, enthusiastically, Garion thought, to stand watch. "Where are you going?" he asked, sitting down on a rock to eat.

"We're going to nose around a bit," Belgarath replied.

"Good idea. You want me to come along?"

"No. You'd better stay here and keep your eyes open. Warn the others if anybody comes up the ridge." Then the old man led Garion a few hundred feet up the ridge line, and the two of them made the change into their other forms. Garion had changed back and forth so many times in the past few months that at times the distinction between the two shapes had begun to blur and, oftentimes, even when he was in his human form, he found himself thinking in the language of wolves. He loped along behind the great silver wolf, considering this peculiar loss of identity.

Belgarath stopped. "Keep your mind on what we're doing," he said. "Your ears and nose won't be much good to us if you're woolgathering."

"Yes, revered pack-leader," Garion replied, feeling very embarrassed. Wolves seldom needed reprimanding and they were covered with shame when it happened.

When they reached the spot where the side of the ridge had been sheared away by the earthquake, they stopped. The foothills that sloped down toward the plain were dark. Urvon's army was obviously under orders to build no fires. Out on the plain itself, however, the watch fires twinkled in profusion like small orange stars.

"Zandramas has a big army," Garion sent his thought quietly to his grandfather.

"Yes," the old man agreed. "That battle tomorrow morning might take quite a while. Even Nahaz's demons are going to need a lot of time to kill that many people."

"The longer the better. They can take all week, if they want to. We could be halfway to Kell by then."

Belgarath looked around. "Let's go on up the ridge a ways and have a look."

"All right."

Despite Beldin's warning that there might be scouts from the two armies here in the higher foothills, the two wolves encountered no one. "They probably went back to report," Garion heard Belgarath's voice speaking in his mind. "They'll be out again first thing in the morning, most likely. Let's go on back to the cave and get some sleep."

They rose early the following morning, long before first light. They were all subdued as they ate breakfast. Although the two armies facing each other below them were composed entirely of enemies, none of them took any particular pleasure in the prospect of the bloodshed the day would bring. After breakfast, they carried out the packs and their saddles and, last of all, they led out the horses.

"You're quiet this morning, Garion," Zakath said as the two were saddling their mounts.

"I was just wondering if there might be some way to stop what's going to happen today."

"Not really," Zakath told him. "Their positions are too firmly fixed. It's too late to turn it back now. The Darshivans will advance, and Urvon's army will ambush them. I've organized enough battles to know that at a certain point things become inevitable."

"The way Thull Mardu was?"

"Thull Mardu was a blunder," Zakath admitted. "I should have gone around Ce'Nedra's army instead of trying to go through it. The Grolims had me convinced that they could hold that fog in place all day. I should have known better than to believe them. And I definitely shouldn't have underestimated the Asturian bowmen. How can they possibly shoot arrows that fast?"

"There's a knack to it. Lelldorin showed me how it's done."

"Lelldorin?"

"An Asturian friend of mine."

"We've always been told that Arends are stupid to the point of imbecility."

"They're not overly bright," Garion admitted. "Maybe that's what makes them such good soldiers. They don't have enough imagination to be afraid." He smiled in the darkness. "Mandorallen can't even conceive of the possibility that he could lose a fight. He'd attack your whole army—all by himself."

"The Baron of Vo Mandor? I know his reputation." Zakath laughed wryly. "It's entirely possible that he'd win, you know."

"Don't ever tell him that. He has enough problems as it is." Garion sighed. "I wish he were here, though—and Barak and Hettar and even Relg."

395

"Relg?"

"He's an Ulgo mystic. He walks through rock."

Zakath stared at him.

"I don't know how, so don't ask me. I saw him stick a Grolim into a large boulder once. Then he just left him there with only his hands sticking out."

Zakath shuddered.

They mounted and rode slowly up the ravine with Ce'Nedra's carriage jolting along behind them. The sky gradually grew lighter overhead, and Garion saw that they were approaching the edge of the cliff that overlooked the site of the impending battle.

"Belgarath," Zakath said quietly, "would you mind a suggestion?"

"I'll always listen to suggestions."

"This is probably the only place where we'll be able to see what's going on down below. Wouldn't it be a good idea to stop and make sure that the armies down there are fully engaged before we move on? If the Darshivans outflank Urvon's ambush, we'll have them no more than a few leagues behind us. We'll need to run at that point."

Belgarath frowned. "You might be right," he conceded. "It never hurts to know the whole situation." He reined in. "All right," he said, "we'll stop here and go ahead on foot. There's cover enough at the edge of that cliff so that we can watch without being seen." He swung down from his horse.

"The ladies and I will wait here, father," Polgara told him. "We've seen battles before. I don't think we need to watch another one." She glanced at Eriond. "You stay with us, too," she told him.

"Yes, Polgara."

The rest of them moved forward at a crouch and took cover behind the few boulders at the edge of the cliff. The gloomy overcast that hung perpetually over Darshiva covered the blasted and decaying plain below with a sullen twilight. Out on the plain, Garion could make out tiny-appearing figures moving forward at what seemed no more than a crawl.

"I think I've detected a flaw in what was otherwise an excellent plan," Zakath said wryly. "They're too far away to make out any details."

"I can take care of that," Beldin growled. "A hawk's eyes are about ten times more acute than a man's. I can circle over them at a few hundred feet and pick out every detail."

"Are you sure your feathers are dry?" Belgarath asked.

"That's why I slept near the fire last night."

"All right. Keep me advised."

"Naturally." The grim hunchback crouched and blurred. With an agile leap the hawk settled atop a boulder, his fierce eyes looking out over the plain. Then he spread his wings and dropped headlong off the cliff.

"You people always take that so casually," Zakath noted.

"It's not really that," Sadi murmured, rubbing his scalp. "It's just that we're numb. The first time I saw him do it, my hair stood on end, and for me that's a neat trick."

"Urvon's army's hiding in shallow pits along the ridge tops on either side of that long gorge," Belgarath repeated the silent words of the hawk soaring through the murky air far below them, "and the elephants are moving directly toward the same gorge."

Zakath leaned out over the edge and looked down.

"Careful," Garion said, catching the Mallorean's arm with one hand.

"It *is* a long way down," Zakath agreed. "All right then," he said. "Now I see why the Darshivans are making for that gorge. It branches at the foot of this cliff, and one branch goes north. It probably connects with the main caravan route." He thought about it. "It's actually a good strategy. If Nahaz hadn't driven his troops so hard, the Darshivans would have reached the caravan route first, and they could have set up an ambush of their own." He pulled back away from the edge of the cliff.

"That's one of the reasons I always hate to operate in rough terrain. I got a number of very nasty surprises in Cthol Murgos."

"The elephants are starting to form up into a column," Belgarath reported, "and the rest of the Darshivans are strung out behind them."

"Are they putting out scouts?" Zakath asked.

"Yes, but they're only scouting along the floor of the gorge. A few of them went up to the ridge tops, but the Hounds eliminated those."

They waited as Beldin circled above the two armies.

"They're committed now," Belgarath said sadly. "The elephants are starting into the gorge."

"I feel a little sorry for the elephants," Durnik said. "They didn't volunteer for this. I wish they didn't plan to use fire on them."

"It's fairly standard, Goodman," Zakath said calmly. "Fire's the only thing elephants are really afraid of. They'll stampede back down the gorge."

"Right through the Darshivans," Silk added in a slightly sick voice. "Nahaz should get his fill of blood today."

"Do we really have to watch this?" Durnik asked.

"We have to wait until it gets started," Belgarath replied.

"I think I'll go back and wait with Pol," the smith said, edging back from the cliff top. Then he and Toth went on down the ridge.

"He's a very gentle person, isn't he?" Zakath said.

"Usually," Garion replied. "When it's necessary, though, he can do what needs doing."

"You remember the time he chased that Murgo into a quicksand bog," Silk said with a shudder, "and then watched him sink?"

"It shouldn't be too long now," Belgarath said tensely. "The last of the elephants just entered the gorge."

They waited. For some reason, Garion felt suddenly cold.

Then, even though what was happening was more than a league away, they heard a thunderous rumbling sound as Urvon's troops began to roll huge boulders down on the advancing elephants. Faintly they could hear the agonized screams of the huge beasts. Then, smoke and flame began to boil up out of the gorge as the brutish Karands rained huge piles of burning brush down on the helpless animals.

"I think I've seen enough," Sadi said. He rose and went back down the ridge.

The surviving elephants, looking almost like ants in the distance, wheeled and fled in panic back down the gorge, and the agonized squeals of the animals were suddenly accompanied by human screams as the great beasts crushed their way through rank after rank of Darshivan soldiers.

Beldin came soaring up from below and settled back on the boulder from which he had started.

"What's that?" Silk exclaimed. "There at the mouth of the gorge."

There seemed to be some vast disturbance in the murky air at the edge of the plain, a sort of shimmering filled with flickering, rainbow-hued light and sullen flashes of heat lightning. Then, quite suddenly, the disturbance coalesced into a nightmare.

"Belar!" Silk swore. "It's as big as a barn!"

The thing was hideous. It had a dozen or more snakelike arms that writhed and lashed at the air. It had three blazing eyes and a vast muzzle filled with great fangs. It towered over the elephants and kicked them aside contemptuously with huge, clawed feet. Then with thunderous stride, it started up the gorge, walking indifferently through the flames and paying no more attention to the boulders bouncing off its shoulders that it might have to snowflakes.

"What *is* that thing?" Zakath asked in a shaken voice.

"That's Mordja," Belgarath told him. "I've seen him before—in Morindland—and that's not the sort of face one forgets."

The demon in the gorge was reaching out with his many arms now, catching whole platoons of Karands in his clawed hands and almost casually hurling them with terrific force against the surrounding rocks.

"It looks to me as if the tide of battle just turned," Silk said. "What's our general feeling about leaving—along about right now?"

The Demon Lord Mordja raised his huge muzzle and thundered something in a language too hideous for human comprehension.

"Stay put!" Belgarath ordered, catching Silk's arm. "This isn't played out yet. That was a challenge, and Nahaz won't be able to refuse it."

Another of those flickering disturbances appeared in the air above the upper end of the gorge, and another towering form appeared out of its center. Garion could not see its face, a fact for which he was profoundly grateful, but it, too, had snaky arms growing in profusion from its vast shoulders. "Thou darest to face me, Mordja?" it roared in a voice which shook the nearby mountains.

"I do not fear thee, Nahaz," Mordja bellowed back. "Our enmity hath endured for a thousand thousand years. Let it end here. I shall carry word of thy death back to the King of Hell and bear thy head with me as proof of my words."

"My head is thine," Nahaz said with a chilling laugh. "Come and take it—if thou canst."

"And thou wouldst bestow the stone of power on the mad Disciple of maimed Torak?" Mordja sneered.

"Thy sojourn in the land of the Morindim hath bereft thee of thy wits, Mordja. The stone of power shall be *mine*, and I shall rule these ants that creep upon the face of this world. I will raise them like cattle and feed upon them when I hunger."

"How wilt thou feed, Nahaz—without thy head? It is I who will rule and feed here, for the stone of power shall lie in my hand."

"That we will soon discover, Mordja. Come. Let us contend for a head and for the stone we both desire." Suddenly Nahaz spun about, his baleful eyes searching the top of the cliff where Garion and his friends lay hidden. A volcanic hiss burst from the demon's distorted lips. "The Child of Light!" he roared. "Praise the name of the King of Hell, who hath brought him within my reach. I will rend him asunder and seize the stone which *he* carries. Thou art doomed, Mordja. That stone in my hand shall be thy undoing." With hideous speed the Demon Lord Nahaz clambered over the tumbled rocks at the foot of the cliff and reached out with his dozens of clawed hands at the sheer rock face. His vast shoulders heaved.

"He's climbing straight up the rock!" Silk exclaimed in a strangled voice. "Let's get out of here!"

The Demon Lord Mordja stood for a moment in stunned chagrin, then he, too, ran forward and began to claw his way up the face of the cliff.

Garion rose to his feet, looking down at the two vast monsters clambering up the sheer rock. He felt a peculiar detachment as he reached back over his shoulder and drew his sword. He untied the leather sleeve covering the hilt and slipped it off. The Orb glowed, and when he took the sword in both hands, the familiar blue flame ran up the blade.

"Garion!" Zakath exclaimed.

"They want the Orb," Garion said grimly. "Well, they're going to have to take it, and I may have something to say about that."

But then Durnik was there. His face was calm, and he was stripped to the waist. In his right hand he carried an awesome sledgehammer that glowed as blue as Garion's sword. "Excuse

401

me, Garion," he said in a matter-of-fact tone, "but this is my task."

Polgara had come with him, and her face showed no fear. She had drawn her blue cloak about her, and the snowy lock at her brow glowed.

"What's happening here?" Belgarath demanded.

"Stay out of it, father," Polgara told him. "This is something that has to happen."

Durnik advanced to the edge of the cliff and looked down at the two horrors struggling up the sheer face toward him. "I abjure ye," he said to them in a great voice, "return to the place from whence ye came, lest ye die." Overlaying his voice was another voice, calm, almost gentle, but with a power in it that shook Garion as a tree is shaken by a hurricane. He knew that voice.

"Begone!" Durnik commanded, emphasizing that word with a dreadful blow of his sledge that shattered a boulder into fragments.

The demons clawing their way up the cliff hesitated.

At first it was barely perceptible. At first it seemed that Durnik was only swelling his chest and shoulders in preparation for an impossible struggle. Then Garion saw his oldest friend begin to grow. At ten feet, the smith was awesome. At twenty, he was beyond belief. The great hammer in his hand grew with him, and the blue nimbus about it grew more intense as he expanded and grew, thrusting the sullen air aside with his massive shoulders. The very rocks seemed to cringe back from him as, with long sweeps of his dreadful, glowing hammer, he loosened his arm.

The Demon Lord Mordja paused, clinging to the rock. His bestial face suddenly showed fear. Again Durnik destroyed whole square yards of rock with a single ringing blow.

Nahaz, however, his eyes ablaze and empty of thought, continued to slather and claw his way up the rock face, screeching imprecations in that dreadful language which only demons know.

"So be it, then," Durnik said, and the voice in which he spoke was not his own, but that other, more profound voice, which rang in Garion's ears like the very crack of doom.

The Demon Lord Mordja looked up, his terrible face filled with terror. Then suddenly he released his grip on the face of the rock cliff to topple and tumble to the rocks below. Howling, and with his multitudinous arms covering his scabrous head, he fled.

Nahaz, however, his blazing eyes filled with madness, continued to sink his claws into naked rock and to haul his vast body up the cliff.

Almost politely, it seemed, Durnik stepped back from the awful brink and wrapped both enormous hands about the glowing handle of his sledge.

"Durnik!" Silk cried. "No! Don't let him get his feet under him!"

Durnik did not reply, but a faint smile touched his honest face. Again he tested his vast hammer, swinging it in both hands. The sound of its passage through the air was not a whistle, but a roar.

Nahaz clambered up over the edge of the cliff and rose enormously, clawing at the sky and roaring insanely in the hideous language of the demons.

Durnik spat on his left hand; then on his right. He twisted his huge hands on the handle of his sledge to set them in place, then he swung a vast, overhand blow that took the Demon Lord full in the chest. "Begone!" the smith roared in a voice louder than thunder. The sledge struck fiery sparks from the demon's body, sullen orange sparks that sizzled and jumped on the ground like burning roaches.

Nahaz screamed, clutching at his chest.

Unperturbed, Durnik swung again.

And again.

Garion recognized the rhythm of his friend's strokes. Durnik was not fighting; he was hammering with the age-old precision of a man whose tools are but an extension of his arms. Again and again the glowing hammer crashed into the body of the Demon Lord. With each blow, the sparks flew. Nahaz cringed, trying to shield his body from those awful, shattering strokes. Each time Durnik struck, he roared, "Begone!" Gradually, like a man splitting a huge rock, he began to hammer Nahaz into pieces. Pythonlike arms fell writhing into the abyss, and great, craterlike holes appeared in the demon's chest.

Unable to watch the dreadful work any longer, Garion averted his eyes. Far below, he saw Urvon's throne. The two dozen bearers who had carried it had fled, and the mad Disciple capered on the rocks howling insanely.

Durnik struck again. "Begone!"

And again. "Begone!"

And again. "Begone!"

Beaten beyond endurance, the Demon Lord Nahaz flinched back, missed his footing, and toppled off the cliff with a howl of rage and despair. Down and down he plunged, glowing with green fire like a streaking comet. As he drove into the earth, one snakelike arm lashed out and caught the last Disciple of Torak in a deathly grip. Urvon, shrieking, was pulled along as Nahaz sank into the earth like a stick into water.

When Garion looked back, Durnik had resumed his normal size. His chest and arms were covered with sweat, and he was breathing hard from his exertions. He held his glowing sledge out at arm's length, and its fire grew brighter and brighter until it was incandescent. Then the fire gradually faded, and the smith was holding a silver amulet in his hand with its chain draped across the backs of his fingers.

The voice which had overlain Durnik's during his awful encounter with the Demon Lord now spoke in no more than a whisper. "Know that this good man is also my beloved Disciple, since he was best suited of all of ye for this task."

Belgarath bowed in the direction the voice was coming from. "It shall be as You say, Master," he said in a voice thick with emotion. "We welcome him as a brother."

Polgara came forward with a look of wonder on her face and gently took the amulet from Durnik's hand. "How very appropriate," she said softly, looking at the silver disc. She lovingly hung the chain around her husband's neck, then she kissed him and held him to her tightly.

"Please, Pol," he objected with flaming cheeks, "we're not alone, you know."

She laughed her warm, rich laugh and held him even tighter.

Beldin was grinning crookedly. "Nice job, brother mine," he said to Durnik. "Hot work though, I'd imagine." He reached out his hand and took a foaming tankard out of the air and handed it to Aldur's newest Disciple.

Durnik drank gratefully.

Belgarath clapped him on the shoulder. "It's been a long, long time since we last had a new brother," he said. Then he quickly embraced Durnik.

"Oh," Ce'Nedra said with a little catch in her voice, "that's just beautiful."

Wordlessly, Velvet handed her the wispy little handkerchief. "What is that on his amulet?" the blond girl asked, sounding just a bit awed.

"It's a hammer," Belgarath told her. "What else could it be?"

"If I might make a suggestion, Ancient One," Sadi said diffidently, "the armies down there on the plain seem to be in a state of total confusion. Wouldn't this be an excellent time to depart—before they regain their wits?"

"My thought exactly," Silk approved, putting his hand on the eunuch's shoulder.

"They're right, Belgarath," Beldin agreed. "We've done what we were sent here to do—or Durnik has, at least." The hunchback sighed and looked over the edge of the cliff. "I really wanted to kill Urvon myself," he said, "but I suppose this is even better. I hope he enjoys his sojourn in Hell."

A shrill laugh suddenly came from the top of the ridge, a laugh of triumph. Garion whirled, then stopped, frozen with surprise. Atop the ridge stood the black-robed figure of the Sorceress of Darshiva. Beside her stood a blond little boy. Geran's features had changed in the year and more since he had been abducted, but Garion knew him instantly. "Ye have done my work well," Zandramas declared. "I myself could not have found a more fitting end for Torak's last Disciple. Now, Child of Light, only thou standest between me and Cthrag Sardius. I will await thy coming in the Place Which Is No More. There shalt thou be a witness when I raise up a New God over Angorak, whose dominion over all the world shall endure until the end of days!"

Geran reached out his hand imploringly to Ce'Nedra, but then he and Zandramas vanished.

"How remarkable," the she-wolf said in surprise.

Here ends Book IV of *The Malloreon*.
Book V, *The Seeress of Kell*,
will take up the final result
of the War of Destinies
and of the people involved.